Point Horror

COLLECTION 7.

A terrifying trio in one!

Have you read these other fabulous Point Horror Collections?

Point Horror

COLLECTION 7

A terrifying trio in one!

The Window
Carol Ellis

The Train
Diane Hoh

Hit and Run
R.L. Stine

■ SCHOLASTIC

Scholastic Children's Books,
7–9 Pratt Street, London NW1 0AE, UK
a division of Scholastic Publications Ltd
London ~ New York ~ Toronto ~ Sydney ~ Auckland

First published in this edition by Scholastic Publications Ltd, 1995

The Window
First published in the USA by Scholastic Inc., 1992
First published in the UK by Scholastic Publications Ltd, 1993
Copyright © Carol Ellis, 1992

The Train
First published in the USA by Scholastic Inc., 1992
First published in the UK by Scholastic Publications Ltd, 1993
Copyright © Diane Hoh, 1992

Hit and Run
First published in the USA by Scholastic Inc., 1992
First published in the UK by Scholastic Publications Ltd, 1993
Copyright © R.L. Stine, 1992

ISBN: 0 590 13182 6

Contents

THE WINDOW

Chapter 1

Jody Sanderson closed her eyes, but it didn't help. The van had just hit a patch of ice and was sliding to the right. It veered across the frozen surface toward the safety rail separating the highway from a rocky gorge forty feet below. In her mind's eye, Jody watched the silver-gray van gliding almost gracefully across the ice, bursting through the flimsy rail, and soaring into the air where it hung suspended for a few seconds, streamlined and glinting in the pale sun. Before she could picture its terrifying, deadly plunge toward the rocks, Jody felt the tires regain their traction. Releasing the breath she'd been holding, Jody felt her body lean with the van as it pulled left, back toward the safety of the highway.

Jody opened her eyes and looked around. No one else in the van seemed to have suffered from the same flight of imagination she had. In the seat across from her, Christine Castella was still holding her paperback, although the main focus of her attention was obviously Drew Hansen, across and up one seat. Jody couldn't blame Chris for not concentrating on her book; Drew was very good-looking, in a brown-eyed, brooding sort of way. He'd attracted the attention of Ellen Cummings, too, Jody'd noticed earlier. All Jody could see of Ellen at the moment was the top of her light-brown hair above the seatback ahead, but she was willing to bet that Ellen was staring at the seat across from *her*, wishing hard that Drew would turn and talk to her.

Behind her, Jody could hear the sound of Billy Feldman's even, slightly stuffy breathing. If he was asleep, then he hadn't noticed how close they'd come to disaster, and if he was awake, then it must not have bothered him in the slightest.

It hadn't bothered the driver of the van, either, Jody noticed. Sasha Wolf, her long dark hair spilling down her back in shining waves, turned her head to the side just long enough for Jody to see that she was smiling. Her twin brother, Cal, smiled back.

"They're beautiful," Jody's friend Kate had said of her neighbors, the Wolf twins. After meeting them earlier that morning, Jody had agreed. Tall and slender, dark-haired and blue-eyed, Sasha and Cal Wolf were beautiful, all right. Whether Sasha was a good enough driver to keep them alive the rest of the three-hour drive to Brevard Pass remained to be seen.

Scrunching down in her seat, Jody told herself that she really didn't know any of these people well enough to be making judgments about them. She had to give them a chance. Still, she wished Kate had been able to come on the ski trip. After all, *Kate* was the one who'd invited her. Sasha and Cal had rented the cabin, and invited Kate, who in turn had invited Jody. But now Kate was sick with the flu, and Jody was stuck with a bunch of strangers.

Well, they weren't *all* strangers. She knew Billy and Chris a little from school. Billy was kind of a klutz, that's all she really knew about him. But Chris, with her spiky blonde hair and blue eyes that always stared at the air above your head, was *not* the kind of person Jody was dying to spend five days in a cabin with.

But as Kate said when she'd called the night before to say good-bye, this wasn't just any ski trip. This was Brevard Pass, *the* place to go skiing. Jody couldn't pass it up. Besides, Kate said she *needed* Jody to go. Leahna Calder was going to be there. Jody had never heard of Leahna Calder. Kate said she was poison. She said she needed Jody to keep an eye on Cal and let Kate know if Leahna started sinking her claws into him.

Jody grinned to herself. Kate had told her at least a thousand times how she'd die for Cal Wolf, and from her first look at him, Jody couldn't blame her. But she had no intention of keeping an eye on Cal and Leahna. This was a ski trip, not an undercover assignment.

The last thing Kate had said the night before was not to worry about not knowing anyone, that she'd have a great time. Now, as the van barreled along the highway, Jody looked around and tried to decide if these were people she could have a great time with. When they skidded across another patch of ice, Jody closed her eyes again. With Sasha's driving, she'd be lucky if she got the chance to find out.

About forty miles later, the highway narrowed from four lanes to two. Looking out the window, Jody saw a small white sign bordered in dark green. Black lettering announced that Brevard Pass was ten miles away.

"Brevard Pass," Billy said from the seat behind her, obviously having seen the sign, too. "It used to be just what it says, a plain old mountain pass used by wagons. Named after Charles Brevard. He was the first guy to cross it, back in 1852, something like that."

"Thanks for the history lesson," Chris said.

Jody twisted around and looked at Billy. "This is my first time here," she told him. "It's so popular, I guess I expected bells and whistles. Or at least a bigger sign."

"Neon?" Chris asked sarcastically, never taking her eyes off Drew.

"Just bigger." Jody decided her snap impression of Chris had been right on the mark. The girl's personality was as spiky as her hair.

"I know what you mean, Jody." Sasha took her eyes off the road and smiled warmly in the rearview mirror. Her voice was low and throaty. "You hear so much about Brevard, you expect bells and whistles, like you said. I think the people who live here all year-round didn't want it to turn into another Aspen."

"But that's what it is, almost," Billy said. "It's got night skiing, it's got a lodge that looks like a mansion, it's got famous people buying up land and spending millions."

"Yes, but it's not flashy." Sasha peered at him in the mirror. "Brevard's got class."

"Okay. Just as long as it's got snow, too." Billy laughed a little too loudly at his small joke. His liquid brown eyes reminded Jody of a puppy's. The poor guy, she thought, he's got a thing for Sasha. She hoped he realized he'd probably have to wait in line.

"There'll be plenty of snow," Ellen said seriously. Her voice was airy and kind of singsongy. "I listened to the weather report this morning and Brevard got two inches last night. The base is packed, and it's almost eighty inches, they said."

Sasha and Cal exchanged another quick smile. Jody could almost hear them saying, "Great! The slopes are going to be perfect." At least that's what she imagined they might be saying. The two of them seemed to communicate without words half the time. Kate said they were really close, being twins and all. Jody supposed it was normal, considering, but it made her feel a little left out. Why couldn't they talk out loud, like everybody else?

As if he felt her watching him, Cal turned around in his seat and looked down the aisle toward Jody. His light-blue eyes were sparkling. "Kate told us you're a pretty good skier," he said. "Are you ready for the Jaws of Death?"

"The *what*?"

"He means one of the runs." Drew's dark-blond head appeared over the rim of his seat. "The hard one."

"Drew!" Sasha called out. She lifted her hand and waved, a wide silver bracelet shining on her wrist. "I was wondering when you'd surface. Have you been asleep or were you just sunk in one of your moody spells?"

"Neither, Sasha. I was praying we wouldn't go off the highway whenever you didn't bother to slow down for the ice." Drew's head sank down behind his seatback again.

Jody grinned. At least one person was on her wavelength.

Sasha laughed, strong and full. "You should have told me you were worried, Drew. I would have slowed down if I'd known."

"That would have spoiled the thrill," Drew's disembodied voice said.

Sasha laughed again. "Was anybody else scared?" she asked. "Come on, you can tell me. If you were, I'll let Cal drive on the trip back home. He's much more cautious than I am."

"I don't even want to think about the trip back," Chris whined. "We've been in this van forever, it feels like. Are we almost there?"

"About five more minutes." Cal pointed out the window to where several long lines of almost identical A-frame cabins were strung along a snowy hillside dotted with pine trees. "We're in one of those. Which row, Sash, the third?"

"Mmm, the third. Cabins above and below us,"

Sasha said. "Big windows and no curtains. Don't walk naked to the shower . . . unless you *like* being watched," she added.

Jody thought that was sort of an odd thing to say. But everyone else laughed, Billy the loudest. "I'd rather *do* the watching," he said. "Anybody bring binoculars?"

"Who'd want to spend their time staring into windows?" Ellen asked. "We came to ski."

"There's always nighttime," Chris reminded her. "Unless you plan to ski then, too."

"Oh, sure I do." Ellen's voice got higher and much more animated. "That's the most beautiful time."

"Yeah," Drew murmured. "Down the slopes in the moonlight. Nothing better."

"There's more floodlight than moonlight, but I know what you mean," Sasha said. "No skiing tonight, though." She glanced at Cal.

"I knew it!" Cal laughed. "You set it up, didn't you?"

"I told you I would."

"Set what up?" Billy draped himself over the back of Jody's seat. "Set what up, Sasha?"

Cal answered him. "Party time, my friend. Sasha's been on the phone all week, talking to everybody we know who'll be here."

"Most of them are coming, too, and we'll invite a bunch more this afternoon. Whoever looks interesting and fun," Sasha said. "The main lodge does five-foot submarine sandwiches — I'll order a couple as soon as we get to the cabin. It'll be perfect."

"It'll be wild," Cal added.

"Oh, definitely wild," Sasha agreed. "So everybody save the moonlit slopes for another night."

"Do we have a choice?" Drew asked.

Chris snickered.

Jody saw a small frown flit across Sasha's face, but it disappeared quickly, and she laughed. "I was doing it again, wasn't I, Cal?"

"Mmm." He turned around and grinned at the rest of the passengers. "Sasha's into taking charge, in case nobody could tell."

"I get a little pushy sometimes," Sasha admitted. "*Of course* you don't have to be at the party, Drew." She eyed him in the mirror, her beautiful face slightly flushed. "It's strictly voluntary."

"Good, I'm glad we've got that straight." Drew subsided again, and Jody thought he was finished talking. Then he added, "A party sounds fine. Count me in, Sasha."

"I never seriously counted you out," Sasha told him with a grin, and Jody heard Drew laugh for the first time.

"Hey, we're here!" Billy called out as they passed a sign welcoming them to Brevard Pass. "Look, there's the lift."

Off to the right, Jody saw the lift moving slowly up the mountainside, the skiers' jackets bright splashes of color against the snow beneath them. She watched excitedly, as Sasha pulled the van into the parking area at the base of the cabin-dotted hill.

It was almost noon. Nobody wanted to unload and waste time trekking with their bags to the cabin; everyone wanted to get on the slopes. But leaving everything in the van, even if it was locked, wasn't such a great idea.

"I'll carry the stuff," Drew volunteered as they all piled out of the van. "I want to check out the cabin."

"Third row, remember," Sasha said. "You'll see the number eight on the deck railing. That's the one." There were keys for everyone staying at the cabin, and she tossed Drew's to him. "And could you call the lodge and order the subs for tonight? And be sure to turn up the heat?"

"I'll help, too," Chris said, flashing a smile at Drew. "I'm going to need to go into town before I can start skiing, anyway. My dog chewed up my best gloves last night, and I have to buy another pair." She held up her hands. Her arms jingled with bracelets, and every finger except her thumbs had a ring on it.

"You'll both get rewards," Cal told them. "I don't know what, but we'll think of something."

"How about if you pay for our lift tickets?" Drew suggested.

Cal laughed. "How about if I carry my own bags, instead?"

Drew laughed, too, shaking his head. Then he turned to the van and started lifting the skis off the top.

The joking around helped Jody feel loose for the first time since the trip had started. She reminded herself that she probably wasn't the only one who'd been uncomfortable; they'd all been circling each other a little, trying to feel each other out, deciding if they could be friends, or at least stand each other for the five days they'd be at Brevard.

"Who's got the Heads?" Drew asked, propping a pair of skis against the van.

"I do." Jody finished pulling on her ski pants and walked over to him. "Thanks." She pulled out her wallet, took the money she'd need for the lift ticket, and handed the wallet to him.

"You sure you trust me with this?" Drew asked seriously.

Jody grinned. "I trusted Sasha to get us here in one piece, didn't I?"

Drew laughed and leaned his head close to Jody's. "I guess Cal's got your vote to drive back," he said softly.

Jody nodded, enjoying the conspiracy. Enjoying his closeness, too.

"That makes two of us," he said. "Let's try to talk the others into coming over to our side. Deal?"

"Deal." Jody laughed, then reached past him to take her skis. As she turned around, she saw that Chris was watching her. All Jody's good feelings froze like the hard-packed snow under her feet. Chris's face was a mask of hate.

Chapter 2

Riding up in the lift, Jody breathed deeply, taking in a great gulp of the cold air. She kept telling herself she'd only imagined the hatred in Chris's eyes. Chris was probably just squinting in the sun, and that always distorted people's faces. Still, Jody couldn't help feeling that Chris wanted Drew for herself, and thought Jody was butting into her territory.

Jody shivered as she watched the skiers below making their runs. She was anxious to get off the lift and join them. Thinking about Chris's look bothered her, like remembering a bad dream. Once Jody was up on the slopes, she could forget about Chris and just think about skiing, which she loved.

In a couple of minutes, the lift had reached the top. Jody stood up and slid down the snow-covered, wooden ramp. Then she poled on a few feet farther, where most of the people were heading, toward the intermediate slopes. Once there, she checked her bindings, then maneuvered herself into position.

Just before she pulled down her goggles, she saw Ellen, looking very pretty in pale blue, get off the lift. Behind her came Sasha and Cal. Sasha was wearing red and black, very dramatic, Jody thought. It made her own teal and yellow seem washed out, but Jody figured Sasha probably made most girls feel washed out. She wondered if Cal, long and lean in black and silver, had the same effect on guys.

But Jody didn't stand around wondering for long. There was a whole afternoon of skiing ahead. She still hadn't decided whether she could have a great time with these people, but she knew she could enjoy the slopes. She pulled down her goggles, jabbed her poles into the snow, and pushed off down the slope.

An hour later, Jody came to a perfect stop at the bottom of the slope, slid up her goggles and grinned to herself. This one had been her best run yet; she'd felt completely in control, her body doing exactly what it was supposed to do.

Exhilirated, her cheeks tingling, Jody glanced up the slope and tried not to laugh. Here came Billy, floundering in the powder, his legs straight as sticks. Jody felt like shouting at him to bend his knees, but he was too far away. She covered her eyes, then slid her fingers apart and watched as Billy came up over a small rise. His body was ramrod straight, and his poles were dragging. He didn't stand a chance.

Jody covered her eyes again, cringing in sympathy for what she knew was coming. When she finally looked, Billy was spitting snow and trying to pick himself up from a tangle of skis and poles.

Once he got himself together, he trudged down the rest of the way and stopped in front of Jody, breathing heavily.

"That *was* the Jaws of Death, wasn't it?" he asked.

Jody laughed. "I hate to tell you . . ."

"I know, I know. I belong on the beginners' slope," Billy said. He brushed more snow off his hair. "It's too humiliating, though. Some of those kids in grade school are better than I am."

"I guess I'd feel the same way. You've probably heard this before, but you should bend your knees, go into a sort of semi-crouch." Jody found herself cringing again: Billy's lips were chapped, and his forehead and nose were sunburned. "And wear some sunscreen," she added. "Your face is going to be sore."

"Yeah? That'll be nothing, compared to the way the rest of me feels already." He started putting his skis back on. "Give me a minute, okay? I'll walk over to the lift with you."

"You're going up again?"

"You're surprised? I don't blame you." Billy was tightening his bindings, his goggles dangling from one ear.

"Well, a little," Jody admitted. "But at least you don't quit."

"That's not it. I have a reputation to keep up." The goggles plopped into the snow, and he got his skis crossed shuffling around to pick them up.

"Don't move," Jody said. She bent easily, got the goggles, and held them out to him. "What do you mean, a reputation?"

"I'm the laugh man," he said as they headed for the lift line. "I either tell jokes or — "

"Or what?"

"Or I *am* the joke." Billy's smile had faded, and, for an instant, Jody thought he looked almost angry. "Haven't you figured that out?" he asked.

Jody shook her head, embarrassed. "We hardly know each other," she reminded him. "What about the others? Do they know you really well?"

"Nope." Billy looked at her. "Why'd you ask that? No, wait, I know. You're saying I could make a new image for myself, become a new Billy Feldman, at least while we're here?"

"No, but now that you mention it, I guess you could," Jody said. "I mean, if you wanted to." She bet he wanted to, especially with Sashá. Jody felt funny giving him advice. Besides, she didn't think he stood a chance with Sasha Wolf, no matter what kind of new image he came up with.

They were at the lift line by now, but suddenly Billy shuffled to the side. "On second thought, I think I'll sit out for a while, anyway, give myself a break. See you later, Jody."

There's definitely more to him than that clownish image he puts on, Jody thought. Just before she got on the lift, she turned around and looked at Billy. He was standing where she'd left him, watching a skier coming down the slope. A skier in dramatic red and black with perfect form and dark, gleaming hair whipping out behind her. It was Sasha. Billy gaped up at her, his skis pigeon-toed. Jody hoped he remembered to straighten them out and close his mouth before Sasha reached him.

By late afternoon, the sky had clouded over and a few snowflakes were whirling around in the wind. Jody came out of one of the warm-up huts, where she'd just gulped down some hot chocolate, and tried to decide whether to go back up. A nice warm cabin, a hot shower, and a change of clothes were tempting. Maybe one more run, she decided. Then she'd call it quits for the day.

She hadn't seen Drew or Chris since she'd left them at the van earlier, but when she got off the lift, she saw both of them at the top of the ridge. In fact, the entire group was there.

"Jody!" Sasha called out as Jody slid toward them. "Come on, you're just in time!"

"For what?"

"Sasha just had a brilliant idea," Cal said. "Well, *she* thinks it's brilliant. I think it's a little crazy, myself."

"Come on!" Sasha gave her brother a light punch on the arm. "You love it, I can tell." She tossed her head and laughed. "You're just scared you won't be able to do it."

"I *know* I won't be able to do it," Cal said.

"Do what?" Jody asked.

Ellen touched her lightly on the arm. "Look down the slope," she said, pointing with her pole. "There's that bunch of trees and then there's a little rise. What do you see?"

Blinking the snowflakes off her eyelashes, Jody squinted down the slope. At first she didn't see anything but snow. Then, just past a group of pines, she thought she saw a small rock. It was awfully bright for a rock, though. "I give up," she said. "What is it?"

"An orange peel," Ellen said.

"Okay," Jody laughed. "What's the brilliant idea?"

"A contest," Sasha said excitedly. "You have to ski down, stab the orange peel with your pole, go around the trees and then over the rise. The run flattens out for a few yards after that and there's a place where you can stop, so you don't have to go all the way down. Whoever makes the fastest time wins."

"Whoever makes it down *alive*, you mean," Cal said. "You'll be coming around the trees, there's no time to stab an orange peel and get set for the rise. Your balance will be all wrong."

"Oh, come on," Sasha said. "It'll be fun!"

"Great," Chris muttered, completely without enthusiasm. "An orange-peel slalom."

"All you have to do is holler when you've stopped." Sasha walked over next to Billy and threw her arm around his shoulders. "Billy, you'd like to be our timekeeper, wouldn't you?" She pulled off her watch and handed it to him. "It works as a stopwatch, too," she explained, pointing to a little button on the side.

Billy took the watch, his face even redder than it had been earlier. Probably because Sasha was so close, Jody thought. "Sure, Sasha," he said. "I'll keep time for you."

"Smart man, Billy," Cal said. "Good way to get out of it."

"Hey, somebody's gotta punch the button," Billy said with a grin. "Besides, I defy anybody to equal my finesse with a stopwatch."

"Well, come on, you guys!" Sasha urged. "Drew, don't you want to try?"

Jody wasn't sure Drew had been listening. He hadn't greeted her when she arrived, and even though Chris had planted herself right next to him, Drew hadn't said a word to her, either. While the rest of them had been discussing the orange-peel slalom, he'd been staring off into the distance.

Jody wondered if he thought this whole thing sounded dangerous, like she did. Skiing around the trees and getting set for the rise was hard enough. Trying to stab an orange peel could make you shift your balance so much that you'd come over the rise all wrong. If you landed badly, you might do more than just take a spill.

Or was there something else bothering Drew, Jody wondered.

"Drew?" Sasha said again. She sounded excited and a little impatient. This was her idea, Jody thought; she wanted everyone to think it was as great as she did.

"Why don't you go first, Sasha?" Chris sneered a little.

"We could draw straws," Billy suggested, when Sasha didn't say anything to Chris. "Well, not straws. How about pine needles?"

Sasha ignored him. *"Of course* I'll go first," she said, pulling down her goggles and getting into position. "I *expected* to go first." She looked over at her brother, and Jody saw that Cal was already getting ready to go next. She couldn't tell if he'd decided on his own or if Sasha had somehow egged him on without saying a word. Or maybe he was just silently sticking by her.

Drew finally spoke up. "Don't get all bent out of shape, Sasha. Most of us just hadn't planned on breaking a leg our first day out, that's all."

Sasha smiled around the group. "Nobody *has* to go, really. I'm sorry if I got pushy again." With that, she was off, down the slope and around the trees. She missed the orange peel, kept going, and a moment later they heard her call out, "Come on, Cal!"

"Here goes nothing." Cal took off in a flash of silver and black. His form was as good as Sasha's, but he didn't get the orange peel, either.

The snow was coming down more heavily now, and not many other skiers were up on the slopes. Billy reset the stopwatch. "Okay, who's next?"

Chris sighed loudly. "I just want to get this over with," she said, stomping into position. "Don't bother to time me, Billy. I'm not even going to try for the dumb orange peel."

But at the last minute, coming around the trees, Chris must have changed her mind. She swung her right pole out toward the orange peel and jabbed down.

"Hey!" Billy shouted. "I think she got it!"

But the rise was coming up fast, and Chris had to shift her weight back to the left to be ready for it. She bent her knees, leaned left, and brought her right pole back to tuck it under her arm. She took the rise in good shape, but she left the orange peel about a foot farther to the right than it had been.

Drew looked at Jody. "She just gave us the perfect excuse not to try for the orange peel."

"That's what I was thinking," Jody laughed.

"Yeah?" His dark-brown eyes flickered over her face, and he smiled a little. "Looks like we're on the same wavelength again."

Jody watched him push off, feeling a little excited. He was awfully good-looking, and when he wasn't being quiet and moody, he seemed really nice. She wasn't going out with anybody right now, but she hadn't come on the trip to find a guy. Still, if something started to happen between her and Drew, she might have trouble resisting.

Remembering that Ellen had seemed interested in Drew, too, Jody stopped grinning to herself and glanced at her. Ellen wasn't shooting her a look that could kill, at least. She just looked sad. Ellen was thin, almost frail-looking, and the disappointment in her soft hazel eyes gave Jody a twinge. But the twinge didn't last long. She didn't know Ellen, she didn't really know Drew, she didn't even know if he was interested in her or not. And she wasn't going to get all upset worrying about it.

"Do you want to go now, or shall I?" she asked.

"I'll go." Ellen dug in her poles and pushed off. Jody hadn't seen her ski before now. Jody was surprised to learn that for somebody so frail-looking, Ellen was smooth and strong and sure of herself.

"What about you?" Jody asked Billy. "Can you get down okay?"

"Oh, sure, I'll make it. I'll hike down if I have to."

Jody laughed and pushed off, not even glancing at the orange peel as she came around the trees. She took the rise and landed a little shakily, but managed to keep her balance. The run flattened out, as Sasha had said, and a few yards away, Jody saw the group waiting for her.

Jody heard laughter as she came to a stop; even Chris had a smile on her face. Somebody should tell her to smile more often, Jody thought. It was a refreshing change from the prickly look she usually wore.

"I don't know what happened to me," Chris was saying. "When I started, I was just going to ignore the orange peel, but then I couldn't resist taking a stab at it."

"How far away is it now?" Cal asked Jody.

"Too far," Jody laughed.

"We can always move it back," Sasha suggested.

"Well, it's snowing too hard now, anyway," Cal said. "Let's wait for Billy and go to the cabin. My toes are numb."

"Right, my face feels like a slab of ice," Drew said. "I could use something hot to drink. Where is Billy, anyway?"

Jody started to say it might take him a while to get down, but just then, a skier appeared over the rise. For a second, she thought it was Billy, but she changed her mind fast. The skier looked like an ad for the best in style and form: bright white outfit with neon-green stripes, knees bent perfectly to absorb the impact of the landing. Besides, this skier was a girl. Thick, taffy-colored hair swirled out behind her as she dug in her poles and pushed toward them.

"Look, I don't believe it!" Chris said. "She's got the orange peel!"

Sure enough, as the skier lifted her left pole and waved it triumphantly, everyone could see the glistening orange peel stuck to the end of it.

"Hey, is that who I think it is?" Cal said.

Drew's expression hardened, and he frowned at the skier. "Couldn't be anybody else," he said, his voice tight.

"Who?" Chris asked.

"It's Leahna," Ellen said softly.

"Yeah. Leahna." Cal breathed out her name on a sigh.

Leahna Calder. Jody suddenly felt very sorry for Kate. From the look on Cal's face, he was more than just "interested" in Leahna. He was crazy about her.

Chapter 3

Thawed out from a hot shower, Jody left the bathroom and padded up the open-tread stairs to the
cabin's second floor. It was dark out now, and remembering Sasha's comment about the windows,
Jody kept a tight hold on the king-size bath towel
she'd wrapped around herself.

Reaching the second floor, she stopped and
looked over the railing, down to the living room
below. The floor was wood, scattered over with
American-Indian-type rugs. The chairs and couch
were covered in bright blue corduroy, and a fire
was burning in an orange, free-standing fireplace.
Underneath where she was standing, was the
kitchen, gleaming white and modern. The place had
everything, right down to extra goggles and tooth-
paste. All they'd had to bring was food.

Jody knew from Kate that the owners were
friends of Cal's and Sasha's parents, which was why
they'd gotten a nice break on the rent. Thank God
for that, she thought. She'd never have been able
to afford whatever they charged strangers.

As she was turning to go into the girls' half of the upstairs sleeping loft, Jody saw a movement out of the corner of her eye. She looked back down and saw Sasha stride into the living room from the back of the cabin. She was carrying two wooden bowls, one each of chips and pretzels, which she set down on the coffee table. Behind her came Cal, his arms full of logs for the fireplace.

Sasha dropped onto the couch and stretched her long legs out. "Listen," she said.

"I did. I don't want to listen anymore." Cal dumped the logs into a brass holder and walked out.

Jody followed his dark head until it disappeared, then she looked back at the couch. Sasha was sitting up now, staring at the fire. Jody couldn't see her face, but from the way Sasha's shoulders were hunched, she knew she wasn't happy.

Trouble in twinland, Jody thought. The two of them seemed like such perfect soulmates, it was almost reassuring to see that they could argue, just like a normal brother and sister.

In spite of the closeness that shut everyone out sometimes, Jody liked them. Sasha tried to take over a lot, but she was so charming when somebody called her on it, you couldn't hold it against her. And Cal was even better: looser, funnier, and really sexy. Jody might have been interested in him herself, but after watching him practically drool over Leahna Calder earlier, she figured everyone else's romantic chances with him were close to zero.

Not wanting to get caught staring, Jody turned away and went down the hall that divided the two big sleeping lofts, frowning as she thought of Drew's reaction to Leahna. He'd looked angry at her, but he hadn't been able to take his eyes off her, either. It was almost as if he couldn't decide whether he loved her or hated her.

Chris was in the girls' half of the loft, stretched out on the floor with a magazine. Jody stepped over pillows and duffel bags and went to the end by the window, where she'd dumped her stuff on one of the low beds.

"Is Ellen in the shower now?" Chris asked.

"Mmm. She said she wouldn't be long." Jody pulled on jeans and a pink wool sweater, sitting on the floor to do it. Sasha hadn't been kidding about no curtains. The window was big, too, covering almost the whole end of the room. Standing up, Jody looked out and up, right into the brightly lit window of the cabin above theirs. A figure crossed the room, and Jody turned away. Then she laughed.

"What?" Chris asked, licking her fingertip to turn the magazine page.

"I just noticed those binoculars," Jody said, pointing to a pair hanging by their leather strap from a hook on the back of the door. "They must belong to the owners. I saw somebody in the cabin out there and actually wanted to get a better look." She laughed again. "I sound like Billy."

"Umm." Chris turned another page, then glanced at Jody. "What did you think of the Lovely Leahna?"

Uh-oh, Jody thought. She wasn't sure she wanted to get into this conversation. "Well, she

. . ." Jody rubbed her hair with the towel and tried to think of something diplomatic to say. "She's a good skier."

Chris laughed. "Right. She's also gorgeous and rich and spoiled rotten."

"You know her?"

"I've met her a few times. She goes to the same school with Cal and Sasha and Drew and Ellen." Chris flipped the magazine aside and stood up, stretching. "Cal's obviously wild for her, but I was hoping Drew was smarter than that."

Jody sat on the bed and started combing her hair. "What do you mean?"

"I mean, Drew and Leahna were seeing each other for a while," Chris said. "He was crazy for her, and I guess while it lasted, it really sizzled." She snorted. "Of course, it didn't last long. Nothing ever lasts long with Leahna."

"What happened?"

"What do you think?" Chris asked. "She dropped him. She got him to where he couldn't think about anything but her, and then she told him to get lost."

"Why?"

"Because," Chris said impatiently, "that's what she likes to do — play with people's feelings. From what I heard, it was a pretty ugly scene — Drew shouted at her and called her every name in the book, told her she'd be sorry some day."

Remembering Drew's reaction to Leahna on the slopes, Jody's heart sank a little. He probably *did* hate her, she thought. But he certainly wasn't over her.

"Anyway," Chris went on, "like I said, I was hoping Drew had gotten smart. But I'll bet he's down in the kitchen right now, trying to get Leahna on the phone to invite her to the party again." Chris obviously didn't care much about the windows. She undressed in the middle of the room and walked casually to the bed where she'd flung her robe. "Didn't you hear him and Cal inviting her before?"

Jody shook her head. "I saw them talking to her, but they were too far away for me to hear."

"Well, I heard them." Chris tossed her head and changed her voice. " 'A party sounds wonderful, but I don't know. I might be flying to Antigua tomorrow, and I'll need to get to bed early.' Antigua, can you believe it?" Chris said in her own voice. "I wish she was there right now."

"Well, maybe she will be tomorrow," Jody said. "Then you can . . ." she stopped, but Chris picked up on it.

"I can go after Drew again?" she asked. "Yes, I plan to. The question is, will I be the only one?" Chris eyed Jody, a small smile on her lips.

It was a challenge, Jody knew it. She was tempted to say something, but the thought of exchanging nasty remarks with Chris was really kind of disgusting.

Chris was still watching her. The look in her eyes made Jody nervous, so she got up and started rummaging through her duffel bag for some eye makeup.

"I probably won't be the only one," Chris said,

answering her own question. "Ellen's been hanging around him as much as possible. I don't think I have to worry about *her*, though. But I'll have to keep my eye on Leahna." She laughed a little. "What about you, Jody?"

Chris's tone still made Jody nervous, but she could feel herself starting to get mad, too. She slammed down the little eye-shadow compact and took a deep breath. "No, I'm not worried about Leahna," she said. "I'll leave that to you. I'm sure you can handle it."

"Yeah?" Chris laughed again, maliciously. "So am I."

Ellen came into the room then, bundled in a thick white bathrobe and carrying a telephone. "Jody, your friend Kate's on the phone," she said, looking around for the wall plug. "Cal found this extension in one of the kitchen cabinets, so you can talk up here."

Ellen found the plug and hooked up the phone, and Chris gathered up her shampoo and conditioner and left the room. Jody settled on her bed and picked up the receiver. "Hi, how are you feeling?"

There was a click; someone had hung up the phone in the kitchen. "Worse than yesterday," Kate said. "I didn't think that was possible. Cheer me up and tell me what's happening."

"Well, the skiing's been great so far. It's snowing now, so there's not any skiing tonight," Jody said. "That's okay, though, because Sasha already organized a party. There are two gigantic subs stuffed with ham and cheese and salami sitting in the kitchen right now. I think I could eat one of them by myself, I'm so hungry."

Jody heard herself babbling on and knew she was trying to keep Kate from asking about Leahna. "We had this contest on the trail before," she went on, watching Ellen towel her wet hair. "It was crazy, but nobody got hurt. Nobody fell, even. What we did was — "

"How are you getting along?" Kate broke in. "I mean, with all those strangers you were so worried about?"

"Fine."

"What do you think of Cal? Isn't he incredible? Drew's not bad, either, you notice."

"Yep."

"Chris'd die for him."

"Uh-huh."

"Oh," Kate said. "Somebody's in the room with you, am I right?"

"You got it." Ellen was pulling clothes out of her bag now, obviously trying not to listen. But Jody knew it was impossible. How could you not listen when the only person in the room with you was talking on the telephone? "Like I said," she added, "it's been great so far."

"Okay, I'll get to the point," Kate said. "Leahna. She showed up, didn't she?"

"Well, yes." Here it comes, Jody thought.

Kate let out her breath. "Well? Oh, right, you can't talk. Okay, did anything happen? Did she come on to Cal?"

"Not that I could see." That was being honest, at least. As far as Jody could tell, Leahna had acted kind of aloof.

"Never mind, she doesn't flirt," Kate said. "She just stands back and waits for guys to act like idiots around her, like she deserves their attention or something. Then she looks amused." She paused. "Did Cal? Fall all over her, I mean?"

"Uh, no, nobody fell."

"You know what I mean," Kate said sharply. "He did, didn't he? I knew he would. She's so great-looking, guys don't bother to find out what she's like. And by then it's too late. Is she coming to the party?"

"I don't know." Jody suddenly hated the way Kate sounded, so mean and vicious. Maybe Leahna was a beautiful creep, but there was nothing Kate could do about her. Or about Cal, either. "I really don't know," Jody said again. "Listen, I think I just heard a bunch of people come in downstairs. I guess the party's about ready to start."

"Okay. Let me say hi to Sasha, will you?" Kate said. "I'll talk to you again, tomorrow, maybe."

"Okay. I hope you get better fast." Jody lay the phone down quickly before Kate had a chance to say anything more. She went out to the railing over-looking the living room, and saw Sasha talking to some kids she didn't recognize. "Sasha?" Jody called. "Kate's on the phone, wants to say hi."

"Thanks, I'll get it in the kitchen."

Back in the bedroom, Jody waited until she heard Sasha's voice on the extension, then hung up and went over to the mirror hanging above a low, white chest of drawers. Her hair, dark-brown and naturally curly, was almost dry. She leaned close to the mirror and started putting on some eye shadow. Ellen was standing behind her, in the middle of the room, and their eyes met.

Ellen smiled. "I wish my hair would curl like that."

"It's murder in the summer," Jody said. "Curls so tight I have trouble getting a comb through it."

Ellen ran a comb through her own hair, which was fine and straight. "Jody? Could I ask you something?"

"Sure."

Ellen glanced at the door and bit her lip. Then she said, "Do you think I could ever have a chance with Cal?"

"*Cal?*" Jody almost dropped her makeup brush. "I thought you . . ."

"I know. You thought I was in love with Drew." Ellen smiled again. "Drew's a friend. I've known him a long time. I'm not comfortable with very many people, but I am with him."

Jody turned around and leaned against the chest. "Drew's . . . well, he doesn't seem like the most comfortable person to be with."

Ellen's laugh was as airy as her voice. "I know, it's funny, isn't it? His moods go up and down like a roller coaster. I guess I'm just used to them and they don't bother me." She looked down and picked a piece of fuzz off her navy sweater. "But it's Cal I love," she said in a low voice.

Jody cleared her throat. Talk about feeling uncomfortable. "Well, I don't really know Cal at all," she said. "Is he going out with anybody?"

Ellen shook her head. "He'd like to be going out with Leahna, anybody can see that."

"Well, but maybe he just likes the way she looks," Jody said. She knew it was more than that, but Ellen sounded so sad, she wanted to cheer her up. "I mean, she *is* beautiful."

"Sure. She's beautiful like Snow White's stepmother," Ellen said. "Inside she's rotten. I can't believe Cal doesn't see it."

"Chris told me about how she dropped Drew," Jody said. "It sounded pretty awful."

Ellen nodded. "She does things like that all the time. I don't mean just dropping boys, though. Once I thought she was my friend. She acted like one, anyway. We went to the library together and to the movies a couple of times, stuff like that." Ellen was staring into the distance, remembering. "She was in between boys at the time, so I should have guessed. But I didn't. She knew I'd been working on this essay for a statewide contest, and she offered to read it and make suggestions, you know. So naturally, I let her. And she stole it."

"What do you mean? You mean, she wrote the same thing?" Jody asked. "How come the teacher or judges or whatever didn't notice?"

"First we had to submit an idea to our English teacher," Ellen said. "The teacher told me my idea was good, but Leahna had had it first." Ellen's lips curled in a little smile. "She beat me to it. And her essay got into the finals."

"What did you say to her?"

"Nothing."

"Nothing?" Jody couldn't believe it. "Why didn't you tell the teacher? How come you let her get away with it?"

"Because I was afraid." Ellen blinked and shifted her gaze to Jody. "But she'll pay for it some day, you know. She'll pay for everything, I'm sure of it. I just hope it happens before she gets to Cal, because she'll hurt him, too. She takes and takes and never gives. She's rotten."

Ellen was talking softly, as usual, but there was ice in her voice. Jody shuddered a little.

"I'm sorry," Ellen said. "I shouldn't have said anything."

"It's okay. It's just that I can't tell you anything about Cal or what he's thinking. I don't know him," Jody said. "I don't really know you, either, or anybody else, hardly." She realized she sounded kind of cold. "Couldn't you ask Sasha about this?"

Ellen burst out laughing.

Jody looked at her curiously.

"Sorry, I'm not laughing at you, not really." Ellen took a deep breath. "Never mind, Jody. I should never have asked you. It wasn't fair, because you're right, you don't know any of us." She laughed again, almost a giggle, then stopped herself. "I think I'll go down and get something to eat before the food disappears. Thanks for listening to me, Jody."

When Ellen had gone, Jody leaned against the

chest and closed her eyes. First Chris, then Kate, then Ellen. One friend and two people she barely knew, and they were all obsessed with Leahna Calder. She shuddered, remembering the way they'd sounded, so full of bitterness. Her head was starting to ache — the last half hour had been a little too much.

A blast of music suddenly thundered up from below, and Jody fluffed up her hair and headed for the door. She was ready for a party. With dozens of people around, she could hide in the crowd and not get too close to *anybody*.

Chapter 4

The party *should* have been great. It started out exactly as Jody wanted. But by the end, she began to wish she'd never been a part of it.

At first it was fun. There were at least twenty people, not counting Jody's group, and she didn't know a single one. Nobody was being serious, either. Well, Drew had a frown on his face, but Jody decided that was normal for him half the time.

Jody enjoyed herself, just wandering around from group to group, listening but not talking much. It was almost impossible to talk, anyway, the music was so loud. But that was okay. She wasn't in the mood to talk.

Sasha was the center of the party, which didn't surprise Jody a bit. Dressed in sweatpants and a sweatshirt, with no makeup and her hair tied back with a piece of yarn, she still managed to look more beautiful than anyone. She danced a little and laughed a lot and was constantly on the move, her pale blue eyes searching out everyone, as if she wanted to make sure they were having fun.

Everyone was, at first. Well, Chris looked a little glum because Drew wasn't paying any attention to her; she prowled the edges of the room and always kept coming back to Drew, who was slouched in a low chair near the fire, watching the front door. Cal kept a hopeful eye on the door, too, Jody noticed. He was waiting for Leahna, she thought. She guessed Drew was, too, but he didn't look hopeful. He looked edgy, as if he wasn't sure whether he wanted her to come or not. But everybody else kept shouting at each other over the music, joking and swapping ski stories.

"Jody!" Billy called out when she walked into the kitchen. "Better hurry, the subs won't last forever."

Jody grabbed a wide wedge of one of the sandwiches and bit into it. She was famished.

"There's lots to drink," Billy told her, opening the refrigerator. "Coke, 7-Up, diet, regular, caffeine-free?"

"Later," Jody mumbled, her mouth full. People were milling around, brushing past her to get to the food. "I was wondering where you were," she said to Billy. "How come you're hanging out in here?"

"Sasha asked if I'd sort of take charge of the food, make sure we don't run out." Billy smiled, his mouth glistening with lip balm. "I guess my new image needs some more work. But hey, did you notice how I made that run today without crippling myself?"

"You did great." Jody didn't think Sasha had noticed, though. She'd been watching Leahna, like almost everyone else. "What happened, anyway? With Leahna, I mean?"

"I was just getting up the nerve to go down, and she came along," Billy said. "Kind of surprised me because nobody else was coming up on the lift by then. Anyway, we could hear you guys laughing, and she asked me what was going on, so I told her about the orange peel. So she goes, 'What's the prize if you get it?' And I said I didn't know if there was one, but Sasha would probably come up with something. She acted really excited when she found out it was Sasha and Cal down there. I was telling her about how Chris had knocked the orange peel out of reach, but she just laughed and said, 'Watch this.' Then she took off." Billy shook his head in wonder. "I couldn't believe it when she actually stabbed the thing."

"Nobody else could, either," Jody said. "Do you know her?"

"Not really. I've seen her around, though."

"I was just wondering if she's as bad as she sounds," Jody said. "I got an earful about her from Chris and Ellen."

"Well, I got the feeling Sasha isn't crazy about her, either," Billy said. "I heard her tell Drew the party wouldn't be ruined if she didn't show up."

"Listen," Jody said, "you shouldn't be staying in here all the time. People can find their own food. Why don't you go ask Sasha to dance or something?"

"I dance about as well as I ski," Billy said. He looked hopefully toward the living room. "But maybe I'll go talk to her."

After Billy left, Jody got herself a can of Coke and was just about ready to go back into the living room when Drew and Cal came into the kitchen. "Jody, how's it going, you having a good time?" Cal asked. Without waiting for an answer, he crossed to the telephone and started dialing. Jody looked at Drew, but he was watching Cal. Jody shrugged and left the room.

Over by the fireplace, Billy had edged close to Sasha and was gesturing wildly with his hands as he talked to her. Jody winced when one of his flying hands hit Sasha's cup, sending it halfway across the room where it landed with a splash at someone's feet.

Sasha laughed and patted him on the shoulder, then she leaned close and said something in his ear. Billy scurried off toward the kitchen, passing Jody on the way. "Did you see that trick?" he asked, his face redder than ever. "I've got a million of them."

"It could happen to anybody," Jody said.

"Yeah, but not on somebody's Navajo rug." Billy gulped a little. "Sasha said there's some kind of special cleaner in the kitchen. I hope it works." He turned and hurried on, almost bumping into Cal, who was on his way back in.

Jody spotted an empty chair near the fireplace and got to it fast. She sank down and closed her eyes a minute. The cold air and the skiing before, and now the heat of the room, were making her sleepy.

"You should see yourself, Cal," Jody heard Sasha say. "You keep watching the door like you're waiting for the Second Coming or something."

Jody kept her eyes closed.

"I'm not the only one," Cal said. "But Drew's not watching the door anymore. He just went over to her cabin."

"Fine, wonderful. That'll be one less person dragging the party down."

"Yeah, but what if he comes back with her?"

Sasha didn't answer, at least not directly. "I wish you could just forget her."

Cal was quiet for a minute. Then he said, "So do I, Sash. But things change."

He sounded so sad, Jody thought. She opened her eyes and looked around. That's when she saw Ellen standing nearby. Ellen had obviously overheard the conversation, too. She was staring into the distance the way she had earlier, but her jaw was clenched tightly, as if she were trying not to scream in anger.

"You're right, things do change." Sasha's voice was suddenly loud and excited. "And I think it's time for a change right now. Everybody!" she called out over the music. "Time for games, okay? Party games!"

Jody opened her eyes and saw Sasha striding toward the wall unit, where she shut off the CD player. She whirled around and faced everyone, her cheeks bright with color. "Enough standing around mindlessly stuffing yourselves, let's do something really fun!"

"I'm having fun already," someone quipped.

"Maybe, but look at Billy." Sasha pointed to Billy, down on his knees with a sponge, rubbing at the rug. "He can't possibly be enjoying himself. Billy, I'm sure you've got it, if you keep going, you'll rub a hole in the rug." She laughed and pointed to a chair in the center of the room. "Go sit there, okay, and we'll start the game."

Still holding the sponge, Billy took the chair. Sasha rummaged around in a drawer of the wall unit and came up with her hands full of pencils and small pads of paper.

"Pictionary?" someone asked. "I hate that game."

"That's okay, we're not playing it." Sasha looked at Cal, and they smiled at each other. Whatever was wrong between them seemed to have been forgotten. "This is much better."

"So what is it?" Chris asked.

"Truth," Cal said.

Someone groaned, but Cal ignored it. "One person sits in the chair and the rest of us write something down about him. Somebody reads the statements, and the person has to say whether they're true or not."

This time it was Jody who groaned, but she did it silently. She'd played this game before, or at least a version of it, and it always got embarrassing. Just because it was a game, people seemed to think it was okay to dredge up all kinds of secrets. You could lie, of course, but half the time your face gave you away. And whoever'd written the secret would call you on it.

Looking around the room, Jody saw that there weren't as many people as there had been earlier. She guessed some of them had gone on to other parties, or maybe to the lodge, or just to bed. She was tempted to go upstairs to bed herself, but she didn't want to get caught trying to sneak out of this. She sank down farther into the chair.

Sasha went around the room, passing out pencils and paper. When she was finished, she went over and stood next to Billy. "This is Billy Feldman," she said. "He's sixteen, and if you don't know him, then just take a guess at something."

Billy watched as people started scribbling on their pads. He looked like he was on trial.

"Remember," Sasha said, "you can't write easy stuff like 'You'd like to be rich.' This game is supposed to force people to be honest, even if it's embarrassing. And there's nothing embarrassing about wanting money."

Jody thought a minute, then wrote, *You sometimes wish you were somebody else.* From what she knew of Billy, it had to be true. And it wasn't prying, either. Lots of people wished that.

After a moment, Cal gathered the slips of paper from everyone. "Ready?" he asked Billy.

"Aren't I supposed to get a hearty meal first?" Billy said. "No, I already had one. Actually I had three. Okay, okay, go ahead. Let me have it. How bad can it be?"

The first statement was *You never lie.*

"Obviously, somebody took a guess," Billy said, looking relieved. "Not true. I do lie. I admit it."

Cal read the next statement. It was Jody's. Billy listened, then shook his head. "Not true." He grinned. "I *always* wish I were someone else."

"Go on, Cal," Sasha urged.

"If you didn't laugh at yourself, you'd be the only one not laughing," Cal read.

Somebody whistled. Jody looked at Chris, wondering if she'd written it. Chris was picking at a fingernail, looking bored.

"I knew something like this was coming," Billy said. He squeezed the sponge, dripping water on his jeans. "Well. How do I know? I mean, I can't speak for everybody. I can't answer it."

"But you have to," Sasha said softly. She was sitting on the rug, her long legs curled under her.

"Okay, true," Billy said quickly. He was starting to look trapped. His soft brown eyes darted around the room as if he were looking for a way to escape. "Next question, please."

Cal looked at the next slip of paper. "Um . . . it says, *You hate Sasha.*"

Sasha's eyes widened, but she looked eager to hear the answer.

Billy leaned over until his forehead was touching his knees. His shoulders shook a little, and Jody thought he must be laughing. It was a ridiculous question, she thought. Anyone with eyes could see that Billy was wild about Sasha.

"Billy?" Cal said.

Billy slowly raised his head. His eyes were bright, but not with laughter. He glanced around the room again and stopped when he saw Jody. He looked straight at her. "I thought we could be friends," he said, his voice pleading.

Jody felt like someone had punched her in the stomach.

No one else seemed to have noticed that Billy was speaking directly to Jody.

"Does that mean it's not true?" Cal asked.

"What?" Billy blinked. Finally he looked away from Jody. "Oh. Yes. Not true."

"Well, that's a relief," Sasha said, with a light laugh. "Of course we can be friends, Billy. We *are* friends."

"Great." Billy stood up, the sponge still gripped in his hand.

"Hey, where are you going?" Cal jabbed him playfully on the shoulder. "Your time's not up yet, buddy."

Billy started to say something, but before he could, the front door opened and Drew came in, a gust of cold wind blowing behind him. He was alone.

"Drew!" Sasha said, leaping to her feet. "You're just in time. We're playing Truth. You can join us."

Drew didn't answer at first. He was stomping snow off his boots, his head down. When he looked up, he and Cal exchanged glances. Drew's face was dark with anger. Cal's shoulders sagged, and the hopeful expression disappeared from his face.

"Hey, what's it like out there now?" someone asked Drew. "Still snowing?"

"I didn't notice," Drew said shortly. As he shrugged out of his jacket, several kids went to the front window, cupping their hands against the glass so they could see outside, talking about what the slopes would be like tomorrow.

But Jody didn't join in. Billy had taken advantage of the break to slip out of the room and go into the kitchen, and Jody decided to follow him. She had to straighten things out.

On her way through the living room, she got stuck for a moment behind Cal, who had moved over next to Drew.

"Is she leaving tomorrow?" Cal was asking Drew.

"You think she'd be straight and tell me?" Drew said. "She laughed and said she wasn't sure. Like you can just pick up and fly from Brevard to Antigua without having to plan ahead."

Jody put her hand lightly on Cal's back, thinking he'd step aside, but he didn't seem to notice.

"Maybe I'll go over, talk to her," Cal said. "You don't mind, I mean . . ."

"Hey, I'm through, she's all yours, buddy," Drew said bitterly.

"Come on, Drew," Chris said, brushing past Jody and slipping her arm through Drew's. "There's an empty chair by the fireplace. Come sit down."

Drew glanced at her, then back at Cal. "Go if you want to," he said. "But if you want my advice, don't waste your time."

"Come on, Drew!" Chris gave his arm an impatient tug, and finally the three of them shifted, and Jody was able to get by.

"Jody, if you see Billy, would you bring him back?" Sasha called out to her. "We're going to get started again."

"I'll tell him, but I have the feeling he doesn't want to sit in the hot seat anymore."

"No?" Sasha looked surprised. "Why?"

Jody stared at her. Had she really missed the trapped look on Billy's face? "I just don't think he was having any fun, that's all."

"Oh, sure he was. Everybody knows it's just a game. Nobody takes it seriously." Sasha smiled and spun back toward the rest of the group.

Maybe she's right, Jody thought, heading on to the kitchen. Maybe Billy hadn't really been looking at Jody when he'd said he thought they were friends. Nobody else had picked up on it, so maybe she'd just imagined the whole thing.

The kitchen was empty, except for Billy. He was standing at the sink, splashing water on his face.

"Billy?" Jody said.

He held up a hand, gesturing for her to wait. Then he reached for the paper towel holder, which spun out of control, sending about twenty of the towels into a pile on the counter. Billy fumbled at them, tore off too many, and blotted his face. His back was still to Jody.

Finally, he turned around, crumpling the towels into a ball in his fist. "How did you know?" he asked quietly. "Until tonight, I didn't even realize that I hate Sasha. So how did you figure it out?"

Chapter 5

Jody felt as if the wind had been knocked out of her again. Coming from Billy, the word *hate* sounded foreign. He was too soft, too puppy-doggish for such a strong word. But there he was, his jaw tight, his eyes hard. He didn't look soft at all. He looked perfectly capable of hating, maybe even hating Jody herself.

"You look surprised," Billy said. "Actually, you look shocked. Why?"

Jody felt behind her for one of the kitchen chairs, swung it around to face him and sat down. "I came in here to tell you that I didn't write that — about hating Sasha," she said. "I never expected you to say you do."

Billy leaned his head back and stared at the ceiling. "Me and my big mouth," he said, his chin still in the air. "I should have let you talk first. Then I could have laughed the whole thing off."

"Jody, Billy!" Ellen's voice was calling from the living room. "Everybody's ready to play again."

Jody turned sideways and shouted, "I dropped

47

the potato salad, and we're cleaning it up. Go ahead, start without us!" When she turned back, Billy was grinning at her.

"You lie, too," he said.

"Sometimes, but I'm not lying about what I wrote," Jody said. "I wrote the one about wishing you were somebody else."

"Well, like I said, I thought you'd guessed the truth about Sasha. I don't know why, maybe it's because you listen and watch a lot," he said.

There was laughter from the living room, and they heard Ellen saying, "Oh, no, do I have to answer?" She giggled, and Jody could almost see her blushing.

"Hey, why don't you go back in?" Billy said, tossing the wad of paper towels into the wastebasket. "I can tell you're embarrassed to be with me, now that you know my big secret."

"I'm not embarrassed," Jody told him. "I'm shocked. I thought you were crazy about Sasha."

"Me, too. It's wild, isn't it?" Billy said. "I think it was the rug."

"The rug?"

"Yeah, when I was cleaning it up, it just kind of hit me — there I was, down on my knees, scrubbing away so she wouldn't be mad. So she'd thank me, notice me, whatever. Then I realized it couldn't be a *real* Navajo rug. If it were, it would probably be on the wall, not the floor. But she let me believe it was priceless." He shrugged. "I usually hate myself when I get into a situation like that, but this time I hated *her*. For making me feel like a nerd."

Billy turned back to the sink and stared out of the window above it. "Leahna," he said.

"What?"

"That's Leahna's cabin, right across from us," Billy said. "I saw her through the window just before you came in. She's not there now." He turned around. "She's like Sasha, I've decided. The way she talked to me up on the slope today, like I was invisible. They're two of a kind, and I hate them both."

"Billy . . ."

"Hey, don't look at me like that," he said. "*I'm* not the one who treats people like dirt."

There was another burst of laughter from the living room.

"Go on, Jody," Billy said, turning his back on her again. "Just go on."

Shaken by the anger in his voice, Jody got up and left the room. Sasha was coming toward the kitchen and immediately asked about Billy.

"He's . . . I think he's tired," Jody said, moving farther into the living room, away from the kitchen.

"No, I've been thinking about what you said, and he *was* upset, wasn't he?" Sasha asked. "I wish I knew who wrote that, about how if he didn't laugh at himself, he'd be the only one. It wasn't very nice."

"No," Jody agreed. She started to say what he was *really* upset about, but then she changed her mind. Here was Sasha, looking worried and sorry that Billy might be upset. Was that the kind of person who treated people like dirt? Maybe Billy had her all wrong. Jody didn't know and suddenly didn't want to think about it anymore.

"Well, maybe we should just leave him alone," Sasha said. "Come on, let's see how Ellen's holding up."

Jody was hardly excited about more Truth, but she let herself be pulled back into the living room. The crowd had gotten smaller now. There were only three or four kids left who weren't actually staying at the cabin.

Ellen was in the hot seat, tugging at a strand of her light-brown hair. "I hope I'm almost finished," she said shyly to Cal. "I don't think I can stand much more." Actually she looked pretty happy, Jody thought, probably because Cal was standing so close to her.

"Three more to go, then you're free," Cal told her, glancing at his watch. He looked down at the next paper and read, *"You're in love with Drew."*

Drew snorted.

"Hey, wait," Cal said, "the next one says you're in love with me!"

Sasha laughed. "Maybe she loves both of you."

"Give her a break," Drew said.

Chris looked at him sharply, but she kept her voice light. "No, she has to answer."

Ellen's face was bright red, and she covered it with her hands. "Not true," she said.

"Which one?" Sasha laughed.

"Not true," Ellen said again, her voice muffled by her fingers.

"Does that mean both?" Chris asked.

"Let's say it does and get this over with." Cal

flipped to the last piece of paper, started to read, and then stopped. "This isn't funny," he said quietly.

"None of it's been that funny," Drew commented.

"Go on, Cal," Sasha said. "You're the one in a hurry. Read it."

Cal crumpled the paper and let it drop, but Chris snatched it up. "I'll do it," she said, smoothing it out. Her eyes widened, and she gave a short laugh. "Are you ready for this? It says *You wish Leahna Calder were dead.*"

Ellen lowered her hands and stood up. Her face was white now. "But that's . . ." She gave her head a shake. "That's enough."

Jody thought Ellen would go upstairs, but instead she took her jacket and walked out the door. Jody wondered who'd written that one. Whoever it was must know Ellen pretty well. Except Ellen didn't really want Leahna *dead*. She just wanted her punished, maybe, or paid back.

The three people who weren't staying at the cabin stood up. "Listen, I think we'll be going," one of them said. "See everybody tomorrow, probably."

When the door shut behind them, everyone was quiet for a minute. Then Sasha said, "I feel awful." She looked disappointed. "And this was going to be such a great party."

"Can't win 'em all, Sash." Cal was rummaging through the puffy down jackets by the door. He dug his out and pulled it on.

"You're going out?" Sasha asked. "Cal, I — "

"I know." He zipped up his parka and smiled at

her, his eyes bright. "Cheer up, Sasha. Maybe I won't be long." He left, slamming the door behind him. Jody wished he were going after Ellen, but she was pretty sure he was heading for Leahna's place.

Sasha stared at the closed door for a second, then she swung around, moving gracefully from table to table. "Time to clean up. I'm sorry the party turned out this way," she said, her long fingers quickly gathering up empty cups and stacking them together. "Maybe we'll have another one tomorrow night. A better one. I'll talk to Cal about it. Or maybe somebody else will have one. There's always a party going on around here." Her cheerful voice trailed off as she went into the kitchen.

Jody decided not to volunteer for kitchen duty. She'd had enough — of everything — for one night and she was suddenly so tired she wasn't sure she could make it up the stairs.

The girls' bedroom was dark, and Jody left it that way while she got undressed and into a pair of light-weight sweatpants and a soft T-shirt. Switching on a light, she gathered up her toothbrush and tooth-paste, then went down to the small half-bathroom at the end of the hall. The guys' half of the top floor was dark, too, and she wondered if Billy was in there, asleep. She brushed her teeth and walked back, her legs feeling like lead.

Jody turned off the light, unfolded a heavy blanket, and crawled into bed, spreading the blanket out on top of her. Her bed was under the eave; if she turned toward the wall, her head would hit the sloping ceiling. She rolled over onto her stomach, sure that she'd be asleep in a few seconds.

But as soon as she closed her eyes, images started flashing through her mind: Billy hanging over the van seat, eagerly talking to Sasha. Chris looking daggers at her because of Drew. Ellen's white face when she left the living room. Drew, stomping angrily into the cabin after going to Leahna's. Sasha and Cal, their identical blue eyes sending messages to each other. And Billy again, licking his chapped lips, scrubbing at the rug, and later in the kitchen, his eyes dark with hatred.

Downstairs, a door slammed. Jody opened her eyes and listened, expecting to hear footsteps on the stairs. But the cabin stayed quiet. She rolled onto her back and closed her eyes again, but this time, her thoughts kept her awake. The game of Truth should be banned, she decided. Too many ugly feelings came out when you played it. If there was really so much hate around, it should be kept hidden. People had bad thoughts about other people all the time, but they were private, not party material.

The door to the bedroom swung open, and Jody sat up, bumping her head on the ceiling. "Who is it?" she asked, rubbing her head.

"Chris."

In the light from the hallway, Jody saw Chris move like a shadow toward her own bed. "You going to sleep?" Jody asked.

"Not yet. It's not even midnight." There was some shuffling, and Chris clicked her tongue impatiently. "Where are they?"

"What?"

"My gloves . . . oh, there they are."

Jody blinked. "You're going out?"

"Why not? It stopped snowing. Everybody else did."

"Everybody?"

"I don't really know, it seems like it." Chris sounded in a hurry; she was moving back toward the door now. "This place is dead. I'm walking down to the lodge — maybe there's some action there." She went out, shutting the door behind her, leaving Jody in the dark.

Jody lay back down, carefully avoiding the ceiling. Maybe she'd just imagined all those hateful feelings swirling around the cabin like smoke. Maybe everyone had laughed it all off and they were down at the lodge having fun, while she was up here, knocking her head against the ceiling. It would serve her right for taking everything so seriously.

For a second, Jody considered going to the lodge, too. But she'd warmed up the bed already, and she was feeling too lazy to get dressed and pull on boots and stuff. Besides, she wasn't even sure where the lodge was.

She felt lazy, but she was also wide awake now. Rolling over, she propped her chin in her hands and looked out the window. Chris was right: It had stopped snowing.

The view into Leahna Calder's cabin window was crystal-clear.

The Lovely Leahna, Jody thought. And just as she thought it, there Leahna was, moving across the room. It looked like she was getting ready to go out. Jody's eyes widened, then squinted, so she could see better. She scooted up a little until her forehead was pressed against the cold glass.

Suddenly Leahna turned her head and looked off, toward the door, Jody guessed. Then she walked out of the room.

Jody's eyes drifted away, toward the other cabins and the snow-covered paths between them. She could see a few people walking, slipping along like dark ghosts. She could even see the frosty puffs of their breath in the cold air.

A movement caught Jody's eye, and she jerked her head toward Leahna's window again. Leahna was back, but not alone. Someone was with her.

Jody pushed her head closer to the window, mashing the tip of her nose. Leahna's visitor hadn't come far enough into the room for Jody to see much. Even so, she could tell that this was not a friendly visit.

Leahna shook her head. Her visitor jabbed the air with a finger. Jody saw something flash, a chain, maybe, or a watch. Leahna took a few steps back, then shook her head again.

Jody's breath had completely fogged up the glass. She wiped it away and covered her nose.

Leahna had tossed her head back; was she laughing? She pointed toward the door, maybe telling the visitor to go. The visitor didn't move.

As Jody wiped the glass again, Leahna strode toward her visitor, making a shooing motion with her hands. The visitor's arms shot out, and suddenly Leahna was stumbling backward, tripping and falling onto the floor.

The visitor stood still for a moment, then turned and disappeared from view.

Leahna was out of Jody's view, too. But then Leahna was standing up again, her eyes on the spot where the visitor had been. She rubbed a shoulder, ran her fingers through her hair, and shrugged.

Then she came to the window and cupped her hands against it, almost mirroring Jody.

Jody immediately ducked down, then laughed at herself. She was in the dark and couldn't be seen. She popped her head back up.

Leahna's window was empty.

Jody felt almost disappointed. She had no idea who Leahna's visitor was or what they were arguing about, but it had been an exciting little drama and it was over too fast. Too bad she hadn't been able to hear them, or at least read their lips.

Suddenly Jody tensed. Was that somebody coming up the stairs? She listened closely, but the cabin stayed quiet. Nobody came.

Jody let her breath fog the window again and then wrote her name in it. She suddenly felt ashamed of herself, playing the peeping Tom, safe in the dark, looking at two people who had no idea they were being watched. She'd had no right to do that. She sure wouldn't want anybody watching *her*.

With a sigh, Jody put her head down and pulled the blanket up over her shoulders. Billy had said she listened and watched a lot. She'd never realized it, but maybe he was right. She sure had done enough of it tonight, and look what had happened. She'd seen people crying and arguing, heard them saying ugly things they probably didn't mean. Tomorrow, she decided, she'd keep her ears closed and her eyes on the snowy slopes of Brevard Pass.

But even as Jody drifted off to sleep, the scene in Leahna's window flashed through her mind. She saw the visitor's arms reach out and shove Leahna away, hard enough to make her fall.

Jody shivered a little. It hadn't really been an exciting drama. It was actually kind of scary, knowing that somebody was mad enough to do that.

Leahna should be careful, Jody thought. She has a lot of enemies.

Chapter 6

Bright sunshine woke Jody up, streaming through the big glass window onto her face. She turned over and looked out, and the first things she saw were her name streaked across the window and the big smudge on the glass where she'd kept wiping the fog away. The memory of last night came flooding back, and she moved over and tried to see into Leahna's window. But the glare of the sun made it impossible, and she felt disappointed. Maybe she'd uncovered a dark secret about herself — Jody Sanderson, window spy.

Hearing soft, even breathing in the room, Jody sat on the edge of the bed and looked around. At the other end of the room, Chris was almost buried under her blanket, one spike of bright blonde hair sticking out. On the bed next to hers, Ellen was curled on her side, clutching the pillow in both hands. Sasha's bed was empty.

Not wanting to wake anyone, Jody quietly eased out of bed. The room was cold, and she shivered as she pulled on a sweatshirt. She went out and brushed her teeth, then headed for the stairs, smelling coffee the closer she got to the kitchen.

"Hi, Jody." Sasha greeted her from the kitchen table, where she sat with her hands around a cup of coffee. She looked tired, with shadowy circles under her eyes. "I'm glad somebody else is up. I hate sitting alone."

There was a box of blueberry muffins on the counter. Jody took one and poured herself some coffee. "I'm surprised anybody's up but me," she said, pulling out a chair and sitting down. "When I went to sleep last night, I was still the only one in the room." She wolfed down half a muffin. "Chris said she was going to the lodge. Is that where everybody else went? Did I miss anything great?"

"I don't know, I didn't go there," Sasha said. "I went to some friends' cabin. But there's always something going on at the lodge, so if you missed anything last night, you can try it tonight." She got up and spilled the last of her coffee into the sink.

"It's too early to think about tonight," Jody said. "All I can think about now is getting down the slopes. It's going to be a great day."

"Yes. I hope so." Sasha picked up a towel draped over one of the chairs and went to the door. "Time for a shower. See you later, Jody."

A couple of minutes after Sasha left, Drew came in, followed by Billy. Then Ellen came downstairs, and then Cal and Chris, and the kitchen was full of hungry people. Jody'd told herself last night that she wasn't going to do so much watching and listening. But she couldn't help trying to get a sense of their moods, to see if there were any bad feelings left over from the party.

It was hard to tell. Ellen and Drew were quiet. In fact, no one talked much at all. Chris looked a little grumpy, but that was her usual expression. Billy yawned most of the time and avoided looking at Jody. Cal didn't say a word, and Jody wondered if he'd gone to see Leahna last night.

Maybe he had. Maybe he was the one she'd seen in the window.

The house had warmed up by now, but the mood in the kitchen was cold and unfriendly. For a while, the day before, Jody had felt like she was getting to know these people and to like some of them. Now she felt as if she were in a room full of strangers again.

But it was morning, she told herself. Everybody had just gotten up and they were barely awake. Maybe she was exaggerating things.

Of course, she hadn't exaggerated the argument she'd seen between Leahna and her visitor. That had been ugly and *real*. And the harder Jody tried to forget it, the more she thought about it.

The snow had added an inch of powder, but the night had been cold, and the slopes were icy and incredibly fast. The sun didn't help much; it was still so cold the snow squeaked. It was too fast for Jody; she fell three times during a single run. As she picked herself up from the last fall, she decided to get something to eat. Food might not help her ski any better, but at least it would cheer her up.

Rather than go back to the cabin, Jody decided to check out the lodge. It was a big wood-and-stone building with tall windows, and she figured she'd sit and watch everyone else skiing while she got warm and full.

The dining room was enormous, with a big stone fireplace blazing away, and it was crowded. All the window tables were taken, and most of the others were, too. Jody was looking for someplace to sit when she heard her name called.

"Jody, over here." It was Drew, sitting at a window table with Chris, waving for her to join them.

Jody waved back and started threading her way through people and tables. Chris probably wasn't thrilled to have her sit with them, but Jody was too hungry to care.

"Thanks," Jody said when she got to them. "I was beginning to think I'd have to eat standing up."

Drew pushed a chair out with his foot, and Jody sat down and looked around.

"This place is huge," she said. "Big enough for a band and stuff." She looked at Chris. "Was there one last night?"

"You were here last night?" Drew said to Chris. "I was, for a while, but I didn't see you."

"Too bad," Chris murmured. "I guess we were here at different times." She frowned at her menu.

Jody picked up her own menu. If Chris wanted to ignore her, fine. Jody could ignore with the best of them. "What's good to eat here?" She asked Drew.

"Stick with the hamburgers," he advised.

"Everything else is too expensive and not that great."

Jody ordered a cheeseburger, and because she was still cold, some cream-of-mushroom soup. When the soup came, she tasted it and wished she hadn't. She reached for her water and caught Drew looking at her. One eyebrow was raised. "Okay, okay," she laughed. "You told me so."

"I didn't say a word," he protested.

"You didn't have to. I knew you were dying to."

"True," he admitted. "Are you always that good at figuring out what people are thinking?"

"It didn't take much to figure that out." Jody snuck a look at Chris. It didn't take much to figure out what *she* was thinking, either. She was wishing Jody would conveniently disappear.

In spite of Chris, Jody was enjoying herself. Drew in one of his good moods was very nice to be with.

Unfortunately, his good mood lasted about as long as his hamburger, which he demolished before Jody was even a third of the way through hers. Drew was teasing Jody, daring her to try the slope known as the Killer, when Chris, who'd been picking at a grilled cheese sandwich, suddenly laughed out loud. It was a short, sharp, bark of a laugh.

"What is it?" Drew asked.

"Nothing. I just saw something." Chris tore a strip of crust off her sandwich and nibbled on it, smirking a little. "I thought it was funny."

"Well?" Drew sounded impatient.

"Look." Chris pointed out the window to where a skier was trying to pick herself up after a fall. Jody wasn't surprised that Chris got a kick out of something like that — she probably laughed at old ladies falling down, too — but it was the kind of thing she thought even Chris would keep to herself. Then she saw who the skier was: Leahna Calder, dressed today in blue and neon-green, with a wide chartreuse headband holding back her long hair.

"She was almost at the bottom when she fell," Chris said. "She's probably wishing she did go to Antigua today. Look! Billy's helping her up."

Sure enough, Billy Feldman had come to Leahna's aid, standing pigeon-toed again, holding out his hand. Jody didn't understand why he bothered, after what he'd said the night before. Leahna waved him away and got to her feet alone.

Jody started to feel sorry for Billy, and then told herself to stop. She could only see what was happening, she couldn't hear. Leahna might have thanked him and said it was easier to get up by herself.

"Well!" Chris said, cheerfully polishing off another piece of crust, "I'm ready for some hot chocolate. What about you, Drew?"

But Drew just shook his head, his teasing, lighthearted mood gone. "I think it's time to get back on the slopes," he said grimly. He pushed his chair back and stood up, dropping a dollar bill on the table for a tip. Then he nodded at the two girls and left. Chris was on her feet before he was halfway across the dining room, hurrying after him. She didn't bother to say good-bye to Jody. She didn't add to the tip, either.

Sighing, Jody picked up her cheeseburger and bit into it, looking out the window. Billy had disappeared, but Leahna was still there. Cal was with her now, and the two of them were talking. Jody wondered again if Cal had gone to see her last night, like he'd said he was going to. Could he have been the visitor she'd seen through Leahna's window?

Jody dropped her burger into her plate, narrowing her eyes to get a better look, to see if she could tell whether their conversation was friendly. Leahna's visitor had shoved her backwards, made her fall. Would Cal do something like that? If he had, they'd hardly be talking to each other now, would they? Unless Cal was apologizing. Maybe . . .

Jody suddenly realized she was doing it again — watching through windows. She really ought to learn to mind her own business. She forced her eyes back to the table and deliberately thought about something else. Like whether or not she should add two dollars to the tip — one for herself and one for Chris. Or whether she should just add a single and let the waiter think she was the cheap one.

Jody had compromised on the tip — a dollar-fifty — and by the time she was outside again and riding up in the lift, everyone from the cabin was out of sight. Not out of mind, though, not completely. Jody couldn't help being curious about all the little dramas that seemed to be going on around her. But she'd compromised on that, too — as long as she just thought about them, but didn't say anything, then she wasn't being nosy.

Midway through the ride, the man next to her on the lift said, "Is it my imagination or has it gotten colder?"

"It's getting cloudy, so you're probably right," Jody said.

"Good. The skiing's going to get fast."

"It already is." Jody peered down, wondering if she'd made a mistake coming up again. She'd already fallen because of ice, and if it was getting worse, she'd definitely fall again. Well, she didn't have much choice. She could ride the lift down, of course. But nobody did that unless they broke a binding or something. Jody'd never been much of a risk-taker, but she wasn't ready to face total humiliation by riding an empty down-lift, either.

Once she got off the lift, she asked a couple of people about ice and they said some places were flagged, but it really wasn't any worse than it had been before.

They were wrong.

As soon as she pushed off, Jody knew this wasn't going to be an easy run. Twice she almost lost control, and when she came to a flat stretch, she stopped and got off the trail, into the powdery snow that hadn't been tamped down and hardened into what felt like a skating rink. She watched another skier whiz by, then took a deep breath and pushed off again.

The patch of ice took her by surprise, and as soon as Jody hit it, she knew it was all over. Her left ski shot out from under her, and she felt her body lifting into the air. She got rid of the poles and told herself to relax, go with the fall. But the edge of her right ski caught on something — ice, dirt, a root, she didn't know — and her right leg was dragging, going the wrong way. It finally joined the rest of her, but not before Jody felt a sharp pain in her ankle, a pain that shot halfway up her leg and made her cry out even before she'd hit the ground.

The landing knocked the breath out of her, and she was dizzy. She lay sprawled in the snow, black spots dancing behind her closed eyelids. She couldn't remember hitting her head, but she must have. Afraid to lose consciousness, she opened her eyes. The tops of the pine trees spun sickeningly in the bright blue sky, and a wave of nausea hit her. She closed her eyes and panted, frightened and hurt.

The next thing she felt was a hand on her arm. "Don't move," a voice said.

"No, the only thing I hurt is my ankle, and maybe my head," Jody said. She hadn't even heard the skier arrive — she must have blacked out for a second — but she leaned gratefully on the skier's arm and pushed herself to a sitting position. "I might be sick," she warned.

But she wasn't. Her stomach churned ominously for a few seconds, then settled down. Jody took a chance and opened her eyes. The first thing she saw were blue-covered legs with patches of neon-green on them. Then she looked up, into a lovely face framed by thick, taffy-colored hair pushed back with a chartreuse headband.

Leahna Calder. Everybody's enemy was now Jody's hero.

Leahna helped her get semi-comfortable, leaning against a tree trunk, then she said, "I'll go down and get the patrol." Her voice was matter-of-fact, as if she did this kind of thing all the time.

Jody watched as Leahna found her skis and poles and put them next to her, near the tree. She felt safe now, sore and cold, but safe.

Another skier came down the slope then, swooshed to a stop, and raised her goggles. "Jody!" Sasha cried. "Are you hurt bad?"

"I don't think so," Jody said. "My right ankle got it, but I think everything else is in one piece." She suddenly realized she hadn't even thanked Leahna for helping her, but it was too late, now. Leahna was already pushing off down the slope in a flash of blue and green, her long hair whipping out behind her. And then she was gone.

Chapter 7

Jody's ankle was sprained, not broken. A doctor at the lodge wrapped it up and then suggested she stay at the lodge overnight so the medical team could keep an eye on her.

"I don't understand," Jody said, leaning on Sasha for support as she got off the examining table. "Even if my ankle were broken . . ."

"Not your ankle," the doctor said. "Your head. There's no evidence of concussion but that doesn't always rule it out. You should be watched for twenty-four hours, just in case."

Jody was worn out. "Watched for what?" she asked tiredly.

"Dizziness, blurred vision, tingling in your fingers or toes, vomiting, unconsciousness." He reeled them off like a chant.

"She's staying with six other people," Sasha told him. "We'll check on her all the time, and if anything looks funny, we'll get her over here right away. That'll be all right, won't it?"

Sasha sounded responsible and competent, and

the doctor gave them both his blessing to go back to the cabin.

"I feel ridiculous," Jody said as she hobbled out of the room, leaning heavily on Sasha. "I knew the slopes were icy; I should never have gone back up." If she'd been in the mood, she might have laughed at herself: They hadn't had to take her down on a stretcher — she'd ridden the empty lift down, the humiliating ride she'd thought about taking on the way up.

"Don't be silly," Sasha said. "They weren't any worse than they were this morning. You didn't do anything stupid. It was just bad luck."

"I guess I should go back home," Jody said glumly. "I mean, I can't ski, so what's the point of staying? But my parents are away." Since she was taking a vacation, they'd decided to take one, too, and had flown to Arizona to visit some friends.

"Well, you shouldn't go tonight, anyway," Sasha said. "You should lie down and relax and then see how you feel tomorrow."

Jody didn't argue. Sasha was right — she had to stay overnight, at least. She couldn't go back to an empty house the way she felt right now. And what if she got worse on the bus or something? Still, she wanted to go home in the worst way. She was shivering and her ankle throbbed and her head ached. She wanted to be in her own bed, not in a strange bed, in a strange cabin, being watched over by people she hardly knew.

By the time Jody *was* in bed, though, she stopped feeling so sorry for herself. The rest of her group came back soon after she and Sasha did, and they all went out of their way to make her comfortable, offering to bring her magazines and hot chocolate and food. Even Chris didn't make any nasty remarks, which for her, *was* going out of her way, Jody figured, and probably took a supreme effort. Jody was grateful for all their attention and felt a little less lonely and homesick.

"So," Drew said, dropping a pile of magazines on her bed, "you had to do it, didn't you?"

"Do what?"

He grinned. "You mean you weren't on the Killer run?"

"Very funny, you know I wasn't." Jody picked up one of the magazines. "*Popular Mechanic?*"

"Hey, it was in the cabin. For all I know you could be a whiz in the garage." He chuckled and headed for the door. "Actually, I'll be glad to get you something else. I'm going out in a little while."

"No, that's okay, thanks." Jody was rifling through the pile of magazines. "There's other stuff here, and Sasha brought me some books." She scooted farther up on her pillow and winced.

Drew noticed. "I could get you some aspirin. You look like you could use it."

"Thanks, but I have aspirin. And the doctor gave me those." Jody pointed to a brown bottle on a low stool by the bed. "Pain pills. I'll take one later if I can't sleep."

"Looks like I'm useless," Drew said. "I'll stop by later, anyway, okay?"

"Sure." Jody smiled at him, hoping he would.

Ellen and Cal came in just as Drew was leaving. "She's not rational," Drew told them with a straight face. "I'm afraid it's just a matter of time." He shook his head sadly and went out the door.

"I don't know, you seem okay to me." Cal walked closer and peered at her. "Of course, your eyes are crossed, and you've got this huge point coming up out of your head, but that doesn't mean your mind is going."

"What do I have to do to get a little sympathy around here?" Jody laughed, and so did Cal, a little too hard. Even though he was joking, his voice sounded strained, and his eyes didn't light up when he smiled.

Ellen gazed at Cal. "You're terrible," she said to him. "Poor Jody's got enough to worry about."

"You're right," Cal agreed. He laughed again, sounding forced. "The point isn't that big."

"Cal!" Ellen covered her mouth and giggled. "Anyway, Jody, do you need anything else? Before dinner, I mean?"

"I'm fine, really," Jody said.

"How'd it happen?" Cal asked as they both sat on the floor next to the bed. "Give us the gory details. That's what we really came for."

"I just lost control on some ice," Jody said. "My right leg went one way and the rest of me went the other. I don't even remember hitting my head. Leahna told me not to move, but I was pretty sure nothing was broken, except maybe my ankle."

There was a silence. Jody looked at them and realized neither one of them knew Leahna had been there. Cal's face had tightened, closed up, and his light-blue eyes seemed darker. Jody wished she could read his mind. Was he still crazy about Leahna, or had he come to hate her, too?

Ellen was watching Cal with a smile that looked painted on. When she finally spoke, her voice was hard and brittle, the way it was when she'd talked about the essay. "Leahna? I thought Sasha found you."

"No, Leahna was the one." Jody felt uncomfortable, but she went on. "Then Sasha came and Leahna went down for help." She spread her hands and shrugged, laughing a little to fill up the silence. "That's it, the whole gruesome story."

Cal had been staring up at the window, frowning. Now he got to his feet, lithe and graceful, like his sister. "Well, I'm going to head down and see what's for dinner," he said. "Glad you're okay, Jody."

Ellen stayed where she was, picking at the rug with thin fingers. "So it was Leahna to the rescue," she said with a twisted smile.

Jody shifted in the bed, the bitterness in Ellen's voice making her uneasy. "Maybe she'll go to Antigua tonight or tomorrow."

"Maybe." Ellen's mouth twisted again.

Without thinking, Jody said, "I didn't thank her."

"Who. Sasha?"

Jody shook her head.

"Oh. Leahna." Ellen got up and looked out the window. "Well, you'd better do it soon, Jody, before it's too late." Without looking at Jody again, she turned and left the room.

Jody blew out her breath and leaned back against the pillows. What had Ellen meant by not waiting until it was too late? Did she mean before Leahna left for Antigua? That was the obvious answer, but that wasn't the way it had sounded. It had sounded like a threat.

"Hey, are you asleep?" Billy's round face peered around the door. "If you are, just say the word and I'll disappear."

"I'm asleep," Jody said.

"Too bad." Billy was speaking in a stage whisper. "I've brought food — soup, bread, salad, Chips Ahoy. I guess I'll have to eat it myself."

"I'm awake now. Bring it in." Jody held her breath as he came in, biting his lip, keeping his eyes on the tray. He made it without tripping and set the tray down on her lap. "Thanks, this looks great."

"I opened the soup can and shook the salad-dressing bottle myself." Billy started to sit on the bed, caught himself, and stayed standing.

"You can sit," Jody told him. "My ankle's against the wall. I don't think you'll hit it."

"No, that's okay. I'm going down and eat with the rest of them in a minute. Sasha . . ." He stopped.

Jody could have finished the sentence for him: "Sasha asked me to bring it up." She didn't say it, though. Billy was obviously embarrassed about last night. He probably regretted it but didn't know how to say so. Let it slide, Jody told herself. She spooned up some soup. Beef barley, much better than the stuff she'd tried at lunch. She discovered that she was ravenous and swallowed several more spoonfuls before she said another word.

"I feel like a pig," she said at last. "Don't tell me I look like one, please," she added. She offered Billy a cookie.

"Thanks." Billy took it and munched on it while Jody ate her dinner. "Actually, you look pale," he said. "I heard we're supposed to watch and see if you throw up." He looked a little sick at the thought.

Jody laughed. "It's been four hours," she said. "And I just stuffed myself. If I can keep this down, then I'll be fine."

"Good." Billy hesitated. "Jody, about last night. I kind of lost my sense of humor there for a while. I didn't mean the things I said." He smiled nervously. "Gotta go," he said quickly. "Watching you eat made me realize I'm starving."

Jody frowned as she watched him leave. Last night, when Billy had talked about hating Leahna and Sasha, he'd sounded a lot more honest than he had just now. He said he'd lost his sense of humor, but Jody couldn't help wondering if he ever really had one. She didn't know if he was really a joker, or if it was just an act, a cover for some very *un*-funny feelings.

A half hour later, Chris, Ellen, and Sasha came into the room. "We came to ask if you think you can get downstairs," Sasha said.

"Sure, I suppose so. Why?"

"There's a party tonight." Sasha was changing clothes, putting on a black wool sweater. "Everybody's going, and we don't want to leave you alone."

"Oh." Jody shook her head. "I can get downstairs, but I don't think I want to hop over snow and ice to somebody's cabin."

Chris was brushing her hair.

"I'll stay," Ellen said.

"No, that's dumb. I mean, thank you," Jody said. "But I'm okay, really. I'm not dizzy anymore, and the only thing that hurts is my ankle."

Ellen looked doubtful, but Sasha came up with a solution. "We'll call, every hour or so," she said, putting the phone on the floor next to Jody's bed. "If there's no answer, we'll call back in fifteen minutes, in case you're in the bathroom."

"I don't think you even have to do that," Jody said.

"Yeah, what if she's just sleeping normally?" Chris asked.

Ellen frowned at her. "Just to be safe, it's better to wake her up."

"Right, so it's settled." Sasha picked up her makeup kit and turned toward Jody. She started to say something else, but then she stopped, frowning at the window.

Jody shifted and looked. So did Ellen and Chris. There was Jody's name, spelled out clearly on the glass. "My mother used to get furious when I did that," she joked. "I'll clean it off."

Sasha laughed. "Don't be silly. After we leave, the maid will come in and do the whole place." She turned away and headed for the door. "Take care, Jody. One of us will call you."

Chris followed Sasha, and after a minute, Ellen

left, too, assuring Jody that they'd call. Drew stuck his head in a few minutes later and said good-bye. So did Cal and Billy. Jody lay back and listened to the clatter of feet on the stairs and the shuffling as people tugged on their parkas. The door slammed three times. Then the cabin was quiet, and Jody was alone.

The minute they left, Jody started wishing they hadn't. It felt creepy, lying alone in an empty cabin, listening to the wind making it creak and groan. And what if something happened? What if a fire started or somebody broke in? How would she get out with her ankle like this?

Her ankle was throbbing worse than ever now. Looking for distraction, Jody picked up a *People* magazine and read it from cover to cover. Her ankle still hurt. She thought about taking one of the pain pills, but decided to wait and see if the pain got any worse. If it didn't, aspirin would be enough.

Talking would definitely take her mind off her ankle. Maybe she'd call Kate. She didn't want to get her riled up by mentioning Leahna, but she could just leave her out of the story. "Sorry, Leahna," she murmured, reaching for the phone.

She got an operator so she could charge the call to her home phone, then waited impatiently for Kate to answer. But the phone kept ringing, and after a full minute, Jody hung up. She thought for sure Kate would be there. After all, her flu was only two days old, and Kate's mother'd been sick for a week. Maybe Kate had gone to the doctor. But no, it was so late. Well, maybe she'd had a miraculous recovery and was on her way to Brevard Pass this very moment.

Jody wished she could call her parents, but she knew it would just worry them. Sighing, she flipped through another magazine. Then she drank some water and reached for a book. It was a self-help book — ways to improve your outlook on life. Jody read a little, and took one of the quizzes to see if she was an optimist or a pessimist. She came out an optimist and decided her outlook on life must be okay, so why bother with the book? She couldn't concentrate anymore, anyway. Her ankle was still bothering her a lot.

It was a quarter after nine, and she decided to go ahead and take a pain pill. The doctor told her it would probably make her sleepy, which was one reason she'd been holding out — she didn't want to go to sleep too early and wake up at four in the morning.

After swallowing the pill, Jody snapped off the reading lamp, got as comfortable as possible, and waited for sleep to come.

Twenty minutes later, Jody still felt wide awake. But the next thing she knew, a bell was ringing in her ear. Everything felt heavy — her arms, her legs, even her eyelids. She dragged them open and finally realized she was hearing the phone. Fumbling in the dark, she picked it up and said hello.

"I was just about to give up," Ellen said. "Were you in the bathroom?"

"No, I . . . wait a sec." Jody's mouth was dry. She turned on the lamp and took a sip of water. "I was asleep," she said. "Actually I was knocked out. I took a pain pill and those things are lethal!"

"What do you mean?"

"One minute I was awake and the next minute — wham!"

"But you're okay?" Ellen asked.

"I guess. Yeah, I am. Just groggy," Jody said. She could hear music and loud voices in the background. "What time is it?"

"Not quite ten. Did anybody else call yet?"

"If they did, I didn't hear the phone. Why?" Jody asked. "Isn't everybody there?"

"Yes, but so are about a million other people." Ellen sounded tired and unhappy, and Jody thought she'd probably lost sight of Cal. "As soon as we got here, everybody split up and I couldn't find anyone to see if they'd called."

"You're the first, I think. Thanks," Jody said. "I'm fine, not frothing at the mouth or anything."

"Okay. Well, I guess I'll call you again in a while. Or somebody will." There was a loud burst of laughter and Ellen raised her voice. "Sorry I woke you up. 'Bye, Jody."

Jody hung up and turned off the light. She still felt thick-headed and heavy, and she expected to fall back asleep in a minute. But she discovered that the pain pill didn't really take the pain away, it just made the rest of her numb. Her ankle was still throbbing away. She didn't dare take another pill, though, or she'd never wake up and whoever called next would get worried.

She turned on the light and tried to read, but

after about fifteen minutes, she gave up and lay in the dark again. Restless, she shifted around in the bed, trying to find a good position. She was sick of lying on her back, but nothing else felt any better. Maybe she was just sick of lying down, period. She slid to the edge of the bed and swung her legs over the side. Gingerly, she stood up, leaning forward so she wouldn't bump her head on the ceiling.

The pill had made her dizzy, though. Quickly, Jody sat back down. As she did, her arm brushed the window, and she leaned her head against the cold glass and looked out.

Suddenly her head felt clear as a bell. Looking into the window of Leahna's cabin, she saw two figures. One of them was Leahna. And even though she couldn't tell exactly who it was, Jody recognized the other one, too.

Jody's heart started pounding and her mouth went dry.

Leahna's late-night visitor was back.

Chapter 8

Like a television viewer with the sound turned off, Jody leaned against the glass and watched the drama play out in front of her.

They were having another argument. Or maybe this was just a continuation of the previous night's.

Leahna seemed to be doing most of the talking at the moment, sometimes pacing around the room, sometimes standing still, one hand on her hip, the other gesturing in the air.

Like last night, her visitor stayed in one place, just inside the doorway. Jody couldn't tell whether it was a guy or a girl; the only reason she even knew the other person was Leahna was because of her hair. From this distance, their faces were nothing more than pale smudges, and the visitor's head and hair were covered by what looked like a black ski cap.

The window started to fog again, and Jody impatiently wiped it off. Finally she leaned her head at an angle so her breath blew away from the glass. Her neck was going to get stiff, and she had to watch out of the corners of her eyes, but she could see.

The argument was still going on. Leahna still appeared to be doing all the talking — or shouting. She turned from the visitor and strode across the room, bent down and picked something up, waved it in the air. White. A piece of paper, Jody thought. A letter?

Still holding the piece of paper, Leahna advanced toward the visitor, until they were about a foot apart. Then she put out her hand, almost shoving the paper into her visitor's face.

Like lightning, the visitor's arm shot out, batting Leahna's hand away. The paper must have fluttered to the floor. Leahna looked down, then tossed her head back. Laughing?

Swiftly, the visitor knelt down, then straightened up, the paper clutched in one hand. Wearing gloves, Jody decided. She couldn't see any skin at all, only the flash of something — maybe metal — that she'd seen the night before. Without looking at the paper, the visitor slowly crumpled it in one fist, opened the fist, and let the small white ball drop to the floor.

Jody could barely feel her ankle anymore, but her neck was killing her. She pulled away from the window, scrunched up her shoulders and turned her head back and forth, easing her neck. Just as she was getting into position again, she froze.

Had someone come back? She'd heard a noise — the door, maybe, or boots dropping — downstairs. Not wanting to get caught spying out the window, she slid back and lay down on her side on the bed.

A couple of minutes went by.

Nobody came upstairs, but maybe they'd gone into the kitchen. Jody sat up, leaning on an elbow, and listened.

Nothing.

"Hello!" Jody called out. "Anybody here?"

Still nothing.

She took a deep breath and shouted again, louder than before.

There was no answer.

Slightly ashamed of herself, but not ashamed enough to quit watching, Jody scooted closer to the window and looked out again.

Things had changed. The visitor was still there, but Leahna was out of sight. The visitor had moved, too, to the other side of the room, near the wall. Just standing there, back facing Jody, head bent down. Standing there like a lean black shadow, not moving at all.

Jody ticked the seconds off — one, two, three — waiting for the visitor to move, or for Leahna to come back. Nothing happened.

Shifting position to ease her neck again, Jody turned her head just enough to see something hanging on the back of her door, something that had been there all along.

Binoculars.

Should she get them? No. It was one thing to look when you couldn't see all that clearly because of the distance. Binoculars would bring it too close, make her really guilty of spying. She wouldn't get them.

Yes, she would. Might as well stop trying to fool herself. She wanted to see what happened next, and she would have watched without the binoculars, so why split hairs?

Jody stood up, steadied herself on one foot and hopped over to the door. She unhooked the binoculars, tucked them under one arm and hopped back to the bed, the other arm waving in the air for balance. It took about half a minute.

It took another half minute to find the right window. How come it was easier without the binoculars? Jody kept having to take them away, look without them, bring them back up without moving her head out of line. She saw a deck, a black mass that must have been a tree, lots of snow. Finally she found Leahna's window.

Too late.

The window was empty.

The visitor was gone and Leahna hadn't come back. Had Jody missed a big make-up scene? Somehow, she doubted it. Even without binoculars, the argument had looked too fierce to end with a quick apology. Probably Leahna had stormed out, leaving the visitor alone. But what had the visitor been looking at?

Jody moved the glasses slowly across the room. She couldn't see the floor. She couldn't even see the furniture, really, except for the tops of a couple of chairs, and books, and a vase of flowers on what must be a low bookcase. The binoculars were great — she could even tell what kind of flowers they were.

Roses. Long-stemmed red roses. Jody wondered for a moment who they were from. Drew? Cal? Or maybe one of Leahna's many other admirers?

Still wondering what the visitor had been staring at, Jody panned around the room a second time, stopping when she got to the spot where she'd last seen the visitor, standing alone. Pretending the visitor was still there, she focused just behind the spot. It was just like the room she was in — a low white wall met by a sloping white ceiling.

There. There was something. A streak of red on the wall. Thick, dark red, darker than the roses, glistening like nail polish. Had it been there before?

Jody moved the binoculars away and looked without them. She could just make out the streak. But could she see it only because she knew it was there? Was it new or had it been there all along?

And what was it? Nail polish, paint?

Blood?

Jody shook her head. She'd been watching too many late-night horror shows. It couldn't be blood. Could it?

Jody felt a shiver run up her spine.

Last night, the visitor had shoved Leahna down. Tonight, he'd knocked her arm away. Not just pushed it aside, but knocked it, violently. What if he'd hit her again, while Jody wasn't looking? Hit her so hard she fell and cut her head? It was possible, wasn't it? And if it *wasn't* blood, why would the visitor be staring at just a blob of paint or nail polish?

On the floor by her bed, the telephone suddenly

rang, blaringly loud in the quiet room. Jody jumped, hit her head, and had to let it ring twice more while her breath got back to normal. She wasn't sure her heart ever would.

"Good," Sasha said after Jody answered, "you're alive."

Jody put her hand on her chest, felt her heart still pounding. "Yes, I'm alive and kicking." She laughed too loudly. "Not exactly kicking, but you know what I mean. I'm fine."

"Good. Were you asleep?"

"Uh, yeah, but that's okay." It was quiet on the other end. "What happened?" Jody asked. "Is the party over? I don't hear any music or anything."

"It moved to somebody else's cabin," Sasha said. "I don't think they've found the stereo yet." She laughed. "There's been a little beer-drinking and a few people aren't seeing too straight."

Jody picked up the clock on her bedside stool. Eleven. "Is everybody else there, too?"

"It's hard to tell, there are so many people all over the place. Why?"

"I was just thinking you could tell them not to call me anymore," Jody said. "I know the doctor said twenty-four hours, but I feel great. Well, not great. My ankle still hurts. But my head's fine, even after that pain pill."

"Oh, you took one?"

"Yes, and it knocked me out. Ellen called and woke me up and at first I was really groggy from it," Jody said. "But I'm not anymore, and I don't think anyone should bother calling."

"It's not a bother," Sasha said. "But if you want, I'll tell everybody. Well, everybody I see," she added. "It's a crazy night, and I might miss a few, so don't be surprised if someone else calls."

"Okay." Jody scooted back on the bed. Without thinking, she used her bad foot to push with and took a sharp breath when the pain hit her.

"Your ankle must be worse than you said," Sasha remarked. "Take another pill, why don't you, and go to sleep. I'll try to find everyone so they won't call and wake you."

"Maybe I will. 'Bye, Sasha."

The minute she hung up, Jody lifted the binoculars and swung them back toward the window. Nothing had changed. No one was in the room. The roses still bloomed in their vase.

The streak of red was still on the wall.

Jody watched a minute or two longer, waiting to see if Leahna would come back, but she didn't. Jody kept watching, almost willing Leahna to appear so she'd know she was all right.

But the room stayed empty, like a stage set waiting for the actors to make their entrance.

Suddenly Jody was very tired. The binoculars felt heavier in her hands, and her arms ached from holding them. She lowered them into her lap, trying to get up the energy to put them back. The last thing she wanted was for somebody to come back and figure out what she'd been up to. But her eyelids were so heavy, and her body just sank farther into the bed, not listening to her brain. Finally she stretched out, covered the binoculars with the blanket, and went to sleep.

Blood. Not one red streak, but a river of it, dark and glistening, dripping down the white walls, pooling on the floor at her feet. Where did it come from? If she didn't get out of the room, she'd drown in it. But she couldn't make herself move, couldn't make herself walk through the blood to escape. It was getting deeper, rising up the walls, flooding across the floor to the one dry spot where Jody was standing. She opened her mouth to scream.

Her heart pounding, Jody lay still for a minute, trying to push the nightmare out of her mind. The room was still dark, and she didn't hear anybody else breathing. Was she still alone? She turned her head, stretched out an arm toward the lamp.

Suddenly her heart seemed to stop completely.

Someone was standing in the doorway, motionless, dark as a shadow.

Jody screamed.

"Jody? It's me, Cal."

"God, you scared me to death!" Jody flopped back down, her heart still racing, the ugly feeling of the nightmare still with her.

"Sorry." Cal didn't move. "I came back to get some CDs and thought I'd check on you." He laughed quietly. "There's nothing wrong with your voice, I can tell that. How's your ankle?"

"What ankle? Seeing somebody in the doorway in the middle of the night took my mind right off it." She rubbed her face and pushed her hair back. "What time is it, anyway?"

"Midnight. The witching hour."

"Thanks for reminding me," Jody said with a shiver. "I guess Sasha didn't find you, huh?"

"What do you mean?"

"She called about an hour ago, and I told her to tell everyone not to bother with me anymore." Actually Jody was glad he had. The nightmare had been horrible. She could still see the blood drifting toward her like an ocean of red.

Cal was quiet for a moment. Then he said, "Sorry. It's been a crazy night — people all over the place."

"Mmm, that's what Sasha said." Jody suddenly felt the binoculars next to her, pressed against her side. Even though they were still hidden under the blanket, she was glad the room was dark. "I didn't mean to sound so grouchy," she said. "Thanks for stopping by, Cal. Go back to the party and have fun."

"Okay. I'll try to pass the word along, about not calling anymore." Cal finally moved, turning to go out the door. "Go back to sleep," he called back as he walked down the hall.

"Right," Jody murmured, already closing her eyes. She heard the door slam downstairs, but she was halfway back to sleep, and it sounded distant, like something under water.

The telephone didn't sound distant at all, though, and it wasn't. It was two feet from her head, ringing again. Jody dragged her eyes open and glared down at it, but it didn't shut up. Who was it going to be this time? She hoped it was Drew. A late-night chat with him was worth losing sleep over.

Jody picked up the phone and heard an impatient sigh. "Hi, Chris, I'm fine," she said.

"How'd you know it was me?"

"Lucky guess." Then Jody realized Chris hadn't been sighing. She was panting. "You must have just been dancing."

"Huh? Oh, right, I was." Chris's breathing slowed a little. "Anyway, I just ran into Ellen and she said I should call."

"Well, you did. And I'm okay." Jody didn't even bother to tell Chris to get the word out to the others about *not* calling. They obviously weren't connecting tonight. "See you later."

"Sure. 'Bye."

Now Jody realized that this party might go on all night, which meant she could be waking up every hour on the hour. She could always take another pain pill, maybe even two. Then she wouldn't hear the phone, and everyone would rush back.

After what she'd seen at Leahna's, and her nightmare, that didn't sound so bad. At least she wouldn't be alone anymore.

Jody was tempted, but she decided not to take another pill. They were too strong. Besides, what was the harm if she lost a night's sleep? Her ankle wasn't hurting as badly now, anyway.

Okay, she thought. As long as her ankle wasn't bothering her so much, and she was definitely wide awake, this was a good time to put the binoculars back.

But the minute Jody sat up, she knew what she had to do — take one last look through the window. She didn't even bother excusing herself this time. She wanted to know if Leahna was back, wanted to know if she was all right, so she simply looked across, started to raise the binoculars, and stopped.

The light was off. Leahna's room was dark, as dark as Jody's. The moon was up, but its light didn't reach into the room. There was nothing for Jody to see.

She felt disappointed and annoyed, as if she'd gone to the refrigerator during a commercial and come back to find she'd missed the good part. While she'd been sleeping, or talking to Cal or Chris, Leahna must have come back. Jody wondered what she'd done — changed her clothes and gone out, talked on the phone a while, gone to bed? None of that really sounded like the "good part." Face it, she told herself — there probably wasn't any good part. Leahna and someone else had had an argument and now it was over. She should stop thinking about that red streak on the wall, too. All it did was cause nightmares.

Jody stayed where she was a moment, staring across at the darkened window. Then she gave herself a mental shake and finally looked away. Her eyes roamed over the other cabins in the row, along the snowy paths between them, up at the sky, back to Leahna's cabin.

That's when she saw the movement.

Not in the window — it was still pitch-dark — but outside the cabin. Something glinting in the moonlight had caught Jody's eye, and she quickly raised the binoculars. She'd gotten good at finding Leahna's window, but it took a lot of panning with the binoculars to finally locate the spot outside her cabin.

Whatever she'd seen wasn't in the moonlight anymore, but something was still there. No, not something. *Someone*. Someone moving slowly away from the cabin. It couldn't be Leahna or her visitor. This person looked fat.

Wait a minute, though. The person wasn't fat, he was just bent over. Or she, Jody reminded herself. Maybe it was Leahna; after all, it was her cabin. Sort of hunched over, dragging her feet. But why was Leahna walking like an old person with a bad back?

Because she — or whoever it was — was dragging something. Pulling something along behind her.

Frustrated, Jody wished the person would get into the moonlight again, so she could see him or her better. But there were trees all over the place now, blocking the light. Jody wanted to see who it was and what they were dragging.

It had to be heavy. The person took a few steps, tugged, took a step, tugged. Jody swept the binoculars back to the ground behind and was just able to make out a big, dark, lumpy thing, like a big garbage bag, maybe. Then the person, moving slowly but steadily, was out of sight.

A garbage bag. Leahna was taking out the garbage. A big clean-up, lots of garbage, because she was leaving for Antigua first thing in the morning. That had to be it. Jody felt ridiculous as she hopped across the room and hung the binoculars back on the door. The big window spy had sat and watched somebody take out the garbage.

But as she got back into bed, Jody remembered something. All the other cabins had garbage cans right outside their doors. So why was Leahna dragging hers so far away? And wouldn't she have at least turned on an outside light to see by?

So maybe it wasn't Leahna.

Who was it, then, and what were they trying to get rid of?

And if it wasn't Leahna, what had happened to her?

Chapter 9

The questions kept Jody awake well past two. No one came home, and no one called again. All she had for company were the unanswered questions buzzing around in her head.

Now, waking up with sunlight on her face, Jody realized that sleep hadn't helped clear her mind. Even before she opened her eyes, she thought of that hunched-over figure she'd seen in the snow outside Leahna's cabin — definitely coming from *Leahna's* cabin — dragging away something heavy.

It couldn't have been garbage, she kept telling herself. It just didn't make sense. What it was, she didn't know. She didn't know why she thought there was some connection between that figure and the argument between Leahna and her visitor, either. But the whole thing had spooked her, and she couldn't forget about it. She'd probably never learn everything about what had happened, but until she saw Leahna again, or heard that she'd left for Antigua, she knew she couldn't let it go.

The first thing to do was find out if maybe Leahna

was at the party last night. She'd gone somewhere after leaving the visitor alone in her room, and the party made sense.

Jody sat up and looked around. It was almost nine. The cabin was completely quiet. Ellen, Chris, and Sasha were all in their beds, all still sleeping deeply, and the guys probably were, too.

She scooted up and started to look out the window, but one of the others turned over in bed just then, mumbling something in her sleep. Jody still didn't want to be seen window-watching. She stood up slowly, taking a quick glance outside — that was perfectly normal — but she didn't take time to really look. She'd wait until she was alone for that.

She was hungry, and her hair felt greasy. Food and a shower were both downstairs. Towel draped around her neck, plastic bag with shampoo clutched in her teeth, she hopped to the landing and slowly made her way down the stairs on her rear.

She unwrapped the bandage from around her ankle and took a long, hot shower. It washed away the dirt but not the questions that still lingered about Leahna. The first thing Jody did when she hopped back into the kitchen, towel wrapped around her head, was lean on the counter and stare across to Leahna's cabin.

Just like at every other cabin, two orange plastic garbage cans sat outside on a little wooden platform. Jody wasn't surprised to see them. But now she was more sure than ever that no one in their right mind should have been lugging garbage in the middle of the night.

It was impossible to see into Leahna's window at this time of day, so Jody turned away and got busy tending to her stomach. She started the coffee and drank some orange juice while she waited for it to brew. When the coffee was done, she sat at the table with a cupful, a bowl of cornflakes, and a leftover muffin. She was just polishing off the last of the muffin when Ellen came in.

"I don't believe it," Jody said. "You couldn't have gotten in before three. What are you doing up?"

"I don't really know." Ellen gave her a tired smile. She looked pale, almost sick.

"Was the party fun?" Jody asked. "It must have been, or nobody would have stayed, right?"

Ellen shrugged and poured some juice. "It was okay. Kind of crowded. For me, I mean." She shrugged again. "I don't know why I stayed, really."

Jody knew. Ellen had stayed because of Cal, because she wanted to be wherever he was. From the look on Ellen's face, all she'd gotten out of it was a short night's sleep. If Jody had known Ellen better, she might have tried to talk to her about it. Or she might not. Ellen was quieter than usual; it was obvious she didn't want to talk.

Still, the only way to find out what she wanted to know was to ask. She'd just have to let Ellen think she was an insensitive jerk. "Listen," she said, "did you see Leahna last night?"

Ellen was reaching for her juice glass and hit it with her fingers. It toppled over, sending an orange puddle spreading across the white countertop. Jody shuddered. She couldn't help thinking of the red streak she'd seen on Leahna's wall and the river of blood in her nightmare.

Ellen tore off some paper towels. "Why do you want to know?" she asked slowly, her back to Jody as she mopped up the juice.

"Well, like I said last night, I never thanked her for helping me yesterday." Ellen's back was straight and stiff. It was clear that she didn't even like the sound of Leahna's name, but Jody plowed ahead anyway. "So I thought if she was at the party, then she hadn't left for Antigua yet, and I could thank her today."

"She could have left this morning," Ellen said.

"Sure, I know. I was just wondering if you saw her, that's all."

Ellen finally turned around and looked at Jody. Her jaw was tight, as if she was clamping her teeth together. Her eyes were rimmed with red, but they were dry. "Why are you *really* asking me, Jody? Why do you care so much? Leahna didn't exactly save your life; all she did was get the patrol. And after everything I've told you about her, I can't believe you really think she's worth thanking. She's not." Ellen tossed down the paper towels and headed for the door. Just before she walked out, she said, "Leahna's not worth your trouble. She's not worth anything, so why don't you forget about her?"

Jody sat alone for a few minutes, stunned by Ellen's soft-voiced hatred. She almost wished she hadn't asked about Leahna, but she knew she wasn't going to stop, no matter how many people got mad.

After a moment, Jody made her way into the living room, where she stretched out on the couch. Maybe she was obsessed, but she had to find out what happened to Leahna, and the only way was to ask.

Cal came downstairs a few minutes later. His reaction to Jody's question wasn't as strong as Ellen's, but Jody knew he was uneasy. His face tightened up, and he stared at her so long she started to get nervous. Finally he asked the same question Ellen had: Why did she want to know?

Jody went through the same explanation of wanting to thank Leahna. "So did you see her?" she asked again.

"At the party?" he asked. He scrubbed at his dark hair with his fingertips, as if he were trying to wake up his mind. "Which one? There were two."

"Oh, I thought the whole thing just moved from one cabin to another."

"Right, that's right, it did." Cal was in jeans and a T-shirt, with no socks. He frowned down at his bare feet, then rubbed his head again. Usually he was pretty cool, Jody thought. But not now. What was the matter with him? It wasn't a hard question. Either he'd seen Leahna or he hadn't.

"What I meant," Cal said, "was that we didn't all go at the same time."

"Okay," Jody said. "You didn't see her then, right?"

"Didn't see who?" It was Sasha, standing at the railing overlooking the living room. "Hi, Jody."

"Hi, Sasha." Jody took a breath and jumped in with the question about Leahna.

Sasha surprised her by laughing. "I thought you knew she's not my favorite subject, Jody."

Jody looked at Cal, who was looking at Sasha. "Yeah, I figured that out," she said. "I just wanted to thank her for yesterday, so I thought if she's still here in Brevard . . ."

"Did you see her, Sash?" Cal asked quietly.

"No." Sasha ran her fingers through her hair. "Don't you remember, Cal? We were together almost the whole time, except when you went to get the CDs. So you didn't see her, either, did you, Cal?"

Cal just stared at his sister, his face blank. Finally he shook his head.

Sasha turned back to Jody. "Well, that's that, isn't it?"

Jody nodded. But that wasn't that, not to her. So far, no one had given her a straight answer, and she couldn't help wondering why.

By the time Jody went upstairs — sitting down again, and scooting up backwards — she'd asked Billy and Chris. Neither one of them had seen Leahna. Actually, what they said was they hadn't noticed if she'd been there or not. Billy said it quickly and headed for the kitchen. Chris almost snarled out her answer. Jody was glad there was only one person left to ask.

Settled in bed again, Jody wondered where Drew was. She wanted to see him, not just to ask about

Leahna, either. When he tapped on the door and smiled across the room at her, she realized how much she was getting to like him.

"Don't you think you're taking this invalid act a little too far?" he teased, gesturing at the bed. "I mean, you could save us all a lot of legwork if you stayed on the couch downstairs."

"Sure, but then I wouldn't get to hear you guys going up and down, just for me," Jody laughed.

"Next thing you know, you'll be asking for a little bell."

"Good idea."

Drew seemed happier this morning than Jody had ever seen him. He'd had flashes of good humor before, but this was different. He was relaxed, loose, a smile playing around the edges of his mouth. It was hard to believe he could ever be in a bad mood.

Jody was lying on top of the covers. Drew sat down and pointed to her ankle. "How is it?"

"It's still there," Jody said. "It hurts, but not so much."

"So where's the bandage?"

Jody had draped it around her neck after the shower. Now she pulled it off. "I tried to wrap it again, but I made a mess of it."

"Let me try." Drew took the narrow bandage from her hand and slipped it under her ankle. Jody kept her eyes on his hands. They were wide and powerful-looking, but very gentle as he wrapped it over and under, finally tucking the end in place. "How's that?" he asked, looking up.

"As good as the doctor's. Thanks." He was watching her. Jody looked away, looked back. He was still staring at her.

"What?" she asked, feeling herself blush.

"You've got green eyes." Drew leaned closer, peering into them. "Pretty."

Please don't let Chris come in now, Jody thought. I'd have an enemy for life.

Drew smiled at her. "They see a lot, don't they?"

Jody thought he'd been going to kiss her. Now she felt disappointed and a little confused. "What do you mean?"

"I mean you don't miss much that's going on," he said.

Jody was suddenly very conscious of the binoculars hanging on the door, and her name streaked on the window. Had Drew guessed what she'd been doing? But if he had, why would he care? Unless . . . unless *he* was Leahna's visitor.

Jody laughed uneasily. "I still don't know what you mean," she said. "I don't see any more than the next person."

Drew stared at her a second, then shrugged. "Okay. How about last night?"

Jody almost jumped. "Last night? What about it?"

"I mean, did your ankle give you much trouble?" He sounded impatient. "Did you sleep okay, were you bored, did you have enough to read, what?"

"Oh." Jody'd been sure he was going to call her on her spying, and now she laughed in relief. "No, last night was okay. I took a pain pill, but they're too strong. I don't think I'll need another one, anyway."

"Good." Drew stood up and looked out the window. Jody watched him as he stared across at Leahna's. His jaw was set, and he had his hands jammed into the pockets of his jeans. Finally he turned back to her. "Better get going. I'll see you later."

"Wait." Jody took a deep breath. "I need to ask you something."

"I knew it," he said, giving an exaggerated sigh. "What'll it be — coffee, ginger ale, something to eat?"

"Nothing. Yet." Jody laughed nervously. "No, really, uh . . . I was wondering if Leahna was at the party last night."

Drew sighed again, but this wasn't a fake one. And he didn't ask why she wanted to know. Instead, he stepped back over to the bed and leaned down, his face near Jody's. "Listen," he said softly. "Don't worry about her. She's out of my life for good."

Before Jody could answer, he leaned even closer, kissed her swiftly on the lips, and walked out of the room without looking back.

Later, when everyone had left the cabin, Jody could still feel the touch of Drew's lips. She'd expected a kiss earlier, when he was talking about the color of her eyes. But when he did kiss her, it was just after he said Leahna was out of his life, *for good*. And he'd sounded so intense, almost mad. The kiss took her completely by surprise, and she didn't know what to make of it. Why would he kiss her when he was angry? She should have been happy, but instead, she felt cold.

Jody pushed the feeling away and thought about Leahna. She didn't know any more about her now than she had when she woke up, and the first thing to do was get the binoculars and check the window.

The sun was higher now, so she could see in. The view wasn't as good as at night, with Leahna's light blazing away, but it would have to do for now.

The room was empty. Nothing new there. The roses were drooping; one of them bent halfway down the side of the vase, only a couple of its petals left.

And the red streak on the wall was — *gone*.

Maybe she was looking in the wrong spot. Jody moved the binoculars back and moved them slowly across the room — the roses, the chair tops, the place where the streak had been. *Had been*. Yes, it was definitely gone.

She lowered the binoculars to her lap and thought about it. She hadn't been watching the window every minute of the night. She'd been asleep or talking on the phone or with Cal part of the time. Somewhere in there, someone had cleaned the wall. The only person staying there, as far as she knew, was Leahna Calder. So either Leahna had come back or she'd left town and someone else had moved in and cleaned up.

Right, Jody thought. Cleaned up at one in the morning, dragging a ton of garbage away from the cabin when there were two perfectly good garbage cans right outside.

Okay, she still couldn't explain the person she'd seen at one in the morning and she didn't know who'd cleaned the wall, either. But she could watch the window all day if she had to. Somebody was obviously staying there, and they'd have to come back eventually.

If only it weren't for her ankle, she'd just go across and knock on the door. There was too much ice and snow, though. If she tried it, she'd probably wind up with two sprained ankles.

The telephone. Why hadn't she thought of it before? This was the twentieth century — she could *call* the stupid cabin.

Jody picked up the phone, got information, and gave the name Calder. It was the only name she had. When the operator said there was no listing under that name, Jody tried to explain where the cabin was. The operator couldn't help.

Jody hung up the phone, then immediately picked it up again. Kate might know. Not the number, but maybe she'd know if Leahna's parents were divorced or if someone else owned the cabin, and she might have another name Jody could use. Besides, Jody hadn't heard from Kate since the first night, and she was starting to wonder why. Before Jody had left on the trip, Kate had promised — *threatened* was more like it — to call every day.

Kate answered on the fourth ring, sounding groggy and confused. "I woke you up, didn't I?" Jody said.

"Jody?" Kate's voice was rough with sleep.

"You must be feeling better," Jody said.

"Why do you say that? I feel rotten."

"Then you shouldn't have gone out last night," Jody teased. "What was it, a party somewhere?"

Kate was silent for a few seconds. Then she said, "I didn't go anywhere last night. What are you talking about?"

"Well, don't get mad," Jody said, wondering why Kate sounded so touchy. "I called you last night, I guess it was about seven, and nobody answered."

"So? I didn't hear it," Kate told her. "I told you what my mother was like when she had the flu — all she did was sleep. That's exactly what I've been doing."

Jody started to ask why Kate heard the phone this morning but not last night. Then she changed her mind. She hadn't called to get into an argument.

"Anyway," Kate went on, "Sasha told me there was going to be a party last night. Why were you calling me instead of out partying?"

"You're not going to believe this," Jody said. "Well, maybe you will. I fell yesterday and sprained my ankle." She launched into the story of her spill, giving all the details except the part about Leahna. "So I was stuck here alone last night," she finished, "and I felt like talking to you." She paused. "I thought for sure you would have called."

"Why?"

Jody rolled her eyes. "Because, Kate, you said you were going to call every day, remember?"

Kate was quiet again. "I remember," she finally said. "I changed my mind."

"Does that mean you've lost interest in Cal?" Jody asked. "Just like that?"

"No. It means I changed my mind about calling every day, okay?"

"Okay, okay." The flu sure had affected Kate's attitude, Jody thought. It was like talking to a grouchy stranger. She decided to get to the point anyway. "Look, there's another reason I called," she said. "It's about Leahna, so don't get all bent out of shape."

"What about Leahna?" Kate asked sharply.

"I said, don't get bent out of shape." Jody took a deep breath, then told Kate about the part Leahna had played in rescuing her, and how she wanted to thank her. "The thing is," she said, "and this is terrible, so don't say anything. But I can see into Leahna's window from here and I saw her last night." She hesitated. Should she tell everything she'd seen? She was still spooked by it all, but Kate wasn't in much of a listening mood. No, Jody decided, she wouldn't tell it all. Not yet.

"Anyway," she went on, "I haven't seen her since, but I decided to call her and thank her. Except I can't get her phone number. You wouldn't happen to know who owns that cabin, would you? Her family, or somebody else?"

"I really don't believe this," Kate said. "You've been watching her through the window?!"

"Sort of." Jody laughed a little. "Hey, there's not

much else to do around here — I'm stuck, remember?"

"What did you see?" Kate demanded.

"Just . . ." Jody sighed. "Well, she had a fight with somebody. I don't know who. Then they left. Look, never mind about that," she said quickly. "What about her cabin?"

"I have no idea about Leahna Calder's cabin," Kate said coldly. "If I were you, I'd forget about thanking her. Forget about watching her, too, Jody. You could get into trouble, you know. I have to go now," she added.

After they said good-bye, Jody hung up, frowning at the phone. What was the matter with Kate, anyway? Since when did the flu cause a complete personality change? They'd have to have a talk when she got home.

The phone was in Jody's lap. She picked it up and started to set it on the floor by her bed, and that's when she saw the shadow move across the rug. It only took a second to raise her eyes, but by then the doorway was empty.

Had she imagined it? Or had someone been standing outside the door, listening to every word she'd said?

Chapter 10

Jody felt her cheeks flame with embarrassment. She'd thought everyone had left! There she was, thinking she was alone, blabbing away about spying on Leahna. And maybe being overheard.

But Jody was more than just embarrassed.

She was scared. Why would anyone stand outside the door like that, unless they didn't want to be seen? Unless they wanted to know what she was up to?

Jody swallowed dryly and yelled "hello" a couple of times.

No answer.

She sat for a minute, straining to hear some sound. She heard a few ticks and creaks, and the hiss of wind in the snow outside. Except for that, the cabin was quiet, like it had been for at least forty-five minutes. Whoever made that shadow was gone now. Unless she'd imagined it. Was she so spooked about Leahna she was starting to see things?

No. Someone had been outside the door, she was

positive. Well, almost positive. To be safe, she hopped over to the door and pushed it closed. If someone came back now, and she didn't hear them downstairs, she'd at least hear the bedroom door open. Then she'd have time to stick the binoculars under her pillow before she was caught.

Back on the bed, Jody raised the binoculars and aimed them at Leahna's window. No change. She watched for a while, then moved them over, to the outside of the cabin where she'd seen the figure dragging the big bag. She wasn't sure, but she thought she could see a depression in the snow, a wide swath like something made by a sled, one of those round plastic ones. It wasn't smooth or even, though, and there were lots of footprints in it from people walking back and forth all morning.

Suddenly Jody gripped the binoculars more tightly and held her breath to keep them still. There was something in the snow, something shiny.

She remembered the glint she'd seen last night on the bent-over figure. She'd seen it on Leahna's visitor, too — a flash of what she thought was metal, like a watch, or a ring. Were they the same person?

The binoculars slipped. The skin around her eyes was getting sweaty, so she took them away, wiped her eyes with the sheet, and clamped them to her face again. Slowly she moved the binoculars around, trying to locate that glint in the snow. But suddenly there seemed to be hundreds of glints in the snow, most of them made by sunlight on ice crystals.

Jody sighed. Maybe she'd imagined the shiny

thing, too. She swept the binoculars up to Leahna's window again. Still no change. She sighed again, and it turned into a yawn. She was beginning to get tired. She hadn't gotten enough sleep last night. She'd take a little nap, then start watching again. Maybe she'd see something then.

But she was almost afraid of what it might be.

Jody woke up to the sound of rustling and shuffling in the room. She was sprawled on her stomach, her chin pillowed uncomfortably against the binoculars. Blinking, she rolled over.

"You snore, did you know that?" Chris said from across the room. She was sitting on her bed, pulling on a pair of thick socks.

"I do now," Jody said. "Thanks a lot for telling me."

Chris sniffed and pointed a finger toward Jody. Her ring — a silver one — flashed, and Jody narrowed her eyes, trying to see if any of Chris's rings were missing. But Chris wore so many and changed them so often, it was impossible to tell.

Then Jody noticed what Chris was pointing at — the binoculars.

Jody slowly raised her eyes and looked at Chris.

Chris didn't say anything, just curled her lips in a knowing little smile.

Jody didn't say anything, either. There wasn't any point. She'd fallen asleep without putting the binoculars back, and now she'd been caught. Chris's smile said she knew Jody had been spying through the window. Jody wondered if this was the first

Chris knew about it. Or had she been the shadow standing outside the room?

When Chris went back to pulling on her socks, Jody started to shove the binoculars under her pillow so no one else would see them. But before she could, Sasha breezed into the room, followed by Ellen.

"We're all going ice-skating!" Sasha announced, and Jody bet it was her idea. "Doesn't that sound great?"

"Great," Jody agreed. Sasha was looking directly at her and so was Ellen. She could hardly try to hide the binoculars now.

Ellen stared at the binoculars for a moment, then looked at Jody. Her expression was startled, Jody thought, as if she were the one who'd been caught. Finally Ellen turned away and started taking off her ski pants.

"Poor Jody," Sasha said. "You must feel kind of left out."

"Oh, no, really," Jody said. "I mean, I do feel left out, but that's not your problem. You guys can't sit around all day and keep me company. Anyway, it's not like I'm sick. I'm just immobile."

"I don't see why you're staying here," Chris said bluntly. She looked pointedly at the binoculars. "You must be bored out of your mind."

"She'd be bored at home, too," Ellen said.

"Right," Jody agreed. "And my parents are away. . . . I guess I just figured it made more sense to stay here."

"So you've decided to stay?" Sasha asked, her

voice muffled as she pulled a dark purple turtleneck over her head.

"Well, it's only for a couple more days," Jody said. "I don't know for sure yet." Maybe she *should* go home, she thought. But she'd have to take the bus, and the long ride would be awful. And she did want to find out what had happened to Leahna, what exactly she'd seen through the window. "Maybe I'll check the bus schedules this afternoon," she said. "Then I'll make up my mind."

"Is your ankle feeling any better at all?" Ellen asked.

Jody hadn't paid much attention to her ankle lately, except to stay off of it. "It doesn't hurt all the time now," she said. "But when I move it wrong, it really zaps me."

"Well, I think you should stay, then," Ellen said. "A bus will be packed. You'll be much more comfortable in the van."

"Oh, definitely, stay," Sasha agreed. She came and sat on Jody's bed to put on her socks. "We're going to eat at the lodge tonight, and tomorrow night I think somebody's having another party. You might be able to hobble along with us." She gave Jody a quick smile and stood up to leave, almost colliding with Billy at the door.

"Sorry," Billy said, stepping aside. Sasha tapped him on the arm as she passed. He looked after her, his eyes narrowed, his hands clenched into fists.

"How come you're always apologizing?" Chris asked Billy. Without waiting for an answer, she walked out the door after Sasha, causing Billy to step aside again. Jody took the opportunity to shove the binoculars under the pillow.

Ellen left, too, and finally Billy was able to come in. He stared out the window toward Leahna's cabin, not saying a word. Then he looked at Jody. "Have you seen her?"

Jody frowned. Why should he care? He hated Leahna, didn't he?

"I mean, I couldn't help noticing the binoculars," Billy went on. "And you were asking about her earlier. So, have you seen her?"

Jody shook her head, not bothering to deny that she'd been looking in the window. Billy's voice was flat, empty of emotion, and it made her nervous. "I guess she left."

Billy smiled strangely. "And with any luck, she'll never come back."

Before Jody could think of what to say, Cal stopped in the doorway. "Do me a favor, will you?" he said to Billy. "Go find Sasha and tell her Drew said not to wait — he'll meet us at the rink."

Billy nodded and left, and Cal turned to Jody. He looked tired and preoccupied. Like Billy, he stared out the window, then at Jody. His eyes were bright, but Jody couldn't tell if he was angry or sad. He started to say something, then stopped. Finally he said, " 'Bye, Jody. See you later."

Jody knew he'd come in for a reason. He'd wanted to tell her something or ask her something, but then he'd changed his mind. What could it have been?

A few minutes later, she heard the downstairs door slam, and a few minutes after that, Drew came in. He had a white pitcher in one hand. The other hand was behind his back. "Are you ready for this?" he asked.

"I don't know," Jody said. "Depends on what it is."

Drew brought his hand out. He was holding a bunch of flowers wrapped in green tissue.

"Oh, thank you!" Jody said.

"Guilt made me do this," Drew explained. "Everybody's having fun, and you're stuck here."

"You don't have to feel guilty. But I'm glad you do. I don't get flowers every day," Jody said, watching him unwrap them and stick them in the pitcher. She sort of wished he'd stay around, even if it was just for a little while. But she didn't know him well yet. Maybe he loved ice-skating. Maybe he couldn't stand being inside for long, even with her, when it was such a great day.

"There." Drew shoved aside some of the stuff on the stool by the bed and put the pitcher down. "When you look at these," he said, bending over to kiss her, "you can think of me." He straightened up and grinned, already backing out of the room. "Bet you didn't think I was so corny, huh?"

Slapping his hand against the doorframe, he hurried down the hall. Jody touched her lips. This kiss had been soft, but it still didn't make her forget the other one, which had been almost angry. She couldn't figure Drew out at all. One minute he was like a storm cloud, dark and swirling and frightening. And the next minute he was sweet, kissing her softly and giving her flowers.

Looking at the flowers now, Jody smiled a little. They looked nice — baby's breath, white carnations, and two red roses.

Red roses. Jody's smile faded. These flowers didn't make her think of Drew at all. They reminded her of the ones she'd seen through Leahna's window. Were those Drew's roses she'd seen through the binoculars? Had he kissed Leahna, too, and then stormed in the other night and pushed her to the floor?

The downstairs door slammed, and Jody jumped. She waited for footsteps on the stairs, and when she didn't hear any, she realized it had been Drew, leaving. She was alone again. Still thinking about Drew and the flowers, she pulled the binoculars out from under her pillow.

Leahna's roses were still there. Two of them had lost all their petals, and the rest were drooping badly. If Leahna — or someone else — had been in there, wouldn't they have thrown out the dying flowers?

Jody spent the rest of the afternoon reading, checking Leahna's window, reading some more, checking the window again. Around four she made her way downstairs and fixed a sandwich. When she got back up, the view hadn't changed.

By five it was starting to get dark, and at six, Drew called. "What do you like?" he asked. "Chinese chicken, barbecued ribs, lasagna, Swedish meatballs?"

"I like them all," Jody said.

"Okay, I'll bring you some of each."

Jody laughed a little. He was obviously still in a good mood. "Great. Where are you?"

"The lodge. It's smorgasbord night," he said. "I went the last time I was up here. They do a good job."

"Is everybody there?"

"I think so. We all came together, anyway," he said. "But the place is packed. I can't see anybody I know right now."

Jody could hear voices in the background. It sounded like a small army. A happy army, though. She heard a lot of laughing.

"Listen, I should get in line," Drew said. "This is going to take a while, I think. In fact, you might be eating meatballs for breakfast."

"Forget the meatballs," Jody told him. "Double up on the ribs."

"Right." Drew's voice was almost drowned out by the crowd in the background. "Later, Jody."

Much later, Jody decided Drew hadn't been kidding about breakfast. It was eight-thirty, and he hadn't come back. No one had. Thinking of the ribs made her stomach growl, so she went downstairs again and brought a package of cookies back up with her. She ate five of them, then shut off the light and looked out the window.

No light coming from Leahna's. Jody used the binoculars to see if she could see light anywhere else in the cabin, maybe the hall, but all she saw was darkness. She moved the binoculars slightly, to where she'd seen the figure last night, and gasped out loud.

Somebody was there.

Jody tightened her grip on the binoculars. The somebody wasn't just walking by. He was bent over, like last night, but not dragging anything. What was he doing? Kicking, that was it. Kicking at the snow and looking down. Looking for something. For that shiny thing? He'd lost something last night when he'd dragged the bag away, and now he'd come back to find it.

But why at night? The moon was out, but so were the clouds, and they kept drifting across the light, making it harder than ever for Jody to see. Half the time she thought the person had gone, but then she'd catch a movement again, and know he was still there, kicking at the snow.

Then the kicking stopped. But the person was still there. She could just make out a dark form, motionless in the snow. Standing there. Staring.

Staring up at *her*.

Jody suddenly shrank back and ducked down, her heart pounding like a drum. She'd been seen. The glass in the binoculars must have caught the moonlight and given her away. And now, whoever was out there knew Jody had been watching everything.

Still feeling nervous, Jody looked around the room. It was completely dark. The moon wasn't coming in her window at all, so how could it have flashed on the binocular glass? She couldn't have been seen. Still, she couldn't shake the creepy feeling that the figure had been looking right at her, that he'd known she was watching and was watching her back.

Enough of this. In the dark, Jody made her way to the door and hung up the binoculars. If they were there, she wouldn't be so tempted to use them. She lay down on the bed and decided to wait a while before turning the light back on.

She was still lying in the dark when Kate called.

"You sound funny," Kate commented after Jody said hello. "Like you've been getting obscene calls or something and you thought I was another one. You sounded suspicious."

"No, but I'm spooked," Jody said, glad to hear another voice. "I've really done it to myself this time."

"What do you mean? What are you spooked about?"

The connection was bad, with lots of crackling, and Jody had to talk loud. "I mean you were right about watching out the window," she said. "I don't think I'm in trouble, but it would serve me right if I were."

"You're not making any sense."

"I know." Jody laughed, a little shakily.

"So tell me what you saw that could get you in trouble," Kate said. "I'm feeling a little better, that's why I called. I'm ready for a good story."

"I don't know how good it is, but it's weird," Jody said. And then, sure this time that she was alone, Jody told Kate everything, starting from the first night she'd seen Leahna arguing with someone, and finishing with the dark figure she'd just seen kicking in the snow. "Tell me it's my imagination," she said. "They weren't looking at me, and Leahna's just a slob, that's why she hasn't thrown out the roses."

But Kate didn't tell her anything of the kind. "I don't believe this," she said angrily. "I call and all you can talk about is Leahna Calder! Why should I want to hear about her? She's — " Kate broke off. "Never mind. Why don't you just get out of there, Jody? Stop wasting your time looking out the window and imagining things."

"Well. Maybe I will," Jody said softly, trying not to get angry herself.

There was a loud crackle on the line. "What?" Kate yelled.

"I said, maybe I will!" Jody *was* angry, and she was glad for the excuse to yell. "But first I — "

"What?" Kate interrupted. "Don't do — " She said something else, but it was lost in the static.

Jody started to ask what she'd said, but decided it was hopeless. She might as well hang up. She heard a click, and the static stopped. Kate had given up, too, she guessed.

But before Jody heard the dial tone, she heard another click, soft but distinct. She hadn't hung up the phone yet.

But someone else had.

Chapter 11

Jody put down the receiver with a shaky hand. She wished her legs could race as fast as her heart was at the moment — she'd be down the stairs and out the door in a few seconds. On second thought, no she wouldn't. Whoever had been listening on the phone was downstairs.

It hadn't been her imagination, she was sure of that. Maybe the shadow was, but not that click. Kate had hung up, and before Jody did, someone else hung up. On the other phone, in the kitchen. Downstairs.

Jody felt sweat gathering at the edges of her hair. Someone was in the cabin, downstairs, right now. She didn't know what to do. Crawl under the bed? No, it was too low for that.

She had to listen, that's what she had to do. Listen for somebody coming up the stairs. Get her heart to stop thudding in her ears so she could hear.

But Jody didn't need to get her heart under control to hear what she heard now — another click:

the door downstairs, shutting click-closed. The listener had gone.

Jody snapped on the light, then dropped to her knees and scurried to the door. It was a little faster than hopping, and she was sure she wouldn't fall. Still on her knees, she stopped at the guys' door, raised up and found the light switch, and turned it on. Back out and down the hall to the railing. A lamp was on in the living room. The room was empty.

Now for the scariest part. Jody bumped her way down the stairs and over to the front door. She turned the lock button. Nobody could get in without a key now.

She held her breath and flung open the two closet doors. Nothing there but jackets and boots. Turning, she went into the kitchen. When she saw the back door, she almost panicked. She'd forgotten about it. But it was locked, too, and bolted on the inside. The listener couldn't have come in that way. When Drew had left to go skating, he must have forgotten to turn the lock on the front door.

Jody turned on another light in the kitchen, and just to be sure, pulled opén the door of the narrow broom closet. A broom, a mop, and some bottles of cleaning stuff. It would be a tight squeeze for someone, anyway.

Okay. Jody was sure she was alone. She'd been alone upstairs. She hadn't met anyone coming down, thank God. And no one else was down here. She was safe.

Safe and still scared. Because if someone had

broken in to rob the place, why had they just listened in on the phone and left?

Jody was lying wide-eyed on the couch in the living room when the others came back. She heard loud voices and footsteps crunching on the icy steps and snapped her head up. Then she heard the key in the lock, and the door opened, letting in a blast of cold air and snow.

"Jody, hi," Sasha said, stomping the snow off her feet. "There's a storm coming, I think. The wind is awful."

"I know, I've been listening to it," Jody said. "Is it snowing?"

"Just starting," Billy told her, pulling his gloves off with his teeth.

Chris, Ellen, and Cal shrugged out of their jackets, their cheeks pink from the cold. Drew stood where he was, his hands filled with a big paper bag. "Your dinner," he said to Jody. "Sorry it's so late. We didn't even eat until nine, and then there was a band."

It was after eleven, but Jody wasn't hungry. "That's okay," she said. She sat up farther and swung her legs to the floor.

"How come you're down here?" he asked. "I know, you were starving. Go ahead, make me feel guilty."

"No, I just got tired of being upstairs." Jody shook her head. "Actually, I got scared. Somebody . . . I'm pretty sure somebody was in here while you were gone."

That got everybody's attention.

"What do you mean, you're 'pretty sure'?" Chris asked. "Either somebody was or somebody wasn't."

"How could someone get in?" Ellen asked. "The door was locked, wasn't it?"

Jody looked at Drew. "I thought I locked it," he said, frowning. "Wait a minute." He closed his eyes, thought a second, opened his eyes again. "I did. I remember turning the little button."

Everyone was looking at Jody now. "I was talking on the phone," she said. "To Kate. And before I hung up, I heard a click. I thought somebody was listening on the phone down here in the kitchen. Then I heard another click. The door."

"You're sure you locked it, Drew?" Cal asked.

"Yes." Drew was still frowning at Jody.

"We shouldn't have left you alone," Ellen said.

"Oh, don't be ridiculous." Chris brushed past Billy, heading for the stairs. "All she heard was two clicks. And nothing happened, anyway."

"Yes, that's the important thing," Sasha said. "Nothing happened. But, Jody, are you sure it wasn't something else you heard? I mean, I used the phone in the lodge tonight and there was so much static on the line, I could hardly hear anything else. Maybe that's what you heard, too."

"What about the door, Sash?" Cal asked.

Sasha shrugged. "I don't know."

"The wind?" Billy suggested.

Cal shook his head. He still looked tired, Jody thought, and now he looked worried. "What are we saying, that Jody imagined it all?"

"Not *imagined* it, Cal," Ellen said, walking over to him and touching his arm. "Just thought she heard it, when it was really something else."

Jody decided not to join in this discussion of what she heard or didn't hear. She didn't have any doubts at all, but if the rest of them wanted to come up with another explanation, they could do it without her. "Sorry if I got everybody all worried," she said as she stood up. "I got scared, that's why I came down here. But now I think I'll go back up and go to sleep."

"What about your ribs?" Sasha asked. "Drew brought you a ton of them."

"Thanks, Drew." Jody was hopping to the stairs. "I'll eat them tomorrow. Good night, everybody."

Chris was already in bed when Jody got upstairs. The light was off, and Jody undressed in the dark. In bed, she listened to the others moving around downstairs, talking a little. She heard Sasha and Ellen come in, but she didn't say anything and after a while, she heard their even breathing.

Jody lay awake a long time, listening to the wind whistle and whine outside. It was an eerie sound, and it made her shiver even though she was warm under the blanket.

Kate said she'd been imagining things. Nobody else really seemed to believe that there'd been someone in the cabin. Jody felt like it was seven against one. Were they right? Had she just gotten so spooked thinking it was blood on Leahna's wall that she was twisting everything around, hearing things that weren't really there, scaring herself so much she couldn't go to sleep?

Why was she staying there, anyway? She wanted to know what happened to Leahna, but not if she was going to be terrified doing it. Maybe she'd imagined that click on the phone line, and maybe she hadn't, but it didn't matter anymore. It was time to get out. She hadn't called the bus station this afternoon, but she'd do it first thing in the morning. She'd take the earliest bus she could, and by lunchtime tomorrow, she'd be home.

Once Jody decided to go, she thought for sure she'd be able to sleep. She still couldn't, though. The wind kept howling, gusting and slamming against the cabin.

But that wasn't what kept Jody awake. What she saw every time she closed her eyes was that figure outside, standing in the snow. What she heard in her mind, louder than the wind, was that click on the telephone. And what kept her awake was the thought that the two things were connected.

She'd been caught spying, and then she'd been spied on.

And now, she herself was in danger.

When Jody woke up after an uneasy sleep, it wasn't to sunlight streaming in, but to the howl of the wind, still whipping around the cabin and whistling through the snow. She turned over and saw the gray sky, then got on her knees and looked out the window.

It seemed to have stopped snowing, but it was

hard to tell. Every time the wind gusted, it sent up a thick spray of snow, filling the air with swirling white flakes and blotting out the line between the sky and the ground.

Leahna's window was covered with a film of frost. Snow had drifted against the garbage cans, and only two small specks of orange still showed. The place where the person had been looking for something was smoothed over with new snow.

Tons of new snow, Jody thought, looking at the drifts that curled up and over like waves in the ocean. It must have been a monster storm.

When she got downstairs and turned on the radio in the kitchen, she found out just how monstrous it had been. More than three feet of snow had fallen during the night, the announcer said, and some drifts were as high as five feet. More snow was coming down, but it was expected to taper off by noon. Telephone lines were down, the ski lift was temporarily out of commission, and roads were closed. Brevard Pass was snowed in.

Jody picked up the telephone, just to be sure. There was no dial tone. She hung up and went back to the table, so nervous her hands were shaking. Last night had scared her badly — she wanted out of Brevard Pass.

But now she was trapped.

All Jody could do was wait, and waiting made her edgy. While Ellen and Billy made pancakes for everyone, Jody sat in the living room, staring out the window and chewing on a fingernail. She didn't pay much attention to the loud talk coming from the kitchen, but she couldn't help hearing Sasha taking charge, as usual, telling everyone to hurry and eat so they could get outside and play.

"We can have a snowball fight," Sasha was saying. "And I bet the snow's deep enough to dig tunnels. Remember, Cal, we did that once? Billy, don't make another stack, we'll be stuck in here forever."

Sasha went on, convincing everybody how much fun they could have, but Jody tuned her out. She was trying to keep her mind blank, trying not to think about last night and how much she wanted to leave, when Drew walked in with a plate of pancakes for her.

"You're mad at me, aren't you?" he said.

"No, I'm mad at the storm," Jody said, taking the plate. "I was going to go home today. You're not stopping me. Why should I be mad at you?"

"Because you think I left the door unlocked and won't admit it."

"No. I think you *think* you locked the door," Jody said. "I *know* somebody was in this cabin, listening on the phone, and then they left. So how did they get in?"

"You're really sure, aren't you?" he asked.

"Yes. No," Jody said. "I don't know. Nobody believes me, and it's making me confused. Forget it."

Drew stared at her, his eyes narrowed. He started to say something, then seemed to change his mind and shrugged. "Maybe you'll be able to go home later today," he said. "The roads might be plowed. So if you do, how about giving me your

phone number? I'd like to call you, if that's okay."
His voice soft, he added, "Hey, come on. I'm not
saying I did leave the door unlocked. But even if I
did, you're not going to hold it against me forever,
are you?"

"I guess not." Jody smiled a little. "Got a pencil?"

Drew found a pencil and paper on the shelf unit,
and Jody gave him her number. He tucked it into
his pocket and went upstairs, whistling.

Jody stayed on the couch, listening to the others
talking quietly in the kitchen. Probably about her
and her overactive imagination, she thought. She
couldn't wait to get out of there.

By eleven, everyone had left. Jody checked that
the front door was really locked, then took her plate
into the kitchen. Afterwards she took a shower and
went upstairs to get dressed, taking the radio with
her for company. This wasn't the Arctic, after all,
and the roads might be plowed in time for her to
take a late bus out.

By noon, it had stopped snowing. Jody didn't
need the radio to tell her that, she could see it out
the window. But the roads were still closed, and
the telephone wasn't working yet. Every once in a
while, she'd pick it up to check, then go back to
reading. For a while, she deliberately avoided looking at Leahna's window. Finally, though, she gave
in and got the binoculars. But the window was still
frosty and she couldn't see in.

Around two, she started to wonder where the
others were. According to the radio, the lift wasn't
running yet. Maybe they'd gone ice-skating, or to

the lodge for lunch. Hungry herself, Jody went downstairs, taking the radio to keep tabs on the road situation. She knew both doors were locked, she knew she was alone, but it didn't make her feel any better. Every time something creaked, she jumped. Every time she looked at the phone, she thought of that click on the line. She *had* heard it, she knew she had. Why did everyone want to talk her out of what she knew was true?

She tried to eat some of the ribs, but her stomach was a knot of nerves, and she couldn't even get through one. She put them away and made a thermos of tea to take upstairs for the rest of the afternoon. She was trying to decide whether to take the radio or the thermos up first, when she heard the door open and the rest of the group came in.

"The lift just started up again," Sasha said as Jody came hopping into the living room. "We came back to change and then we're going back out. Only a few trails are open, but our time's almost up, so we don't want to waste it."

"Are the roads still closed, do you know?" Jody asked.

"I think so," Cal said. "Why?"

"You're not thinking of leaving!" Sasha exclaimed. "Jody, even if the roads were open, they'd be dangerous. You're much safer here."

"I wanted to go home today," Jody said, sinking onto the couch. She didn't bother to say that she didn't feel safe at all.

"Going stir-crazy?" Billy asked. He looked half-frozen from whatever games Sasha had organized. Jody didn't understand why he wanted to go back out skiing. But Billy didn't even wait for an answer, he just hurried up the stairs.

Jody stayed on the couch while everyone else hurried around, running upstairs, going into the kitchen to grab a cookie, going back up. Knowing they'd all be gone soon, leaving her alone in the cabin made her feel more trapped than ever. Trapped and terrified. The last thing she wanted was to spend another evening all by herself here.

"We'll probably be eating at the lodge, since there's not much here," Ellen said as she pulled on her parka. "You can find something, can't you, Jody?"

"Sure, there's a ton of ribs left." Jody took a shaky breath. "Ellen, maybe you'd like to stay and eat them with me. And they have a Monopoly game here. We could play that."

Ellen shook her head, laughing a little. "I always lose at Monopoly."

"I'll let you win." Jody heard herself laugh and realized it sounded desperate. But she didn't care, she just wanted someone with her. "And if I land on Park Place, I promise not to buy it."

Ellen looked at her curiously. She started to say something, and then Cal walked in.

Jody's heart sank. Ellen would go wherever Cal went.

"Okay, we're off," Sasha announced, coming in from the kitchen. "Jody, if the phones start working, one of us will call."

"You don't have to," Jody said. "I'm not going anywhere."

Sasha smiled and tossed Jody a cookie from the handful she was carrying. "If you take a nap, maybe the day will go by faster."

Jody forced herself to smile back and tell her to have a good time. Billy hurried downstairs, but she didn't ask him to stay. She was waiting for Drew. He'd stay, wouldn't he? He'd kissed her; he'd asked for her phone number. If she asked him to stay, he wouldn't mind.

Billy left, and then Drew came downstairs, striding into the kitchen before Jody could say anything. "Drew?" she called.

Silence. Then he called back, "What?"

Jody cleared her throat. "Do you have to go?"

"What?"

Jody took a deep breath. "I was wondering if you'd stay," she shouted.

"I can't hear you, just a sec." There was a clatter in the kitchen, and then he came into the living room. "What did you ask?"

"I wondered — " Jody broke off as Chris came bustling downstairs.

"Come on, Drew," Chris said, smiling at him. "This may be our last chance on the slopes."

Drew gave her a distracted glance. "Yeah, sure, just a minute. What was it, Jody?"

Jody waited for Chris to leave, but she'd planted herself next to Drew and didn't look like she was going to budge. Jody knew Chris would sneer when she asked Drew to stay. But she was too scared to let that stop her. "I was wondering if you'd — "

The door opened and Cal stuck his head in. "Come on, you guys," he said. "Drew, you've got my lift pass, remember?"

Drew reached into his pocket. "You sure?" He checked another pocket. He was moving toward the door now, with Chris right behind him. "I can't find it."

"You'd better," Cal said. "I can't get to the slopes without it."

"Yeah, I remember now," Drew said, pulling open another pocket. "There it is. How come you don't have it on your parka like everybody else?"

The door slammed shut before Jody heard Cal's answer. She leaned forward, watching the door, hoping Drew would come back and ask her what she'd wanted. But after five minutes, she knew he wasn't coming back. She was alone again, and dark was coming soon.

Jody stayed on the couch for a while, too nervous to do anything but listen for sounds. Finally, though, she decided to go upstairs. After making sure the front door was really locked, she went into the kitchen and checked the back door. The radio had a leather strap, so she slipped it over one wrist, picked up the thermos of tea, and made her way up to the bedroom. She turned the radio on and poured some tea into the plastic thermos cup. After a few sips, she poured it back into the thermos — she hadn't put enough sugar in.

Four o'clock and the roads were opening up, but only to emergency vehicles. It would be dark soon, and Jody knew she'd be staying here at least another night. She found a magazine she hadn't read yet and tried to get interested in an article about body language. But her own body was telling her it was tired and wanted to sleep. She didn't know why, since she hadn't had any exercise for days, but she couldn't keep her eyes open and in a few minutes, she'd drifted off to sleep.

She woke up to the dark and the blare of music from the radio. She immediately snapped on the lamp, knocking her bottle of pain pills onto the floor. She started to pick it up, then stopped, leaning toward the floor, her hand halfway to the bottle.

The music had stopped, and an announcer's voice was giving a news bulletin.

"The body of a young woman has been discovered by a ski patrol checking some of the cross-country trails near Brevard Pass. The discovery was made at approximately four-thirty, and police have still not identified the body. The victim is described as white, approximately sixteen to eighteen years old, with dark-blonde hair and blue eyes. Anyone with information is urged to contact authorities. Police have not issued a statement on the cause of death as yet, although a ski accident has been ruled out. Stay tuned for further details."

The music came back on then, but Jody hardly heard it. Something was the matter with her ears, there was a rushing sound, like the ocean or the wind. She sat like a statue, feeling cold and dizzy.

It was Leahna Calder who'd been found, Jody knew it. She didn't need to stay tuned for further details. She could fill in the details herself: Leahna arguing with a visitor, the visitor standing alone, the red streak on the wall that had been washed off, the dying roses, the dark figure dragging something away from the cabin. Dragging Leahna's body away. And Jody had seen it all.

Someone had killed Leahna, and Jody had seen that someone. Seen him come back last night, frantically trying to find something he'd lost in the snow, something that might tie him to the killing. And then he'd stopped, a dark figure in the snow, staring up at the window where Jody was watching.

Jody had seen the killer, and the killer had seen her.

Chapter 12

Still cold and dizzy, Jody reached out a shaky hand for the phone. She had to call the police, tell them what she knew. But there was no dial tone. The phone was dead. Jody slammed it down in frustration and then glared at her ankle. She wanted to move, to pace around the room. Her thoughts were going double-time, it wasn't fair that she had to sit still through something like this.

The radio was still playing music, and Jody shut it off. She had to decide what to do. The announcer said they'd found the body about four-thirty. It was six now, so maybe they'd identified her. Jody turned off the light and snatched up the binoculars. Leahna's cabin was dark. If the police had found out who she was, wouldn't they be there, looking for clues? Could they have come and gone already?

Everything Jody knew about the police she'd learned on television; she had no idea how things really worked. One thing she was sure about, though, was that they didn't just put a dead body on display and ask people if they knew who she was.

So what did they do? Wait for somebody — parents, a friend, a boyfriend — to report that they hadn't heard from her in three days?

It had to be something like that, Jody thought. So where were Leahna's friends? Not in this cabin, that was for sure. Except for Cal. But Cal probably thought she'd gone to Antigua.

What about her parents? Weren't they worried when they didn't hear from her? Where were they, anyway — in Antigua? Jody had no idea. Maybe it was a real loose family relationship and Leahna didn't have to report in.

Leahna wasn't a total stranger to Brevard Pass, though. The police must be asking people who worked here to try to identify her. Maybe some people recognized her, but didn't know her name or something. The police might be using a photograph or a drawing, going around from place to place. That would take time.

Jody tried the phone again. It still wasn't working, but she didn't slam it down this time. She was feeling calmer, at least calm enough to try to convince herself that it didn't have to be *Leahna's* body they'd found.

She turned on the light, poured some more tea, and took a sip. It was still hot, but she'd forgotten how bitter it was, so she set it aside. Then she sat back and started going over everything she'd seen. Leahna arguing with somebody, twice. The red streak on the wall, the hunched-over figure dragging a bag, then somebody kicking in the snow. It could be that the visitor had thrown Leahna against the wall, killed her, and come back later in the night to hide her body up on the slopes. Then he'd come back the next night to search for whatever he'd dropped in the snow.

Or, she told herself, Leahna could have gotten mad, thrown a jar of nail polish at the visitor, missed, hit the wall and stormed out. Leahna could have left for Antigua without throwing out the roses. Like Jody had said jokingly to Kate, maybe she was a slob. A selective slob — she cleaned the wall but left the roses to die. And the person in the snow didn't have to be Leahna's visitor, guilty of murder and trying to get rid of the evidence.

Which was it? Jody didn't know. She wanted to believe the second one, but she couldn't make herself do it. She still wanted to call the police. Let them think she was hysterical, she didn't care. She'd be happy to find out she was wrong.

She looked out the window again. There was no light in Leahna's cabin. She tried the phone. Still dead. She turned on the radio, hoping the body had been identified and it wasn't Leahna. She sat for fifteen minutes, but when the news came on, nothing had changed.

What now? Wait, that's all she could do. When the others came back, she could tell them, and they could go to the police for her. It was six-thirty. They were probably eating now. Maybe they wouldn't take so long tonight.

Having to wait didn't keep Jody calm. She suddenly realized that her muscles were all clenched, even her jaw and her stomach. She tried to make herself relax, but she couldn't. Instead of sitting around, she decided to go downstairs, just to move.

She started to get up and almost fell when her good foot hit the pill bottle she'd knocked over earlier. She sat down again, picked up the bottle, started to put it on the stool. Her hand stopped in midair, and she looked at the bottle. Frowning a little, she shook it.

Something was wrong. Jody started to open the bottle, but her fingers were clumsy with the safety cap, and she bent a fingernail halfway back. She dropped the bottle, grabbed it up again, finally got the top off and looked inside.

The doctor had given her twelve pills. She'd taken one, the first night. She tipped the bottle and poured the pills into the palm of her hand. Four left. What had happened to the other seven?

As far as she knew, nobody in the cabin used drugs. But she wasn't sure. Maybe one of them liked the floaty feeling pain pills gave you before they knocked you out. Or maybe somebody just couldn't sleep.

Jody shook her head and put the pills back, still frowning. Then she picked up the thermos and cup and poured back the tea she hadn't drunk. She was capping the thermos when she thought of something, and the thought hit her like a punch in the stomach.

The tea had been bitter.

She'd thought it was because she hadn't put enough sugar in it. But maybe that wasn't it at all.

Maybe it was bitter because seven of her pills

had been dissolved in it. And maybe if she'd drunk more than a few sips earlier, she'd still be asleep. The thermos held about two or three cups — if she'd had it all, all seven pills, would she be dead? Maybe, if the others didn't come back in time to find her.

The others.

In her mind's eye, Jody saw them moving through the cabin that afternoon getting ready to go skiing. She'd just finished making the tea, and she'd left it in the kitchen.

Nobody else had been in the cabin, nobody else could have taken her pills and put them in the tea.

Only one of the others.

Wait a minute, wait a minute. She didn't know for sure that her tea had been drugged. She was guessing, just like she was guessing that the body of the young woman was the body of Leahna Calder.

But Jody's mind kept pushing on, she couldn't stop it. She'd written her name on the window, and everyone had seen it. She'd used the binoculars, and everybody knew about that, too. She'd asked questions about Leahna, but she hadn't gotten a straight answer from anyone. She'd seen that figure searching frantically through the snow, and later, she'd heard the phone being hung up downstairs, and the door shutting.

Somebody knew.

Somebody knew that Jody had been watching, and they were afraid of what she might have seen. Then they came in and heard her telling everything to Kate.

Drew had been right — he hadn't left the door unlocked. Whoever came in had used a key.

Jody bent over, her head in her hands. She was shaking her head slightly, not wanting to believe what she was thinking.

Suddenly her head shot up and her eyes opened wide and her heart started hammering in her chest. She had heard the door open downstairs.

Someone had come back.

The door slammed, and Jody heard shuffling sounds. Then a fast *thump-thump* as someone trotted up the stairs. Jody stood up, watching the door. She wanted to run, but there was nowhere to go. She wanted to scream, but her mouth was dry. She couldn't make a sound. All she could do was wait.

It was Chris who came through the door. She gasped when she saw Jody standing there. "God, Jody!"

Jody licked her lips and swallowed. "What?"

Chris kept staring at her. Then she said, "You scared me. I didn't think you were awake."

Jody didn't move. "Why wouldn't I be?"

"Because." Chris walked across the room and started rummaging through a pile of clothes she'd left on her bed. "Sleeping's about all you've been doing lately."

Jody watched her, saw her rings and bracelets flashing and wondered again if any of them were missing. "What are you doing here?" That sounded wrong. "I mean, are the others coming back, too?"

Chris's yellow sweater had a dark stain across the front and she was taking it off. She picked up a black sweater and stood there, smiling at Jody. It wasn't a nice smile. "Are you hearing noises again?" She cocked her head, still looking at Jody. "You know, maybe you *should* be scared. They found a body up on one of the trails today. No one knows who it is or what happened yet, but everybody's talking about a maniac running around Brevard Pass. Maybe he was in here last night."

Jody felt her good leg shaking and hoped Chris wouldn't notice. "Why'd you come back?" she asked again.

"Because," Chris said, pulling the clean sweater over her head, "Billy spilled grape soda all over me, and I wanted to change, that's why. Okay?"

"So you're going back to the lodge?" Jody asked. "Is everyone else still there? When are they coming back here?"

"What is this, a test?" Chris was heading for the door now. "I don't know what everybody else is doing, Jody. I only know what I'm doing." She eyed the binoculars on the bed, then looked at Jody. "I know what you've been doing, too. Better be careful, Jody. You might see the maniac." She smiled another nasty smile and left the room.

I've already seen the maniac, Jody thought.

She waited until she heard the front door slam, then hurried across the room and picked up Chris's yellow sweater. The stain smelled like grape soda, but that didn't mean Billy had spilled it. He was a convenient one to blame it on, though. Chris could have spilled it herself and used it as an excuse to come back and see if Jody was knocked out from the tea. Then she would have turned around and left, made sure the others stayed out late. Late enough for the pills to do their work.

Jody wondered what Chris would do now, if she was the one.

But what if she wasn't the one?

Jody dropped the yellow sweater in a heap on the floor and went back to her bed. Chris wasn't alone in hating Leahna. No one in the cabin liked her, except Cal. Sasha didn't bother to keep her feelings a secret. She tried to talk Cal out of seeing Leahna, and she'd come right out and admitted she didn't like her. Maybe it was more than dislike, though. Maybe it was hatred.

Ellen, what about Ellen? She seemed so frail and soft, but Jody remembered what a strong skier she was. And she couldn't forget the way her airy, little-girl voice had hardened when she told Jody how Leahna had used her, and that Leahna was rotten and not worth anything. Jody couldn't forget the way she looked at the party, when Cal had read the statement, *You wish Leahna Calder were dead.* Maybe Ellen did wish it, because of Cal. Because she was jealous and knew she didn't stand a chance with Cal as long as Leahna was alive.

Who else might wish Leahna were dead, wish it hard enough to kill her? Billy. Jody saw his round face, not smiling anymore, as he stared out the kitchen window and said he hated her. He told Jody the next day he didn't mean it, but even then, she didn't believe him. He'd said he was the joker, but he'd dropped the clown mask when he'd said maybe Leahna would never come back.

Cal? Jody thought he was crazy about Leahna. Maybe he'd gone to see her, and she'd laughed at him. Two nights in a row, she'd laughed at him, and then maybe he *did* go crazy. Lost his temper and shoved her, hard enough to kill her.

Then there was Drew. As much as Jody wanted to, she couldn't ignore the possibility that he might be the one. He'd gone over to Leahna's the night of the party, and he'd come back furious. Furious enough to go back and kill her? What had he said to Jody? "She's out of my life."

He'd been so different since that night, the night Jody saw the stranger standing alone in Leahna's room. He'd been easy, funny, romantic, not moody at all. As if whatever had been bothering him had just . . . disappeared.

Jody shook her head a little, almost laughed. Leahna was out of Drew's life and who was in? Jody. Drew could have been coming on to her to keep her off balance, keep her from suspecting him. If he was, then Jody had played right into his hands.

She remembered Drew's hands, wide and strong, wrapping the bandage around her ankle. They'd been gentle then, but they were anything but gentle when they shoved Leahna against the wall. *If* they did. If Drew was the one.

So many people had reasons to hate Leahna Calder, to wish she would disappear. Even Kate. She'd called Leahna poison. Jody had been surprised at how strange Kate had sounded on the phone whenever Leahna's name was mentioned, so cold and mean.

Jody pushed them all out of her mind and picked up the phone. All she heard was silence. She clicked the button a few times and waited, willing the dial tone to come on.

Nothing.

She lifted the binoculars, but Leahna's window was dark. The police hadn't come yet.

Only two people knew Leahna was dead — Jody and Leahna's killer.

It could have been any one of them. During the second party, when Jody was home alone, any one of them could have left and gone to Leahna's. The party moved from one cabin to another, and it was crowded, lots of people coming and going. What had Sasha said? "It was a crazy night." Cal had said the same thing, when he'd appeared in the doorway, a dark shadow that made Jody scream. She wanted to scream now, but there was no one to hear her, no one to help. It was a crazy night, all right. A night for murder.

The next night was the smorgasbord. Another crowd. Plenty of time for somebody to leave and go look for something they'd lost in the snow.

And any one of them could have put the pills in Jody's tea. They were all over the cabin earlier, upstairs and down, in the kitchen and out.

Jody squeezed her eyes shut, trying to remember if there was a time when just one person was in the kitchen alone. She saw Ellen, Sasha, Billy, Drew

. . . what about the others? She couldn't remember.

Her eyes still closed, Jody pictured Leahna's visitor. Wearing black, it looked like, or at least dark clothes. Taller than Leahna. How tall was that? She remembered the day she'd first seen her, coming down the slope with the orange peel stuck on her pole. Then Cal and Drew had gone over to her. They were much taller than she was. That meant Sasha was, too. And Billy and Ellen. Chris? Chris was about Jody's height. About the same as Leahna, maybe a little taller.

Now Jody was seeing the killer's hand. Hand or wrist. A watch, or a bracelet, or a ring. Something the killer had to get back.

Now she was picturing everyone's hands. Chris wore enough rings and bracelets to start a jewelry store. Who else wore rings? Sasha wore a silver bracelet. Ellen wore a gold one, a thin gold bracelet. Was it too small to catch the light? Drew wore a watch. Did everyone else? Jody squeezed her eyes tighter, tried to remember if someone's watch was missing, or someone's bracelet. She had to remember. She just *had* to.

Jody opened her eyes, looked around the room. She was trapped in this room. Trapped in the cabin. If the killer came back now, she wouldn't be able to run.

Get out. She should get out now. She'd go out the back door, and crawl if she had to, crawl through the snow to another cabin, where she'd be safe. Okay, where were her jacket and gloves? Downstairs. Did she need anything from up here? Nothing, she just needed to get out.

Jody decided to try the phone one last time. If it was still dead, she was out of here. If it worked, she'd call the police and then get out.

Jody lifted the receiver. Even before she got it up to her ear, she heard the dial tone. Nothing had ever sounded so sweet.

Chapter 13

The phone was working, but there was still so much static on the line, Jody could barely make herself heard.

"I'm sorry, you'll have to speak up," the operator said.

Jody raised her voice until she was shouting. "I said, I need to talk to the police!"

Another loud crackle. Then the operator's voice. "Police?"

"Yes!" Jody shouted. She couldn't shout any louder. "I need the police!"

More static. Jody almost whimpered in frustration. "Hello? Hello?"

The operator was saying the same thing. "Hello?"

"I'm still here!" Jody shouted. "Did you understand me? Did you hear me?"

There was more crackling. She'd never get through, Jody thought. She was wasting her time.

Then, like magic, the static stopped and the line was clear.

"Hello?" The operator sounded like she was in the same room.

"Yes!" Jody caught her breath and told herself not to yell anymore. "Thank goodness. Yes, I want the police."

"Yes, ma'am, I need to know where you're calling from, please."

"Right, I'm in Brevard — " Jody broke off and stared at the phone.

The line was dead. No static, no dial tone, just dead. She pushed the button down, then listened again. Nothing.

Okay, she'd just go. She probably should have done that in the first place.

Now that she was leaving, Jody couldn't do it fast enough. She hopped across the room, got to the door and had to steady herself against it. Enough hopping. She could move faster on her knees.

Just before she dropped to her knees, she heard the sound in the kitchen, a faint clink, like metal hitting against metal. Jody's heart knocked like a fist against her chest.

The sound hadn't been loud, but that didn't matter. It had come from the kitchen, and whatever it was, Jody knew it hadn't happened by itself.

The phone hadn't just died again, either. The line in the kitchen had been cut.

Someone was down there. Someone who didn't want to be heard.

Now Jody eased down to her knees, trying not to make noise, trying not to breathe. She stayed where she was a few seconds, wishing she could think better. Should she go back into her room or try to get across to the guys' room?

When she heard the creak of the stairs, she stopped trying to think and scooted back into her room. Where, though? There weren't any closets to hide in. The beds were too low to crawl under.

Another creak of the stairs sent Jody scrambling toward her bed. She shut off the lamp, wincing at the noise it made. Then she grabbed the binoculars. She'd hide behind the door, swing them at whoever came in, and run out.

She was just about to move when she saw the shadow out in the hall. Long and tall, moving quickly and quietly against the wall, coming toward Jody's room. Jody stuffed the binoculars under her pillow. She might get a chance to use them and she didn't want to be forced to give them up.

Then the shadow filled the doorway, only it wasn't a shadow anymore. Somebody long and lean, dressed in black. Cal? Jody heard the rushing sound in her ears again, felt her heart thudding, made herself stand still and wait.

"Oh, Jody, you're awake," Sasha said in surprise.

Jody's mouth was dry, and she had to swallow before she could talk. "Yes."

Sasha laughed, that throaty, infectious laugh that nobody could resist. "Poor Jody. You must be getting sick of this room."

"Yes," Jody said again.

Sasha reached a hand up to her head, and then her long hair fell free. She'd had it up, that's why

Jody'd thought it might be Cal at first.

"You sound kind of funny," Sasha said. "Are you feeling okay?"

Jody licked her lips. "I'm . . . just tired of being here, like you said."

Sasha nodded. "I don't blame you. That's why I came back, to see how you're doing."

Jody felt her heart slow down a little. Maybe Sasha wasn't the one after all. She sounded normal, friendly the way she always was. "Actually," Jody said, "I'm not just tired of being here. I was nervous, too."

"Really? Oh, after last night, you mean." Sasha nodded again. "Yes, I would be, too."

"I guess everybody thinks I was imagining it," Jody said cautiously.

"Oh, well, you know. It's hard to think something like that could really happen," Sasha said. "I mean a robber, yes. But a robber who listens in on a phone conversation? That's pretty weird."

"Yeah," Jody agreed. She suddenly realized she was still standing in the dark. She bent a little and stretched her hand toward the lamp.

"Oh, no, leave it off," Sasha said. "I won't be staying long, and it'll be easier in the dark."

Jody wasn't sure she'd heard her right. "What'll be easier? What do you mean?"

But Sasha didn't answer.

And suddenly, the meaning of her words hit home. Sasha wouldn't be staying long.

Just long enough to kill Jody. And it would be easier to kill her in the dark.

Jody felt her knees shaking, and her heart raced so fast she thought it would burst. She saw Sasha's lips move, and knew she'd said something, but her ears were roaring again and she couldn't hear. For a second Jody was afraid she might faint. She was so scared she wanted to cry.

But she couldn't. She couldn't do any of that.

If she wanted to live, she had to hold on.

Jody was shaking so badly she wondered why she didn't fall. But somehow she managed to stay upright. Gradually the roaring in her ears stopped, and she was able to hear what Sasha was saying.

"Well, Jody, I see you've figured it out," Sasha said. "Just like you figured everything else out when you started spying out the window."

Jody hugged herself, trying to stop the shaking. "Why?" she whispered. "Why'd you do it?"

"Kill Leahna, you mean? Well." Sasha leaned against the doorframe as if she were settling down to have a friendly chat. "It was Cal."

"Cal?" What did she mean? Did they do it together? "I don't understand," Jody said.

"No, you probably don't." Sasha ran the fingers of one hand through her hair. Jody saw her silver bracelet shimmer for a second. Sasha must have seen her notice it, because she said, "Yes. I found it, Jody. I was lucky wasn't I, that the storm didn't come any sooner? I must have looked ridiculous, stomping around in the snow like that. Did I?"

"No, just in a hurry," Jody said. "I couldn't tell who you were."

"No. But you've got a busy mind, you would have

figured it out. Once I found the bracelet, I only had to worry about you."

Sasha turned her head for a second, to look out in the hall. Jody sat down on the bed, slipped her hand under the pillow, and touched the binoculars.

"I was going to tell you to go ahead and sit," Sasha said. "You've been standing like a statue. Your good leg must be tired."

"How thoughtful." Jody bit her lip, wishing she hadn't said it.

But Sasha just shook her head. "Oh, Jody, don't be sarcastic," she said sadly. "That's not like you. Leave that to Chris. You know, I wish it *were* Chris, not you. I liked you. For a while."

Jody didn't want to hear about Sasha's regrets. "You were going to tell me about Cal."

"Yes, Cal." Sasha shifted in the doorway, and Jody tensed. But she was only leaning the other way now, her arms crossed, one leg bent. She looked relaxed, but Jody didn't dare make a move yet. Jody sat still, not taking her eyes away from Sasha.

"I love Cal," Sasha said. "We were always so close. Well, you probably guessed that. We didn't have to talk half the time. Our minds just seemed to communicate without talk. We argued plenty of times, but we always stuck up for each other against somebody else. No one could come between us."

Jody remembered something: At the party, when Cal and Sasha were standing near her, talking. Jody didn't know what they'd been talking about, but Cal had sounded sad. And he'd said, "Things change."

Now, Jody said it out loud. "Things change."

Sasha nodded. "I told Cal that Leahna wasn't any good for him. And she wasn't — he knew she wasn't. But he wouldn't stop hoping. He wouldn't listen to me."

"But . . ." Jody knew she shouldn't argue, but she couldn't help it. "You mean, you killed her to get her out of his life? Sasha, there'll be other girls after Leahna."

"Sure there will." Sasha sounded so reasonable. "You don't understand, Jody. I don't want to keep girls out of Cal's life. Don't be silly."

"You're right, I don't understand."

"Stop interrupting and maybe you will!" Sasha's voice was harsh and cold, and Jody shrank back from the sound of it. She wrapped her fingers around the binoculars and held on tight.

When she spoke again, Sasha sounded back to normal, whatever that meant. "Leahna didn't care about Cal. She didn't care about any guy, really, but Cal's the one who mattered to me. See, Jody, he was crazy about her. He actually thought he was in love with her, that he had a chance with her. I tried to tell him he didn't. But he wouldn't listen. I told him he'd get hurt, and he said he didn't believe it. And he didn't care. But I cared!"

Was Sasha crying? Jody hoped so. Let her cry, she thought. Let her get hysterical, fall on the floor sobbing. Anything so Jody could get away.

Sasha might have been crying, but she was still in control. And she didn't move from the doorway. "He sent her flowers. He sent her a note," she went on, her voice calmer. "And then he went to see her after the party. When he came back, he said he'd asked her to stay another day or two. Do you know, he actually told her he thought he loved her? Poor Cal."

What was that sound? Jody tensed up again, listening hard.

But Sasha was shaking her head. "It was only the refrigerator coming on, Jody. I know you're hoping somebody will come to the rescue, but that's not going to happen. Do you really think I'd be standing here explaining things to you if I didn't think I had the time?"

Jody had to ask. "How do you know they won't come? How can you be so sure?"

"Because I told Cal and Billy to keep everybody there, at the lodge," Sasha said simply. "I told them I was coming to get you, that I'd bring you back with me, and we'd have a little surprise party for you. They all thought it was a great idea."

"Even Chris?"

"No, not Chris," Sasha laughed. "She's not there. She latched on to a new guy tonight, and I have the feeling she won't be back here at all. But the others? They're all there, waiting for us, Jody. I told them it would probably take a while," she added. "But they've got plenty to do — bribe the kitchen for a 'get well' cake, find some balloons if they can. I put Billy in charge, that made him feel good. It cheered Cal up, too. He likes you."

Yes, Sasha was good at organizing things, Jody thought. A ski trip, a party, a murder. "What happens when I don't show up with you?" she asked. She couldn't believe she sounded so calm, as if she'd asked about the weather.

Sasha didn't answer, didn't even act as if she'd heard. "Cal told Leahna he loved her," she said, picking up the story again. "And she . . . Cal said she laughed at him! Jody, you should have seen the look in his eyes when he told me!"

Sasha was quiet for a moment, and Jody heard her swallow. Then she said, "So I went over to her cabin. I told her — I *warned* her — she shouldn't treat Cal like that, and she said it wasn't any of my business, that Cal could stick up for himself if he wanted to." Sasha was talking faster now. "I didn't do anything that night. I waited, to see what would happen. Maybe Cal *would* stick up for himself. Or maybe he'd cheer up and laugh it off. But he didn't. He was thinking about her every minute, I could tell. Remember, I've always known what he's thinking, and I couldn't make him stop."

Jody remembered the way Cal had acted after he'd seen Leahna. Yes, he'd talked and joked, but he'd been forcing himself, and she'd known something was bothering him. But he didn't act devastated. If only Sasha had left things alone, Jody thought, Cal would probably have been fine. He was growing away from Sasha, changing. It was Sasha who wanted things to stay the same, always wanted to protect him. Cal would have been fine by himself. He was strong enough. In a way, Sasha was the weak one.

Sasha wasn't leaning against the doorframe anymore. She'd straightened up, and Jody could tell how stiff she was, stiff with anger.

"Before, I could always make him see things my way. But not this time," Sasha said. "And it was Leahna's fault. She'd hurt him. Nobody hurts Cal, Jody. So I went back, the next night. And she laughed at him again. Said he was so cute, though, she just might have some fun with him. She liked his note, she said. It reminded her of the love notes she used to get in grade school. She made Cal sound like a little boy, a toy she was going to play with. And I knew he'd get hurt even worse if I didn't stop her!"

So you stopped her, Jody thought.

As if she could read Jody's mind, too, Sasha said, "Yes. I think her neck broke when I threw her against the wall. There was a nail in the wall, too, but that didn't kill her, I could tell. It just cut her head. That's where the blood came from. Did you see it, Jody?"

Jody didn't answer. There was Sasha, calmly talking about broken necks and blood on the wall. The way she talked — sometimes mad, sometimes as if this were a perfectly normal discussion — was the most frightening thing Jody had ever heard.

"I mean, did you see me kill her?" Sasha asked.

Jody shook her head. "I saw you standing there alone. I didn't know it was you. I didn't know it was you in the snow, either. I never saw your face."

"But you tried, didn't you?" Sasha's voice had a smile in it. "You and your binoculars. I'll bet you're sorry you ever found them."

Jody didn't answer. What was the point?

"I don't blame you, naturally," Sasha said, leaning against the door again. "You must have been awfully bored, sitting around with nothing to do. You must have been surprised when you realized what you'd seen with those binoculars."

"I never did realize it," Jody said. "Until I heard about Leahna on the radio. I thought something had happened to her, but I never really knew. And I never thought anyone here did it. Until the tea."

"Yes, the tea. I wonder if that was a mistake." Sasha thought about it for a moment. "No. After you heard about Leahna, you would have figured it out. Like I said, you have a busy mind. And if you didn't, you still would have gone to the police and told them what you saw. Then there would have been all kinds of questions."

The word *police* made Jody want to look out the window and see if they'd finally gotten to Leahna's. But she was afraid to stop watching Sasha. Sasha hadn't made a move yet, but she would, and Jody had to be ready.

"It's taking the police a long time to identify Leahna," Sasha said. "I'm afraid when I dragged her up the hill, her face . . . well, you can imagine, Jody. There was ice and rocks. Did you see me taking her away?"

"Yes. I didn't know what you were doing, though."

"That was hard," Sasha said. "I never realized it would be so hard. I wanted to take her farther away, so they wouldn't find her for days, but it was impossible."

Without thinking, Jody said, "You shouldn't have moved her at all."

"Oh?" Sasha tilted her head. "Tell me why." She sounded curious, interested in Jody's opinion.

Fine, Jody thought. The more they talked, the more chance there was that someone might come. "I didn't see you actually kill her," she said. "All I saw was someone I didn't know standing in an empty room. I saw something red on the wall, and I thought of blood, but I didn't know that's what it was. Then it was gone. Sure, I tried to see Leahna again. I was curious about what had happened. I even thought it might have been something bad, but there was no way I could *know*."

Sasha moved a little, and Jody stopped talking. But Sasha was only rubbing her foot against her leg. "Keep going," she said.

"If you hadn't taken her away, if you'd left her there, it might have been days before anybody found her," Jody said. "Nobody came to the cabin that I saw. I don't know anything about her family, but they must not have been worried because nobody was asking any questions or knocking on her door. If you'd left her there, we might have gone home before she was found."

"And you might never even have heard that she was dead," Sasha went on. "Who would have told you? Kate, I guess, but she wouldn't find out for days, maybe even longer. By then . . ." she laughed softly. "Very good, Jody. Too bad I didn't think of that, isn't it?"

Yes, Jody thought. Too bad.

"Well," Sasha sighed. "I think we've talked enough now. I should be getting back to the lodge to break the news."

Sasha pushed herself up straight, moved her arm, and Jody saw something flash again. Not the bracelet this time. Something silver. Something metal. Jody remembered the sound she'd heard in the kitchen, and she knew what it was even before she could really see it.

Sasha had a knife in her hand.

Chapter 14

The sight of the knife in Sasha's hand sent a wave of fear through Jody. The fear was hot; she felt the sweat break out at the edges of her hair, and her hands were clammy. But her arms were cold, prickly with goose bumps, and she was starting to shiver. If she tried to move, she thought she'd collapse. She clamped her jaws together and held herself rigid, every muscle as tight as she could get it, trying to keep herself from shaking.

As much as Jody wanted to scream and cry and crawl under the covers, she didn't take her eyes away from that slender figure across the room.

Sasha hadn't moved. She was still standing in the doorway, her arms hanging loose at her sides, the knife pointing toward the floor. She rubbed her thumb back and forth on the knife handle, but she didn't move.

Jody's mind was starting to work again. She felt the binoculars in her hand, under the pillow, and she slid her hand a little until it touched the leather strap. She curled her fingers around it and held on tight. When Sasha came for her, she'd fling the pillow with her other hand first. That would throw Sasha off balance, wouldn't it? By then Jody would be on her feet, and she'd use the binoculars.

What should she aim for, Sasha's head, the knife? Her arm, that would be best. Hit the arm holding the knife and run. Hit her anywhere and run. But don't throw the binoculars, keep hold of them, she might need them again.

"I can imagine what's going through your mind, Jody."

Jody jumped.

"You've been thinking so hard, I can almost hear the wheels turning," Sasha said. "You're trying to figure out how to get away, aren't you?"

What was she doing? Jody wondered. Why was she starting up a conversation again? She'd said it was time. Not that Jody was ready, how could she ever be *ready* to fight off somebody with a knife? But she'd been holding herself together so tightly she was afraid that if she didn't move soon she might snap apart.

Afraid. Maybe Sasha was afraid, too. After all, slamming somebody against a wall was very different from looking someone else in the eye and knifing her. Jody didn't doubt that Sasha was going to try, but she might be talking just to put it off for a little longer.

"Aren't you, Jody?" Sasha asked again. "Aren't you looking for a way to escape?"

"Sure." Jody's voice sounded shrill in her ears,

and she took a deep breath. "Wouldn't you be?"

Sasha laughed. "Yes, I guess I would."

"I've also been wondering." Jody hadn't been wondering about anything except how she was going to get out. But if Sasha was willing to talk, Jody would think of something to wonder about. "You said you killed Leahna because of Cal, because she hurt him."

"Yes, nobody hurts Cal," Sasha said again.

"But how's he going to feel when he finds out?" Jody asked. "Don't you think what you've done is going to hurt him? You're twins, you're really close. What's going to happen to Cal when you get caught?"

"Cal won't know, Jody. I thought I already told you," Sasha said patiently. "Nobody will know. You're the only one who does, and you . . . well, I already explained that, too."

Jody shook her head. "I think you're wrong, Sasha. Once they identify Leahna, and once they find me . . ." Jody's voice rose a little, but she took another deep breath. "Once they find me, they're going to start asking questions. They're going to ask everybody questions, including you."

Sasha tilted her head. "Well, I'm very good at answering questions." Jody could almost see her smile.

"Maybe, but what about Cal's questions?" she asked. "Will you be able to answer those?"

Sasha was quiet.

"He's not stupid," Jody went on. "I think he'll

have lots of questions for you about Leahna, and about me. What are you going to tell him when he starts asking, Sasha?"

"It doesn't matter." Sasha's voice was low now, almost a whisper. "It doesn't matter what anybody asks. I did all this for Cal, and he'll understand, Jody. Don't you get it? Don't you remember? We stick up for each other, we always have. You're right — Cal's not stupid — he might start to wonder. But he'd never do anything about it. He'll understand, Jody, and he'll stick by my story. He'll stick by me."

Sasha was going to move now, Jody could feel it. Her hand had tightened around the knife handle, and she was going to start moving any second.

Jody slid her hand across her lap and took hold of a corner of the pillow.

Sasha took a step. She was bringing the knife up, taking another step.

Jody saw something move out in the hall.

And Sasha stopped and whirled around.

They both saw Cal standing in the doorway.

"Sasha?" Cal's voice was hoarse, his breathing ragged. "Sasha, you have to stop. Please, you can't do this!"

"Don't be silly, Cal, of course I can do this." Sasha's voice was high and singsongish. "You don't have to worry about me, Cal. I've got it all worked out. It's going to be just fine."

"Fine?" Cal's voice broke. "Sasha, you killed Leahna, and you're trying to kill Jody."

"Yes, but it'll be all right." Sasha was standing sideways now, her glance going from Cal to Jody and back again. "It'll be just great. You'll get over Leahna, Cal, you know you will."

"Sasha!"

She didn't seem to hear him. "Everything's worked out," she went on. "I'll explain it afterward so you'll know what to say."

Cal was shaking his head, back and forth. "Sasha, I can't stick by you on this. This is murder. *Murder*, Sasha! Please, put the knife down!"

Instead, Sasha raised her arm, and with a scream, she rushed toward Cal, the knife high in the air. Jody screamed, too, as Sasha brought the knife down, its blade flashing in the light, heading for his neck.

Cal sidestepped, but not fast enough. The knife plunged into his upper arm, and he staggered back and fell.

Jody heard herself scream again as Sasha whirled on her, now, raising the bloody knife again.

Jody threw the pillow and missed. Sasha was still coming at her. Jody shot off the bed, swung the binoculars back and brought them around again, forgetting about trying to hit Sasha's arm, just praying she'd hit her somewhere. She felt the strap slip out of her fingers, then saw the binoculars hit Sasha on the side of the head, heard a cracking sound.

Sasha dropped to her knees, and Jody scrambled around the room, trying to get to Cal and the door.

But Sasha was starting to get up. She swayed a little, but she was getting up. And she still had the knife.

Jody limped around to Cal, tried to help him get up. Jody was gasping, tugging at Cal. He was dizzy and hurt and fell against her. Sasha was straightening up now.

Then there was a horrible cry from the doorway, and Billy was there. Drew was behind him. But it was Billy who threw himself at Sasha, knocking her down again, twisting her arm painfully behind her until she had to drop the knife. Billy was crying and shouting, even after Sasha was down, and Jody knew she'd never forget the look on his face as he put his hand on Sasha's head and stroked her long, dark hair.

The police didn't leave until after midnight. Jody was so exhausted her face was numb, and she couldn't speak right. Her mind was numb, too, and she didn't want to wake it up. She'd knew she'd be thinking about what had happened for a long time, but not tonight. Tonight she'd sleep.

Not upstairs, though. She'd never sleep upstairs. She was in the living room, that's where she'd been since it was over, and that's where she'd sleep. The others were in the kitchen — she could hear them. Cal wasn't; he'd gone with Sasha. No, Jody wasn't going to think about that tonight.

She closed her eyes, felt herself drifting off. Then she felt something on top of her, light and soft. She tried to open her eyes.

"Ssh, it's just a blanket," Drew said. "Go to sleep."

Jody felt his lips brush her forehead, and then she did what he said.

Jody woke up to the sound of thumping. She opened her eyes and looked around. Chris was standing at the closet near the front door, pulling out boots. *Thump, thump.*

Jody yawned. "They sounded like they were right by my head."

Chris jumped a little and turned around. "Sorry. I didn't mean to wake you." She chewed nervously on a fingernail for a moment. "I'm leaving in a few minutes. I got a ride," she said. "I can't stand to stay here another second."

"I don't blame you."

Chris blushed. "I didn't mean to sound that way." She spiked up her hair, her bracelets and rings flashing, then glanced around the room, finally looking at Jody. "What happened was awful. I'm glad you're okay."

"Thanks, Chris."

"Yeah. Well." Chris shrugged. Then she pulled on her boots and jacket and opened the door. "See you."

" 'Bye."

After the door slammed, Ellen came in from the kitchen. "Who was that?" she asked.

"Chris. She got a ride," Jody said.

"Yes, I know, I just thought it might be Cal." Ellen smiled weakly. "How are you?"

"I don't know yet," Jody said. "I think I'm still numb. How's Cal?"

"Well, his arm's okay. But he's . . ." Ellen's eyes filled with tears. "Oh, Jody, he feels terrible. And he can't help worrying about Sasha. I mean, she's his sister."

"How did he know?" Jody asked. She hadn't talked to Cal much at all after the police came. "When he came last night, he already knew Sasha had killed Leahna."

Ellen nodded. "We were all at the lodge when someone told us they'd identified the body, and it was Leahna Calder, and it looked like murder. I didn't believe it at first, I thought it was just a rumor. But Cal believed it. Last night, he told me he'd suspected something had happened to her. And when he found out, he couldn't stop thinking that Sasha had something to do with it."

"Did he say why?"

"Different things," Ellen said. "The way Sasha hated Leahna, the way she tried to tell Cal not to have anything to do with her. How mad she got when Cal told her Leahna was the one who didn't want anything to do with *him*."

"Sasha told me Leahna had laughed at him."

"She probably did," Ellen said. "And Cal said it made him feel terrible. But it made Sasha *furious*. He said Sasha's always tried to protect him, but he didn't need her that way anymore." Ellen was staring at the fireplace, her eyes still shiny with tears. "Anyway, after the night — I guess the night Sasha killed her — Cal knew something was wrong. He didn't know what, but he knew. He could read Sasha's feelings, he said, and even though he never thought of murder, he knew she'd done something."

"Just feelings?" Jody asked. "That's all he had to go on?"

"Well, he knew Sasha hadn't been where she'd said she was sometimes," Ellen told her. "The day you were asking about Leahna, Cal told me Sasha said they'd been together all the time. And Cal said it wasn't true. And then there was her bracelet." Ellen rubbed her eyes. "Cal knew she'd lost it, even though she said she just wanted to give it a rest. He gave her the bracelet, see, and she always wore it. Those things made him suspicious. But a lot of it was feelings." Ellen smiled sadly. "They're so close, it's hard to understand, isn't it?"

Jody nodded. "What's going to happen?"

"I don't know. Their parents are on their way here," Ellen said. "Cal's staying with Sasha, and I'm going to stay, too."

Jody smiled. Maybe Ellen could do Cal some good. He needed it, and Ellen would certainly try.

Ellen left then, to go be with Cal, and Jody went into the kitchen. She saw the cut phone cord and shuddered a little. Then she found some bread and was making toast when Billy came in.

They looked at each other and then Jody limped over and hugged him tightly. "Thank you," she murmured. "I know you feel terrible, Billy, but thank you."

She felt Billy's hands press against her back, felt him sigh. Then he held her away from him. "I can't talk about it yet," he said, his brown eyes shiny like Ellen's. "But maybe when I can, I can talk to you?"

"Sure," Jody said. "Of course."

"Thanks, Jody." Billy kissed her on the cheek and hurried out of the room.

Jody heard him running up the stairs, and heard someone else running down at the same time. Another few seconds and Drew was in the kitchen. He was carrying two duffel bags. One of them was hers.

"You ready?" he asked, putting the bags down. "I called a friend from the lodge, he's letting me take his car, and he'll get a ride with someone else. We can leave any time."

"You packed for me?"

"Yeah, well, Ellen told me what was yours, and I just threw everything in," he said. "It'll probably be pretty wrinkled."

"That's okay." Jody started to eat some toast, then decided she didn't want it. "Is Billy coming with us?"

"I asked, but he's taking a bus." Drew picked up her toast and took a bite. "He said he doesn't want to be with anyone he knows right now."

"How is he? Is he going to be okay, do you think?"

"He's kind of broken up," Drew said. "Poor guy. He loved Sasha, but he hated her, too."

Jody nodded. "I thought he might . . . last night, when he pushed her down, at first I thought he was going to hit her."

"Yeah, but he didn't. I think he realized she's

sick, and he stopped hating her and felt sorry for her. He'll be okay, I bet." Drew looked at Jody, his dark-brown eyes watching her closely. "What about you?" he asked. "Are you going to be okay?"

For the first time since it was over, Jody thought she might cry. She felt her face crumple. "I don't want to start," she said, blinking back the tears and taking a shaky breath. "I might never stop."

Drew took a few steps and put his arms around her. "Hey, I'll be driving," he said. "You can cry all you want."

Jody laughed a little. "Thanks." They stayed where they were for a few moments, not talking. Then Jody said, "I'll be okay. I'll be even better when I get home."

Drew pulled back a little. "I guess you're not going to want any reminders of this place, huh?"

"I'll have them whether I want them or not," Jody said. "I'm going to be remembering this for a long time."

"I know." Drew kissed her forehead the way he had the night before. "That's not what I meant, though."

"No?"

"No." He looked away from her, then looked back. "I was trying to find out if you still want to see me, at home," he said. "I guess I'm afraid you won't, because I was here, and I'll remind you of it."

Jody smiled, remembering the way he'd covered her with a blanket last night, and the gentleness of his hands when he'd wrapped her ankle. "You won't remind me of anything bad," she told him.

He put his arms around her again. They held each other for a long moment, and then it was time to go home.

THE TRAIN

Chapter 1

Hannah Deaton surveyed the crowded train station in dismay. Flanked by a pair of friends, she stared at the scene in front of her and thought of an old western she'd seen on television recently. "The cattle are about to stampede," she joked as their small group moved hesitantly forward to join the rest of Parker High School's Teen Tour from Chicago to San Francisco.

The train station was noisy with clusters of students weighted down with backpacks and shoulder bags and suitcases stuffed to excess. Most of the travelers had gathered in groups. Hannah couldn't help feeling sorry for the handful who stood apart from the safety of a cozy, friendly group. Caroline Brewster, a girl in Hannah's geometry class, waited off in a corner by herself, continually glancing at her watch as if she were waiting for someone to join her. Hannah knew she wasn't. She was just pretending.

An unhappy-looking trio caught her attention. Eugene Bryer, a thin, quiet boy with sun-bleached hair and a sullen expression on his pale face, stood off to Hannah's right. With him was Dale Sutterworth, a huge boy with dark hair and glasses, and Lolly Slocum, a stocky girl with sad eyes and lank blonde hair. They weren't talking or laughing as the other groups were, and Hannah couldn't help wondering why they were taking the trip. They didn't seem the least bit interested or excited and she knew they would never be included in the fun.

What was it like to always be on the outside looking in?

Grateful that she and her little group didn't fall into that dismal category, Hannah returned her attention to her own friends and to the excitement of the moment.

The tour's chaperones, two young teachers, Clara Quick and Benjamin Dobbs, stood in the center of the throng, armed with clipboards and looking bewildered. Thirty students were taking the end-of-summer train trip to the West Coast. Ms. Quick, in a pale flowered dress and high heels, and Mr. Dobbs, wearing jeans and a short-sleeved white shirt and blue tie, looked like they'd been slapped with a pop quiz and weren't at all sure they knew the answers.

"Poor Ms. Quick," Hannah murmured. "She looks like she'd rather be home cleaning her oven."

"Yeah," Mack McComber agreed, tossing an arm carelessly around Hannah's shoulders. "I'll bet Dobbs would volunteer to scrub every restroom at school with a toothbrush if it would get him out of this."

"I can't believe we were only allowed one suitcase!" complained Kerry Oliver, who was standing beside Hannah. Kerry was a tall, olive-skinned girl with waist-long, straight black hair that glistened like patent leather. "A whole week on one suitcase? It can't be done. I'll have to wear the same outfit at least twice . . . maybe *two* outfits twice."

The boy next to her gasped in mock horror and clutched at his throat. "Oh, no! Kerry Oliver wearing an outfit more than once?" He was Kerry's height, and stick-thin. A wild jumble of carroty hair threatened to engulf his narrow, tanned face. Warm gray eyes behind wire-rimmed glasses reflected amusement. "Cable cars will stop in their tracks," he teased. "The Golden Gate Bridge will collapse into the Bay. The earth will shake, all because Kerry Oliver could only bring one suitcase to San Francisco."

"Lewis Joseph Reed," Hannah said, her lips curved in a gentle smile, "quit teasing her. We all know you get a kick out of dating the best-dressed girl in school."

"Darn straight!" Kerry said, yanking playfully at a lock of Lewis's burnt-orange hair. "Hannah's right. You love it and you know it. Anyway, don't worry. At least I won't embarrass you on the train by showing up in grubby clothes." Pointing to the bulging maroon bag at her feet, she added, "We're allowed one carry on during the trip." She grinned. "No one said what *size*. Ms. Quick said if we could carry it, we could bring it."

Lewis hefted the bag, testing. He barely raised

it an inch off the tile. Groaning, he glanced around the station before asking, "So where did you park the crane that hauled this over here?"

Hannah laughed.

"Mack will carry it," Kerry said lightly with an unconcerned shrug. She smiled at the tall, husky boy with the dark hair and a strong, rugged face. "He has all those muscles, he might as well use them someplace besides on the football field."

"You must have me mixed up with someone who's all brawn and no brain," Mack McComber said with a grin. "If you think I'm some dumb jock you're going to sucker into carrying that ten-ton piece of baggage you were dumb enough to bring, think again. The rules say, 'if *you* can carry it,' not if someone else can."

Before Kerry could protest, the chaperones, looking grimly determined, took command and began shepherding their charges toward the blue and silver train waiting on the tracks beyond the terminal.

Lewis dragged Kerry's bag, while she danced lightly ahead of him, ignoring his groans. Anxious to get on board the train and "check it out," she hurried ahead, not noticing when Lewis, hampered by the heavy burden, fell behind.

Hannah approached the elephantine coach with mixed feelings. The lure of San Francisco, the city on the Bay, had enticed her into taking this trip. Her parents had visited there several times, and loved it. They assured her she would, too.

But she had been dreading the train ride. Trains

scared her. They went awfully fast, their coaches swaying dangerously as the wheels sped over the tracks. It was a long way from Chicago to California. Was it possible to sleep on a train that was moving so fast and rocking back and forth?

Approaching the steps leading into the coach, Hannah glanced nervously down at the wheels. They were comfortably wide and, made of metal, looked strong enough. But how did they stay on that narrow metal rail when the train reached top speed?

Sometimes, they didn't. She knew that. She had heard about derailments, some almost as devastating as a plane crash. Some people said you were safer on an airplane than you were on the ground.

But this tour had been planned, according to the brochure she'd received in the mail, so that students could "see the country." You couldn't do that from an airplane. So, here she was, at three o'clock on a Wednesday afternoon in late August, boarding a huge, blue and silver train with her friends from Parker High.

Hannah pushed an errant strand of naturally wavy, chocolate-ice-cream-colored hair behind her ears and, urged gently onward by Mack, climbed the steps into the coach.

When everyone was on board, the conductor — a tall, heavy man with a tiny black mustache, and a perfectly pressed blue uniform — led them on a brief tour of the train.

Hannah found it did little to ease her fears. The coaches weren't bad, wrapped in windows that provided lots of light and an all-encompassing view. But the narrow corridors between the sleeping compartments were cramped and dark. The walls were covered with a dark paisley print of rust, deep gold, and navy blue. The carpet underfoot shared the same gloomy pattern. Hannah felt a grim, heavy feeling descend upon her each time they entered a new car.

Mack noticed her nervous shivers. "You cold?" he asked with concern.

Hannah shook her head. "No. It's just . . . nothing. Never mind." She wasn't about to let a silly case of jitters spoil Mack's fun. *He* wasn't afraid of anything. At least, she didn't think he was. She'd only gotten to know him about six weeks before, in the middle of summer. But she'd never seen him frightened. Maybe that came with his size. What would anyone so big have to be frightened of? While she, on the other hand, barely came up to Mack's armpit and weighed only ninety-six pounds, soaking wet.

Shaking aside her gloomy feelings, Hannah continued onward with the group. But she let Mack fold her hand inside his, telling herself it was so they wouldn't become separated as Lewis had, struggling somewhere behind with Kerry's bag.

The Cafe, Hannah decided upon seeing it, was a fun place. No dark paisley here. Instead, the walls were panelled in a warm, light wood, and the stools, tables, and booths were a vivid red. Skylights and windows made it feel light and airy. A cheerful tune played in the background while passengers separate from the Teen Tour sat at the bright-red Formica counter sipping cold drinks.

Everyone wanted to order something to eat or drink, but Ms. Quick insisted they "get settled first." A special low tour rate had allowed the students to be housed in compartments rather than coach, which Hannah appreciated. She and Kerry would have more privacy in a compartment. And Kerry had insisted that she never could have slept in "one of those chair-beds. I need to lie *down* to sleep!"

Lewis met them in the corridor. He was empty-handed and he looked worried.

"Where's my bag?" Kerry asked him immediately, her eyes going from one of his hands to the other. "Did you put it in your compartment?"

Lewis shook his head. Rusty strands fell against his forehead. He shoved them back nervously. "No . . . I . . . the conductor made me stow it in the baggage car, Kerry."

Kerry shrieked.

"He said it was too big to be a carry on. I argued with him," Lewis added desperately, seeing the flush of anger begin on Kerry's face, "but it was no go. He just took it from me and headed for the baggage car. But," he added hopefully as Kerry drew in a breath in preparation for another shriek, "the baggage car isn't locked. You can go get what you need from your bag."

"Lewis," Kerry cried, her cheeks deepening in color, "my *face* is in that bag! And most of my clothes for the trip!"

Lewis frowned, uncomprehending. "Your face?"

But Hannah understood. Kerry's makeup and hair care supplies were in that bag. Kerry would have to boomerang back and forth between their compartment and the baggage car every time she wanted to change her "look." Which, knowing Kerry, would be often.

Hannah knew Kerry wouldn't accept this arrangement.

She didn't. "This is ridiculous!" Kerry said, turning away from Lewis. "Ms. Quick said we could have a carry-on bag and that's what I brought! Who does that conductor think he is, anyway? Lewis, you have to go get that bag. I *need* it!"

"Kerry," Hannah offered, "you can share my stuff."

Kerry stared at her. "*Your* stuff? Hannah, you only wear mascara, and you use that cheap stuff. It gives me a rash."

Hannah flushed and fell silent.

"Lewis?" Kerry turned a stern gaze on her boyfriend.

"Look," he said, "I told you, you can go get what you need when you need it. Quit making such a big deal out of it. The conductor said you can't have that bag on the train, so live with it."

Kerry's mouth fell open. Then, just as quickly, she clamped it shut. She turned to Mack. "Mack?"

He shook his head.

"All right. All *right*!" Kerry said grimly. "I'll get it myself. I need that bag, it's mine, and I have a right to have it with me."

And, swinging her black hair angrily, she stomped off down the corridor, heading for the baggage car.

She was back only minutes later, before Hannah, who had gone into their compartment, had had time to open her own small tote bag.

Kerry pushed the compartment door open and immediately sank into one of the seats. Her face was an odd pea green, her dark eyes wide.

She did not have the carry-on bag.

"What's wrong?" Hannah asked. "Did the conductor yell at you?"

Kerry shook her head. "No," she said almost in a whisper, "I didn't even see him. But Hannah . . . Hannah, you won't believe what's *in* there. You won't . . ."

"In the baggage car?" Hannah smiled. "Luggage, I guess."

"It's not funny," Kerry snapped, surprising Hannah. Hannah took a couple of steps forward and sat down beside her.

"Kerry, what's the matter? Why are you acting so weird?"

Kerry lifted her head and looked straight at Hannah. Then she said with horror, "Hannah, there's a *coffin* in the baggage car!"

Chapter 2

"*A coffin?*" Hannah repeated in response to Kerry's grim news.

Kerry nodded. "Yes. In the baggage car. It's sitting up on a table that's draped with a long black cloth." She shuddered. "A coffin! A *dead* person is on this tour, Hannah! It's disgusting."

Hannah sat in thoughtful silence for a moment and then said, "Kerry, maybe there isn't anyone *in* it. Someone along the train route could have ordered a coffin from Chicago. You know . . . someone from a little town where they don't *have* coffins. So they have to send away for them when someone . . . dies."

Kerry sent her a skeptical look. "Hannah, how can a town not have coffins? One thing people do absolutely *everywhere* is *die*. Even the tiniest town would have to have a funeral parlor, and funeral parlors have coffins."

Hannah wasn't ready to surrender. "Well, maybe someone's relatives didn't *like* the coffins in their town, so they sent away for a fancier one. Someone with a lot of money . . . that's possible, right?" She paused, and then added, "I'll bet there isn't anyone in that coffin. It's just an empty box, Kerry. So quit worrying."

Who are you trying to convince? she wondered. Kerry or yourself? Hannah tried never to think about dying, or dead things. They frightened her. Maybe that was childish, but she couldn't help it.

Kerry shivered. "I've never been around anyone dead before. Gives me the willies."

Hannah nodded. "When I was six," she said, the words dragging with reluctance, "my grandmother died. I went to the funeral parlor with my parents. They didn't make me do anything gross like kiss my grandmother when she was in the coffin, but I hated being there. Everyone kept saying how natural she looked, how peaceful. But she didn't. I stayed overnight with her lots of times when I was little and she'd fall asleep in her chair while we were watching television. She looked peaceful then. But in her coffin, she looked . . . mad. Like . . . like she hadn't been ready to die."

"Hannah, cut it out! You're giving me the creeps!" Kerry sat up straighter. "I think we should go find out if someone is in that coffin."

Hannah drew in her breath sharply. "You're kidding, right? You'd better be."

Kerry stood up, tossing her black hair as she always did whenever she changed positions. "If I'm going to have a good time on this trip, I have to be sure that coffin is empty. You should want to know, too, Hannah. We do *not* want to share this tour with a dead body. Besides," Kerry added, "every time I want something from my bag, I have to go into the baggage compartment to get it." She shuddered again. "I couldn't stand it if I knew a corpse was in the room with me."

Hannah knew what Mack would have said. He would have said, "Kerry, don't you *get* it? A person inside a coffin can't possibly hurt you. You couldn't *be* any safer."

Hannah didn't say that, because she shared Kerry's uneasiness. Maybe it was silly — Mack would say it was — but she couldn't help the way she felt.

"I'm not going with you," she announced as firmly as her voice would allow.

"Oh, yes, you are!" Kerry grabbed Hannah's hand and pulled her up out of the seat. "I'm not going in that room alone. You're my best friend, Hannah Deaton. You wouldn't want me to worry through this whole wonderful trip, would you?" Kerry's voice changed from one of command to one of pleading. "C'mon, Hannah! I'm sure you're right. The coffin is probably empty. We'll just pop in, I'll grab a white sweater from my bag, we'll see if there's a tag on the box, and once we know for sure that it's just an empty coffin, we'll head for the Cafe and some fun."

"What if — what if it *isn't* empty?" Hannah asked. "It's not like we can do anything about it."

Kerry's mouth tightened. "It *will* be!"

The train began to move then, catching them by surprise. It moved slowly at first, making its way out of the station, and then quickly picked up speed.

It was surprisingly quiet, Hannah thought, and there was less movement than she'd feared. The cars didn't sway back and forth as if they were getting ready to tip over. Beneath her feet she could hear the wheels. They didn't make the loud, annoying clackety-clack she'd expected. Instead, the wheels provided a steady but muted background sound, a soft, constant *ga-dink, ga-dink, ga-dink*.

Kerry sighed impatiently.

Hannah wished fervently that she could believe her own theory about the coffin being empty. But she knew people were often shipped back to their hometown for burial in a family cemetery plot. No matter how many years they'd spent in other places, they wanted to be buried close to where they'd been born. It seemed odd to her. It wasn't as if they'd *know* . . .

Stalling for time, she said, "Kerry, how are we going to know if the coffin's empty without opening it?"

"New stuff that's being shipped to somewhere else has an invoice taped to it," Kerry told her knowingly. "I had to push aside a whole bunch of boxes to get to my bag. The boxes all had invoices wrapped in plastic taped to the side. If you're right about the coffin being shipped empty, it'll have one of those invoices taped to it."

Hannah nodded. "And if I'm wrong?" she couldn't help asking as Kerry reached for the handle on the compartment door. "What will the tag say then?"

Kerry shook her head. "Don't think about it. I refuse to accept the possibility. Come on."

As they left the compartment and entered the corridor, Hannah felt her stomach begin to churn. She hated and feared small or narrow spaces. The dark walls and floor seemed to press in on her, cutting off the light, as if she were walking through an airless underground tunnel.

By the time they reached the baggage car at the far end of half a dozen coaches, Hannah was having trouble breathing.

"What's the matter with you?" Kerry asked as she pushed the heavy door open and peered inside. "You're wheezing. You sound like my brother when he has an asthma attack."

"Claustrophobia," Hannah answered with difficulty. "There's not enough room. . . . I feel closed in, and I hate it."

"You'll feel better in the Cafe," Kerry said confidently. "It's lighter and brighter and there's room to move around. This'll just take us a minute, then we'll head for the bright lights, the music, and the fun." Kerry lowered her voice to a whisper. "Now where are the lights?"

There were no windows in the baggage car. "Wasn't it dark when you were here before?" Hannah asked.

"No. The light was on. C'mon, help me find the switch."

After several moments of creeping around in the dark, Kerry found the switch and flicked it on. A lone ceiling fixture cast eerie shadows over their faces and over the long, narrow room half-full of suitcases, boxes, crates, and cartons.

Hannah spotted the coffin right away. It was, as Kerry had said, on a long, narrow table that was covered with a floor-length black cloth. Although Hannah's eyes immediately darted over every inch of the wooden box's surface, she saw no sign of an invoice, and her heart sank.

Closer examination confirmed that there was no invoice. The coffin was not empty.

In the chilly, shadowed room, Hannah and Kerry stared at each other with dismayed faces.

"Look," Hannah finally said, her voice not as steady as she would have liked, "we're being silly. Nothing in this room can hurt us, Kerry. Let's just get out of here."

"No, wait! There's a tag, there, on the corner." Kerry hesitated, clasping her hands together and then, before Hannah could stop her, she lunged forward to read the small, square white tag hanging at one end of the coffin.

"Kerry, let's *go*!" Hannah cried. An overwhelming sensation of dread began to sweep over her like a chill fog. She began backing away, her eyes fastened in morbid curiosity on Kerry, bending to read the tag.

"Oh, my God!" Kerry bolted upright and turned to face Hannah. Her hands flew up to cover her mouth and her skin became gray.

Hannah, watching, saw the scene in slow-motion. "What?" she whispered, continuing to back away, "what's wrong?"

Kerry opened her mouth, but no sound came out. She tried again, sidling sideways away from the coffin.

"Hannah," she said hoarsely, "it's someone we *know*. Knew. I never thought it would be someone we *knew*."

Confusion flooded Hannah's face. "But . . . but no one we know died, Kerry. No one."

Kerry nodded grimly. "Oh, yes, someone did, Hannah. Don't you remember? *Frog* died."

Hannah frowned. "Frog?"

Another nod. "Yes. The tag on the coffin has his name on it. Frederick Roger Drummond. On its way to San Francisco, where his parents live."

Speechless, Hannah stared at the coffin.

Kerry did the same. "Hannah that's . . . "

Hannah finished the sentence for her. "That's Frog in there."

Chapter 3

In the stunned silence that followed, the steady *ga-dink*, *ga-dink*, *ga-dink* of the train wheels racing along the rails seemed to send Hannah a warning: *Go-back, go-back, go-back* . . .

But we *can't* go back, she thought as she reached out to clutch Kerry's hand. They won't take the train back to the station just because Kerry and I don't want to travel with . . .

"How could they put it on this train?" Kerry cried, still staring at the coffin. "It's just not *right*! Why didn't they put it on a regular train with people who never knew Frog? Why did they have to put it on this one and ruin our trip? It's not fair!"

"I don't know," Hannah whispered. But the part of her that hadn't been shocked senseless pointed out silently that maybe there wasn't a lot of choice when it came to shipping a body. You probably couldn't sit around and wait for a particular train. Arrangements would have to be made, grieving relatives would be waiting . . . you probably had to use the first train that was going in the right direction.

Would there be grieving relatives for Frog? There would have been for her: her parents, her younger brother, Tad, her grandfather. Even her parakeet, Disraeli, would miss her and probably wouldn't eat for a while. Kerry, too, had parents, grandparents, cousins. And Mack and Lewis had tons of friends and relatives who would mourn if anything terrible happened to them.

But Frog? Did he have anyone? In California or anywhere else?

He must, or he wouldn't be on his way west.

But it was hard to imagine.

"Do you think Lolly and Eugene and Dale know Frog is on the train?" Kerry whispered. "He was their best friend. They never went anywhere without him. That's creepy."

Was that why the trio had looked so glum in the terminal, Hannah wondered? Because they knew Frog's coffin was on the train?

"Maybe there's a memorial service in California. Maybe they're going for that."

"Let's get out of here," Kerry said finally, breaking the silence. She began backing away, as Hannah had earlier, as if turning her back on the coffin would be inviting trouble. "Let's go tell Mack and Lewis."

"They won't care. They'll think we're silly for getting upset. They'll say Frog can't hurt anyone now, so why let it bother us that he's on the train? That's what they'll say."

* * *

Hannah was right. That was exactly what the boys said.

They were in the Cafe, sitting with Jean Marie Westlake, a red-haired girl who had once dated Mack. Hannah felt no pangs of jealousy upon seeing the two together. That was history and, besides, Jean Marie was too nice a person to flirt with someone else's boyfriend.

Hannah quickly glanced around. She saw no sign of Lolly or Eugene or Dale. But the backs of the shiny red booths were very high, hiding people from view.

"You will never," Kerry breathed as she and Hannah slid into the booth occupied by their friends, "guess what's in the baggage compartment. Never!"

"Baggage?" Lewis quipped, sliding over to make more room. Mack started to laugh, and then caught the expression on Hannah's face.

"What's wrong?" he asked her quietly, and Jean Marie looked at Hannah with concern in her eyes. "Are you sick?" she asked. "You look like you've seen a ghost."

"That's what I'm trying to *tell* you," Kerry said. "Not that we've seen a ghost," she added hastily, "but it's almost that bad." She took a deep breath and exhaled before saying dramatically, "Frog's coffin is on this train!"

"Yeah, I know," Mack said calmly. "I was out there when they loaded it on the train."

Hannah looked at him sharply. "Why didn't you say anything? Maybe if we'd known ahead of time . . ."

"Sorry." Mack shrugged. "It's not the kind of thing you bring up in ordinary conversation. It would sound pretty weird to say, 'Hey, let's have a good time on this trip — even though Frog's coffin's on board.' "

Kerry sent him a disgusted look. "You wouldn't have had to say it like that. But you still could have told us. I can't believe you didn't say anything."

"How would I know you were going to pack your entire wardrobe in a carry-on bag? Is it my fault you have to run back and forth to the baggage car every five minutes?" Mack asked. "I never expected you or Hannah or anyone else to know the coffin was there. So why would I mention it?"

"I don't see what the big deal is," Lewis said to Kerry. "The guy is dead. Burned to death when his car hit that wall. It's not like he's going to be bugging you during the trip."

"Lewis!" Hannah cried. "That's gross!"

Jean Marie nodded. "He was only seventeen, Lewis. What happened to him was horrible. I know he wasn't very nice, but nobody deserves to die that way." She paused, and then added, "My dad said the firemen worked for forty minutes to get him out of that car. It was twisted like a pretzel and they couldn't open the doors. Then it burst into flames — " She stopped, so appalled by the image that she couldn't continue.

"I know he lived with his grandmother," Hannah

said, feeling better now that Mack's safe, solid bulk was there beside her, close enough that she could feel its warmth, "but he must have family in California." She glanced around the table. "He wouldn't be on the train if there wasn't someone there, waiting . . ."

"His parents," Jean Marie offered. "They couldn't cope with him, so they sent him here, to live with his grandmother. But . . . she had a heart attack right after Frog's accident. She's in the hospital."

"They dumped him?" Lewis said, incredulous. "His folks dumped him?" Lewis's own parents were fiercely proud of their son, and would have fought anyone who tried to take him from them.

Hannah didn't blame them. Lewis was neat. A great kid. Not at all like Frog . . .

"You know, my mother works in the school office," Jean Marie said. "Well, she said his records showed that he skipped school a lot in California and he was picked up by the police a couple of times for stuff like speeding and shoplifting. I guess his parents got tired of the hassles, so they shipped him here."

They all fell silent then, thinking about Frog.

After a few moments, Mack said slowly, "I remember the first class I had with him. Bio. He showed up in December, right before the midterms. Here was this big, hulking kid with long greasy hair and bad skin and anyone could see he had an attitude problem, and here he was coming in in the middle of the year — social death for a junior in high school. Everyone checked him out real quick and then wrote him off, know what I mean?"

They all nodded silently. They knew.

"Brutus" — Mack's nickname for their biology teacher — "told him to write his name on the blackboard. Frog made a face, but he did it. When he went up to the board, everyone could see his jeans were filthy and he hadn't shaved in a couple of days." Mack grinned slightly. "And we're not talking fashion statement here, guys. He just didn't *care*."

More nods. Whatever it was that Frog *had* cared about, it hadn't been his appearance.

"He wasn't poor," Kerry said. "His grandmother had money . . . that big house and a new car every year. He didn't have to be a slob." There was awe in Kerry's voice as she tried to comprehend appearance not being important to someone.

"Anyway," Mack continued, "Frog started to write his name, Frederick Roger Drummond. He never used the Frederick, so he wrote the initial F, then R-O-G. And when he got that far, I yelled, 'Hey, the guy's name is Frog!'" Remembering, Mack flushed with shame. "I don't know why I did it. It was a rotten thing to do. But some guys wouldn't have minded. If Frog had laughed, maybe everyone would have liked him even though he looked pretty scuzzy, and things would have been different. But he didn't laugh. Everyone else did, though. And the name stuck."

No one said anything. Hannah told herself Mack hadn't meant to be cruel, but she couldn't help thinking what it must have felt like to Frog, being the target of everyone's laughter on his first day at Parker.

"I keep seeing his face when he finished and turned away from the blackboard," Mack added, his voice quiet and serious. "He looked like he was going to explode: red face, eyes popping, fists clenched . . . like he wanted to smash someone's face in. Mine, I guess. Every time I passed him in the hall after that, he looked at me like he'd love to crush me under the heel of his boot."

Another long silence passed, broken only by the carefree sounds from other tables, where no one was thinking of a dead boy or a coffin.

Finally, Kerry spoke up. "You weren't the only one who was mean to Frog," she said, her eyes on the bright red tabletop. "I was, too."

Then she fell silent.

Chapter 4

When Kerry didn't elaborate, Lewis volunteered, "Don't waste time on guilt, Kerry. I don't think anyone at Parker qualifies for the Be-Kind-To-Frog award." He glanced around the table, mild annoyance on his face. "But what good does it do Frog to spin your wheels feeling guilty now?"

Kerry flushed an unhappy scarlet. "I didn't *say* it did any good! I just meant, after seeing that . . . coffin . . . I couldn't stop thinking about what I did to him."

"It couldn't have been anything so terrible, Kerry," Hannah said loyally. "You're not a mean person." She meant it. Kerry was spoiled and a little shallow, but she wasn't mean.

"Before he started dating Lolly Slocum," Kerry said, "Frog asked me out."

Lewis laughed out loud, and Mack whistled.

"It's not funny! He made me mad right at the start, acting like he was doing me a favor. Strutted right up to me, hands in his pockets, the whole macho routine." She made her voice go very deep.

"Hey, babe, how about a movie tonight?" Kerry sighed. "I've never been rude to boys, even when I couldn't stand them. I know it's hard for them, never knowing if they're going to be shot down when they ask a girl out. So I try to be nice when I say no."

"You weren't that terrific when I asked you out the first time," Lewis teased. "You said you had to wash your hair. We all know what *that* means. It means you find us totally repulsive."

Kerry didn't laugh. "I *did* have to wash my hair. Anyway," she added crossly, "you were just too sure I'd say yes. That bugged me."

"If you were nice to Frog when you turned him down," Jean Marie said, "you don't have anything to feel guilty about."

Kerry lifted her head. "But that's just it. I *wasn't* nice! He was so creepy-looking. Something about his eyes. They were empty — nothing there, you know? And I don't think I ever saw him smile." Kerry shuddered, remembering. "When I said no, I couldn't go out with him, he actually *argued* with me. He asked me why I wouldn't, and I gave him some stupid excuse like I had to go shopping with my mother or something, but he still didn't leave. He said he was as good as anybody else at Parker and if I didn't give him a really good reason why I'd said no, I'd be sorry."

Hannah gasped. Frog had threatened Kerry? "You never told me that, Kerry. Why didn't you?"

"I forgot about it. Really."

"So far," Lewis said, "I haven't heard word one

197

about how you were mean to Frog. Sounds to me like it was the other way around."

"I laughed at him." Kerry shifted uncomfortably in her seat. "He made me so nervous, making this big fuss right there in the hall with a whole bunch of people around staring at us, that it was either laugh or cry. I look awful when I cry, so I laughed."

"*Now* I hear mean," Lewis said grimly. "Something every guy lives in terror of is being shot down with *laughter* when he asks a girl out."

"I *know* that, Lewis!" Kerry cried. "And I'd never, ever done it before. And I'll never do it again. The look on his face . . . it was like you said, Mack — like he wanted to strangle me, right there in front of everybody. It made my blood freeze." She frowned. "I never could understand what Lolly saw in him. She was so quiet, like she was afraid of her own shadow, and Frog . . ." Kerry fell silent.

No one said anything, and after a minute or two of silence, Kerry added, "I knew it was rotten to laugh at him. And now he's dead, and I can't tell him I'm sorry."

"Would you have if he'd lived?" Lewis asked pointedly.

Kerry thought for a minute and then said softly, "No. I guess not."

"Then quit thinking about it now when it doesn't do any good."

Hannah was surprised by his tone of voice. It wasn't like Lewis to be unsympathetic, especially with Kerry.

She learned why a moment later. Lewis sank

back in the booth and let out a long breath of air. "Okay," he said, his mouth tense, "since this seems to be true confession time, and since Kerry seems determined to beat herself up as if she were the only person in the world who eighty-sixed Frog, I don't mind admitting that she *wasn't*."

"I know that, Lewis," Kerry said quietly. "Nobody liked him. Except for Lolly — and Eugene and Dale. And that was only because they didn't have anyone else."

"I didn't just dislike him," Lewis persisted. "I got him kicked out of gym class."

Surprise flooded Kerry's features. "You did? Really?" She knew, as did Hannah and Mack and Jean Marie, that Lewis brought home every stray animal he came across, had once torn down his treehouse and rebuilt it elsewhere because it was interfering with the home of an owl and its family, and coached Little League baseball during the summer. If Lewis had a mean bone in his body, it was well-hidden.

But Lewis nodded. "I was captain of one of the basketball teams in gym when Frog showed up. Coach told me to pick him, so he'd feel at home." Lewis shook his thatch of rusty hair. "But the guy looked like he had two left feet, and I had a bet with Mack that my team would win. Anyway, I knew if I picked the new guy, we'd lose. We had a good chance against Mack's team, but putting that Neanderthal on the team could have screwed things up. So I gave Coach a hard time about it. And Frog heard us arguing."

Hannah listened silently. Her stomach was churning again. She told herself it was from the gently rocking motion of the train as it sped along the tracks, but she didn't quite believe it. Was that really it? Or was it because they kept talking about Frog? She knew *he* couldn't hear them. Hannah glanced around nervously. She wouldn't want Frog's friends overhearing this conversation. It would upset them.

"I remember that day," Mack was saying to Lewis. "Frog's first day in gym. And he wasn't the only one who heard you, Lewis. We *all* heard you. When you get excited, your voice really carries."

Lewis nodded in agreement. "I know. I guess I got carried away. Didn't even think about how the guy might be feeling if he overheard me. Geez, why didn't you stop me, Mack?"

Mack leaned back against the booth and laughed. "Are you kidding? You were on a roll, Lewis. There's no stopping you when you get wound up like that."

"Also true. Anyway, the guy heard me and stomped over. Started calling me names. He got madder and madder and when it looked like he was about to take a swing at me, Coach kicked him out. Sent him to Decker's office."

Decker was Parker High's vice-principal. No one liked him, possibly because he was an effective disciplinarian.

"I heard later that he suspended Frog for two days," Lewis added, his voiced edged with regret.

"A crummy way to start school in a new place, right?"

Hannah thought so. But she said nothing. Lewis was feeling bad enough.

"If you were the one who was arguing with Coach," Jean Marie asked, "why weren't you kicked out of gym, too?"

"Because he's a varsity basketball hotshot," Mack said with a sardonic grin. "Coach is no fool. He *needs* Lewis this season. He knew he didn't need Frog. You could tell just by looking at the guy that he'd be a disaster out on the floor."

"That shouldn't have mattered," Jean Marie argued. "Coach should have given Frog a chance. And so should you, Lewis."

He didn't argue with her. There was a bleak expression on his face that made Hannah want to reach out and pat his hand. But she said nothing. All she wanted now was a change of subject.

"I'm starving!" she announced, although the very thought of food made her ill. "Let's order something to eat, okay?"

But, lost in guilt, Lewis and Kerry shook their heads silently and Jean Marie said, "He came into the journalism office, too, asking if he could be a reporter."

Jean Marie was the editor of the *Parker Pen*, the school newspaper. "I took one look at him and knew I couldn't use him." Her hands, wrapped around a glass of soda, tightened until the knuckles turned white. "It was so unfair of me. I never even asked him if he'd worked on a school newspaper before or if he was interested in writing. I just told him, flat out, that there weren't any openings for reporters. I said they'd all been assigned at the beginning of the year, and he was too late."

"Well, that's true, isn't it?" Kerry asked.

Jean Marie shook her head. "No, it's not. Students can come in any time and sign up. And Frog probably found that out soon enough. He would have figured out then, if he hadn't earlier, that I just didn't *like* him."

After another long silence broken only by the train wheels whispering to Hannah, *Go-back, go-back, go-back*, Kerry turned to her and said, "Hannah? You're the only one who hasn't said anything. Wasn't Frog in your English class? Did you ever talk to him? What I really want to know is, did you make him mad like the rest of us? What's *your* story?"

"I don't have one," Hannah replied. Then saying, "Excuse me," she slid past Mack and out of the booth to hurry to the counter.

"Well!" Kerry cried, offended.

Hannah ignored her. She didn't turn around in an effort to make amends. She stood stiffly at the counter, her back to her friends, listening as the train wheels repeated their warning.

Go-back, go-back, go-back . . .

Chapter 5

Hannah stood at the counter, alone, sipping the Coke she'd ordered. Laughter and music and chatter surrounded her, but she heard only the warning of the wheels telling her to go back.

Everyone seemed so happy. The Cafe was cheerful and lively in its coat of bright red, and sunshine and light streamed in through the windows and skylights. Each round red table, every booth, was occupied by a group of four or five laughing, joking students, every bright red stool filled, and the upbeat music inspired more than one foot to tap out the beat on the red-and-white checkered floor tiles.

So much life here. But at the other end of the train, in the baggage car . . . there was a coffin.

Go-back, go-back, go-back . . .

She couldn't go back any more than Frog could. Frog — Frederick Roger Drummond — dead at seventeen, killed in a horrible, fiery crash not far from her house. They heard the sirens, she and her friends, and had dismissed them. Busy, she thought, we were busy and we paid no attention.

Not that they could have helped. Jean Marie had said the car was a blazing mass of melting metal when help arrived.

Poor Frog. Kerry had said, "He shouldn't have been going so fast. He always drove too fast. He almost hit me once, roaring out of the school parking lot. I screamed at him, but he didn't hear me."

But Frog couldn't have known that on this particular Friday night, driving too fast was going to kill him. If you were only seventeen and you knew absolutely, positively that something was going to take away the rest of your life, you wouldn't do it, would you? Not even if you were unpopular and unhappy, like Frog. Not at seventeen. Not unless you didn't want to live anymore.

Could Frog have been *that* unhappy, that night? Guilt and shame washed over her. Could she and her friends have made the new boy so miserable that he would actually end his own life?

We didn't mean to, she told herself quickly to ease the pain that washed over her. We didn't *mean* to. We didn't know.

But the police hadn't mentioned suicide. No one had. She was imagining things. A guilty conscience . . . ?

"Penny." Mack came up behind her, startling her out of her morbid thoughts.

Hannah looked up at him. "What?"

"I'll give you a penny if you'll tell me what you're thinking about. My grandmother used to do that, offer me a penny for my thoughts."

Hannah smiled. "A penny won't even buy chewing gum now, Mack. Inflation. You'd better up the price."

"Okay, a nickel then, but that's my top offer."

"I was thinking about Frog," she answered reluctantly.

"Don't."

"I can't help it. Everyone talking about him just now . . . we really weren't very nice to him."

"Hannah, he was a creep. Don't make him a saint now because something awful happened to him."

"I'm not." Hannah's tone was more defensive than she'd meant it to be. She wanted Mack to understand what she was feeling. But how could he? None of them had liked Frog, that was the truth, and Mack was being more honest about it than she was.

Still, she couldn't shake the eerie feeling that Frog was listening to every word she said. The thought raised the flesh on her arms in tiny bumps.

"Hannah and Mack," Kerry cried, "come on back here! Lewis is telling incredibly stupid jokes and if you don't get on over here, he'll keep it up. Save me!"

Hannah turned, Coke in hand and, at that instant, without warning, the cheerful light allowed by the huge windows and the ceiling skylights disappeared as the train entered a tunnel. A split second later, the overhead lights went out, and the entire Cafe was plunged into total darkness.

There were screams and voices saying, "What the . . . ?" Hannah clutched for Mack's sleeve. The utter blackness, combined with the hollow sound of the train rattling through the tunnel, made her breath catch in her throat. She hated tunnels. There was no way out of them — you couldn't just decide halfway through, I don't like this tunnel anymore, and leave it by a side exit. There was only the entrance and the exit, and some tunnels were very, very long. There was no space, no air, and you were surrounded on all sides by concrete or rock. Sometimes there was water above and on both sides of the tunnel, and Hannah found those the scariest of all. Did this train go through that kind of tunnel? She didn't know.

Why had the Cafe lights gone out?

The screaming and shouting was followed by a bewildered, shocked silence. Into it rang Ms. Quick's voice. "All right, everyone, calm down! You've been in darkened rooms before, and you survived."

Her weak attempt at humor fell flat. When no one laughed, and a few boys yelled complaints, Mack calmly asked the chaperone, "Any idea what the problem is? We know the tunnel is dark, but what happened to the lights in here?"

"I don't know," Ms. Quick answered, her voice close enough to Hannah that she thought she could probably reach out and touch the teacher if she chose. She didn't. Mack's sleeve was enough for now.

A startled gasp came from somewhere off to Hannah's left. She peered through the darkness but could make out only the bulky shadow of a booth.

The train left the tunnel as suddenly as it had

entered, and natural light and sunshine flooded the Cafe through the skylights and windows.

Ms. Quick went immediately to the light switch on the wall beside the entrance to the Cafe and flicked it, bathing the already bright room in artificial light.

"Well, honestly!" the teacher exclaimed in disbelief, "someone turned off the switch!"

When she realized that no one was listening to her, she clucked in annoyance. Then her eyes followed theirs, and she gasped in horror. Everyone in the Cafe was staring in mute shock at Lolly Slocum, sitting alone in a bright red booth off to Hannah's left.

Hannah thought, Did she hear all the things we said about Frog?

And then the horror of the scene before her obliterated all thought.

What everyone was staring at was a bright red print bandana, twisted into a "rope" and wound around Lolly's neck so tightly that her round, plain face was rapidly turning purple and her eyes, wild with desperation, were bulging dangerously. Her fingers clawed frantically at the brightly-colored noose, but in vain. Her mouth opened and closed silently as she struggled for precious air.

Like a dying fish, Hannah thought numbly.

Lolly Slocum was choking to death.

Chapter 6

While everyone watched, transfixed, Mack took two huge steps forward and began working on the bandana knot digging into the back of Lolly's purple neck.

A waiter whispered, "What should we do?"

The elderly man working behind the counter gave no response other than to continue staring, wide-eyed, at the victim.

"Someone get the conductor!" Ms. Quick barked. "See if there's a doctor on board!"

Lewis whirled and ran.

The only sound in the room as Mack struggled with the stubborn knot was the ugly, tormented gurgling coming from Lolly Slocum.

This isn't happening, Hannah thought, sickened by the sight of Lolly's bulging eyes rolling back in her head. This can't be happening. It can't be real.

"I think she's had it," someone said softly, eyes on Lolly. Then someone else said, "Well, who *is* she? Is she with our tour?"

The question saddened Hannah. Lolly's fellow students didn't even know who she *was*. Parker High wasn't such a big school. Shouldn't they all know each other? Shouldn't the people watching Lolly fight for her life at least know who she *was*?

When at last the bandana gave way under Mack's fingers, Lolly took one deep, grateful gasp of air, and fainted. Her head fell forward like a sack of sand. There was a loud, sickening thunk as her forehead slammed into the red Formica tabletop.

Several girls screamed.

"She's dead!" one cried, and then the same voice asked tremulously, "*isn't* she?"

Ms. Quick checked Lolly's pulse. "She's alive. But she needs a doctor. *Where* is Lewis with that conductor? Oh, I do hope there's a doctor on board."

There was. A tall, gray-haired woman in a dark suit arrived with Lewis and the conductor. She was carrying a fat black bag. Lolly was beginning to stir, moaning hoarsely, when they burst into the Cafe.

"Everybody out!" the doctor snapped, hurrying over to help the victim sit up. Singling out an adult in the group, she turned to Ms. Quick and added, "Except you! I want to know what happened here."

With the doctor's help, Lolly leaned her head back against the seat, her mouth working furiously to gulp in air. An ugly necklace of raw, wounded skin encircled her throat.

Flushing guiltily, Ms. Quick waved everyone else out of the room. "Go straight to your compartments and stay there until you hear from me," she ordered in a shaky voice. Then she turned her attention to doctor and patient.

Shock slowed the steps of the tour group as they left the Cafe. "Is that girl going to die?" someone whispered as they made their way through the cars.

"I don't think so," Mack said. "If she was, she probably wouldn't have regained consciousness."

That remark broke the stunned silence. Everyone began talking at once, some softly, some more loudly, about what had happened to Lolly. There was disbelief in every comment.

When the door had been closed and latched from the inside, the compartment felt safe. But Hannah knew that Lolly's attack had changed the tour for all of them. Looking at the pale, drawn faces of her friends as they collapsed onto the maroon velour seats, she knew they were still seeing Lolly's mottled, swollen face.

"You think she'll live?" Lewis asked Mack, his voice subdued.

Mack shrugged.

"I keep seeing her face," Kerry said, leaning her head back against the seat and closing her eyes. "It was . . . it was awful." She trembled. "Horrible!"

"It must have hurt," Hannah whispered, sitting down beside Mack. "She looked like she was in such terrible pain. Who would . . . ?" She couldn't finish the question, but they all knew what she had been about to say.

Who would do such a terrible thing?

Kerry opened her eyes. "Maybe one of those

weirdos she came with did it. That Eugene character was Frog's best friend. Maybe he freaked out and decided Frog wants Lolly with him. I've heard of weirder things."

Mack and Lewis clucked in disgust.

But Hannah remained silent. Once, when she had visited her grandmother's grave in the cemetery, she had come upon Eugene, sitting with his back against a tree. Thinking he was there for the same reason she was, she had said politely, "It's kind of nice that we can bring flowers here. I think it sort of helps, don't you?"

And he had looked at her with pale, cool eyes and said, "I just come because I like it here."

Hannah found herself wondering how Lolly had ended up with three such strange boys as her only friends. Unlike Frog, Lolly wasn't really unattractive. She was a big girl, but it seemed to Hannah that she at least made an effort to look her best, wearing neat, clean clothes, trying to jazz them up a little with a colorful scarf around her neck or a pretty pin on a blouse collar. Hannah remembered seeing her once in the hall in a plain, short-sleeved white blouse, a small bunch of artificial violets pinned to the collar, repeating the color of the purple corduroy skirt Lolly was wearing. She had looked almost pretty.

So it wasn't appearance that had set Lolly apart. And it wasn't attitude, the way it was with Frog. Lolly Slocum was pleasant enough in classes and in the halls, nodding or smiling at people she passed.

"Why don't any of us like Lolly?" Hannah asked

quietly as Mack and Lewis, Jean Marie and Kerry continued to sit in shocked silence. Their faces were still gray with shock and disbelief.

Kerry stared at her. "What?"

"Why isn't Lolly more popular? Most of the people in the Cafe didn't even know who she was. I mean, she seems nice enough. So why doesn't anyone like her?"

"Because she dated Frog," was Kerry's immediate answer. "And Frog was a creep."

"No, I mean, *before* that. Before she dated Frog. Why didn't we like her then?"

Her friends exchanged confused glances. Kerry shrugged. "How should I know? I don't remember. I think . . . I think she was just . . . not *fun*. Too . . . quiet or something. What's the difference, anyway? Even if we *had* liked her, when she started going out with Frog we would have changed our minds, right?"

"Maybe if we'd liked her," Hannah said slowly, "she wouldn't have gone *out* with someone like Frog. Maybe she wouldn't have had to."

Lewis groaned. "More guilt? Look, some sick nut turned off the lights and wrapped a noose around that girl's neck. But it didn't happen because of the way we treated Frog or his girlfriend Polly."

"Lolly," Hannah said, agitated. "Her name is *Lolly*."

"Actually," Jean Marie said, "it's Louise. Her real name is Louise. She was in Choir, and Mr. Foley called her Louise."

"I didn't know she was in Choir." Hannah

frowned. "Did you ever talk to her, Jean Marie?"

A pink flush of shame colored Jean Marie's cheeks. She shook her head. "No, not really. But," she added quickly, "she was only there a couple of times. Then I guess she quit, because all of a sudden, she didn't show up. Foley was really mad. She had a nice voice. Alto. We're short on altos. I heard she'd joined the Drama Club instead."

A sudden rap on the door ended the conversation about Lolly. Startled, they all stared at each other and no one moved.

Chapter 7

"It's me!" Ms. Quick's voice called from beyond the door. "Let me in!"

Hannah jumped up and opened the door.

The teacher stood in the hallway. "Lolly is going to be all right," she said, relief in every syllable. "The doctor said she could continue the trip, but we're having trouble calming her down, and she wants to go back home. I can't blame her. We're sending her back on the express train."

I want to go, too, Hannah thought. I want to go back home.

Ms. Quick glanced around the room. There was dismayed awe in her voice as she said, "Isn't this the most awful thing? I can't believe . . ." Then she took a deep breath and said in a monotone, "I want you all to stay here until it's time to go to the dining car for dinner. No running around the train alone, not until we find out who's behind this horrible business. Dr. Lindsay has volunteered to return to Chicago with Lolly so that Mr. Dobbs and I can stay with all of you."

"So what happens next?" Mack asked.

"We're asking everyone on the tour if they have any idea who might have done this. They've all said no. What about you five — any ideas?"

They all shook their heads.

"Well, then, since no one knows anything, the conductor will be calling in a detective to get some answers. He'll come on board first thing tomorrow morning when we arrive in Denver. Until then, I must urge all of you to please stick together, okay?"

They all nodded solemnly, and Ms. Quick left to continue spreading the news.

Thoroughly shaken by the disastrous way their trip had begun, they all sat quietly, gazing out the window at the speeding landscape and the rapidly descending twilight.

It was ten minutes past eight o'clock when Ms. Quick rapped on the door and said it was time to head for the dining car, reminding them once more to "stay together."

The thought of eating dinner turned Hannah's stomach. But the others eagerly got up to go. "I need to stop back at our compartment first," Lewis told Mack. "Need anything there?"

"I'd better come with you. I think Ms. Quick is right. We shouldn't be wandering the train alone. Not after . . ." Mack didn't finish the sentence. "I guess two qualifies as a group. Let's go."

"Walk me back to my compartment?" Jean Marie asked. "Sherry and Ann are probably already there. I can go to dinner with them, but I don't want to walk back there alone."

The three left together, with Lewis and Mack promising to return to go with Kerry and Hannah to dinner.

A few minutes later, the train slowed gradually and came to a complete standstill. Hannah went to the window and watched as Lolly, flanked by the doctor and the conductor, was helped out of the tour train and into a red and silver train standing at the station and aimed in the opposite direction. As she watched the unfortunate girl collapse into a seat in the well-lighted train, Hannah couldn't help thinking she looked relieved. She's *glad* to be off our train, glad to be going back home.

No wonder, after what had happened to her.

Was it really safe to wait until morning and let the detective figure things out?

It didn't feel safe. How could they be sure that Lolly's attacker had left the train?

They couldn't.

Dinner in the dining car would be creepy, Hannah thought. Everyone would be watching everyone else, trying to decide if anyone looked suspicious. There wouldn't be any laughing, the way there had been in the Cafe earlier, and if people talked about anything at all, it would be the attack on Lolly.

Hannah didn't want to go to the dining car. But anything was better than staying in the compartment alone. That, she could *not* do.

Soon they were on their way again, the wheels droning their steady *ga-dink, ga-dink, ga-dink.*

Go-back, go-back, go-back . . .

Hannah turned away from the window. "It was

nice of the doctor to go back with Lolly. So she won't be alone."

"Yeah, but what if she was the only doctor on board?" Kerry asked. "Let's just hope nothing else bad happens. I hope whoever was after Lolly knows she's not on *this* train anymore." Kerry pulled the barrette out of her hair and then replaced it carefully. "I wonder who it was? Why would anyone want to kill Lolly Slocum?"

She means, Hannah thought with sadness, that Lolly wasn't interesting enough or important enough to have something like that happen to her. How awful. Hannah sighed, and slowly began to unpack her small suitcase.

Chapter 8

It seemed to Hannah that it was taking Kerry forever to get ready for dinner. Mack and Lewis came to get them twice. Both times, Kerry sent them back to their own compartment, insisting that she needed a few more minutes. They left grudgingly.

"Kerry," Hannah finally said, "you've changed your hair four times. After what's happened, how can you stand there fussing with your hair as if life were totally normal? It's *not*."

But, in truth, she was grateful. . . . The thought of leaving the safety of the compartment for those dark, narrow corridors made her palms sweat. There would be no bright sunshine relieving the darkness now. The windows and skylights would reflect only empty darkness. The corridors would seem airless, confining . . .

"You're right, Hannah. I'm being petty and shallow and silly." But in the next second, Kerry peered into the mirror over the small sink and cried, "Look at this purple eye shadow. Purple! I feel like a peacock. Wait just one minute, let me try this beige.

The salesgirl at Bonham's talked me into the purple. I could strangle her."

The word "strangle" hung in the air and Kerry's eyes widened as she realized what she had just said. "Oh," she said softly, glancing guiltily at Hannah, "sorry. I wasn't . . ."

"It's all right. Just hurry up, okay? Mack and Lewis must be starving. If you send them away one more time, they'll go without us." And I don't want that, Hannah added to herself. I definitely don't want that.

The minute Kerry finally finished primping, she became impatient. "Where are those guys, anyway?" she complained. "I've been ready for five minutes and they're still not here. Let's go get them."

Lolly's swollen, purpled face danced before Hannah's eyes. "You know what Ms. Quick said. And you *told* the guys to give you more time. They'll be here. If we leave first, we could miss them."

"Hannah. There is only one way to get from their compartment at the other end of the car to ours. It's not like the train has side streets. C'mon, we'll surprise them. It'll be fun."

"No. Ms. Quick said — "

"Hannah, the guy who tried to throttle Lolly left the train when she did, I'm sure of it. Why would he hang around here?"

"Okay," Hannah said, "you're right. We'll probably run into Mack and Lewis on the way."

But as they left the compartment, her stomach began churning again. The corridor was so dark, and completely empty. Kerry had taken so long making herself beautiful that everyone else had already left for the dining car.

They had gone only a few steps when Kerry let out a piercing shriek and stopped in her tracks.

Hannah gasped and whirled, expecting to see a crazed maniac holding a knife against her best friend's throat.

"I forgot my gold chain," Kerry cried. "The one Lewis gave me for my birthday. I never go anywhere without it. I promised him I wouldn't. But I took it off when I was brushing my teeth because it kept dangling over the stupid little sink and I didn't want to get toothpaste gunk all over it. Wait here. I'll be right back."

"I am not waiting in this hall alone," Hannah said, "and do not ever, ever shriek like that again on this train!"

"Sorry. It was dumb. You okay?"

"Yes. But I'm coming with you."

"Hannah, don't be silly." Kerry was already backing away. "Our compartment is only a few inches away. I'll be right back. I know exactly where my chain is. And Mack and Lewis should come along any minute now."

Their compartment was more than "a few inches" away. More like a few *hundred* inches. But Hannah *did* feel silly refusing to wait alone in the corridor. Hadn't she already decided that Lolly's attacker had left the train when Lolly left?

"Okay," she agreed, "but hurry up. Are you *sure* you know exactly where that chain is?"

"Of course I do. Wait right here. Back in a sec."

And Kerry hurried away, her black hair swinging behind her like a pendulum.

The minute Hannah stood alone in the corridor, lost in a sea of dark paisley, her nerves tightened like piano wires. She couldn't help it.

The train wheels whispered, *ga-dink*, *ga-dink*, *ga-dink* . . .

When Kerry didn't return immediately, Hannah, restless and impatient, moved on down the hall to the door at the end of the car. Its window looked out upon a dark, moonless night, but in the distance, lights appeared and disappeared, blurring into one, long, pale gold ribbon. The black and gold panorama was hypnotizing and Hannah became lost in it, unaware of the passing minutes.

A sound behind her snapped her out of her trance.

"It's about time," she said, as she began to turn around. "Couldn't you find the chain?"

Without warning, something thick and fluffy and cottony covered her mouth and nose, stifling her cry of surprise.

A strong arm fastened itself around her chest, pinning her arms against her sides. The arm began dragging her backward, her legs dangling helplessly. She fought to touch the ground with her feet, but when she did, the only result was the sound of her sneakers hitting against the dark carpet.

Help me! Hannah tried to cry out, but her mouth, mashed cruelly into the cottony fluff, made no sound.

And it occurred to her dazed, terrified mind that even if she could scream, there was no one to hear her.

The corridor was empty.

Snapping out of her paralysis of fear, Hannah began to fight back. She tried frantically to slow their progress by digging her heels into the carpet, but the soft rubber soles of her sneakers were useless. Her attacker plodded onward, toward the baggage car. Hannah's desperate attempts at resistance seemed to go unnoticed.

Why hadn't Kerry returned? Hannah wondered. She had said, "Back in a sec." She'd been gone much longer than a second. Much longer . . .

She heard the door to the baggage car slide open.

If only someone . . . a porter . . . the conductor . . . someone was in the baggage car to help her.

Hannah realized they had moved inside the car. A booted foot pushed the door closed. Hannah's eyes, seeking help, darted wildly about the room.

There was no help. There were only boxes and cartons and containers, which offered no help at all. There was no porter, no conductor . . . no one to help her.

They shouldn't leave all this luggage unguarded, she thought angrily, crazily. When I get out of here, I'm complaining to the conductor.

Complain? I'm losing my mind. I probably won't even get out of here . . . alive.

Lolly's tomato-hued face danced before her, and nausea rose in her throat. Calm, calm . . . must stay calm . . . mustn't panic . . . must think . . . think . . . think . . .

Think, Hannah! Think or die!

How could she think when she was so scared?

Because she was being dragged backward by the grip around her chest, she couldn't see where they were headed; which only made her feel more helpless.

Who was this person dragging her along? And what were they planning to do with her? Was she going to die here?

Suddenly, the dragging stopped and the hand that was gagging Hannah removed the cottony wad over her mouth. Stunned by the unexpected release, Hannah found herself standing upright, freed from her awkward backward-tilt. But her arms were still imprisoned.

Immediately, she opened her mouth to scream for help.

The blow came from behind. Hannah never saw the arm descending, never saw the blunt object that slammed against her skull, sending a sickening shaft of pain zig-zagging, like lightning, from the top of her head all the way down to her toes.

No scream left her lips. Before any sound could escape from her open mouth, darkness swooped down upon her.

Chapter 9

Hannah awoke into a blackness that was as thick and cloying as tar. Her eyes, aching from the blow on her head, searched for the tiniest sliver of light, and found none. She closed her eyes again, hoping that when she opened them, the darkness would be gone.

It wasn't. Wherever she was, there wasn't so much as a pinprick of light. She felt like a mole burrowed into the deepest part of the earth.

Her head hurt terribly. Sharp shafts of pain stabbed at her skull. She put her hands, unfettered now, to her forehead. They were cool, almost clammy, but soothing. Slowly, maddeningly slowly, her mind returned to full consciousness.

Where *was* she?

She was lying flat on her back, legs stretched out, on something soft and silky . . . so slippery that when she tentatively bent her leg at the knee and slid it up toward her, her sneakered foot promptly whooshed back into a flat position again as quickly as if she were lying in melted butter.

She raised the other leg. But this time, she didn't bend it at the knee. Instead, she lifted it higher and higher, testing, until the foot touched something, some kind of cover over her head — over her body — over all of her. The cover felt very solid. Maybe . . . wooden. She pushed against it with her foot. But the wood covering her remained firmly in place. There was no "give" to it. She pushed hard, then harder still, using all of the strength in her legs. But whatever was lying over her, covering her in the dark, was solid and thick and . . . sliding her hands over it . . . wooden. Satin-smooth wood. Thick . . . solid . . . totally immovable wood.

Where *was* she? What was she doing in all this cold blackness?

She raised both legs and pushed once more against the overhead surface with all of her strength.

Nothing. The wooden covering remained firmly in place.

Hannah's left arm moved away from her forehead to reach out to the side. Another solid surface, this one close, very close. *Too* close.

Her nerves began to sing out an alarm as her right arm followed the motion of her left, sliding along her right side until she touched solid wood. Again, too close . . . no more room than a few inches on either side.

Not enough space . . . too narrow . . . something solid over her head and on both sides of her, keeping her in . . .

Not enough room . . . not enough space . . . not enough air . . .

Hannah's breathing began to quicken, coming in shallow little gasps.

Easy, easy, she warned herself. Don't panic. Do *not* panic. Take it easy. Find out where you are, that's the first thing.

What *was* this place? Why was she lying down? Had she fainted? No, she never fainted. Sometimes, when claustrophobia hit her in an elevator, she hyperventilated, but she never fainted.

Her head throbbed. She remembered, then, being struck on the back of her skull. Whoever had done that had put her in this . . . this place. *Why?* And how could she get out when the top wouldn't budge?

Her hands moved more quickly now, seeking, searching for the key to freedom, a way out so that she could begin to breathe normally again. So small, this place . . . so small, so narrow, so dark. Hannah knew in her heart that it would only be seconds before she panicked in earnest. It wasn't as if she could help it. It wasn't something she chose to do, breathing erratically in small, confined spaces. She always tried to fight it, but it was no use. And now her breathing was already out of control, and unless she found an escape soon, her heart and lungs would begin to career around in her chest on a wild rampage.

If she only knew where she was, maybe she could find a way out.

Forcing herself to take a few slow, deep breaths,

she slid down on the silky fabric underneath her, until her feet touched another solid surface. Then, pushing against that "wall" with her sneakered feet, she slid her body back up, arms at her sides, until the top of her head gently bumped into more solid wood.

She did this twice, sliding to one end of the darkness, then back up to the other end, her hands exploring the smooth wooden sides as she went, until she had a clear picture of the dimensions encasing her in wood.

And that picture, when it was complete in her mind, caused her breath to catch in her throat. Her chest began rising and falling far too rapidly as Hannah realized that she was lying in a long, narrow, wooden box with an unyielding wooden roof. No windows, no doors, not nearly enough space or air. Where was the way out? Her hands continued to flutter about, touching . . . exploring . . . sliding along the slippery folds of the melted-butter fabric under and around her.

It felt like . . . it felt like . . . satin.

Hannah's breathing quickened. She scrambled upward, slamming the top of her head against the heavy wooden cover. She cried out in pain. A lid . . . the wooden cover over her head was a . . . lid. She was in a long, narrow wooden box with a lid, and she was lying on . . . folds of . . . satin . . .

Her eyes, in the darkness, widened and her mouth opened. No . . . nonononono . . .

Her grandmother's funeral zoomed, unbidden, into her mind — Nanny lying there in that long, narrow, wooden box, the curved lid raised so that everyone could see her artificially made-up face, lying there, unmoving, on folds of rippled . . . white . . . satin—

Oh, God, no . . . No!

Hannah opened her mouth and screamed and screamed and screamed . . .

Her head tossed crazily from side to side. Her fingernails began clawing and scratching and tearing at the solid wood surrounding her. Finding no escape, her screams escalated to high, thin, keening wails . . . the wild cries of a newly caged animal.

Her legs thrashed frantically, slamming repeatedly against the lid of her prison. Her hands dug and clawed, searching for a way out. Her breathing became so shallow and rapid, there was no air left for screaming, and her wailing descended into a guttural, pained moan.

Hannah fought to remain conscious. But she was hyperventilating, and purple and red dots danced before her eyes.

When she heard voices, she thought she was hallucinating. Using what little strength she had left, she lifted her legs and slammed her feet against the lid hard, once, twice, three times.

Then, telling herself the voices weren't real, Hannah gave up the fight and passed out, sliding down along the white satin with a sob and letting the blackness swallow her up.

Chapter 10

When Hannah struggled back to consciousness, it took her some moments to realize she was free. Out of the horrible box — free! Someone was holding her. . . . Mack . . . Mack was holding her in his arms, her face against the softness of his flannel shirt.

Hannah's eyes struggled to focus. Slowly, the milky cloudiness disappeared as realization dawned. As it did, the sensation of being trapped in the long, narrow wooden box returned in vivid detail. Hannah began shaking violently. Covering her eyes with both hands, she began to moan.

"It's okay, Hannah, it's okay," Mack murmured. "You're out of there now, you're safe, it's okay." None of which did any good. Hannah continued to writhe and moan.

Lewis arrived with Ms. Quick in tow, followed closely by the conductor. Their faces registered hope that Lewis's jumbled story involved only a cruel prank, a joke.

That hope vanished when they saw the state Hannah was in.

"Goodness!" the teacher cried, hurrying to Mack's side. "*Look* at her! This is *not* funny!" She fixed a steely gaze on Mack. "What's been going on in here?"

"Someone shut her in there," Mack said, pointing to the now-closed coffin. "We'd been hunting all over the train for her. This was the only place left to look, and Kerry thought she heard something when we first came in here. It stopped right away. Hannah must have passed out. But we had to check it out."

Ms. Quick paled. "Hannah was in *there*?"

Mack nodded grimly. "And she's claustrophobic. That's why she's so out of control. She needs a doctor." He looked at Lewis. "Did you find one?"

"Aren't any," the conductor offered, his eyes on Hannah, whose moans had dwindled into a soft, anguished sobbing. "Only doctor on board left with that other girl. We have a first-aid kit, but," he shook his head ruefully, "I don't think there's anything in there for this kind of thing. Girl needs a sedative. Calm her down. She's in a bad way."

"You would be, too," Kerry spoke up, "if you'd been trapped in someone's coffin."

The conductor nodded. "Might be I could find a tranquilizer, something like that, on board. Passengers might have something. Want me to ask?"

"No," Hannah whispered, lifting her head and surprising all of them. "I don't want any pills." Thin

streaks of watery mascara veined her bloodles[s]
and her eyes were red and swollen. But her breathing was steadier and she tried to sit up in Mack's
arms. "Someone hit me on the head. When I woke
up . . ." she shuddered, "I was . . . in *there*."

She stopped to take a deep breath. "Whoever did
it is probably still on the train. If he . . . if he comes
back, I don't want to be asleep from some pill." She
made no attempt to leave Mack's arms. "I want to
be able to defend myself," she added in the same
hoarse whisper.

"You won't have to," Mack said. His voice was
full of determination. "I'll be here."

"Someone struck you?" Ms. Quick asked in a
shocked voice. "Then this wasn't just a stupid joke?"

"If it was a joke," Lewis said, "it's not funny.
Not funny at all."

"It wasn't a joke," Hannah said softly. "I was
waiting for Kerry in the corridor and someone
grabbed me from behind and dragged me in here.
Then something slammed against the back of my
head. The next thing I knew, I was . . ." she swallowed hard and continued in barely a whisper, "in
there."

"Did you see who it was?" Lewis wanted to know.

"No, I didn't see anything," Hannah said. "I told
you, he came from behind. Can I go back to my
compartment now, please? I need to . . . I need to
wash my face. I . . . I need to . . . sit down or
something."

"I'll take you," Mack said. "Come on." But before

they left the baggage car, he turned to Ms. Quick and asked, "So what are we going to do about this? Hannah could have died in that . . ." — he couldn't bring himself to say coffin — ". . . in there. We have to *do* something."

The teacher nodded. But it was clear that she was at a loss, still shocked by what had happened to Hannah.

"Serious business," the conductor said glumly. "That detective is meeting us in Denver, first thing tomorrow morning. Have to leave it to him to find out what's going on."

"I guess we'll have to." Mack's arm around Hannah's shoulders tightened. "We'll look out for each other until the guy gets here."

"You're sure this wasn't a crazy kind of stunt?" the conductor pressed. "Bunch of kids on a train trip, high spirits, that kind of thing?"

The teenagers shook their heads vigorously. "No joke," Lewis said, "absolutely."

The conductor nodded, and left the car, shaking his head as he went.

Ms. Quick was shaking her head, too, and her expression clearly said, How did I get myself into this? But she was concerned for Hannah, too, and followed closely behind Mack as he led Hannah from the car.

Hannah's mind whirled in confusion. She had been in a coffin. Frog's coffin. But there was something very, very wrong with that, something more than the awful horror of her imprisonment. There shouldn't have been room for her in that awful box.

Coffins weren't made for *two* people. Only one person . . . one body.

What had happened to the body that was supposed to be in the coffin? Where had it been while she was struggling so hard to get out?

Where was Frog?

Chapter 11

"You need a doctor," Ms. Quick told Hannah, as she and Mack helped her to one of the seats. "Your color is very bad."

"I'll see a doctor in Denver in the morning," Hannah said, closing her eyes again. "But not tonight. I just want to sleep. I'm so tired."

"Hannah," Kerry said suddenly, "your hands . . ."

They all looked at Hannah's hands. Every nail was torn, many of her fingers were bloody, the knuckles scraped raw.

Kerry ran to the sink and quickly wet a washcloth with cool water. Returning to Hannah, she knelt and carefully, gingerly, began wiping the wounded hands clean. Each time Hannah winced in pain, Kerry did the same. "I'm sorry." She said it several times. "I'm really sorry it hurts."

But when she had finished, Hannah's hands felt better, and she said so with gratitude in her voice.

"I hate to leave you," the teacher said. "You will lock your door?"

"We'll be fine," Hannah assured her. "All I want to do is sleep. Kerry, you're staying, right?"

Kerry nodded. "I wouldn't leave you here alone, Hannah."

The boys offered to stay, too, but Ms. Quick nixed that idea. They left reluctantly, especially Mack. Hannah promised him she would sleep, but he still looked worried as he stepped out into the corridor.

"Close your eyes," Kerry commanded gently as she released the upper bunk and climbed into it. "You don't want that doctor in Denver finding you a total wreck and shipping you back home like Lolly, do you?"

Hannah wasn't sure. In spite of her uncertainty about the safety of rail travel, she had looked forward to this end-of-the-summer excursion with her friends. She had been especially excited about seeing San Francisco. But now it looked like train travel could be dangerous in more ways than one. And where did you run to on a train when you were in trouble? There wasn't any place to *go*! You were trapped . . .

When Hannah was twelve, her family had moved from the small town in Idaho where she was born to the suburbs where they now lived. To her dismay, she'd suddenly found herself traveling to and from school on a big yellow bus. She was the only "new kid" in the area that year, and still had braces and wore glasses. She'd been teased unmercifully, made the butt of everyone's jokes for weeks until she was no longer so "new" and they'd accepted her.

But while it lasted, the worst part of all that misery had been the fact that there was no way to escape. There was no place to run to on a school bus, no place to hide. She'd had to sit there and take it, fighting tears of loneliness and pain until suddenly, for no apparent reason that she could see, it ended and she became one of them.

What she felt now, huddled on her bed shrouded in the blanket, was that same sense of trapped-animal fear. If she continued with the trip as planned, how could she feel safe again? Where could she hide? Where could she run to if she was attacked again?

Only a lunatic would jump from a speeding train.

Maybe she should give up now, while she was still in one piece, and go back home. I never thought I would envy Lolly Slocum, she thought, but I do now. I want to be safe, too.

But . . . something in Hannah bridled at the idea of some hateful, crazy person she didn't even know driving her away from the tour, scaring her away from her friends and her trip. That wasn't fair. It wasn't right.

She had her friends around her, and Ms. Quick and Mr. Dobbs, and soon the detective would arrive.

She was staying on the train. She would be very, very careful, but she was staying. For now, anyway.

Exhausted, aware that the door was locked and Kerry was close by, Hannah fell asleep.

* * *

When she awoke the following morning, the first thing she heard was the whisper of the train wheels: *Go-back, go-back, go-back.*

No, she thought clearly. No, I won't go back. Not yet, anyway.

On the bunk above, Kerry hadn't stirred. It was too early to get up.

I should go back to sleep, Hannah thought. I'm still tired. And I want that doctor to think I'm in good shape so he won't send me back home.

Going back to sleep was easier said than done. Thoughts of Frog, unbidden, crawled furtively into her mind . . . first on the edges of it and then, when she was unable to resist, into the middle of it, taking up every inch of her thinking space. Because . . .

Because where *was* he? If he'd been in his coffin where he belonged, there wouldn't have been room for *her.*

The idea that someone might actually have moved Frog's remains made her physically ill.

What kind of person would do such a ghastly, disgusting, horrific thing?

Well, then, where *was* he?

Hannah was reminded of her mother's standard comment whenever Hannah misplaced something: a sneaker, her locker key, a favorite sweater . . . "Well," her mother always said, "it couldn't get up and *walk* away."

Neither could Frog. Not now. Not ever again.

Unless . . .

The thought came into Hannah's mind like a snake slithering through deep grass, arching its narrow head to snap, sending its venom coursing through her veins. The stunning, incredible thought stabbed her, venom-like, with a sharp and wicked pain.

No — impossible! How could she even think such a thing?

But . . .

Frog had burned to death. How many times on television had someone supposedly burned to death in a car or plane crash and then turned up alive later? Happened all the time, didn't it? It always turned out that someone else had died in the character's place and no one suspected.

Could someone other than Frog have died in that crash?

Who? A hitchhiker? Had Frog stopped to pick up someone that night — some innocent person wandering the highways — just before the car crashed? Had Frog himself escaped a split second before the wreck burst into flames? No one would have checked the identity of the driver. No dental records would have been examined. The police would have assumed that, of course, it was Frog driving the car. They had no reason to think anything else.

Hannah bit her lower lip. No. It couldn't be. It was too bizarre. It was *Frog's* car that had crashed and burned. Frog would have been driving it, so Frog would have died . . . no question about it.

But if that were true . . . Frog would have been in the coffin. And he wasn't. Hannah was.

He's here, she thought clearly, her head snapping

up so suddenly she smacked it against the upper berth. He's *here*. Somewhere. And he's . . . he's *angry*.

We shouldn't have been so mean to him, she thought, her heart slamming so wildly against her chest she expected Kerry to lean over the upper bunk and cry, "What's that horrible noise?"

But Kerry slept on.

Frog is out to punish us, Hannah thought with sickening conviction. Those stories we all told in the Cafe . . . they were awful. Cruel. He's not going to let us get away with that.

But Hannah, the nasty little voice reminded her slyly, *You* didn't *tell* a story. You were the only one who made no confession. So why would Frog be out to punish *you*?

For that matter, an even bigger question was, Why would he want to hurt Lolly? Lolly wasn't part of Hannah's group. She was Frog's own girlfriend.

I *know* what we all did to Frog, Hannah thought. But what was it that Lolly did to make him angry enough to hurt *her*?

A sharp rap on the door interrupted Hannah's thoughts.

"Time to get up, girls!" Ms. Quick's voice called. "Denver in an hour." Then, "Hannah? Are you awake? How are you feeling?"

"I'm okay," Hannah answered, forcing a casual tone of voice. Why worry Ms. Quick? She was frantic enough already.

Besides, Hannah could just imagine the look on the teacher's face if she knew Hannah thought Frog was alive. The woman would have a stroke and the whole trip would be cancelled.

Maybe that wouldn't be such a bad idea.

Hannah didn't say anything about Frog being alive to Kerry, either. What if Kerry thought Hannah had freaked out completely because of last night? She couldn't stand the thought of Kerry looking at her as if she had left her mind behind in that coffin.

Besides, saying it aloud would make it so . . . *real*. And now that it was daylight, now that she was washing her face and combing her hair and slipping into a pair of jeans and a red long-sleeved sweatshirt, now that Kerry was up and chattering about how "totally starving" she was, thoughts of Frog being alive seemed *Twilight Zone*-ish.

An hour later, she had convinced herself that her morbid thoughts about Frog had been irrational. Because she felt safe with Ms. Quick at her side as they waited at the doctor's office in downtown Denver, she insisted that Mack go with the others to eat breakfast in a nearby restaurant.

"You'd be bored waiting here for me," she told him, "and I'm not the least bit hungry. I couldn't eat anything. Go ahead."

"I don't want to go until I'm sure you're okay," he argued, lingering by her side.

"Mack," she said with a wan grin, "Go eat! I'll wait for you here when I'm done with the doctor."

Mack finally agreed, and left with Kerry, Lewis, and Jean Marie. Hannah's expression was wistful as she watched them troop off down the street. If it hadn't been for last night, she'd be going with them on this crisp, clean morning in Colorado, having the time of her life instead of waiting to see a doctor.

The doctor gave Hannah a clean bill of health and some aspirin for her headache.

As they left his office, Ms. Quick said, "You know, Hannah, if you want to return home, we can put you on a train to Chicago this morning. If that's what you want."

"No," Hannah said, recalling her resolution from the night before not to let some crazy person force her off the trip. "I'll stay."

"All right," Ms. Quick said, as she and Hannah waited outside in the sunshine for Hannah's friends to appear.

Other students, checking out Colorado's capital city, passed them. Several threw curious glances Hannah's way and she realized the word was out. News of the attack on her had been making the rounds. She hated that. It was humiliating.

Dale Sutterworth and Eugene Bryer, looking odd without Lolly walking between them, passed by.

Eugene looks mad, Hannah thought as his eyes briefly met hers and then quickly moved elsewhere. Was he still angry about the attack on Lolly? Having no one but gloomy Dale as a traveling companion couldn't be much fun.

A little while later, Kerry and Lewis came sauntering up the street with Jean Marie tagging along behind, studying the storefront windows.

But there was no Mack with them.

He's late because he's ordering take-out coffee for me, she told herself even as her heart began pounding in her chest.

"Where's Mack?" she asked and to her surprise, the words sounded perfectly normal.

"Not here yet?" Lewis asked, surprise on his face. "That's weird. When we came out of the restaurant, we started to head this way and all of a sudden, Mack yelled something and took off down the street. We figured he'd decided to jog or run back here, maybe for the exercise. Then," he added with a grin, "we figured, he'd been away from you for more than five minutes, and was feeling Hannah-withdrawal pains, so he decided to race back here to relieve his symptoms." The grin disappeared as Lewis frowned. "But he's not here. That's weird. Where could he be?"

Hannah sucked in her breath. When she spoke, her voice was little more than a whisper. "I don't know," she said. "I don't *know* where he is."

Chapter 12

"Perhaps Mack misunderstood," Ms. Quick told Hannah. "He might have thought he was supposed to meet you back at the train. Why don't we go back there?"

"He promised to meet me here. And that's what he'll do," Hannah insisted. "I'm waiting."

Realizing that there was no changing Hannah's mind, and anxious to return to her other duties, Ms. Quick volunteered to return to the train station to see if Mack had arrived there. "Don't wait too long," she warned before she left. "The train will be leaving as soon as that detective arrives."

Hannah knew the train would never depart without all of its Parker passengers. Ms. Quick would lie down on the tracks, if necessary, to prevent that.

And it didn't matter, anyway. Hannah was far more worried about Mack than she was about being stranded in Denver.

She turned to Lewis. "Why did you let Mack leave like that?"

"Like I could stop him," Lewis replied drily. But

his gray eyes searched the avenue for any sign of his best friend. "I told you, he just took off. He acted like a man on a mission. If we had a clue about what that mission was, we'd know where to look for him."

Hannah began pacing back and forth in front of the doctor's red brick office. She didn't know what to think. What had gotten into Mack? Splitting from Kerry and Lewis like that, making them all worry — after everything that had happened.

It was mean of Mack, that's what it was!

But Mack wasn't a mean person. He was smart and funny and kind.

Ah, but he was mean to Frog, a voice inside her head taunted.

"Hannah," Kerry said, "we have to get back to the station. Mack must already be back there."

"He couldn't have gone back without us seeing him," Hannah argued.

"Probably found a shortcut," Lewis said with one final glance up the street. There was no sign of Mack. "We can't wait here forever, or we'll have to hitchhike to California."

"I'm not leaving without Mack," Hannah said stubbornly.

Lewis was patient with her. "Let's just go back to the station and check, okay? If Mack's there, no problem. If he isn't, we'll tell the conductor and the detective and they'll hold the train until he shows up. And they'll help us look for him. We can't search this town by ourselves."

Hannah knew he was right. It would be stupid to separate and search for Mack in an unfamiliar city. If he wasn't at the station and they did have to look for him, they'd need help.

She nodded slowly, and they began walking. But she kept glancing back over her shoulder with anxious eyes. "He could be hurt," she murmured as they hurried along the street toward the station. "Something terrible could have happened to him." Like something terrible happened to Lolly and me, she added silently.

Lewis patted her shoulder sympathetically. "Listen, Hannah, if anyone can take care of himself, it's Mack. Quit worrying. He'll be at the station, I know he will."

But he wasn't.

The platform was crowded with noisy Parker High students, many of whom fell silent as she approached. Embarrassment washed over her. She hated everyone knowing how helpless she had been.

But she had more important worries now. Not one of the students staring at her was wearing a light blue shirt and a grin that curled her toes.

Dale was leaning against the railing opposite her. He was alone. She couldn't remember ever seeing him alone before. He'd always been with Frog or Lolly or Eugene, or, most often, all three.

Where was Eugene? Hadn't the two of them passed her only five or ten minutes ago? Maybe he'd stopped to buy gum or candy or mints in the terminal.

If only Mack had, too. But Lewis had checked, and there was no sign of Mack inside the building. Where *was* he?

Her face crumpled. "Oh, God, Lewis, he's not here!" she whispered, clutching at Lewis's sleeve. "He's not *here!*"

Frog's got him, came the voice in her head. Frog's got your precious Mack and it serves him right. Serves *you* right, too. You're as bad as he is.

"Don't panic," Lewis said, but his thin face was as anxious as Hannah's. "We'd better tell Ms. Quick. She'll freak, but she needs to know. And she'll have to tell the conductor to hold the train for Mack."

How long was a train allowed to wait before someone high up in the company gave the order to move it? she wondered.

"If Mack isn't on the train when it leaves," she announced, "I won't be, either."

"I heard Ms. Quick tell the conductor we weren't leaving without him, schedule or no schedule," Jean Marie said. "That should make you feel better."

Frog's got him, Frog's got him . . . the voice hissed in Hannah's ear. He's doing something terrible to your precious Mack while you stand around doing nothing. Some friend *you* are.

Hannah couldn't stand the thought of Mack in pain. She closed her eyes and leaned against the platform railing for support. Mack . . .

"Here he comes!" Lewis cried jubilantly. "And he's okay, Hannah, look!"

Hannah's eyes flew open. They fastened on a red-faced, breathless Mack as he ran up the platform steps. His hair hung, wet with sweat, on his forehead, and his face was flushed with exertion. But he didn't look bruised or bloody.

Hannah was the first to cry, "Where have you *been*?" as she ran to him and dove into his chest, wrapping her grateful arms around him. "We thought something horrible had happened to you!"

"I got lost," he said quickly. "You okay? Did the doctor find anything wrong?"

"Never mind me, tell me where you *were*! You got *lost*?" Her relief was rapidly becoming overshadowed by annoyance. He had scared her half to death and now he didn't want to talk about it? Maybe — maybe because it was so awful, he *couldn't* talk about it? Or so bizarre that he was afraid no one would believe him?

"We were so worried," she said, backing away from Mack and waiting for his explanation. "Lewis said you yelled something and ran off. Why?"

Mack shrugged. "I feel like a fool — " he began.

But he was interrupted by Ms. Quick calling out to the conductor, who waited on the train steps, "Everyone present and accounted for!"

The conductor nodded and called, "All aboard!" adding, "C'mon, folks, we're behind schedule. Let's get a move on."

The crowd surged forward, taking Mack and Lewis with them and leaving Hannah behind with Kerry and Jean Marie.

"Mack!" Hannah cried, but he gave no sign that he'd heard her.

As the crowd propelled Hannah forward, she realized she hadn't accepted Mack's story about getting lost. Lost? When all he had to do was go straight up the street to the doctor's office? No way. He wasn't telling the truth, she was sure of it.

Why would Mack lie about where he'd been?

She had to know.

Taking a deep breath and extending her elbows on either side of her, Hannah pushed with all her might, creating a tiny space that allowed her to inch forward a little. She pushed again, and took another step. Mack and Lewis mounted the iron steps. She had to catch up to them.

"Hannah, wait up!" Kerry called from behind, but Hannah kept going. Mack and Lewis had their heads together, like two people sharing a secret. What Mack was saying was important, she knew it. And he didn't want her to hear, she knew that, too. Or he would have told her back at the station. He wouldn't have let himself get swept up by the crowd.

She tried to move closer, where she'd be able to overhear what he was telling Lewis. She was careful not to get too close — that was easy. All she had to do was mingle with the crowd heading from one car to the next. What wasn't so easy was inching her way toward Mack and Lewis. But she kept trying, and finally found herself separated from them by only one person, a small girl with a blonde ponytail.

Mack and Lewis didn't turn around.

By focusing her attention upon them, blocking out the rhythmic *clackety-clack* of the wheels, Hannəh managed to make out what Mack was saying.

"Why are you arguing?" he asked Lewis, "I told you, I *know* it sounds crazy. But I could have sworn . . ."

The girl with the ponytail sneezed. Once. Twice. Three times.

Hannah felt like screaming. She had missed hearing whatever Mack could have sworn.

They entered a new car.

" . . . me get this straight," Lewis was saying. "We came out of the restaurant and started for the doctor's office to meet Hannah and you thought you saw . . . *what?*"

"Not what," Mack's voice replied clearly. "*Who.* I told you . . ." Hannah strained forward to hear.

"Someone was coming out of the drugstore on the corner. There was something about the way he walked, the way he moved, his hair . . . I would have sworn . . ."

Hannah held her breath. But she knew what Mack was going to say before he said it.

" . . . I would have sworn it was Frog."

Chapter 13

Hannah would have fallen to the floor if Mack hadn't heard her sharp intake of breath and turned to see her wavering in the aisle. He lunged for her, catching her before she could fall.

"You . . . saw . . . *Frog*?" she gasped, leaning into him.

"Oh, gosh, Hannah, no, you thought . . . geez, I'm sorry. I didn't know you were listening." Kerry and Jean Marie arrived in time to hear Mack add, "I *thought* it was him, but of course it wasn't."

"Who?" Kerry asked, seeing the look on Hannah's face. "Thought it was who?"

"*Frog*," Hannah breathed. "Mack saw Frog."

Kerry and Jean Marie gasped in unison even as Mack protested. "No! No, I didn't. How could I? This guy came out of the drugstore in town and he looked a lot like Frog. Dressed like him, too. Jeans and a plaid shirt with the sleeves rolled up, baseball cap. He looked so much like him, I lost my head and took off after him." Mack shook his head. "I don't know what I was thinking. I feel like a total jerk."

"But you're *not!*" Hannah cried. "It *was* him! I know he's alive, I can feel it. I didn't say anything because I knew you'd all think I was crazy, but now that Mack's *seen* him — "

"But I didn't!" Mack insisted. "That's just it. That's why I feel so foolish — "

"Did you catch up with the guy? Did you talk to him?" Hannah asked feverishly. "Did you *see* his face?"

Mack hesitated. "Well, no, but — "

"Then it *could* have been Frog! I knew it, I just knew it!"

"Hannah," Kerry warned, her eyes wide with bewilderment, "get a grip! What's wrong with you? Frog is dead. His coffin is right here on this train, remember?"

Hannah pounced. "Yes, but he's not *in* it! No one is. *I* ought to know. I was in there! So don't tell me Frog is dead. Someone else must have died in that car crash and Frog let everybody think it was him."

"Hannah," Jean Marie said softly, "that really doesn't make any sense. Why would Frog do that? If everyone thought he was dead, he'd never be able to show his face in town or at school, he couldn't go out or see people — why would someone do something so crazy?"

"That's just it," Hannah answered, her eyes glittering with fear, "he *is* crazy! Don't you get it? He faked his own death so he'd be free to get even with all of us for the nasty things we did to him. He knew that no matter what happened to any of us, no one would suspect him because everyone thinks he's dead. It's perfect." Her eyes traveled from one face to the next. "Can't you see that?"

Kerry shot a worried look at Mack. "But Hannah," she said, "*you're* the one who got locked in the coffin. And you're the only one who didn't have anything to confess in the Cafe. You're the only one who didn't do something terrible to Frog. So even if he is alive — and I don't think for one single second that he is — why would he hurt *you*?"

Hannah's cheeks blazed. "I have to get out of this awful hallway," she said quickly. "I can't breathe in here. Can we go back to our compartment, *please*? I'll feel safer there."

No one said anything as they all hurried back to the compartment, but Hannah knew what they were thinking. Their thoughts circled around her head like vultures about to descend: Hannah's losing it, Hannah's one slice of bread short of a loaf, Hannah thinks a dead guy is alive and walking this train. Poor Hannah!

Hannah bit down hard on her lower lip. She couldn't help how she felt, could she? *She* was the one who had been shut up in that horrible coffin, *she* was the one who knew better than anyone else that Frog wasn't in there. What was she supposed to think? That a dead person got out to make room for her?

That idea was even crazier than what *she* was thinking!

When they reached the compartment, she turned to face Mack. "So you ran after Frog," she said, biting off her words carefully. "That doesn't explain where you were all that time."

Mack's face flushed as he opened the compartment door and let them all step inside ahead of him. "I . . . I told you, I feel like a fool. What happened was, I ran after this . . . this person, whoever it was, and he went into a little wooden shed in one of the alleys. At least, I thought he did. But when I followed him inside, the place was empty. The door closed behind me and stuck. . . . I tried to get out and couldn't. The hinge was all rusty . . . guess the place hadn't been used much. Some kind of storage shed, I think. Anyway, I pounded and yelled and pushed, but nothing worked. I was stuck in there."

"Or *locked* in," Hannah said triumphantly. Her cheeks as flushed as Mack's, she turned to Kerry and said, "See? He was locked in that shed just like I was shut up inside the coffin. And I don't care what any of you say, it was *Frog* who did it!"

"No, Hannah," Mack protested, "no, it wasn't. I told you, the door was *stuck*, not locked. I got out by breaking a window and I went around to the front and checked the door. It wasn't locked."

"That doesn't mean it wasn't locked in the first

place," Hannah persisted. "He could have unlocked it after a while. And you never got close enough to get a good look at the person you were following, did you?"

"I didn't have to. I realized when I was in that shed that it was a crazy idea. We all know what happened to Frog."

"We all know what we *think* happened to Frog." Hannah, her arms folded against her chest, stood firm in the middle of the small, wood-panelled room. "Exactly what Frog *wanted* us to think."

Mack sighed heavily. "I give up. Think what you want to. Me, I'm going to check with that detective, see if he has any idea what's going on around here."

"Me, too," Lewis agreed. "I'll go with you."

When the compartment door had closed after them, Hannah turned to Kerry and Jean Marie and rolled her eyes heavenward. "They want me to admit that my theory is nuts," she said in exasperation, "and I just can't do that. I don't think it's nuts, do you?"

Their faces told her they thought exactly that.

Hannah's heart descended into her toes. She desperately wanted someone on her side.

Maybe it *was* a crazy theory. How could Frog fool the whole town into thinking he was dead? Didn't medical examiners check out things like that?

"Hannah," Kerry pointed out, "suppose, just suppose, you were right. Why would Frog hurt Lolly? She was the first one attacked, remember? But they were friends. More than friends. She was the only girl at school who would go out with him.

So why would he try to strangle her?"

"Well, I don't know about strangling, but they did have an awful fight," Jean Marie said.

Hannah stared at her. "They did? Frog and Lolly?"

"Well, she didn't call him Frog, Hannah. She called him Roger. Yeah, they did. Really nasty."

"How do you know?"

"I heard them. I mean, I wasn't eavesdropping, not on purpose. I was trying on jeans at The Gap, in the dressing room, and I heard these voices. I recognized Lolly's right away. She kept saying, 'You're not going, are you? Are you, Roger? You *can't* go!' "

Kerry looked interested. "Go where?"

Jean Marie shrugged. "How should I know?"

"What else did they say?" Hannah asked. Frog and Lolly had had a fight? She needed to know how *bad* the fight was.

"She kept saying he couldn't go, and he kept saying he was going. Then she said she was sure it was a joke and he was stupid not to see that and he screamed at her not to call him stupid, and then the clerk came over and threw them out. Told them to take their argument outside. The last thing I heard was Lolly saying something like, 'Then I'm going with you' and Frog saying 'You're not, you'll ruin everything.' Then she said, 'You're not going without me, Roger.' But their voices got too far away for me to hear the rest."

Hannah sank down onto one of the seats. Jean Marie had just answered for her the question of why

Frog would hurt Lolly. He'd been mad at her, maybe even as mad as he was at Hannah and her friends.

"When was this?" she asked quietly, her eyes on Jean Marie.

"Gosh, I don't remember, Hannah. I mean, why would I? It didn't matter to *me*." Jean Marie concentrated for a minute. "I think it was the Saturday before the trip. That morning."

Hannah exhaled deeply. She *knew* what Lolly and Frog had been fighting about.

That fight was *her* fault.

"Hannah," Kerry said, "quit looking so glum. A fight doesn't mean anything. I'm always arguing with boys and so far, not one of them has wrapped a noose around my neck."

"Not one of them was *Frog*," Hannah murmured stubbornly.

"Look, this is silly." Kerry grabbed her purse. "Come on, Jean Marie, let's leave Hannah here to rest — nobody needs rest more than Hannah does. I'll walk you back to your compartment. Then I'm going to take a shower."

"We're not supposed to go anywhere alone," Hannah reminded Kerry, alarm in her voice. "We promised Ms. Quick."

Kerry sighed in annoyance. "You're right. I forgot. Okay, then, Jean Marie needs a shower, too, don't you, Jean Marie?" Without waiting for an answer, she tugged at Jean Marie's sweater sleeve. "C'mon, we'll both take a shower. You rest, Hannah. I know you're nervous, so lock the door after us and, when we come back, I'll knock twice, then three times so you'll know it's me. Okay?"

Hannah nodded reluctantly.

Kerry collected her cosmetic case and towel, and then she and Jean Marie left the compartment.

Chapter 14

Hannah stood alone in the center of the small room, wishing briefly that she'd gone with them. But she was too worn-out to take a shower. Kerry was right: who needed rest more than Hannah Deaton?

She locked the door to the compartment. She would stay here, safe and sound, until Kerry and Jean Marie came back. She would rest, as promised.

The knock on the door as she was about to pull down the window shade wasn't Kerry's. No two-rap, three-rap deal, as Kerry had promised. It was an ordinary knock.

Backing away from the door, Hannah cried, "Who's there?"

"It's Ms. Quick, Hannah. I have the detective with me. He'd like to speak with you if you're feeling up to it."

Hannah let them in.

"I know it's hard to believe right now," Ms. Quick said, "but I actually have good news. I've received word that Lolly arrived home safely. Her parents were distraught, of course. Can't blame them. Now, if I can only get the rest of you to San Francisco intact. . . . Hannah, this is Detective Tesch. He has been assigned to help us. Please try to answer any questions he might have."

But, Hannah thought in silent protest, *I'm* the one with all the questions. Maybe this detective can give me some answers.

The man was short and balding and dressed in a neat brown suit and brown shirt, holding a round brown hat in his hands, which, Hannah noticed, were also brown: tanned and freckled. His brown shoes were shined to a high gloss. He didn't look anything like the detectives she'd seen on television.

As long as he could answer her questions, she didn't care *what* he looked like.

But he couldn't answer her questions. He was very nice, speaking softly and clearly, turning his brown hat around and around in his hands as he spoke, but he had no answers for her. He only had questions.

And Hannah had no answers. None that she could tell him. With Ms. Quick watching her with that frowny, worried look on her face, if Hannah told him what she was really thinking she knew she'd find herself off the train and in a padded cell before you could say, "Frog Drummond is alive and out for revenge."

The detective, whose name was Mr. Tesch, but whom Hannah had already named Mr. Brown, asked Hannah if she had seen the person who had imprisoned her in the "wooden box." He did *not* say "coffin." Maybe he thought it would upset her. He seemed like that sort of person.

When she told him no, she hadn't seen a thing, he nodded and asked her if she had any idea who it might have been. She had to bite her tongue.

"No," she lied. "I can't imagine . . ."

Her friends would have disagreed with that. They would have said the problem was, Hannah *could* imagine, and was doing just that.

But she *wasn't* — was she?

Mr. Brown-Tesch was no help. But he promised that he would check out the baggage car and "the . . . ah . . . place where you were held prisoner."

He made it sound like a jail, with bars and a sheriff and three meals a day. It hadn't been that nice.

"Why are you here alone?" Ms. Quick asked disapprovingly as they got up to leave.

"Kerry's taking a shower. It's okay. I'll keep the door locked. Where's Mack? Why isn't he with you?"

"He's talking to some of your classmates," the detective answered. "Helpful young man. Cares about you." He flushed slightly and shuffled his shiny brown shoes. "Grateful for the help. Don't you worry, miss, we'll find out how this happened. Could be a joke, maybe."

A sigh of disgust escaped from Hannah. He couldn't seriously think it was a joke, could he? Why did adults always think that bad things involving teenagers were just "jokes"? As if everyone Hannah knew was running around stuffing people into coffins, just for laughs.

She couldn't think of a single person who would think that was funny.

Well . . . scratch that. Maybe *one* person.

The two adults left, both visibly disappointed that Hannah hadn't had any answers. Ms. Quick warned her to stay in her compartment until her friends returned, and the detective asked her to "keep thinking. You might remember something that you've forgotten because you've been upset."

She closed the door after them, feeling more frustrated than when they'd arrived. She had expected so much help from the detective. But he, like everyone else, believed that Frog was dead. So how could the detective help her?

How could anyone?

Despondent, she stood looking out the window at the passing landscape for a few minutes before deciding she wasn't accomplishing anything. Better to rest as she'd promised. She'd be able to think more clearly when her mind was fresh.

It was too bright in the room for sleep. Hannah pulled the shades, plunging the room into an artificial "night." In the train station she and Kerry had tossed a coin to decide who got the upper berth. Kerry had lost. The climb up the little ladder was hers.

But I would feel safer up there, Hannah thought decisively, and moved to open the latch that held the upper bunk flat against the wall when not in use.

It seemed wrong, somehow, to be wasting time on sleep during her "educational excursion." But so far, the only education she'd received was the knowledge that someone was out to get her. She might not be learning any geography while she was napping, but at least she'd be *safe*.

The bunk, already made-up, fell forward, and Hannah clambered up the ladder and onto the bed.

Her knee hit something. She couldn't see, but she knew there was a small reading light up there. Her hand reached out, her fingers searching the wall for the switch.

As her fingers fumbled along the panelling, she noticed a sharp, oddly unpleasant odor. In the darkness, she tried to make out the shape of the long, bulky object on the bed. Had Kerry sneaked in a garment bag full of clothes and stashed it up here, figuring she'd move it before they went to bed that night? It seemed like the kind of thing Kerry would do. At last Hannah's fingers found the light switch. She turned it on.

It wasn't much of a light. The little bulb provided only a faint, sickly glow.

But, faint though it was, the glow illuminated the thing in Kerry's bunk.

And it wasn't a garment bag.

Hannah's mouth dropped open, but no sound emerged. Her eyes fastened in horror on the disgusting thing lying there on its back, stiff and unforgiving, emanating a strange odor. The eyes stared, unseeing, up toward the ceiling and the face was raw and ruined — a face she had once known —

a face almost unrecognizable because of the blazing inferno that had tortured it, and nearly consumed it. . . .

She had been right, after all.

Frog Drummond was not in his coffin where he belonged.

Frog Drummond was in Kerry's bunk.

Chapter 15

Voiceless with horror, Hannah toppled backward off the berth. When she hit the floor, she scuttled, crablike, until her back smacked up against the seat opposite the bunks. Eyes and mouth wide open in shock, she crouched there, silent and trembling.

Minutes passed. Hannah sat frozen, her eyes rivetted on the upper berth, her fisted hands pressed against her mouth.

Then she began shaking her head from side to side. The sound she uttered was a muted grunt of denial that, once started, she couldn't stop. "Uhuhuhuh," she moaned, head swinging from side to side, eyes dull with shock. "Uhuhuhuh."

But the dull glaze in her eyes quickly changed to bright, blazing terror.

She had to get out of there. Away from . . . *it*.

When she finally moved, she was no longer making a sound. She had sealed her lips, as if staying really, really quiet, might keep the thing on her bunk from coming after her. She crawled, sideways, still staring at the upper berth, until she was at the door. Reaching up, she unlatched it and yanked it open. Still mute, she threw herself out into the hall.

The door swung shut behind her.

For several seconds, Hannah lay on the dark carpet in the empty corridor, now allowing herself an anguished moan.

But the room right behind her held such horror, she couldn't stay there. She had to move, to escape, to seek safety. Away from that . . . that *thing*.

Scrambling to her feet, Hannah stumbled down the aisle. She still didn't scream. She was afraid to. It . . . might hear her.

She had half-run half-stumbled all the way to the end of the car when she realized she was headed in the wrong direction. Both Mack and Lewis's compartment and the showers were at the opposite end of the car.

Hannah groaned in dismay. She sagged against the wall. Why didn't someone come to help her? Where *was* everyone?

She couldn't stay here. Turning, she reversed her steps.

But when she reached a point of several feet beyond her compartment, she found that she couldn't continue. Her feet came to a complete halt on the carpet and refused to move.

"Help me," Hannah whispered, and began weeping.

She was still standing there, still weeping in despair when Kerry, in her white terrycloth robe, and Jean Marie, in her hot pink robe, emerged from the showers and saw her.

Kerry waved, Jean Marie called out something friendly, and Hannah watched through a haze of tears. They don't know, she thought dully. They don't know that I'm paralyzed here and they don't know what's waiting for them in the compartment. I can't tell them. I can't!

But she knew she would have to.

"Hannah?" Jean Marie asked as they approached and realized she wasn't directly outside the compartment as they had first thought. "What are you doing?"

"You're crying," Kerry said, hurrying over to Hannah. "What's wrong? I thought you were taking a nap." Alarm slid into her voice. "Hannah? *What?*"

"I . . . I . . ." Hannah swallowed hard. "Frog . . ."

"Get someone!" Kerry ordered Jean Marie. "Hurry!"

Jean Marie ran.

All Hannah could do was point toward the compartment with a shaky finger.

"I don't know why you're such a mess," Kerry said, putting an arm around Hannah's shoulders, "but from the look on your face, I'm guessing we won't go back into the compartment until Jean Marie gets here with help." With an edge of the wet towel hanging over her arm she swiped gently at Hannah's tear-streaked face. "Okay, Hannah?" Kerry asked softly, patting Hannah's shoulder.

"We'll just wait right here in the hall for Jean Marie."

Gulping gratefully, Hannah nodded in relief.

A few minutes later, Jean Marie ran down the corridor, followed by Mack and Lewis.

"Where *were* you guys?" Kerry demanded. "Something's happened. Why didn't you hear anything?"

"Playing pool," Mack answered. "In the rec center. Everybody's up there. What's going on?" His eyes went to Hannah's face. "I thought you were sleeping or I'd have been here. What happened?"

Alerted by the commotion, the conductor and Ms. Quick arrived.

All Hannah could say was, "In there," pointing to the compartment, "in the upper berth."

Kerry swallowed her curiosity and stayed with Hannah while the others opened the door and went inside.

They were only in there a few minutes. When they emerged, every face registered bewilderment.

"What?" Mack asked Hannah again. "We didn't see anything. What are we looking for?"

"In . . . in the upper *berth*," she managed. "I told you, in the upper berth."

Mack nodded. "Yeah. We looked. Nothing there."

Hannah blanched. "What? No, no, that's not right. Look again, Mack, please! There's . . . there's something there, there *is*! I *saw* it . . . I felt it . . ." her voice fell to a murmur.

His mouth grim, Mack turned and went back

inside the compartment. Ms. Quick and the conductor looked at Hannah, and then at each other, but no one said anything.

When Mack came back out, he was shaking his head. "There isn't anything there, Hannah, honest. I looked. I can tell someone was sleeping there, because the sheets are all messed up. But that's it. Come see for yourself."

"No!" Hannah shrieked, recoiling. "No! I'm not going back in there. Frog was there, he was! He was in my bunk just lying there, staring up at the ceiling and his face . . ." She sobbed, and her hands went to her mouth . . . "His face . . . it was horrible . . . all burned . . ."

"Hannah, stop this right now!" Ms. Quick said sharply, coming over to put an arm around her. "You fell asleep, you had a nightmare . . . understandable considering what you've been through. But you're going to make yourself sick. You must calm down."

Hannah lifted her head. "A dream?" she cried. "A dream? I hadn't even," she bit off the words, "*gone to sleep!*" She looked from one person to the next. "How could I? I couldn't climb onto the berth because he . . . he was in the way! So how could I have gone to sleep?"

Ms. Quick patted her shoulder. "Many times in nightmares we believe that we were awake the whole time. You must know that, Hannah. I'm sure this isn't the first bad dream you've ever had."

"It wasn't a dream!" Hannah shrieked. "I keep telling you — " But she could see no one believed her. Pulling free of Kerry's arm and Ms. Quick's hand, Hannah shouted, "I'll *show* you! I'll go back in there if that's the only way I can prove . . ." Taking a deep breath, she ran to the compartment, yanked the door open and burst inside crying out, "Come! Come and look and you'll see!"

Her heart was thudding sickeningly, her breathing labored as she stopped short directly opposite the upper berth, still suspended like a roof over her own, exactly as she had left it.

No, *not* exactly.

Except for rumpled white sheets, the bunk was empty.

Chapter 16

Hannah stared, disbelieving, at the empty berth.

"But I . . ." she whispered. "I . . ."

"It's okay, Hannah," Kerry said quickly, pushing Lewis and Mack aside to wrap an arm around Hannah's shoulders, "you just had a really rotten dream, that's all. Because of last night, I'll bet. I mean, you couldn't be over that horrible business already. I'd have nightmares, too, if I were you. We shouldn't have left you here alone."

Mack nodded agreement. "I can't believe we were playing pool and having a high old time while you were wrestling with demons. I'm sorry, Hannah."

"Me, too," Lewis said solemnly. "We'll stick together from now on, I promise."

Unable to speak, Hannah stared silently at the berth. *I wasn't even asleep yet. I was still awake when I saw . . . that* thing.

But there was nothing there. How could she argue with that? She saw it, they all saw it: the empty berth, with the sheets rumpled, as if someone had been sleeping in it. That someone had been her.

A dream? It had been a dream — a nightmare? She hadn't really seen it?

A long, deep shudder escaped from Hannah. She *had* seen it. Let them think what they wanted. She knew what she'd seen with her own eyes. But if she kept arguing, if she insisted that she had seen a dead person in her bunk, everyone would think the train had taken her into the *Twilight Zone* for good.

But, the thing was, it hadn't *been* a dead body. She knew that now. At first, when she'd seen it, of course she'd thought it was dead. Oh, it was burned, all right — horribly. But it had to be alive. How else would it have gotten up into the upper berth, and then gotten away. It was just *pretending* to be dead, to scare her. And scare her it had. No wonder there had been room for her in Frog's coffin. *He* wasn't using it. *He* was roaming around the train, hurting people and trying to scare them to death. Now Hannah knew for sure that Frog was alive and on the train. She had *seen* him.

She should have left the train when Lolly did. By the time they arrived in San Francisco, if they ever did, the last shred of her sanity would be gone like the landscape that whizzed by as the train raced across the tracks.

"I can't get through this day." Her voice was solemn and soft. "I can't. I don't want to be on this train anymore."

Everyone started talking at once, reassuring her, telling her they would stay with her and keep her safe. Mack said he wouldn't leave her side,

Lewis nodded agreement, Kerry held her hand and Ms. Quick thrust two aspirin and a paper cup full of water in Hannah's face.

None of it helped. How could they keep her safe from Frog when none of them believed he was after her? She wasn't going to bring it up again. She couldn't bear the looks that would appear on their faces. She would just do what they had told her to, go where they wanted her to, say what she thought they wanted to hear — but stay alert and on guard every single second, watching for him . . . waiting.

Sooner or later, he'd show up.

"You should sleep," Mack said. "You look really beat."

Hannah lifted her head. She wiped her face free of tears with the tissue Kerry had given her, tossed her head to shake her hair in place, and stood up. "I can't sleep. Let's do something. You said everyone was at the rec center. Let's go there."

Mack frowned. "You sure? Look, I'll stay here while you sleep."

"No. I don't want to sleep." She tried to smile brightly at the cluster of people gathered around her in the compartment. "You guys were right. It was just a bad dream. But I don't want to have it again. So let's play. That's what we're here for, right?"

Kerry looked at her with a quizzical expression on her face and said, "Well, if you're sure that's what you want, they're showing a movie this afternoon. We could grab some lunch in the Cafe and then watch Schwarzenegger get the bad guys."

"Sounds great!" Hannah said. "Let's go!"

The relief that appeared on every face told her she was doing the right thing, although Mack still looked uncertain. She could practically hear them thinking, Oh, good, everything's okay now. Everything's back to normal.

She would keep to herself the belief that absolutely *nothing* was normal. "Well, let's go!" she repeated, and led the way out of the compartment.

When they entered the recreation area where the movie was being shown, everyone seemed to be having a good time. Except for Dale and Eugene, who sat together off to Hannah's left staring stonily at the blank screen, everyone had apparently suspended all thoughts of danger. They cheered happily when the room went dark and the screen lit up.

Hannah didn't cheer. Sitting in a pitch-black, crowded room watching bodies being blown into oblivion was not what she needed. By concentrating with all of her might, she was able to tune out the on-screen mayhem and listen for a sound out of the ordinary, a movement that might be threatening, any sign that danger could be approaching in the total darkness.

That sound, when it came, wasn't the scream or shriek of pain that she was expecting. It was a sharp, *whizzing* sound that sent Hannah's head into an instinctive ducking motion. It came during the last few seconds of the film and no one around her seemed to notice the sound or the startled "Uh!" that followed. Afterward, Hannah would remember thinking at that exact moment, There! There it is! Something bad has happened.

And, following that thought came another: He's here. Frog is here.

She sat perfectly still, waiting, as the movie ended and people around her clapped and shouted their approval. The credits rolled, the lights came on, and she didn't move. Her eyes blinked steadily, but she was waiting.

People stood up, stretched, yawned, grinned at each other.

Mack stood up. Kerry and Jean Marie stood up.

Lewis did not stand up. He remained sitting in his chair.

And he said, slowly and with awe in his voice, "I think I've been stabbed." Hannah's silent reaction was, Well, of course you have. That sound I heard was the knife whizzing through the air. Then I heard you cry out. And I know Frog is here, so I'm not the least bit surprised.

Outwardly, she did what everyone else did. She hurried to Lewis's side in alarm.

The weapon wasn't a knife, after all. It was an ice pick. The thick wooden handle protruded from the back of Lewis's leather theater seat, while the sharp, narrow pick itself had penetrated the seat and impaled the flesh near Lewis's collarbone. A small but vivid red stain etched a half-moon, like some trendy trademark, on his white sweater. The half-moon was slowly oozing into a three-quarter moon, and Lewis's face was the murky beige of swamp water.

"Oh, my God," Kerry breathed.

"I don't think it's that bad," Mack hastened to reassure her. He knelt beside Lewis. "Too high. Hit the bone, I think." The crowd moving up the aisle past them, preoccupied with discussing the movie, seemed unaware of anything unusual until Mack called out, "Someone get the conductor! And Mr. Dobbs or Ms. Quick. Hurry up!"

Kerry lifted a pale face to Hannah and said angrily, "I *knew* we'd need that doctor! And now he's not here, all because of Lolly!"

But it wasn't Lolly's fault she almost got strangled, Hannah thought, and wondered if now someone would believe that Frog was alive and on the train.

Not that it mattered. She had already made up her mind. She was going to make sure, once and for all, that she was right.

There was only one way to do that.

She was going to open Frog's coffin.

Chapter 17

The fact that Lewis's wound proved to be minor, speedily disinfected and bandaged by Ms. Quick, failed to change Hannah's mind about making a trip to the baggage car.

And the fact that the detective had no answers for them, except to say that the ice pick had been stolen from the dining car, only intensified her determination to see for herself whether or not Frog was in his proper place.

If I don't, she thought as they all accompanied a shaken Lewis back to his compartment, I will *not* make it through the rest of this trip. One way or the other, I have to know.

She didn't want to tell anyone what she was planning. Their response, she was positive, would be disheartening. But there was no way on earth she was going into that baggage car alone.

They all went back to Lewis and Mack's compartment.

Hannah waited until the color had returned to Lewis's face. Then she announced firmly, "I'm going to the baggage car after dinner. I want to see for myself that Frog really is dead and he's where he belongs."

Lewis, Kerry, and Jean Marie gasped. But Mack only nodded. "I knew that's what you were thinking," he said. "I saw the look on your face when you spotted the ice pick in Lewis. You're going to open the coffin?"

Hannah nodded. "I have to." She knew that had Mack not been on her side, she wouldn't have had a chance of talking the others into joining her. She reached out and touched his arm in gratitude. "I have to know."

Kerry was still aghast. "Hannah, you *know* it's going to be horrible! He *burned* to death, for pete's sake!"

Hannah opened the door. "You're forgetting, Kerry, I've already *seen* him. Nightmare or not, what I saw in that upper berth is what Frog would look like now. So it won't be a complete shock to me. Are you coming with me?"

"I am," Lewis said, getting to his feet. He didn't waver, and seemed his old self. "I want to know who thinks I'd make a great ice cube."

"If Lewis can go when he's been hurt," Jean Marie said, "I'm not going to chicken out. I'm with you, Hannah."

"Well, I'm certainly not going to wait alone somewhere for you guys," Kerry exclaimed. "I think the whole idea is totally repulsive and useless. Frog is dead as a doornail and isn't bothering anyone. But if you have to, Hannah, you have to. So I'm going, too." But she added grimly as she stood up, "Just don't expect me to look, that's all. I'd die first!"

If we *don't* look, Hannah thought as they left for the dining car, you might die anyway, Kerry. Lolly almost did and I could have suffocated in that coffin, and an inch or two lower with that ice pick would have left you with no boyfriend. Whether Kerry thought so or not, they were doing the right thing.

They told no one of their plans.

Everyone at dinner was glad to see that Lewis was okay. To Hannah's surprise, Dale and Eugene stopped him at the entrance and asked how he was feeling. Lewis was as surprised as Hannah. "Fine," he mumbled.

"You were lucky," Dale said, moving away. "An inch or two lower or higher and . . ."

Eugene raised a hand to make a slicing motion across his own throat. "Yeah, you'd be up in heaven right now with good old Frog," he said with a grin. Then the two left to take a table at the rear of the car.

"Those two are weird," Lewis murmured. "In heaven? Aren't they awfully optimistic about Frog's final destination?"

"They're assuming an awful lot just by believing that he's *dead*," Hannah said sharply. "We won't know that for sure until we check that coffin."

There was a lot of complaining among the students about the detective asking too many questions and getting too few results.

"Some fun trip," one girl groused loudly. "I was just about to take a nice, long shower when he showed up at my door, asking me if I'd seen or heard anything unusual. Is he kidding? This whole *trip* is nuts!"

Another girl at the same table nodded in agreement. "I'm afraid to step outside our compartment alone. At first I thought what happened to that girl in the Cafe was somebody's idea of a sick joke. But what happened to Lewis sure wasn't funny."

Everyone agreed that it wasn't the least bit funny.

There was no laughter or light chatter in the dining car that night. Hannah couldn't help thinking how different the atmosphere was from the way it had been in the Cafe that first morning — before the attack on Lolly. She knew why they were all afraid.

Because there was no place to run to on a train.

After dinner, they gathered in Mack and Lewis's compartment, which was closest to the baggage car, until their fellow passengers had taken refuge in their own secure little rooms.

"We have to be quiet," Hannah warned, opening the door and peering out. "Ms. Quick is a nervous wreck. The slightest sound will set her off and she'll be hot on our trail. And that detective is still roaming around, too. Everyone tiptoe, okay?"

They had no flashlight. The corridors were dimly lit but the baggage car would be dark. As they made their way down the corridor, Lewis pointed out in a whisper that if they turned on a light, someone might see it from under the door.

"No one's going to be around," Hannah argued. "Not at this time of the night. Everyone's hiding in their compartments. But we probably shouldn't take any chances. We'll leave the light off."

"Someone should keep an eye out for the conductor," Jean Marie suggested. "I'll do it if you want. I'll wait outside and if I see him coming, I'll knock twice."

"No way," Lewis protested. "No one's doing anything alone. We go in together and take our chances together, period."

"If we get caught," Kerry said, "we'll make up some story. I'll say I needed something from my bag."

"Right," Lewis whispered in agreement. "Nobody will have trouble believing that."

The cars through which they passed were so still, so silent. No happy chatter, no giggling or laughter, no cheerful music sounded from behind closed doors. Only an occasional, nervous murmuring competed with the steady *ga-dink* of the wheels on the tracks.

Slowly, carefully, Mack pulled the baggage car door open. He checked to make sure no porter or conductor was around and then gestured that it was safe to enter.

"Can't see a thing," he murmured. They fell all over each other in the dark, a jumbled mass of confusion, all colliding elbows and knees and shoulders as they tried to get their bearings.

Then they moved off, cautiously, into the thick curtain of darkness.

"I don't need to see," Hannah whispered. "I can find the coffin in the dark. I know exactly where it is."

"How are you going to know if he's *in* there when you can't see?" Kerry asked.

Hannah began to move forward carefully, feeling with her feet for piles of luggage or boxes. "I'll know. I'll know the minute I open it."

"Then I'm *glad* it's so dark in here," Kerry said. "This way, you won't be able to see his face." To Lewis she said, "Under no circumstances let go of my hand. If you do, I'll scream."

With Mack holding her hand, and Lewis and Kerry and Jean Marie holding on to one another, Hannah slowly, carefully led the way across the baggage car to where the coffin was. As her eyes became accustomed to the gloom, she could make out shapes and was able to avoid several piles of luggage and stacks of boxes. Lewis tripped once and uttered a mild oath, and Kerry, following closely behind him, bumped into him and nearly fell.

Hannah knew that under any other circumstances, they all would have been laughing hysterically. But not now. Not in here.

"I don't see why we can't turn on the light," Kerry complained. "You said yourself, Hannah, there's no one out there now. I'm going to trip and break my neck."

Hannah shook her head. "No. I don't want a light on. Because when I lift the lid, if Frog's in there, you'll see him and scream your head off. Everyone on the train will come running. Just watch where you're going."

"How can I watch where I'm going when I can't *see*?" But Kerry subsided then, and they continued picking their slow, careful, silent way through the darkness.

Determined though Hannah was, she was shaking by the time they reached the long, solid shape sitting at chest-level against the wall. For one blank second, she couldn't remember why she was there.

Then she reminded herself, I am doing this so that I will know if Frog is the one who's been terrorizing us.

Hannah turned to peer into the blackness shrouding her friends. "Ready?" she whispered.

"No," Kerry said, "but you're going to open it anyway, so go ahead."

Mack whispered, "Ready? I'll help. You can't lift that lid by yourself." And he moved forward to grip the edge of the lid.

"On the count of three," Hannah said, her pulse racing wildly. "One . . . two . . . three . . ."

They had lifted the lid less than an inch when the click of a switch broke the breathless silence and the overhead light went on.

Blinking in surprise the five whirled simultaneously, as if they were attached.

The conductor stood in the doorway.

"What in blazes do you think you're doing?"

Chapter 18

Hannah flushed guiltily as all four hands instinctively let go of the lid, and it thudded shut. Hannah knew that no excuse in the world would convince the conductor that what they'd been about to do was the right thing. The truth, in this case, wasn't going to do the trick. She'd have to come up with something better.

The angry conductor began striding across the room toward them.

"I asked what you thought you were doing," the conductor demanded. "Am I crazy or were you people about to open that coffin?"

It sounded to Hannah as if he wasn't sure exactly what he had seen. Probably because he couldn't believe what his own eyes had told him. Too gross, even for teenagers.

"We were just looking for something," she said quickly, taking a half step forward. "I'm the one who was shut in the coffin, remember?"

He nodded slowly, suspicion still clouding his eyes.

"Well, I lost a very valuable ring, one my grandmother gave me, and I've looked everywhere else. So I decided it must have come off in here somewhere. My friends offered to help me look."

"You weren't trying to open that coffin?" he asked. It was clear he wanted to believe her, but was still unsure.

Hannah gasped. *"Open* it? You really think after what happened to me, I'd open that thing?" There, she hadn't actually lied. She had simply asked a question.

The conductor looked dubious. "Looked to me like the three of you had your hands on the coffin."

"We were checking the edges to see if maybe it was somewhere around here. But," Hannah said with feigned disappointment, "it's not."

"I don't want you kids messing around in here," the conductor said sternly. "Can't have that."

Hannah's cold bones warmed with relief. He'd bought her story.

"Didn't your teacher tell you to stay in your compartments?" he added, disapproval heavy in the words.

Hannah nodded contritely, her eyes on the floor. "Yes, sir, she did. And that's where we're going, right this minute, I promise. Thanks for being a good guy."

He *harumphed* and stood aside to let them pass.

Flashing him grateful smiles, they all hurried out of the baggage car.

But the smiles quickly faded as they exited into the dim, empty corridor.

"Well, that certainly was a waste of time!" Kerry announced in disgust. "You guys hardly even got the lid open. We almost got into serious trouble, and for nothing!"

"It wasn't for nothing," Hannah said calmly, "and it wasn't a waste of time." She moved ahead to lead the way back. "I found out what I wanted to know."

Chapter 19

Kerry stopped in her tracks. "You couldn't have!" she cried. "How could you have found out anything? That lid wasn't open more than a crack."

Hannah turned to face her friends. "That was enough. Frog was in there." She could hardly believe it herself, but it was true. She had seen it with her own eyes. Still, where had he been while *she* was in there?

Jean Marie moved forward. "How could you tell, Hannah? I agree with Kerry. The conductor turned on the light too soon."

"No. No, he didn't. I saw that tattoo."

Mack frowned. "Tattoo? What tattoo?"

Hannah leaned against the paisleyed wall. "Frog had a tattoo on his left wrist. It was gross. A rat with wings and bared fangs." She shuddered. "It was ugly. And that's what I saw in the coffin. A wrist with a winged rat tattooed on it. Nobody else at school had anything like that. So I knew it was Frog." She shook her head in disbelief. "I was so sure . . ."

"Well, you were the only one who thought he might not be in there," Kerry pointed out. Relief filled her voice as she added, "I'm glad that's over!"

Hannah lifted her head. "Kerry, aren't you forgetting something? All we know now is that Frog really is dead and where he's supposed to be. But that doesn't explain anything else. We still don't know who hurt Lolly and put me in the coffin and stabbed Lewis. Or, for that matter, where Frog's body was when I was in there."

The door to the baggage car opened and the conductor stuck his head out to deliver a stern glare.

"C'mon, let's go," Lewis urged. "We can think better back in one of the compartments. We'll talk about it there."

Hannah insisted they stop at Lewis and Mack's compartment. "I'm not going back into ours," she said firmly. "I couldn't sleep in that bunk no matter how beat I was. Not after this morning."

Kerry groaned. "Oh, Hannah, I thought you agreed that was just a terrible nightmare. Are you telling me we're not going to get a good night's sleep tonight? After the day we've had? I'm not sleeping in that compartment alone! And at least you know now that Frog couldn't possibly have been in your bed, right?"

Hannah didn't answer until they were safely inside and seated, with the door locked. "Kerry," she said slowly, deliberately, "Frog may be where he belongs, but there's someone *else* out to get us. And whoever it is *knows* which compartment is ours." She glanced at the faces of the other three. "I don't think *any* of us should stay in our compartments tonight. It's not safe."

While they pondered that, Hannah stared out the window, filled now with their pale reflections and, beyond those images, the soft golden haze of distant lights. I wish I were there, Hannah thought. I wish I were in that town, in one of those houses or one of those cars on the highway. I'd be safe there.

She couldn't stop thinking about Frog. Okay, he was in the coffin now, where he belonged.

But where had he been while *she* was in there? And how had he appeared in Kerry's bunk that afternoon? The thought that someone might have taken him out, removed his body and placed it elsewhere, was sickening. How could anyone do something so horrible?

Still, was moving a body any more horrible than strangling someone or trying to suffocate someone in a closed box or splintering someone's flesh with an ice pick? Someone who would do one of those things probably wouldn't even hesitate to lift a corpse from its place of rest and deposit it elsewhere.

"I have an idea," Mack said, leaning forward on the seat. "Why don't we go to the Observation Lounge? Nobody will be there this time of night. We won't be able to see anything out of all that glass, but we'll have it to ourselves. No one will expect us to be up there, so we should be safe, right?"

"Is it open?" Lewis asked.

"I think it's always open. Worth a try, right?"

The idea appealed to Hannah. Simply being somewhere unexpected would give them an edge. No one would think to look for them up in the Observation Lounge.

"I'm for it," she said eagerly. "Jean Marie?"

Jean Marie nodded. "But I'll have to go tell my roomies I'm staying with you guys tonight, or they'll call out the guards. I won't say where we're staying, though. Come with me?"

They all went together, first to Jean Marie's compartment, where one of her roommates questioned her three times before finally opening the compartment door less than an inch to peer out. Then they went on to the Observation Lounge.

It was open. And empty.

"Told you," Mack said in obvious relief. The car, decorated all in blue, seemed larger than any of the others because of the wide expanse of glass on ceiling and walls. There were comfortable seats to lounge on and tables and chairs stationed in windowed corners.

"I wish we had something to eat," Lewis said as he took a seat and pulled Kerry down beside him. "I'm starving!"

"They'd feed you here during the day," Hannah said. She and Mack took the seat opposite Kerry and Lewis, while Jean Marie grabbed a seat for herself across the aisle. "Snacks and Cokes. But not now. Too late."

"I could get something to eat in Salt Lake City. We stop there in half an hour."

"Ms. Quick will never let you off the train," Jean

Marie said, curling up in a little ball with her head on the armrest. "No one's supposed to get off. I heard her tell the conductor."

"No one's going to feed you, Lewis," Kerry said, "so you might as well go to sleep."

Hannah had already closed her eyes. She leaned her head against Mack's shoulder and tried to close off her mind as well.

But it wouldn't stop churning. Were they really safe here? Maybe someone had heard them sneaking through the cars for a second time that night. Maybe whoever was after them would check the compartments, find them empty, and begin searching the entire train. Sooner or later, their stalker, whoever it was, would arrive at this car.

I won't sleep, she resolved, I'll stay awake all night. It's the only way to be sure.

But Mack's chest felt safe and solid and she was exhausted . . .

Chapter 20

When Hannah next opened her eyes, it was morning. The others awakened, too, stretching and groaning, to bright desert sunshine blazing down upon them as the train sped across Nevada.

"I feel like I slept in a sandbox," Jean Marie moaned. "I'm all itchy."

"My neck hurts," Kerry complained, and the first words out of Lewis's mouth were, "I'm starving."

But all Hannah could think was, We're all safe. We're all still here and we're safe.

She smiled sleepily at Mack. "You were right about coming here," she said softly. "It was a super idea. Did you sleep?"

He nodded and rubbed the back of his neck. "Yeah. I wasn't going to, but when no one showed up by three in the morning, I guess I relaxed and fell asleep. Not much of a protector, am I?"

"I think you must be," she disagreed, "because here we all are, and we're all in one piece."

"*Five* pieces," Lewis corrected. His curly hair was askew, with little carroty bunches sticking out every which way and he moved stiffly, the result of sleeping sitting up with Kerry's head on his chest. "Now, can we please go eat before I shrivel up and die right here on the spot?"

"I have to take a shower first," Jean Marie announced, standing up and stretching. "I cannot possibly go into the dining car or the Cafe looking like I slept under the train instead of in it. But I'll hurry, Lewis, I promise."

Lewis made a face, but when Kerry and Hannah both agreed that a shower had to precede breakfast, he gave in and agreed to wait for them.

"We'll stand guard," he volunteered, "me and Mack. But we're only giving you five minutes, not a second more, understood?"

What they understood even as they nodded agreement was that Kerry Oliver had never taken a shower and dressed in less than thirty minutes in her entire life. But they also understood that Mack and Lewis would wait outside the shower room for them no matter how long it took.

The girls gathered their shower things and fresh clothing from their compartments.

"You are the only redhead I know who would dare wear that horrible shade of pink," Kerry teased Jean Marie as they hurried to the shower room, robes over their arms.

Jean Marie laughed. "It's just a robe, Kerry. I'm not planning to wear it in public."

"Quit arguing," Hannah said mildly. "If we don't hurry up, the showers will be filled to overflowing with bodies."

But the white tiled room was empty when they arrived. Hannah felt safe with Mack and Lewis stationed outside, and after a night's sleep, restless though it may have been, she felt more optimistic than she had since the attack on Lolly. Frog was where he belonged and as far as they knew, there had been no new attacks during the night. There had been no screaming, no uproar, no commotion — maybe it was all over now. Maybe their crazy tormentor had been scared off by the appearance of the railroad detective and had left the train in Salt Lake City last night.

Comforted by that thought, Hannah stepped inside one of the three shower cubicles. Kerry and Jean Marie did the same.

Jean Marie finished first. Over the roar of rushing water, Hannah heard a shower door close and knew it was Jean Marie's. Kerry had that mane of long black hair to wash and rinse. She couldn't possibly be done already.

Lathering her own hair with shampoo, Hannah thought, Jean Marie and I will both be dressed and ready to go long before Kerry, and then we'll have to be patient while she fools with that hair of hers. Mack and Lewis will go nuts, waiting.

But the aches and pains of an awkward sleeping position disappeared under the soothing hot water. It felt so good, Hannah hated to turn it off. She stayed in the shower longer than usual.

Finally, the thought of Mack and Lewis waiting stabbed her with guilt. Sighing, she turned off the water. Kerry's shower was still going strong.

Hannah fumbled for her towel.

It wasn't hanging on the door where she thought she'd put it.

"Hey, Jean Marie," she called, swiping at the water running down her cheeks, "grab my towel, will you? I think I left it on that little bench over there."

There was no answer. How could anyone hear anything over the thundering rush of Kerry's shower water?

Hannah raised her voice. "Jean Marie? Are you out there?"

Nothing.

She must have already left to join Lewis and Mack. How could someone who always looked so together dress that quickly?

Mumbling under her breath, Hannah left the cubicle and found her towel and her clothes. Drying and dressing quickly, turbanning her hair in the damp towel, she yelled at Kerry to "get a move on" and pulled the door open.

Mack and Lewis were talking to Eugene. When they spotted Hannah, they moved forward eagerly. Eugene left abruptly, as if he was trying to avoid Hannah.

"Finally!" Lewis exclaimed, "now we can go eat." He patted his stomach. "Where's Kerry?"

"Still in the shower." Hannah's eyes surveyed the corridor. "Where'd Jean Marie go?"

Mack and Lewis exchanged confused glances. Mack spoke first. "Jean Marie? She didn't go any-where. We haven't seen her."

Hannah tilted her head. "Very funny. Now, where is she? If she's hiding and it was your idea, your sense of humor is sick. It's not funny."

Mack took a step forward. "Hannah, Jean Marie didn't come out here. She must still be in the shower."

Hannah jolted upright and sucked in her breath. "You're not kidding, are you? She really didn't come out here?"

He shook his head. Lewis did the same.

"But . . . but she's not in here with us." Hannah glanced over her shoulder, into the shower room. "She's *not*. And there's . . . there's no place to hide in here. My cubicle and Jean Marie's are empty and Kerry's still in hers."

"Hannah!" Kerry shrieked, "do you have the door open? I can feel cold air. Cut it out!"

"Wait a sec," Hannah told the boys, closing the shower room door. "Jean Marie?" she called, although it was quite clear there was no place to hide in the tiny room. It held no secret niches, no roomy nooks and crannies. Besides the three skinny cubicles, there was only a small white bench sitting in the middle of the room.

When Hannah said the name again, her voice came out in little more than a tremulous whisper. "Jean Marie?"

There was no answer.

There was only the constant drumming of a steady stream of water pulsating from Kerry's shower head.

Chapter 21

A crowd gathered in the corridor outside the shower room as the railroad detective checked things out. Kerry, her brows knitted in worry, absentmindedly rubbed her wet hair with a towel. Lewis paced, swinging his arms back and forth impatiently. Hannah and Mack stood quietly together, his arm around her shoulders, her face drawn and white.

"Your friend's playing a joke on you," Mr. Tesch said when he came out. He was smiling. "C'mere, I'll show you."

They followed him back inside.

He stood in the center of the small room, pointing upward. "See those plastic panels up there?" He climbed up on the bench under the light, reached up and easily slid one of the lightweight panels sideways, revealing a large opening. "They're very lightweight," he said. "Slide in and out in a minute. The ducts up here lead all over the train. Your friend climbed up there and probably came down somewhere else, maybe in one of the compartments."

"No," Hannah said. "She wouldn't do that. Jean Marie wouldn't. Not ever, but especially not now. She would never scare us like this."

To her surprise, the detective took her seriously. "No? Doesn't have that kind of sense of humor?"

"No. She wouldn't think that was funny, worrying us. If she went up there, and I guess she must have, it was because someone made her do it."

The detective left the bench. "You hear anything while you were in the shower? Sounds of a struggle?"

Hannah shook her head. "No. Too much water running. I only heard Jean Marie's shower door click shut, that's all."

The man frowned. "Seems like you'd have heard someone pushing or pulling your friend up through the ceiling."

Not if she was unconscious, was Hannah's immediate reaction. "No one heard *me*," she said, "when I was being dragged to the baggage car. Whoever grabbed me made sure of that. He could have done the same thing to Jean Marie . . . covered her mouth so she couldn't make a sound."

He nodded. "Good point. All right, we'll get on it right away. Give me a description of the missing girl. And I want all of you to return to your compartments and stay there until I get back to you, okay?"

"We want to help look," Lewis said. "She's *our* friend. We can't just sit around and wait."

After giving that some thought, the detective nodded. "Fair enough. Divide up into groups and stay together, I insist on that. And get back to me if you see or hear anything. We'll find your friend, don't you worry."

When he had hurried away, Mack took charge, dividing the Parker High students into seven groups of four people each. "Spread out," he ordered. "Everybody take a different car. Wherever you find one of those ceiling panels, check that first. Climb up on something, lift the panel, and check it out. If you see *anything* you think you shouldn't, find Tesch and tell him."

Eugene was nowhere to be seen, but Dale asked, "So, if we find her, do we get a reward?" He grinned slyly. "Like maybe a date with the damsel in distress after we rescue her?"

Some people laughed, others tittered in embarrassment for Dale.

Everyone knew Jean Marie Westlake wouldn't be caught dead in the company of Dale Sutterworth, any more than she would have in Frog's company.

Hannah gasped at that thought. Caught *dead*? That no longer seemed like a harmless expression.

The search began.

Hannah pushed the wet hair back from her forehead as their group headed for the Observation Lounge to check it out. Kerry's hair was plastered down her back and had already soaked through her blouse. But she uttered not one word of complaint as they hurried through the cars.

Atta girl, Kerry, Hannah thought.

The Observation Lounge, all glass and sunshine,

was as empty as it had been when they awakened that morning. Everyone was out looking for Jean Marie.

Because the ceiling was mostly glass, there were no panels to check.

"Waste of time," Lewis muttered as they turned to leave. "Should have skipped this car." They all nodded in agreement, but at that very instant, a shrill scream split the air over their heads.

They stopped, frozen in their tracks.

Suddenly, a bright blur of hot pink sailed past the window in front of them, arcing downward like an arrow aimed at the ground, and disappeared.

Instinctively, Hannah's gaze shot to the ceiling glass and for just one tiny split-second, she thought she saw a movement overhead . . . the heel of a boot? Then it was gone, and there was nothing.

"What was *that*?" Lewis asked. "Something fell off the roof?"

Kerry turned to Hannah, her dark eyes fearful. "Pink . . ." she stammered, barely managing to squeeze out the words. "That pink . . . Jean Marie's robe . . ."

Hannah sucked in her breath. Jean Marie? No . . .

"We don't know that was her," Lewis said nervously, peering out the window.

Hannah stood up. "We can't wait to be sure," she said, her lips trembling. "The train's going too fast. We'll get too far away . . ."

Without hesitation, her arm shot up and her hand

closed around the emergency cord overhead. She yanked with great force.

Their ears rang with the agonizingly long, drawn-out scream of the train's wheels. After what seemed like an eternity, the train slowed and came to an angry halt.

Chapter 22

Hannah and her friends sat like statues, scarcely breathing, in the Observation Lounge where Ms. Quick had ordered them to wait for word on Jean Marie.

"I'm sure it wasn't her," she had said emphatically. "Maybe it was a scarf you saw, or even a newspaper blown by the wind."

A newspaper? A *pink* newspaper? Hannah shrank back against the seat then, biting her lower lip to keep from screaming, Just go find out! Hurry! Come back and tell me it wasn't Jean Marie, that she wasn't tossed off the roof of this train, tell me that! That's all I want to hear.

But when Ms. Quick returned, the conductor at her side, their faces told the story.

"I'm sorry," the teacher said softly, "I'm so sorry. Jean Marie is . . . is . . ." She couldn't continue.

Kerry screamed and Hannah's eyes filled with tears and the boys sat in mute disbelief, their hands in their laps.

"Mr. Dobbs is leaving the train now," Ms. Quick

added gently. "An ambulance is coming for . . . for Jean Marie, and he'll be going with it. We can't turn the train around, so we'll be going on to California. Those of you who want to leave the tour upon our arrival in San Francisco this afternoon may do so. The school is arranging plane transportation for anyone who wants it."

"And the detective?" Kerry asked bitterly, tears streaming down her cheeks, "what is *he* doing about this? I thought he came on the train to keep stuff like this from happening. Where *was* he when Jean Marie was thrown from the train?"

"Still looking for her. But none of us thought to look *outside* the train. Whoever did this must have taken Jean Marie up through the panels in the shower room and onto the roof of the train. He's on his way here now to ask you all a few more questions. I'd appreciate it if you'd be as helpful as possible."

Hannah could stand no more. Jumping up, she brushed past the adults and ran from the car. When Mack cried out at her to wait for him, she ignored his shout and kept going.

She ran all the way to the compartment. Sobs of grief and cries of anger rang from behind closed doors. The news about Jean Marie had spread quickly. But Hannah did not stop to talk to anyone. She needed desperately to be alone.

The compartment that had seemed so frightening yesterday — was that only yesterday? — seemed now warm and welcoming and private, so private. Let Mack and Lewis and Kerry answer Mr. Tesch's questions. She, for one, had no answers. None at all.

The very second they arrived in San Francisco, she was going to board a plane to Chicago, even if she was the only one who did.

I should have gone back when the train wheels told me to, she thought. I didn't listen, and I've been sorry ever since.

As Hannah reached her compartment, the train began moving again, quickly picking up speed, leaving behind the sound of the mournful ambulance wail as it arrived on the scene.

I will never see Jean Marie again, Hannah thought, and fresh tears filled her eyes.

When she opened the door, the compartment was dark, the window shade still pulled down from the day before. Hannah took a few steps and yanked the shade upward.

"Hello, Hannah," a voice said from behind her. "I thought you'd never get here."

Chapter 23

Hannah gasped and whirled, her back against the window, to find herself facing Lolly Slocum. She was dressed in boy's clothes — jeans, cowboy boots, plaid shirt and denim jacket — an outfit Frog had often worn. Her lank blonde hair was hidden under a worn felt cowboy hat.

She leaned against the door and smiled. "Hi, Hannah, how's it going? Not too well, I guess." She clucked her tongue sympathetically. "Too bad."

Hannah found her voice. "Lolly? You scared me half to death! What are you doing here? I thought you went home . . ."

"Went home?" The cowboy hat swung from side to side. "Not really. I told that idiot doctor I had motion sickness really bad. She was afraid I'd barf on her shiny black doctor's bag, so she found me a sleeping car and stashed me in a compartment and left me there. Or so she thought. Said she'd be back to check on me, but if she ever did come back, I was long gone. I just walked off that train and got back on this one. No problem." Then she added, in a confidential tone of voice, "I think that bag of hers was real leather, Hannah. Very fancy-schmancy."

Confused, Hannah frowned. "But . . . Ms. Quick heard from your family. They said you got back to Chicago okay."

"I sent that message myself, you twit!"

"You . . . you've been on the train this whole time? No . . . someone would have seen you."

"No one saw me because I didn't *want* them to. Not even Dale and Eugene. It would have spoiled everything." Lolly shrugged. "There are plenty of places to hide on this train."

Hannah's frown deepened, but along with her confusion a new feeling began to stir — an uneasiness, as if she were stepping up to the edge of a cliff and didn't dare look down for fear of getting dizzy. "You got back on the train but didn't tell anyone? You were . . . you were *hiding*?"

Lolly nodded and smirked with satisfaction. "Those ceiling panels in the shower room?"

Hannah thought of Jean Marie, and felt sick. "What about them?"

"They're in every rest room. Along with one of those little benches for people who are old or tired and have trouble bending to tie their shoes. Those benches are great for standing on to move the ceiling panel back, and then it's a cinch to hoist yourself up into the crawl space. It's not bad up there, not bad at all."

Hannah tried to speak and couldn't. She was

seeing Jean Marie plummeting to the dry, hard-baked desert floor from the roof of the train. Nausea threatened to overwhelm her.

Lolly's voice was light, teasing. "Feeling sick, Hannah? Your lovely trip hasn't been so lovely, has it?"

Fighting to stay calm, Hannah said, "Lolly, what are you doing here? You should be home or in a hospital. That noose around your neck . . ."

Lolly threw her head back and laughed. Sunshine streaming in through the unshaded window sent a gold, metallic shimmer into her pale blue eyes. "Oh, Hannah, don't be silly. I did that myself! When we went through the tunnel. Dale and Eugene never saw a thing. Too dark. They're not all that bright, anyway. If they heard anything, they never guessed it was me knotting that scarf around my poor little neck."

Hannah's jaw dropped. She stared, speechless.

"I'm good at knots. I worked on a boat one summer, to earn money." Her voice deepened, took on a note of harshness. "I didn't spend my summers vegging out around a pool, like you guys."

Hannah's face was a study in bewilderment. "You strangled yourself? Why? What for? I don't get it."

Lolly smiled again. "You will. Oh, you *will* get it, Hannah. Everything you deserve. Soon. But it wouldn't be any fun killing you without telling you why."

Killing? Hannah slid down onto one of the seats, her eyes on Lolly's face. "Lolly, what . . ."

"What, indeed?" Lolly laughed again, deeper and

harsher this time. An ugly sound. Looking at Hannah's hands she said, "You really did a number on your fingernails trying to get out of that coffin, didn't you?" And then she added with a sly grin, "You're not as lightweight as you look, Hannah. I had one heck of a time getting you into that baggage car."

When Hannah spoke, her voice came out thin and high-pitched. *"You?"*

Lolly nodded. "You bet! Too bad I missed any vital organs on your friend Lewis." Lolly shook her head regretfully. "I couldn't believe it when I saw him moving around the train a few hours later. I guess I'll just have to practice, practice, practice."

When Hannah didn't speak — because she couldn't — Lolly slapped her knee with her hand and laughed heartily. "Hannah, I wish you could have seen your face when you climbed onto that bunk. Or tried to. It was hilarious. Wish I'd had a video camera."

"You . . . you were there? When I saw . . . Frog?"

"Oh, Hannah, you're so dense! That wasn't him. How could it be? He's dead, thanks to you and your stupid, rotten friends! That was *me* in your bunk."

"But — how . . . ?"

"I wasn't in Drama Club for nothing. I wanted to act but that idiot Gruber wouldn't even give me the chance. Said I'd be perfect for makeup and hair." Lolly sneered in disgust. "Meaning I'd never appear on a stage while *she* was in charge. But . . ." the pale eyes glittered in triumph, "it came in handy after all, didn't it, Hannah? Doing the makeup, I mean. Didn't I look great as Roger — or *Frog* as you all called him? Come on," she said coaxingly, "admit it. I did a super job, right?"

Hannah wanted to stand up. She wanted to stand up and run from this calm, smiling, crazy person who had shut her in a coffin and tried to kill Lewis and . . .

"Mack?" she asked. "You locked Mack in that shed back in Denver?"

"Oh, big deal. I wanted to do something a lot worse, but I never got the chance. I was going to set it on fire. I thought it would be appropriate if Mack died the same way Roger did. But," Lolly sighed heavily, "too many people were passing back and forth at the entrance to the alley. I knew someone would save him.

"Speaking of your buddies, Hannah," Lolly continued, as friendly as if they were discussing a favorite class in school, "Kerry was supposed to find me in that upper berth, not you. I saw you guys tossing a coin in the train station — everyone was doing the same thing to decide who got the top bunk — and I could tell by the look on her face that she lost. Making myself look all burned and gross was aimed at her, not you." Her eyes narrowed. "The little witch. Roger told me how she treated him." Her voice softened, became dreamy, "He told me everything . . ."

"You were hiding in that upper berth all that time?"

"No, dummy! There's a ceiling panel right above it."

"But why?" Hannah whispered, "why are you doing this?"

Lolly snorted, her eyes cold. "Are you kidding? Roger is *dead*, Hannah. Dead! Gone forever! I loved him. And you were all so rotten to him. He didn't deserve that, Hannah. He was new and scared and he'd been dumped by his parents. He didn't deserve to be treated like pond scum."

Hannah hung her head. "We didn't know . . ." she murmured.

In one huge stride, Lolly was in front of her, bringing her arm up to whack Hannah on the side of the head with all her might. It lifted Hannah up and toppled her sideways. Her right ear and cheek cracked sharply against the wooden arm of the seat.

"Don't say you didn't know!" Lolly hissed, bending over Hannah. "You *should* have known! What kind of people *are* you?"

Then the anger seemed, suddenly, to drain out of her and she straightened up, saying sadly, "It doesn't matter. Roger is gone and I don't have anything without him. Dale and Eugene are losers." Then her face darkened and her eyes turned cold and hard as marbles. "But Roger died mad at me, Hannah, and that's *your* fault!"

"No, it's *not*!" Hannah said angrily. No one had ever hit her before in her life, and Lolly had hit her twice, on the back of the head that night, and now on her face. "Why did you kill Jean Marie?"

"Because Roger loved her." Lolly's pale eyes, no longer glittering with triumph, rested on Hannah's face. They were full of a terrible pain. "He really loved her. He only dated me because I was willing and Jean Marie wasn't." Lolly half-turned toward the window and looking out, said dully, "I hated Jean Marie more than I've ever hated anyone."

She isn't looking at me, Hannah thought, every nerve in her body on the alert. She's forgotten I'm here. She's off somewhere else, thinking about Jean Marie. I won't get another chance like this.

Moving like someone shot from a cannon, Hannah flew to her feet and threw herself at the door, unlatching it in one swift, sure motion. She was out in the hall and running before Lolly had even turned around.

Chapter 24

Hannah had fled the length of two cars when she pulled a door open and ran headlong into Mack. Kerry and Lewis were right behind him.

"Whoa!" Mack cried, reaching out to enfold her. "We were just coming to get you. You okay? I thought that detective would never let us leave." Then he drew her away from him and looked down into her face. "Hannah? What's wrong?"

"Lolly," Hannah gasped. She turned and pointed backward. "Lolly — back there . . . she — it's . . . it's Lolly — "

"Lolly?" Kerry echoed. "Hannah, Lolly got off the train. Remember?" Then, "Hannah, have you been napping? Did you have another nightmare?"

"No!" Hannah shouted. "It's *Lolly*! She killed Jean Marie! She told me. Come *on*!" And without waiting for an answer, she turned and began running back to the compartment.

Her friends followed, shaking their heads. Kerry muttered under her breath.

They ran into the conductor on their way and

Hannah insisted he come, too. "You have to arrest her," she babbled, her eyes feverish with intent. "You can do that, can't you? It's *your* train! She's a murderer, you have to arrest her. Get Mr. Tesch, *hurry!*"

Before the bewildered conductor could make sense of all that, Mr. Tesch called out to them from the doorway. He had been looking for Hannah to ask her the questions she'd skipped out on earlier.

"Hurry up," she cried urgently as they reached the compartment. "She's in here!"

She didn't wait for him to join them. Taking a deep breath, she slammed her palm down hard on the door latch and pushed the door open. "She's in here!" she cried, "Lolly's in here. You'll see that I wasn't dreaming."

But as the door swung open, a gust of hot, breathless desert air rushed toward them. It came from a huge, jagged hole in the window. The paisly curtains danced around it. The steady *ga-dink, ga-dink, ga-dink* of the wheels surged upward into the small space.

In one mass movement, they all piled inside, the conductor exclaiming in dismay over the ruined window. Hannah's eyes darted about the room, looking for signs of Lolly.

The room was empty.

"Hannah?" Kerry whispered, pointing. "Look at the mirror."

They all looked.

Slashed across the small rectangle of glass over

the sink, written in bright pink, which Hannah recognized as her own Pink Powderpuff lipstick, were the words:

I'LL BE WITH ROGER NOW.
I'M NOT SORRY FOR ANYTHING
L.

"Oh no!" the conductor breathed. "She threw herself out the window!"

A stunned silence filled the room, mixing with the hot air blasting in through the jagged hole. Slowly, carefully, they all moved as close to it as they dared. One by one, they looked out, expecting to see below them a dry desert floor. Instead, they found themselves gazing down upon a massive crevasse in the earth running for miles alongside the tracks. It was dry and hard and rocky on both sides and appeared to be bottomless.

"Lolly jumped into *that?*" Lewis whispered. "That — that canyon? She must have broken every bone in her body!"

A wisp of torn denim clung to one of the spikes of broken glass. The detective lifted it carefully, held it in his hand.

"She was wearing a denim jacket," Hannah told him.

Kerry's eyes fastened on the conductor. "Aren't you going to stop the train?"

He shook his head. "No point, Miss. We'd never find her down there. I'll put in a call to the local

Search and Rescue back there and give them the location. They'll find her." Then he sighed heavily and left. The detective went with him, promising Hannah he'd be back soon so she could fill him in on everything Lolly had told her.

"You won't be doing any harm by telling me," he pointed out gently, "now that she's dead."

"No," Hannah said softly when the two men had gone, "I don't believe it. She's playing another trick on us. She's hiding. And I know exactly where to look!"

Her friends stared at her as if they weren't sure they'd heard her correctly and hoped they hadn't.

"She *told* me," she explained, "she told me where she'd been hiding all that time." She ran to the upper berth, yanked it down from the wall. "In here." But there was no Lolly looking like Lolly and no Lolly madeup to look like Frog. Nothing.

An embarrassed silence filled the room. "Hannah — " Mack began, but she interrupted him.

"No, no, look, . . . okay, so she's not in there. There are other places — she hid all over the train. Please, we *have* to find her. If we don't, she'll come back and hurt more people. Me — or Mack — she was so angry — "

"I'll help you look," Mack said gently, taking her arm. "Lewis? Kerry?"

Hannah saw the look he gave them, knew it meant, humor her, she's upset. She didn't care. As long as they helped her look for Lolly, it didn't matter *why*.

The search took all afternoon. Every time one of them wanted to give up, Hannah insisted they continue, her voice cracking with anxiety, her eyes burning with determination. "We'll *find* her, I know we will! We have to keep looking."

While they searched, she told them everything that Lolly had said. Kerry was skeptical at first, but Hannah's voice had a ring of truth to it and eventually, it all made sense.

"Did you find out where she put Frog while you were in the coffin?" Lewis asked.

Hannah shook her head. "No. There wasn't time. But when we find her, I'm going to make her tell me."

But they didn't find Lolly.

When Lewis and Kerry stopped to eat something, Hannah refused to join them. "I haven't checked the ceiling in Kitty Winn's compartment yet. You go ahead." They eyed her nervously, but they left.

Mack stayed with her the whole time. He seemed to sense that this was something she had to do, and for that she was grateful.

They found nothing, no sign of Lolly beyond two wrinkled candy wrappers in one of the crawl spaces and a blue comb with two broken teeth in another.

At four o'clock, Lewis and Kerry caught up with them to warn Hannah that they had less than an hour before arriving in California. "We're supposed to get our things together," she said carefully.

"We're going to be leaving the train, Hannah, and all of this terrible stuff will be over."

"Yeah," Lewis added, his gray eyes sympathetic as he looked at Hannah, "and Lolly's gone, Hannah. We proved that, right? Are you still going to fly back home right away?"

Hannah nodded wearily. She was so tired her body felt like rubber. Her head ached. "I just want to go home," she said quietly. "I'm sorry I made you waste your afternoon. You were right. I just didn't want to believe she'd jumped. I should have known. She sounded so sad, so hopeless and she missed Frog so much . . ."

Giving up the futile search, they rested in their compartments during the last hour of the trip.

It was a strange group of teenagers that left the train. People waiting in the train station stared at them: twenty-eight teenagers not making a sound other than soft murmurs. A sight not seen every day.

Hannah, climbing slowly down the metal steps, turned her head to give the train one last, bleak look. She had endured the most horrifying moments of her life, shut up in a dark and airless box, on that train. Lewis had been stabbed. Jean Marie . . . Jean Marie was dead. And Lolly had committed suicide.

She watched with tears in her eyes as several porters unloaded Frog's coffin. I hate Lolly for killing Jean Marie, she thought, but she was right about one thing. We *were* mean to Frog. And it was my guilty conscience that wanted to think he was still alive.

Now they were both dead . . . Frog *and* Lolly.

She saw Dale and Eugene emerge from the train. Both looked thoroughly shaken by Lolly's suicide. Their eyes were clouded, their shoulders slumped. They looked lost and lonely.

The tour group entered the big bus to San Francisco quietly and solemnly.

But during the twenty-minute ride to San Francisco from Oakland, the mood began to change. When they crossed the bridge, windows were opened to allow the fresh, cool, salty air in. It was invigorating, and slowly, gradually, conversation began, a word at a time. Then there was a bit of laughter here and there, and people began craning their necks to see. Little by little, the tension and gloom evaporated like San Francisco fog.

By the time they reached the city and disembarked, the mood had changed to one of excitement and eagerness.

Even Hannah, looking out upon the tall buildings and the choppy waters of the sun-streaked Bay, began to feel her spirits lift.

Mack came up to her outside the Transbay Terminal and said, "I just talked to Ms. Quick. Your plane doesn't leave for three hours, so we thought you might spend them sightseeing with us." Hannah surprised all of them, especially herself, by saying, "Okay. Why not?"

Mack, Lewis, and Kerry stared at her.

"Really?" Kerry squeaked. "You'll come?"

Hannah laughed. "Yes. I've never seen San Francisco, I've never seen the ocean or even a bay and I'm not going to sit here all by myself for three hours. Yes, I'll come. Besides," she added softly, "Jean Marie would want us to do this."

Mack smiled at her and took her hand.

Chapter 25

The place Mack had in mind was called Rockview.

"I read about it," he told Hannah as he led her to the waiting bus. "It's a big old house up on a hill looking out over the water. If we get lucky, we'll see sea lions on the rocks. And if it's too foggy, there's a restaurant and a gift shop upstairs and an arcade downstairs. You can do a lot in a place like that in three hours."

Hannah knew Mack was trying to help her forget everything that happened. She gave him another smile, and he squeezed her hand. Hannah was glad to be off the train, but she knew that memories of that horrible ride would haunt her for a long time to come.

If only Jean Marie could be with them . . .

It wasn't foggy at Rockview when they arrived. But during dinner in the warm, cozy restaurant overlooking the water, they were able to watch in awe as the thick, white cloud appeared and rolled toward them, banishing everything in its path. The distant lights of huge ships out on the water disappeared, smaller boats vanished, even the great brown rocks closer to shore were swallowed up in one quick gulp.

"Weird," Kerry said softly, her fork halfway to her mouth. "It's like a steamroller . . . but it looks so soft and fluffy."

"Now you see it, now you don't," Lewis said, peering through the big picture window into what was now an unbroken blanket of gray-white mist. "I guess we can forget about the sea lions. We can't even see the *rocks*."

By the time they went downstairs to visit the arcade, darkness had enveloped the concrete walkway on three sides of the house, all facing the water.

Because the thick fog had robbed them of any view, they entered the arcade, noisy with calliope music and laughter and thick with bodies. Almost immediately, Hannah became separated from her friends but, rather than being upset, she was grateful. Now she was free to go outside alone. She felt as if she'd been cooped up forever, first on the train, then on the bus. She needed fresh air, even if it was foggy and drizzly.

Without telling anyone she was leaving, Hannah pushed her way through the crowd and went outside to the seawall overlooking the water. Except for the lights shining out from the arcade and the restaurant above them, it was dark, and very cold. Drizzle from the fog moistened her face and lips. It felt very refreshing after the stuffiness of the arcade.

A large section of the stone wall protecting viewers had crumbled into the cold, choppy water. The destroyed area was roped off with a sign reading:

DANGER
DO NOT ENTER

But it was easy to avoid that area. The earlier sightseers had disappeared, leaving the evening chill for the warmth of the arcade or restaurant and gift shop. The walkway was hers alone.

Grateful for the solitude, Hannah moved close to the wall, peering over the edge to watch the pounding surf below her. She felt she would like to remain there forever, watching the powerful, rushing tide collide with the rocks, the resulting foamy spray dancing high up in the air, almost close enough to touch. She licked her lips and tasted saltwater.

Hannah leaned over the protective stone wall and let the sight and sound of the roaring waves crashing against the huge rocks below soothe her shattered nerves.

Mack's right, she thought. It's all over now. She knew that the sadness she felt for Frog and Lolly and especially for poor Jean Marie would remain with her for a long time to come. But slowly, slowly, for the first time since she'd boarded the train, Hannah could feel herself beginning to relax. I should go in and join my friends for the little while I have left here, Hannah thought. Mack will be happy to see me.

She was about to turn around and head for the arcade when an arm fastened itself around her neck and a voice she recognized instantly said softly, "Hi, Hannah. Fancy meeting you here."

The voice belonged to Lolly Slocum.

Chapter 26

"I have a knife," Lolly whispered. Something cold and metallic pressed against Hannah's ear. "Make even the tiniest sound and you'll never make another."

"Don't," Hannah begged when she could speak. "Please, don't. . . ."

Lolly began pulling Hannah sideways, yanking cruelly at her neck. It hurt, but Hannah didn't cry out. She was afraid to.

"Where . . . where were you?" Hannah whispered. "When we were looking for you? We looked everywhere."

"You didn't look everywhere," Lolly said with contempt. "Not in the coffin."

They were scuttling sideways, toward the roped-off area. Laughter and music rang out from the arcade. Hannah fixed her frightened eyes on the windows, trying to will Mack to realize she was missing and come rescue her. But in that crowd . . . would he even realize she was gone?

They reached the rope. Lolly ducked underneath and roughly pulled Hannah with her.

She isn't going to stab me, Hannah thought with rising nausea. She doesn't have to. All she has to do is push me over that broken wall. I'll be smashed to bits on the rocks below.

The roaring surf no longer seemed comforting.

Stall, stall, Hannah ordered herself. Keep her talking until Mack or Lewis or Kerry realizes you're not in the arcade. Keep her talking . . .

So she asked the question that had been torturing her. "Lolly," she said in a trembling voice as Lolly dragged her backward, closer and closer to the crumbled wall and that deadly roar, "if you were hiding in the coffin, where was Frog? Did you . . . did you *move* him?"

Lolly's laughter pealed out into the thick mist, as if slicing it down the middle. "Oh, Hannah, he isn't in that coffin! He never was." Backing Hannah up against the broken wall, Lolly released her grip but stood blocking Hannah's way, an immovable bulk.

She held something up in front of Hannah. The faint glow from the arcade bounced off the metal object she was holding. It wasn't a knife. It was, Hannah realized, peering through the darkness at it, a tin canister, short and squat.

"This," Lolly said triumphantly, "is *Frog!*"

Drizzle coated Hannah's hair and slid down her cheeks. Behind her she could hear the hungry pounding of the waves waiting to swallow her up.

"Frog?" was all Hannah could manage as she stared at the canister. "Frog?"

Lolly nodded. "You don't think anyone cared enough about him to provide a real funeral for him, do you? Too much bother to have him sent home to be buried. They had him cremated!"

"Frog was never in the coffin? Then why was it on the train?"

Lolly grinned. "I ordered it. I'm having it sent COD to his parents. As a reminder. That they had a son they didn't want, not when he was alive and not when he was dead. They'll get a call from the railroad station and they'll come down to see what they're getting and there it will be . . . their son's coffin. Only he won't be in it. They won't care about that, but they sure will be ticked off when they're given the shipping invoice." Lolly giggled with relish.

"How . . . how did you get his ashes?" Mack, where are you? Hannah thought desperately. Why aren't you looking for me?

"*They* didn't care. But I knew exactly what to do with them." Lolly lifted her head, gazed around her. "So they gave them to me. San Francisco was one of his favorite places. He used to talk about it all the time. I knew about the tour, and I knew it wasn't too late to sign up. It would be perfect. I'd bring him back here, where he loved to be, and I'd take care of you guys at the same time. And the great thing about the empty coffin was, I knew it would make a great hiding place." She held up the canister again, shoving it in Hannah's face.

And Hannah saw the tattoo. The winged rat, its fangs bared, exactly like the one Frog had, and in the same place — on Lolly's left wrist.

"That was *you* in the coffin," Hannah said. "But . . . if we'd opened the lid all the way . . ."

"You would have seen exactly what you saw in the berth," Lolly said confidently. "And you thought *that* was Roger, didn't you? I put the makeup on before I climbed into the coffin every time. Just in case. No one would have known I wasn't Roger. I mean," she said with a chuckle, "it's not as though they'd look too closely, know what I mean?

"It's funny," she added then with an evil grin, "that you and Roger are going to end up in the same place, after all. Don't you think that's funny? He always wanted to hang around you guys. I never understood why, considering the way you treated him. We fought about it. A terrible fight." Tears of pain filled her small, pale eyes. "And I never got a chance to say I was sorry. He didn't want me there that night, the night he died . . . I knew that. He wanted to be with Jean Marie. But I showed up anyway, pulled up right behind him when he parked. He was furious when he saw me. But I knew he'd need me when he got hurt. And he *did* get hurt, didn't he, Hannah? Who would know that better than you?"

Then all the fight seemed to go out of her and she added sadly, "But he wouldn't let me take care of him then. He was hurt and angry and he pushed me away when I tried to comfort him." Suddenly, her head flew up and the sadness was replaced again by fresh anger. "*Your* fault, Hannah, all *your* fault!"

Hannah's hands were behind her, trying to keep her body from touching the crumbling wall. One hand reached out tentatively, groping, searching for a piece of loose rock, or a piece of the crumbling wall. At last she found one, and grasped it tightly in her right hand.

"You know, Hannah," Lolly went on confidently, her voice low and sinister, "if the fall doesn't kill you, I've heard there are man-eating fish in these waters. In a couple of days, you're not going to look so pretty — "

The movement was so swift and sudden that Lolly never saw Hannah's arm dart out from behind her back. The chunk of concrete caught her directly above the left temple with as much force as Hannah could muster.

As Lolly reacted, Hannah bent forward and leapt sideways, to crouch, hands over her mouth, on the solid side of the wall.

Lolly grunted in surprise as the rock struck her. One arm flew to her head. But the other arm, the one that had been displaying the canister close to Hannah's face, jerked in a reflex action as the rock hit its target. The involuntary movement sent the canister spurting out of Lolly's hand. It flew up, up, and out over the edge of the crumbling wall.

It was about to begin its descent to the roaring surf when Lolly, with a desperate cry, lunged for it, both arms outstretched.

She caught it.

But to do so, she had to throw her body, full force, against the broken wall.

The crumbling concrete gave way, disintegrating completely under the force of Lolly's strong body.

Still clutching the canister, Lolly plunged forward and plumeted to the rocks and crashing waves below.

Chapter 27

At the very moment that Lolly plunged into the sea, someone called Hannah's name. She heard nothing. Crouched in a wet, miserable little ball against the concrete wall and lost in shock and horror, she was deaf to everything but the roar of the water beneath her as the huge, hungry waves swallowed up Lolly Slocum.

She covered her face with her hands.

"Hannah! Hannah, it's okay! It's okay now!"

She lifted her head. "Mack?"

He reached down and gently pulled her to her feet. She sagged against him, clutching, hugging, so glad to be safe.

Kerry and Lewis were with Mack. "What happened, Hannah?" Kerry asked, patting Hannah's shoulder.

"Lolly . . ." she whispered.

Lewis nodded. "We thought it was Frog when we spotted the two of you from the arcade window. Then her hair fell out of that cap she was wearing and we knew who it was. We ran to get out of there but it took us forever. No one would let us through."

"It's my fault," Kerry said quietly. "I should have made sure you were with me. I didn't realize we'd been separated until I turned around and you weren't there. I thought you were playing video games with Mack and Lewis until Mack showed up and asked me where you were."

"Let's go inside, Hannah," Mack said, leading her away from the viewing area. "You're soaked and you're shivering."

"I don't want to go into the arcade. All those people . . ."

They went to the restaurant instead. It was nearly empty and they sat at a table in the corner. While the others ordered, Mack went to call the police, and Ms. Quick.

"Lolly didn't jump from the train, after all?" Kerry asked when they'd been served with cups of steaming hot coffee.

Hannah shook her head. Mack had made her exchange her wet sweater for his dry one, but her damp hair chilled the back of her neck and her skin felt salty and sticky. "No. She was hiding again."

"I don't get it," Lewis said, shaking his head. "Did Frog's death unhinge her or what? What was she trying to do?"

Hannah leaned back against her chair and closed her eyes. "Get even," she said quietly.

Mack returned and said the police were on their way, as was Ms. Quick.

"Get even for what?" Kerry asked sharply. "Jean

Marie never did anything mean to Lolly. She wouldn't have."

"Not to Lolly. To Frog. All those things we talked about in the Cafe that day . . ."

"But not you, Hannah. You didn't say anything. And you're the one she tried to kill tonight."

Hannah took a sip of coffee, grateful for its warmth. "I didn't say anything," she said quietly, setting her cup back in its saucer, "because I was too ashamed. What I did to Frog was worse than any of the rest of you." Her cheeks deepened in color. "But I'm going to tell you now.

"It was all because of my party," she began, slipping back in her memory . . .

Her father wanted help with the yard work before her party, so he hired Frog. Every day for a week he was there, trimming bushes, mowing, weeding the flower beds, pruning the trees. He worked hard, Hannah had to admit.

She felt sorry for him, so she brought him cold lemonade when he was stringing the colored lights across the lawn. Turned the sprinkler on to cool him off when he was sweating in the hot sun over a flower bed. Fixed a sandwich and some fruit to take to him when he was struggling with the heavy recycling bins her father wanted moved.

It just seemed like the decent thing to do.

"Some bash you're giving here, huh?" he said one hot afternoon when she was sitting at the patio table folding napkins. "The whole school coming or what?"

"Just about," she answered.

"Figured," was all he said.

Hannah couldn't help thinking how awful it must be to be disliked by so many people. Okay, it was his own fault. He could have tried harder to be nice. But she also couldn't help wondering how many people had really given him a chance. The new kid in town . . . hadn't they all judged him pretty quickly?

And he was right about one thing: practically the whole school was coming to this party, the biggest she'd ever given. And he had worked so hard to make the grounds look pretty and nice. . . . One day it just slipped out, before she had time to consider what she was doing, what her friends would say.

Frog had said, for the hundredth time, "I guess just about everybody's coming to this thing, huh?" and that was when she did it. The words slid out of her mouth as easily as if they'd been buttered: "You can come, too, if you want."

Immediately, instantly, they both knew she regretted releasing the awful words.

And they both knew it was too late. She couldn't take it back, and there was no way he wasn't going to come.

Hannah wrestled with it every second of the next few days before the party. Her friends would have a fit when he walked in. No one could stand him. Several of the boys he'd had fistfights with would be there. Kerry would be appalled.

What was I thinking? she screamed at herself. He doesn't belong at this party. He doesn't know *anyone, he won't have any fun. Everyone will be mad at me. It'll ruin everything if he shows up.*

And she knew he would show up. There was no way he wouldn't. The look on his face when those dreadful words slipped out of her mouth had been the same look her brother Tad wore on his face when he finally got the Nintendo he'd prayed for.

He'd come, all right.

And the party she'd planned for so long would become a total disaster.

Hannah was a nervous wreck that night. She paced back and forth in the front hall in her expensive new party dress of deep forest green and her high heels, wearing her mother's jade earrings, with her hair curled up high on her head. She smiled at her guests as they began arriving and directed them toward the food, and when someone came to her and asked where a particular CD was, she told him, smiling, smiling all the while even though her stomach was churning and her teeth kept clenching and unclenching.

Because, how could she possibly allow Frog at her party? How could she let him ruin it?

The invitation had slipped out on an impulse. And it was retrieved in the same way.

When Hannah looked through the front window and saw him get out of his car and start across the street, it was as if her body took over and moved her outside, quickly, quickly, closing the door behind her, standing with her back against it, the sentry at the gate forbidding entry to the new unwanted — oh, so unwanted! — guest.

She hardly saw Lolly tagging along behind him, calling his name.

He was wearing what she was positive was a brand-new sport coat, and his longish hair was slicked down. He walked up the steps with an excited bounce. Lolly, hurrying along behind him, was wearing a ghastly purple dress with huge puffed sleeves.

"Hi," he said with a huge smile.

I can't do this, she thought with certainty, *I can't.*

But she did.

When they got to the door, Hannah said in a low, pained voice, "I'm really sorry, but the party's been cancelled. I'm not feeling well . . . the flu, I think, I've got this terrible headache and my stomach . . . well, I hate to do it, but I have to send everyone home. I was just about to when you came."

Music and laughter rang out behind them, coming, it seemed to Hannah, from each tiny crevice between the red bricks, through every window, beneath every door.

"Sick?" Frog said, disbelieving. "You don't look sick. You look," he flushed and lowered his head, "you look beautiful."

Hannah did feel sick, then. "Thanks, but I really feel awful. And if it's the flu, I don't want to give it to anyone else, right? I'm really sorry, after all that hard work you did. Maybe I can have the party next week."

The look on Frog's face then would haunt Hannah for a long time.

Without another word, he turned and ran down the steps, leaving Lolly behind. He jumped into his car and roared off, tires screeching, not even waiting to see if Hannah's guests really were leaving.

From somewhere far, far away, Hannah was vaguely aware of Lolly's voice shrieking after the speeding car, "See? Didn't I tell you? Didn't I?"

"He didn't have to wait to see if everyone else left," Hannah finished her story, "because he knew no one would be leaving. He knew I was lying."

Her friends knew the rest of the story. Five minutes later, after Lolly had left, her head held as high as she could manage, Frog had crashed his car into a brick wall at high speed.

"We heard the sirens," Hannah reminded them, "but we never gave it a thought. We were all having too much fun."

They sat in silence for several minutes. Then Hannah said softly, "I didn't know Lolly and Frog had fought about it. She didn't want him to come to the party because she knew that . . . we . . . really didn't want them there and that something bad would happen. She was right, wasn't she? And that made him even madder, finding out that she'd been right all along. He was furious with her when he drove off. It must have just about killed her, not straightening things out with him before he died.

"But it wasn't her fault. It was *mine*." Hannah's breath caught in a sob. "And I've been sorry ever since, but what good does that do either of them?"

"Hannah," Mack said finally, "it's over. It's all over now. We were *all* crummy to the guy, and to Lolly, too, and we're all sorry."

"And now we should forget it," Kerry said firmly. "We'll never forget Jean Marie. But, like Mack said, it's over. Finally."

"No," Hannah said softly, lifting her head, her eyes full of regret. "I don't want to forget it. I don't want any of us to forget it. If we do, what's the point?"

"So you're still going home?" Lewis asked.

Hannah thought about it. She was here, in a wonderful, exciting city, with friends she cared about and trusted. Lolly was gone now. So was Frog. Would going back home change anything that had happened? Would it be wrong to stay?

"No," she said. "I'm not going home. I'm staying."

They all smiled.

"But," she added, taking Mack's hand in hers, "I'm not going to forget, either. And tomorrow, while Kerry's shopping, I'm coming back here, to Rockview, to see the ocean in the sunshine. I'm coming back to say a decent good-bye to Lolly and Frog. Then it will really be over."

And Mack said, "I'll come with you."

Kerry and Lewis nodded. "We will, too."

And Kerry added with a grin, "and *then* we'll go shopping."

HIT AND RUN

1

Cassie Martin hung out with three boys.

Cassie had been athletic all her life, playing sports, swimming, bike-riding, and hanging out with the boys in her neighborhood. And when she got to high school, she didn't see any reason to change friends.

Short and thin, with crimped blonde hair, and lively green eyes in a face full of freckles, Cassie looked about twelve, even though she was nearly sixteen.

Cassie had a crush on one of the three boys she hung out with. Scott Baldwin. But it was a secret crush. Scott had no idea. To him, Cassie was just a pal.

Scott was one of those all-around guys who get their picture in about twenty places in the yearbook. Really good-looking in a teddy bear sort of way, Scott was a big, blond jock with brawny shoulders and a broad neck, but he also had brains.

He was starting fullback on the football team and an all-state wrestler. He was also class representative to the Student Government. He had an after-school job in his uncle's hardware store — and he managed to maintain a solid B-plus average.

Just about perfect. That's what Cassie thought.

But no one's perfect. Scott had his faults, she realized. For one thing, he had a really annoying laugh — a high-pitched giggle that made Cassie's teeth itch. For another, Scott was more of a follower than a leader.

Despite his big size, he was more of a sheep than a tiger.

Mainly, he was always ready to go along with the dumb jokes and schemes that Winks cooked up.

Bruce Winkleman was another one of the three guys Cassie hung out with. No one called him Bruce. Everyone called him Winks — except his mother.

Winks had stringy brown hair down to his shoulders, and he wore black-rimmed Buddy Holly glasses that were too big for his slender face. He had only one kind of smile — a devilish grin.

Winks was a good guy, too, after you got to know him. But what a joker. Sometimes Cassie wished he could be more serious. But then he wouldn't be Winks.

Cassie was at Scott's house on a Wednesday evening after dinner. They were supposed to study their government assignment. But Scott's parents had rushed out to go to an early movie, leaving Scott with the dinner dishes to wash, so Cassie helped him in the kitchen instead.

They had just about finished when Winks came marching in through the back door, as usual without knocking. He was carrying a cardboard box, a little smaller than a shoe box, which he set down on the kitchen counter.

It was a chilly winter night, about twenty-five or so outside, and windy, but Winks was wearing the same blue denim jacket he always wore, the one with his father's old war medals pinned up and down the front, and faded jeans with gaping holes at the knees.

He was wearing his devilish grin, too.

"I suppose you're wondering what's in the box," Winks said, pushing his heavy eyeglasses up on his short, pudgy nose.

"Not really," Cassie said, drying the last dinner plate and handing it to Scott to put away.

"You two look like you're married," Winks said.

Cassie tossed down the dish towel. She glanced at Scott, who looked embarrassed. "Yeah. We got married this morning," she told Winks. "But it's a secret. Our parents don't know yet."

Winks's devilish grin became more devilish. "When's the honeymoon?"

"What's in the box?" Scott asked, changing the subject. He took the dish towel and mopped up the countertop.

"Try to guess," Winks said, drumming his fingers on top of the box. "Is Eddie coming over?"

Eddie was the third guy, Cassie's other friend.

"I don't think so. Why?" Scott asked suspiciously.

"Aw, Winks." Cassie made a disgusted face, then lowered her eyes to the box. "Is this another dumb joke you're going to play on Eddie?"

Winks's dark eyes lit up behind his black-rimmed glasses. "It isn't dumb," he said. "It's . . . baad."

Scott let out his high-pitched giggle. He was always ready to play another joke on Eddie.

But Cassie worried that they'd played too many dumb jokes on their friend. Sure, Eddie was a good sport. In fact, he was *too* good a sport. If he'd get really mad once, Cassie thought, Winks and Scott would probably stop.

The only reason kids liked to play jokes on Eddie was because he was so quiet, and sort of timid and frightened-looking. His name was Eddie Katz, and some kids had started calling him Scaredy Katz.

He was short, about the same height as Cassie, and very wiry, with curly black hair. Eddie was one of those guys who blushed very easily. His cheeks always seemed to have dark red circles on them.

Eddie was smart and serious. He wanted to be a doctor, a difficult goal since his family was struggling financially and he'd have to make his own way through college and medical school.

"Call Eddie," Winks told Scott. "Get him over here."

"Okay. Sure." Scott reached for the red wall phone.

"What's in the box?" Cassie asked.

"Guess," Winks insisted.

"Your brain?"

Scott giggled and punched Eddie's number on the phone.

"Close," Winks said, grinning.

Scott got Eddie on the phone and told him to come over. Then he hung up. "He's coming. What's in the box?"

"It's an eyeball," Winks said, removing the lid and starting to lift the box to show them.

Cassie hid her eyes with her hand. "Don't show it to me. That's really gross!"

Scott stared at the box. "From an animal? What kind of animal?"

"From a human," Winks said. He replaced the lid.

"That's a human eye?" Scott asked. He giggled. "It's so *humongous*!"

"Gross," Cassie repeated. "Where'd you get it?"

"From an eye store," Winks cracked. "They were having a sale."

"I just ate," Scott said, holding his stomach.

"Winks — is that really a human eye?" Cassie asked, staring at the box.

He nodded, pleased with himself. "I got it from Eddie's cousin Jerry. He works at the city morgue. Downtown."

"Eddie's cousin gave you an eyeball?" Cassie asked, feeling sick.

"Yeah. He removed it from some corpse."

"Didn't the corpse need it for his funeral?" Cassie asked.

"I can't believe we're discussing this," Scott proclaimed, scratching his blond hair.

"He was being cremated, so he didn't need it," Winks informed them. He shook the box. The eyeball plopped against the sides.

"Yuck! Stop!" Cassie pleaded. "Really, Winks. I mean it."

"Did you ever get that new Polaroid you were talking about?" Winks asked Scott, giving the box one more good shake for Cassie's benefit.

"Yeah, I got it," Scott replied, straightening the sleeve of his blue-and-gold Avondale North High sweatshirt with the North High bulldog growling across the front.

"Well, go get it," Winks said. "I want a picture of Eddie's reaction when I do my eyeball trick."

"Your . . . eyeball trick?" Cassie asked reluctantly.

Winks flashed his evil grin at her. "You'll see."

Scott returned from his room carrying a yellow plastic camera. "All ready," he said.

"Is that a camera or a toy?" Winks asked sarcastically. "What *is* that — My First Camera?"

Cassie laughed. It did look like a baby camera.

"It's a really good camera," Scott insisted defensively. "You can take underwater pictures with it."

"Underwater Polaroids?" Cassie asked.

"Ooh — let's go try it out in the bathtub," Winks exclaimed.

"Don't look at me," Cassie cracked. "I'm not taking a bath with you, Winks."

Winks did an exaggerated pout. "Hold on to the camera, Scottso. And when I do my eyeball thing, get Eddie's face, okay?"

Scott nodded. He always agreed to everything Winks wanted.

"This is really gross," Cassie said, glancing at the box. "I can't believe Eddie's cousin gave that to you."

"He's a good guy," Winks said. "I guess he gets bored working at the morgue. He said business is really dead!"

Scott laughed. Cassie did, too, but she hated herself for it.

Such a bad joke.

A few minutes later, Eddie appeared at the kitchen door. He was wearing his blue down vest over a bulky black-and-red sweater, and a blue wool ski cap. "It's cold," he said, stepping into the kitchen, his cheeks bright red.

"How's it going?" Scott asked.

Cassie looked around. Winks had disappeared from the room.

"Okay, I guess," Eddie said, pulling off the ski cap and straightening his black, curly hair with his hand. He smiled at Cassie. "Hi."

She returned his greeting, lowering her eyes guiltily to the yellow camera beside Scott on the kitchen counter. She had a momentary urge to warn Eddie that Winks was about to play a trick on him.

But it was only momentary.

"Were you doing homework?" she asked Eddie.

He shook his head. "No. I was studying for my driver's test. You know. That booklet they give you for the written exam."

"When do you take it?" Scott asked, his eyes on the doorway behind Eddie.

"In a few weeks," Eddie replied, tossing his vest onto a tall kitchen stool. "It looks pretty easy. It's all multiple choice."

"I took it last week," Cassie said. "I only missed one question. The one about U-turns. I couldn't remember if they were legal or not."

"So you got your temporary? When do you take the driver's test?" Eddie asked.

"In a few days," Cassie replied excitedly.

At that moment, Winks entered from the hallway, holding both hands over his right eye, his head bowed.

"Hey — Winks," Eddie greeted him.

His hands cupped over his eye, Winks groaned.

Here it comes, Cassie told herself, holding her breath.

"What's wrong with your eye?" Scott asked, helping the joke along.

"I don't know," Winks said, stepping up close to

Eddie. "I — I think I got something in it. There! I got it out!"

Keeping his eye tightly closed, Winks lowered his hand, revealing the big, wet eyeball in his palm.

Winks screamed.

Eddie's mouth dropped open. His cheeks blazed. His entire face burned scarlet.

Scott flashed the camera.

Cassie laughed.

But she stopped laughing when Eddie's eyes rolled up into his head and, uttering a low moan, he slumped backward onto the linoleum.

His head hit the floor with a solid *thud*.

Scott flashed the camera again.

"I don't believe it!" Winks cried gleefully, staring down at Eddie's unmoving form. "He fainted! Scott — photo op! Photo op!"

Scott flashed another photo.

"Wait! Stop!" Cassie cried, bending over Eddie. "Eddie, are you okay?"

Eddie didn't move.

She grabbed his wrist. Slapped his face. Felt his red cheek. Shook his head.

"Hey — " The grin faded from Winks's face. He was still holding the eyeball.

"Winks, I — I don't think he's breathing," Cassie cried. She held Eddie's limp hand. "I — I think he's dead!"

2

Cassie let go of the hand, and it fell limply to the floor.

Scott uttered a choking sound. He backed up against the counter, his hands shoved into his jeans pockets.

"Come on," Winks said quietly, staring at Cassie, then moving his eyes down to Eddie's still form.

Eddie's eyes were closed. One leg was twisted at an odd angle under his body.

Winks set the eyeball down on the counter and wiped his hand off on a dish towel. "Come on," he repeated. "It was just a joke."

Pushing his glasses up on his nose, he crossed the kitchen and bent down over Eddie. "Just a joke," he repeated.

Eddie groaned and sat up. "What happened?" he asked, raising a hand to his forehead. "Did I black out?"

The other three all whooped for joy.

"You're okay!" Cassie cried happily.

Eddie lay back down on the linoleum. "I'm not so sure," he said weakly. "My head . . ."

"You hit it when you fell," Cassie told him.

"Do you believe it? He fainted!" Winks cried, shaking his head. "What a man! What a man!"

"Give him a break," Scott said.

"What's the matter, Eddie — didn't you ever see an eyeball before?" Winks asked. He turned to Scott. "I expected a good reaction — but not *that* good!" He and Scott laughed.

"Wish I'd gotten a photo of *Winks's* face when he thought Eddie was dead!" Scott exclaimed.

"Very funny," Winks said sarcastically. "At least I didn't faint like an old lady!" He scooped up the eyeball, which had yellowed quite a bit and appeared to be oozing some kind of clear liquid, and dropped it into the box.

Eddie pulled himself to his feet, still looking pale. "That is really gross," he said to Winks. "Where'd you get it?"

"I made it in shop," Winks cracked. "No. It was on my lunch tray."

"Actually, there were two of them," said Cassie, "but Winks ate one."

"Ohh, gross," Scott groaned and pretended to throw up in the sink.

Eddie reached for his down vest and ski cap. "Well, thanks for the entertainment, guys. Guess I'll get home."

"Hey, you're feeling better? Let's do something," Winks suggested, holding him back.

"I've got a lot of homework," Eddie said, his cheeks reddening.

"So do we," said Scott and Cassie in unison.

"They're married," Winks explained to Eddie.

"Huh?" Eddie scratched his black hair, then pulled the wool ski cap down over his forehead.

"We can do homework any time," Winks said. "Let's do something more worthwhile."

"Like play with an eyeball?" Cassie snapped. She shuddered, thinking about the hideous thing.

"Let's . . . practice our driving," Winks suggested.

"We can't!" Cassie cried.

"Drive what?" Scott asked.

"Your parents' Volvo," Winks said. "It's in the garage. I saw it when I came up."

Scott's parents had two cars. Cassie realized they must have taken the Toyota to the movie.

"We can't," Cassie said again. "None of us has a license. We aren't allowed to drive by ourselves."

"You have a temporary," Winks said. "That's almost a license."

"You have a temporary brain," Cassie cracked.

"I don't think it's a good idea to take my parents' car," Scott said, fiddling with his sweatshirt sleeve. "No. No way. If they found out, they'd *kill* me!"

Fifteen minutes later they were in their coats, rolling up the garage door.

Scott just can't say no to Winks, Cassie thought. We shouldn't be doing this. What if Scott's parents find out? What if the police stop us for some reason, and discover that none of us has a license?

What if we're in an accident?

She had to admit it was kind of exciting, too.

Bad Kids Out for a Thrill Ride.

She was always making up headlines in her mind. She liked the sound of that one.

"Hey, the car is scratched," Winks said, running his hand along a deep scratch in the driver's door. "You do this, Scott?"

"No way," Scott said quickly. "I haven't had a chance to put any scratches on it yet."

"Who's going to drive first? Eddie?" Winks asked, shoving Eddie toward the driver's door.

"Hey — no way!" Eddie backed out of the garage.

"Come on, Eddie," Winks urged. "We'll just drive to the mall. You know. The parking lot behind the stores. It's always empty at night. We can practice parking."

"No way," Eddie insisted. "You drive, Winks. It's your idea."

"I'll take a turn," Winks said, glancing at Cassie, who was already climbing into the back seat of the silver Volvo. "Okay, Scott, you go first. It's your car."

"Fine," Scott agreed quickly. "I've driven this car before. With my dad, I mean. This is the car

I've been practicing in." He slid behind the wheel. "Ooh — it's cold in here."

All four of them were settled now, their breath steaming up to the ceiling. Eddie sat beside Scott in the front, who was struggling to get his shoulder seat belt to click in.

"Peel out," Winks said enthusiastically.

"I can't believe I agreed to this," Eddie said, tugging off the ski hat and tossing it onto the dashboard in front of him.

"We're just practicing," Winks insisted.

Scott stared at the gearshift. "What does 'R' stand for? 'Right This Way'?"

Cassie and Winks laughed. Eddie's face contracted with worry. He stared straight ahead, eyes up as if praying, as Scott backed out of the garage and down the driveway.

"If we get caught, we'll *never* get our licenses," Eddie whined, sitting stiffly, alertly in his seat.

"We won't get caught," Cassie assured him, leaning over the front seat to pat Eddie's shoulder.

"If the cops come after us, we'll just outrace them," Winks said. "Let's see what this thing can do, Scottso."

"Hey — not funny!" Eddie cried, turning back to glare at Winks.

"Don't worry," Cassie said. "Scott's a good driver, Eddie. He's very careful. I've driven with him when we were with his family."

"She's right," Scott said seriously, making a

sharp right turn onto Market Avenue. And, then, suddenly, he lifted both hands high in the air. "Look, Ma — no hands!"

Cassie laughed. Scott can be so cute sometimes, she thought. Like a big, funny teddy bear.

Eddie, she saw, was not amused by any of this. The poor guy was really frightened, she realized.

"Hey, Winks — what'd you do with the eye?" Scott asked, slowing for a red light.

"The eye?" The evil grin returned to Winks's face. "Well, I put it somewhere."

"Somewhere? Where's somewhere?" Scott demanded.

"In your refrigerator," Winks said, grinning at Cassie. "You know. For when your dad comes into the kitchen for his midnight snack. He opens the refrigerator, pulls out the box, licking his chops, and — bingo!"

Everyone laughed.

"Watch out for that truck," Eddie warned, pointing.

"Eddie, that truck is two lanes away!" Scott cried.

"Well, I didn't know if you saw it," Eddie said, adjusting his seat belt.

When they got to the Avondale Mall, it looked pretty crowded, so they kept on driving. Following the old Route 12, they soon found themselves outside of town, in flat farm country, the road smooth and unswerving.

The new expressway had been open for less than a year, but it had already taken almost all of the traffic that had previously traveled on Route 12.

"The road is all ours," Scott said, pulling the silver Volvo over onto the grassy shoulder. "Someone else's turn. Eddie?"

Eddie shook his head. "Not me."

Cassie leaned forward. "You want to pass your test, don't you?" she asked. "This is a perfect place to practice. It's totally straight, and there isn't another car in sight."

"Well, I *do* want to pass," Eddie said thoughtfully.

Scott opened his door, letting in a blast of cold air. The air this far out of town smelled fresh and sweet. Cassie inhaled deeply, smiling.

"Come on, man," Scott urged.

Eddie disengaged his seat belt and stepped out of the car to trade places with Scott.

"I don't believe he's doing it," Winks whispered to Cassie. "Eddie's always such a wimp. But he's got more guts than I thought."

"He's very competitive," Cassie said. "He likes to pass tests."

Eddie slammed the door. The roof light went out. The darkness seemed to close in on them. He was shorter than Scott, so he moved the seat up.

An oil truck roared by, the driver honking as he passed.

"Hey — someone else is on this road!" Winks exclaimed.

"Ease it out slowly," Scott instructed Eddie, turning in the passenger seat to face him. "You don't have to press hard on the gas. The car has lots of power."

Eddie put both hands at the top of the steering wheel and pulled the car off the shoulder and onto the narrow highway.

"That's it. Very good," Scott assured him.

"I'm pretty comfortable with my dad's car," Eddie said, his eyes straight ahead on the twin beams of light from the headlights. "But it's an old Chevy Nova, the kind they don't make anymore. It takes a while to adjust to a newer car."

"You're doing fine," Scott said, glancing back at Cassie.

"Better slow down," Winks urged. "You're already going fifteen!" He laughed.

"I thought I was going faster," Eddie said, sounding nervous, his hands together on top of the wheel.

"You'd better speed up a little," Scott urged.

"Drive at whatever speed is comfortable for you," Cassie said. "There's no one around, so it doesn't matter."

"But you won't pass your test if you go this slow out on the open road," Winks said.

Eddie immediately sped up.

They passed a sprawling farmhouse, all of its

windows bathed in orange light. Log fences rolled by, dark shadows against a darker ground.

A short while later, they drove under the Hanson Underpass, a low stone bridge that had been built over the highway at least a hundred years before.

"I'm starting to feel like I'm in control," Eddie said. He pressed down a little harder on the gas pedal, and the car sped up.

"EDDIE! LOOK OUT!" Winks screamed.

Eddie slammed down on the brake.

"No! Oh, no!" Cassie cried.

The tires squealed in protest, and the car hurtled into a desperate spin.

3

The car spun wildly over the road, then came to a jolting stop on the soft, grassy shoulder.

Cassie lurched forward into the back of the driver's seat. Eddie uttered a small cry as his chest hit the steering wheel. His eyes searched the darkness beyond the windshield.

There was nothing there.

No car or truck in sight.

"April fool," Winks said quietly.

Scott started to laugh.

"Gotcha," Winks said, reaching forward to pat Eddie on the shoulder.

Eddie jerked his shoulder away and spun around, the fear on his face giving way to anger. "Winks — " He was too angry to talk.

Cassie found herself laughing, more out of relief than amusement. "Winks, you could've gotten us

357

killed," she said, giving him a hard shove that sent him sprawling against the door.

"Anything for a laugh," Winks replied. "Ow. That hurt." He rubbed his shoulder.

She shoved him again.

Scott had tears in his eyes from laughing so hard. "I believed you, Winks," he said. "I believed you, man. You're such a good actor. You sounded so panicked."

Scowling, Eddie shoved the gearshift into park, pushed open the car door, and climbed out. "See you guys," he muttered bitterly.

"Hey, Eddie — wait!" Cassie called.

But he started to walk off quickly into the darkness.

"Eddie — come back!" Scott jumped out of the car and went running after him. Cassie and Winks followed behind, leaving their car doors open, dim yellow light seeping out in a small circle, the hum of the engine the only sound except for the crunch of their sneakers on the cold ground.

Scott caught up with Eddie, who kept walking, his breath rising up in gray puffs against the starless black sky. "Wait up, man." Eddie didn't stop.

Scott grabbed the shoulder of his down vest. "It was just a joke, Eddie."

Eddie spun around angrily, quickly raising both arms to break Scott's grip. "Everything isn't a joke," he said angrily. "Some things shouldn't be joked about."

"There was no one around. I knew we wouldn't get hurt," Winks said, breathing hard, ducking his head down into his jacket as he caught up with Eddie and Scott.

Eddie shoved his hands into his jeans pockets and glared at him. "It wasn't funny, Winks," he said softly. He turned and started walking along the road.

"Eddie — come back!" Cassie called. "Come on. It's cold out here."

The three of them hurried after him. Cassie glanced back at the car, a shadow inside a dim circle of light, far behind them.

"I'm sorry," Winks called. "Eddie, I'm sorry. Okay? It was a stupid joke. I'm sorry."

"We've got to get back," Scott said, trying to read his watch in the darkness. "I've got to get the car back in the garage before my parents get home."

"Come on, Eddie," Cassie urged.

Finally, Eddie stopped. He turned to face them, his hands still shoved in his pockets. Cassie saw that he was shivering. From anger? she wondered. Or from the cold?

"Okay. Let's go back," Eddie said quietly, and started walking toward the car, lowering his head against the wind.

They were all cold by the time they got back to the car. Scott climbed behind the wheel and turned the heater up to high. Eddie climbed in back beside Cassie.

"Hey — it's my turn to drive," Winks protested, buckling the shoulder seat belt.

"No way," Scott said, easing the car onto the road. "Driving practice is over for tonight."

"I didn't get a turn, either," Cassie complained.

"Winks took up all our time with his dumb joke," Scott said. And then he glanced at the glowing yellow clock in the center of the dashboard. "Oh, no! Look how late it is! I'm going to be dead meat. Dead meat!"

He jammed his foot down on the accelerator, and the car responded with a roar.

"Whoa!" Winks cried, sliding down in his seat.

"I've got to get home!" Scott said as the car picked up speed.

Cassie leaned forward and glanced at the speedometer. "Scott — you're going eighty!"

"I can't help it," he replied, staring straight ahead into the twin cones of white light from the headlights. "If they get home before I do . . ." He didn't finish his thought.

He didn't have to. They all knew what kind of trouble he'd be in. What kind of trouble they'd *all* be in.

They roared under the Hanson Underpass. A few seconds later, the brightly lit farmhouse slid by, this time on the other side of the car. The low, flat fields gave way to woods, then clusters of houses.

"Slow down," Cassie urged. "We're back in town."

Eddie, she realized, had been silent ever since they'd returned to the car. She glanced over at him. He was staring out his window, his face expressionless, the wool ski cap pulled protectively low over his forehead.

A traffic light appeared up ahead. It blinked from yellow to red. Scott sped right through it.

"Scott — slow down!" Cassie yelled.

"I'm — I'm trying!" Scott cried, gripping the wheel tightly with both hands.

"Huh? What do you mean?"

Scott pumped the brake pedal hard several times. "The brakes — they're out!" he exclaimed.

The car roared through another intersection.

"No brakes!" Scott cried, his eyes wide with horror.

4

"Lame, Scott. Real lame," Winks said, shaking his head.

"But the brakes — " Scott insisted as the big Volvo roared past the Avondale Mall.

"No one is buying it," Winks said, turning to look back at Cassie and Eddie. "You're just not convincing. You're a bad actor."

Scott slowed the car down. His excited face drooped into a disappointed pout. "How about you, Eddie? You believed me, didn't you?"

Eddie stared silently out the window.

"Eddie isn't talking," Cassie told Scott. "Winks is right. That was lame."

Scott giggled and turned sharply onto Market Avenue.

"Some have it. Some don't," Winks said.

"What did I do wrong?" Scott asked seriously. "I even made it look like I was pumping the brakes."

"But you didn't sound scared enough," Winks told him. "It sounded like a put-on."

"I'll bet Eddie bought it," Scott said.

Eddie didn't reply.

A few minutes later, Scott pulled the car up the driveway and into the garage. "My parents aren't back," he said, very relieved.

The four of them piled out of the car. "Nice drive," Cassie said, stretching.

"Yeah. Thanks for the driving lesson, guys," Eddie said sarcastically.

"Hey — it can talk!" Winks said, and slapped Eddie on the shoulder.

"It was kind of fun," Cassie admitted, "in a crazy kind of way."

"I've got to get home," Eddie said.

"I'll drive you!" Winks joked.

Eddie didn't smile. "See you." He jogged down the driveway to the street.

Cassie stared up at the sky, searching for the moon, but could see only shades of gray against gray. She shivered, suddenly chilled. "Guess I'd better get home, too."

"I think Eddie was really freaked," Winks said.

Cassie and Scott quickly agreed. "Yeah, he was freaked," Cassie said.

Winks's face lit up with a truly evil grin.

"Scott, how can you pay forty dollars more for sneakers just because you can pump them up?" Cassie stared down disapprovingly at the gleaming new white sneakers on Scott's feet.

"They feel good," Scott replied. "Real bouncy." He jumped straight up in the air and pretended to shoot a basketball lay-up.

A woman and her two children had to scramble out of his way. "You're blocking the door," she said, flashing him an annoyed look as she ushered her kids away.

"I can jump about three feet," Scott said, looking very pleased.

"Oh, that'll come in real handy during a wrestling match," Cassie cracked. "You just bought those sneakers because everyone else is."

Scott was such a great guy, she kept thinking. If only he weren't such a sheep.

"They're cool," Scott said, admiring his sneakers as he followed her out of the store and into the crowded mall. "They're way cool."

It was Saturday afternoon, and Cassie didn't know what she was doing here with him. There were a hundred more constructive things she could be doing than following Scott around the Avondale Mall, watching him buy ridiculously expensive sneakers.

"Hey — look. A two-for-one sale on sweat-pants," Scott said, pointing to a sign in a window across the wide aisle.

"Ooh. Thrills," Cassie said sarcastically.

He stared at her, surprised. "What's your problem?"

She shrugged. "No problem."

"Well, let's check out the sweatpants, okay?"

"Yeah. Maybe they have ones that inflate," Cassie joked.

"Ha-ha," he said, making a face.

"I'll meet you over there," Cassie said, pointing to a record store. "There's a CD I want to buy."

"Which one?" Scott asked.

Before she could answer, Winks appeared. He was wearing a bright yellow sweater and green corduroys. "How's my favorite married couple?" he asked, leering first at Cassie, then at Scott. "Buying socks together?"

Cassie rolled her eyes. Scott punched Winks playfully on the shoulder. "Where'd you get that sweater, Winks? You lose a contest or something?"

"What's wrong with this sweater?" Winks asked, fingering a sleeve.

"It's a little yellow, isn't it?" Cassie asked.

"A little."

"You look like an Easter chick," Scott told him.

"Happy Easter," Winks said, smoothing the sweater front with one hand. "You hear what happened to Eddie in school yesterday?"

"No. What?" Cassie asked, waving across the aisle to some girls she recognized from Avondale North.

"Someone de-pantsed him," Winks said, grinning.

"Huh?"

"Well, not exactly," Winks said, following Cassie's glance at the girls across the aisle. "Actually, some kid took Eddie's pants from his gym locker. You know, while he was in gym. And he had to go to class the rest of the day in his smelly gym shorts." Winks laughed. "You should've seen Eddie's face. It was as red as a tomato the whole day."

"I can just picture it," Scott said, grinning. He scratched his head. "Poor Eddie."

"Eddie's such a nice guy," Cassie said. "Why is everyone always picking on him?"

"Because he's so easy," Winks replied, pushing his black-rimmed glasses up on his nose. "Remember Wednesday night? I'll bet *anything* Eddie believed that Scott had no brakes. That was so lame, but I just know Eddie believed it."

"So he's a little gullible," Cassie said. "That doesn't explain why everybody has to pick on him all the time."

"There's one kid like that in every class," Winks said. "One kid everyone likes to pound on. Eddie just happens to be that kid. He's used to it."

"You think so?" Cassie asked.

"Yeah, sure," was Winks's reply. He glanced down at the floor. "Hey, Scott — don't tell me. You bought sneakers you can pump up?"

"Yeah. They feel good," Scott said, bouncing up and down in them.

"I knew a guy who couldn't deflate his once he had them on," Winks said. "He had to get the fire department to chop them off."

"Who did it to Eddie?" Cassie asked, interrupting the sneaker conversation.

"What?" Winks was still staring down at the shiny, white sneakers.

"Who took Eddie's pants from his gym locker?" Cassie demanded.

"I did. Of course," Winks said, grinning proudly.

Cassie and Scott took the North Avondale bus from the mall to her house. Actually, it let them off two blocks from her house. And as they walked, the heavy, gray clouds that had darkened the sky all day parted, allowing some reluctant rays of sunshine to poke through.

Cassie unzipped her coat. The air was still cold, but the sun felt good on her face. It had been a long winter — cold, but with little snow.

When Scott stopped at the hedges in front of her house, put his hands on her shoulders, and kissed her, it came as a real surprise.

The kiss was awkward. He missed her lips and got her chin. His face felt cold against hers.

He stepped back, letting his hands drop from her shoulders, staring at her as if waiting to judge her reaction.

Cassie didn't know how to react.

She'd had a secret crush on Scott for months. But she'd had no idea he saw her as anything else except the friend he had grown up a block away from.

"Winks keeps saying we're married," Scott said, blushing, a strange smile on his handsome face.

Cassie laughed. "Then we can do better than that," she said impulsively. And she grabbed the back of Scott's neck, pulled his face down to hers, and kissed him, their lips on target this time.

When it ended and they smiled awkwardly at each other, Cassie felt strangely unsettled.

Maybe this is wrong, she thought. Maybe I'm messing up a good friendship here.

He reached for her again, but she pulled back. "See you later," she said breathlessly and turned and ran up the drive, leaving him standing there, his expression disappointed, almost sad.

That night, the four of them gathered at Eddie's house after dinner. The small house was hot, almost steamy, and smelled of meat loaf.

Huddled in the narrow living room, two on the couch, two on the threadbare carpet, they were discussing what to do.

"We could go to a movie," Scott said.

"There's nothing good playing," Cassie told him. "I checked."

"There's a dance at the school," Scott suggested. "I think they're having a DJ and a live band. You know, the band that plays at that dance club on the south side. What are they called?"

"You mean RapManiacs?" Eddie asked, small circles of red forming on his cheeks.

"Yeah."

"They're putrid," Eddie said. "They really rot."

"Might be a hoot," Winks said thoughtfully.

"No way," Cassie said. "I'd rather read my government text."

Eddie got up from the couch and walked to the picture window in the center of the room. He stared out into a clear, cool night. "We could go for a drive," he said, his back to them.

The other three reacted in shock.

"You want to go for another drive? After Wednesday night?" Cassie asked. She walked over to Eddie and felt his forehead. "No. No temperature."

Eddie laughed. "We could all use some real driving practice," he said. "You know. No fooling around."

"My parents are home," Scott said. "I can't get the car."

"Our car is here," Eddie said, pointing down to the curb. "My parents are at a party two blocks away. They won't be home till really late. We could take it."

"Great!" Scott exclaimed, climbing to his feet.

Eddie turned to Winks. "But you've got to promise no jokes."

Winks put on his innocent face. "Who, me?"

"We won't need headlights," Cassie cracked. "Winks can run ahead of us in that sweater!"

Everyone laughed but Winks. He yanked at the bright yellow wool. "My grandmother bought me this sweater!"

"Your grandmother is color blind," Eddie said.

"How'd you know?" Winks replied.

"Well, how about it?" Eddie demanded, staring at Winks.

"Okay, okay. No jokes," Winks agreed. "As long as I get a long turn."

"We'll all get turns," Eddie said, hurrying to the coat closet by the front door. He tossed Cassie's down coat across the room to her. "We're all taking the driver's test in the next couple of weeks, right? So we need all the practice we can get."

"Where should we drive?" Cassie asked. "There's so much traffic in town on Saturday nights. Someone might recognize us."

"Let's go back on Route 12," Scott suggested. "It's so deserted. And so straight. It's great for practicing."

"Okay," Eddie agreed, pulling the blue ski cap over his dark, curly hair. "Let's do it."

The four of them stepped out of the house and headed down the drive, their sneakers crunching over unraked, dead leaves. The air was cool and crisp. Someone a few houses down had a fire going in their chimney, sending a tangy, pine aroma wafting over the neighborhood.

Cassie took a deep breath. Such a great smell. "So why'd you change your mind?" she asked Eddie as they walked. "I mean, after Wednesday — "

"I was a jerk on Wednesday night," Eddie said, avoiding her glance. "I acted like a baby. So I thought I'd make up for it. And . . ."

"And?"

"I really want to pass the driver's test. I really want to practice so I can get my license," he said, raising his eyes to hers.

Cassie felt a chill as she climbed into the back seat.

This is kind of dangerous, she thought. None of us has a license. If something goes wrong . . . if we're caught . . .

She shook her head hard as if chasing those thoughts from her mind, and slammed the car door shut.

Nothing was going to go wrong, she decided.

Nothing.

5

The streets in town were clogged with cars. Saturday night. Date night. Market Avenue was jammed with high school kids cruising back and forth along the strip at ten miles an hour.

"In a few weeks, I'll be cruising Market, too," Eddie said cheerfully. He slowed for a light, hit the brake too hard, and the tires squealed as the car jerked to a stop.

"Smooth it out," Winks advised him from beside Cassie in the back seat.

"Thanks for the good advice," Eddie said sarcastically, his eyes raised to the traffic light.

"My turn next," Cassie said.

"What *is* this car — some kind of antique?" Scott asked from the front passenger seat, his eyes surveying the dashboard.

"No, it only smells like an antique," Winks cracked.

"It's a Nova," Eddie said, drumming his fingers impatiently on the steering wheel. "An old Chevy. My dad bought it third-hand for two hundred dollars."

"He got ripped off," Winks said.

A horn honked impatiently behind them.

"Eddie, the light's green," Winks said. "Green means go."

Eddie stepped on the gas, and the car lurched forward, sputtering a little as it shifted. "You're full of good advice tonight, Winks," Eddie said good-naturedly.

Traffic thinned out past the mall. Eddie made the turn onto Route 12, glancing in the rearview mirror as if checking to make sure he wasn't being followed.

"No one's on your tail. You're driving like a pro," Winks said.

"I thought I saw a cop behind us," Eddie said, picking up speed on the nearly deserted highway.

"Don't get paranoid," Scott warned, giggling.

"When do I get my turn?" Cassie asked impatiently.

Eddie obediently pulled the car over to the side of the road. A pickup truck with only one headlight rumbled past. Cassie got out of the car and traded places with him.

"Move the seat up if you have to," Eddie instructed.

"No. We're about the same height," Cassie said, studying the dashboard.

"Both shrimps," Winks cracked.

Cassie ignored him. "Okay. Fasten your seat belts. Here we go!" she announced and, pushing down hard on the gas pedal, pulled the car back onto the old highway, the tires whirring, spitting gravel, and then settling onto the road.

Cassie drove smoothly. After nearly half an hour, cruising through several small farm towns, past dark, flat fields that seemed to stretch on forever, she turned the wheel over to Winks.

He kept his promise to Eddie, driving seriously and carefully. In typical fashion, he kept up a running commentary on every move he made — "I'm looking in the mirror now . . . and now I'm sliding my hand down the wheel. . . . I'm scratching my ear with one hand . . . and now I'm checking the speedometer . . . picking my nose now. . . . " — until the other three begged him to shut up.

Finally, he relinquished the driver's seat to Scott, who drove without incident along the nearly empty highway, taking them most of the way back toward Avondale.

"Hey, we're all going to be pros by the time we take the driver's test," Winks exclaimed happily. "I could drive this car with my eyes closed."

"I heard the parallel-parking test is real easy," Scott said, pulling over to the shoulder so that Eddie could drive the rest of the way home.

"If you take the test in a really small car, you can't flunk it," Cassie said, staring out the window at a tall silo, dark against the purple sky. "They give you this much room." She gestured with her hands. "Enough room to park a moving van in."

"That's what I'm taking the test in," Winks said. "A moving van. You know. More of a challenge that way."

"Remind me to laugh later," Cassie replied.

For the ride home, Eddie climbed behind the wheel. Cassie remained in the passenger seat next to him. The other two boys slumped in the back, their knees on the seatbacks in front of them.

"After I get my license, I'd love to get a jeep," Eddie said, glancing in the rearview mirror, then at Cassie. "Maybe a Renegade. Or a Cherokee."

"Those are way cool," Scott agreed from the back seat.

They were approaching the Hanson Underpass. The low, stone bridge loomed gray-green in the yellow headlights.

Cassie yawned. The warm air from the heater was making her sleepy.

But she snapped wide awake when the man suddenly came into view in the middle of the road.

The headlights caught his startled expression. He stood staring at them, frozen, his arms at his sides.

Eddie cried out and slammed his foot on the brake.

The tires squealed as the car began to slide.

To Cassie, her mouth open wide in a silent

scream, it all seemed to happen in slow motion.

She saw that the man was wearing a tie and jacket. And a baseball cap.

She saw his wide-eyed stare. The expression of horror on his face, so bright, so unearthly bright in the glare of the headlights.

Then he appeared to be standing right in the windshield.

Then she felt the bump.

The surprisingly quiet *thud* of impact.

The man's expression didn't change.

His body flew straight up in the air.

The tires squealed again.

Closing her eyes, Cassie continued to scream, but no sound came out.

She felt another bump as the front tires rolled over the man.

And then the car finally came to a stop.

6

When Cassie was a little girl of seven or eight, her parents gave her a white fluffball of a kitten. She named the kitten Fluffy, and it became her constant companion, immediately taking the place of all her stuffed animals.

She treated the kitten like a stuffed animal, carrying it in her arms everywhere she went, even sleeping with it cuddled under her chin.

"She's so attached to it," she heard her mother telling a friend over the phone.

Attached to it. The phrase stuck in her mind.

When her mother warned her not to take Fluffy into the front yard, Cassie ignored her. She was *attached* to Fluffy, after all.

Besides, it was a pretty spring day, the sun warm, the air soft and fragrant. Fluffy shouldn't be cooped up in the house, little blonde Cassie decided. Fluffy should come outside and play with her.

Out in the sunshine, with the apple trees blossoming pink and white all down the block, Fluffy didn't want to stay in Cassie's arms. The kitten wanted to explore.

And run.

And when Fluffy ran into the street, ignoring the little girl's frantic cries, Cassie felt a terror inside her that she had never experienced.

A cold, paralyzing terror.

The sound of the squealing red car. The sight of the black tire track over Fluffy's flattened white fur.

And then the tears.

The tears that wouldn't stop. The tears she didn't *want* to stop.

Cassie saw it and heard it again and again. Whenever she closed her eyes. Awake or in dreams.

The squeal. The black tire track.

The feeling of terror.

The same feeling she was experiencing now as she and the three boys climbed silently out of the old Chevy. The same paralyzing, cold-all-over terror that made her feel as if she weighed a thousand pounds, as if she were a block of ice about to crumble.

They were directly under the Hanson Overpass. The car headlights bounced off the old stones. Someone had spray-painted a name in huge orange letters on one side: MARGO '90.

Silence. The air was still. Not a sound except for their breathing.

"Mister — are you okay?" Eddie was the first to break the silence. "Can you talk?"

The man, on his back in front of the car, stared lifelessly up at them as they huddled over him. Cold, gray eyes. His blue-and-red Chicago Cubs cap had somehow stayed on his head. His navy-blue necktie was lying straight up over his shoulder, the collar of his white shirt unbuttoned.

"Mister — ?"

Cassie wanted to bend over the man, to grab his hand, to say something to him. But she stood there, behind Scott, trembling now, trembling all over, her hands raised to her face.

Standing in front of the twin beams of light, the light bouncing back at them off the old stone bridge, it all seemed so bright. Not daylight bright. But eerily bright, as if they were in a horror movie, an unnatural world where you were forced to see everything you didn't want to see so clearly, so brightly.

Eddie was the first to overcome his fear enough to bend down and grab the man's wrist.

He dropped it immediately.

"He's dead." Eddie mouthed the words.

"He can't be!" Winks cried, standing timidly by the side of the car, behind the others.

"He's dead," Eddie said a little louder. "Look at his eyes."

They looked at the dull gray eyes staring up at the sky, unblinking.

I'll never forget those horrid eyes, Cassie thought.

She pictured the black tire tracks on her white kitten.

I'll never forget those eyes.

Scott put a hand on her shoulder. "Yeah. He's dead," he said, his voice a whisper. He squeezed Cassie's shoulder. "What are we going to do?"

"I — I *killed* him!" Eddie cried, a loud shriek of horror that startled them all. Eddie dropped to his knees on the pavement and buried his face in his hands.

"Eddie — " Cassie started. But the words didn't come. She leaned back against Scott.

"I killed him!" Eddie cried again.

Cassie gulped a deep breath of cool air and pulled away from Scott's grip. She dropped down beside Eddie, surprised at how cold the pavement felt through the knees of her jeans.

"Eddie, stop — "

He dropped his hands to his side and gazed at her, his face swollen and red in the yellow light from the headlights, his dark eyes wet with tears. "Cassie — I ran over him."

"It was an accident," she said softly.

She wanted to hug Eddie, to comfort him somehow. But she couldn't raise her arms, couldn't move. She turned away for a brief second and stared again at the corpse's wide eyes beneath the Cubs cap.

"But he's dead," Eddie wailed. "What are we going to do?"

Cassie raised her eyes and saw Winks walking toward them, a determined look on his face. "Winks — " she called to him. But he ignored her and, with a loud groan, hunkered over the body.

"Winks, what are you doing?" Scott, his face hidden in shadows, called.

Winks grabbed the dead man's waist and pushed him onto his side. Then he reached into his back pocket and pulled out a flat, brown wallet.

"Winks!" Cassie cried, horrified.

Was Winks going to rob a corpse?

"I just want to see who he is," Winks said. Holding the wallet open with both hands, he held it in front of a headlight.

"What is he *doing*?" Eddie asked Cassie, shaking his head, his face twisted in fright and panic.

"Brandt Tinkers," Winks announced. "His name is Brandt Tinkers."

"Is — is there an address?" Scott asked, still hidden in shadows, his voice shrill and high-pitched.

"Why do we need an address?" Eddie exploded. "Are we going to drop him off at his house? He's dead! Don't you understand? I *killed* him!"

Cassie finally managed to reach out and put her hands on Eddie's shoulders. "Be calm," she whispered, even though her heart was thudding like a bass drum in her chest. "Be calm, Eddie. It was an accident. An accident."

Winks returned the wallet to the dead man's back pocket, then made a sour face. "I feel sick. I really do." He gagged, raised his hand over his mouth, his eyes going wide behind the dark-framed glasses, and ran behind the car to vomit.

"When my parents find out I took the car, they'll *kill* me!" Eddie wailed. "How could this happen? How?"

Cassie held on to him tightly, but couldn't find any comforting words. She found herself thinking about what *her* parents would say. They'll never trust me again, she realized. They'll always be suspicious of me, of where I'm going, what I'm doing.

She turned to look down the dark highway. No one coming. No lights. Nothing moving.

"We've got to get out of here," Winks said, reappearing by the driver's side of the car, leaning against the door. "I just puked my guts out."

"What do you mean — get out of here?" Eddie asked, jumping unsteadily to his feet. He looked very confused.

"We can't stay here," Winks said impatiently, pulling open the car door. "We have to go. We *have* to!"

Cassie climbed to her feet, feeling as if she weighed a ton. She stared down at the corpse. "Winks — "

"I know what you're going to say," Winks replied heatedly, speaking rapidly, still leaning against the car. "But we can't do anything for this guy now.

He's dead. We can't get an ambulance for him. We can't help him. It's too late. So we have to help ourselves."

"He's right," Scott said, stepping into the light, his hands jammed into his jacket pockets. "We don't have driver's licenses. The police will fry our butts. Our lives will be ruined. Everyone will know what we did. We could even go to jail or something."

"But we can't just take off," Cassie said, glancing at Eddie, who was now trembling all over, looking very faint. She put her arm around his shoulders to steady him.

"I can't believe it," Eddie muttered, shaking his head. "I killed a man. I killed him."

"We *have* to take off," Scott insisted, staring down the highway. "Now!"

"We can't do anything for this guy," Winks said from the side of the car. "It was a terrible accident. We'll live with it forever."

"Forever," Eddie repeated, staring down at the corpse.

"But we can't let it ruin our lives," Winks continued. "Come on. Get in!"

"I don't know," Cassie said, her mind spinning, the yellow beams of light suddenly growing brighter, then dimmer, as she stared at them.

She saw the black tire track on the white fluffball.

She felt so guilty.

It took her a while to realize that the others were staring at her, waiting for her to decide.

"Okay," she said with a loud sigh. "Let's go."

"Brandt Tinkers," Eddie said, staring at the corpse. "Brandt Tinkers."

"Eddie, come on," Cassie urged, guiding him to the car, her hand gently on the shoulder of his down vest.

"Do you think he has a family?" Eddie asked, not moving.

"Hurry!" Winks cried. "Someone will come along. We've been lucky so far."

"Who's going to drive?" Scott asked.

"Not me!" Eddie cried. "I can't!"

"Then I'll drive," Winks said and jumped behind the wheel, immediately slamming the door after him.

"But we can't just leave him lying in the middle of the highway!" Cassie protested, not recognizing her shrill, frightened voice.

"Help me move him," Scott said, stepping close to her. "Are you okay?" he whispered.

She nodded. "I guess. I don't know."

"We'll carry him to the side of the road," Scott said, staring into her eyes.

"No! Don't touch him!" Eddie screamed.

"Let's get Eddie to the car first," Cassie suggested to Scott. "He's not doing too well."

They each took an arm and walked Eddie to the car. He sagged down in the back seat, crossing his slender arms protectively over his chest, staring down at the floor. Then Cassie and Scott quickly rolled the corpse onto the grassy shoulder of the road.

"I've never touched a dead man before," Cassie said, shuddering, suddenly chilled from head to foot.

Scott put an arm around her shoulders. "Neither have I."

Leaning against each other, they made their way quickly to the car. Winks started up the engine before Cassie and Scott were inside. As soon as they had pulled their doors shut, he sped off, flooring the gas pedal so that the car lurched forward, throwing all of its passengers back against their seats.

"Winks, slow down!" Cassie scolded. "That's all we need is to get a speeding ticket!"

For some reason, this struck Scott as funny. He started to laugh his high-pitched giggle.

Winks laughed, too, high-pitched, nervous laughter. But he slowed the car down to forty.

"Eddie — feeling a little better?" Cassie asked, beside him in the back seat.

Eddie stared straight down.

"Eddie?"

"I guess," he said finally, not looking at her. "This is hit-and-run, you know. We could all be arrested."

"No one saw us," Winks said, slowing even more as they reached town, darkened stores passing on both sides. "No one. There was no one around."

"But we could all be arrested," Eddie insisted.

"We'll be okay," Cassie said softly. "Winks is right, Eddie. There were no witnesses. What happened is terrible. But it was an accident. An accident. You have to keep telling yourself that."

"What was Brandt Tinkers doing there in the middle of the highway, anyway?" Winks asked. He was starting to sound a little more like himself. He slowed and turned the car onto Market Avenue, still jammed with Saturday night traffic.

"He was just standing there in the road," Cassie said thoughtfully.

"And I killed him," Eddie said, shaking his head.

"Stop it, Eddie," Cassie said softly. "We've got to go on, you know. We've got to go on as if nothing happened."

"But how *can* we?" he wailed.

"We have no choice," Scott said firmly, turning to look at Eddie from the front seat.

"In a way, we were lucky," Winks said, sliding his hands nervously back and forth on the plastic steering wheel. "I mean, no one came by that entire time. Not a car. Not a truck. Nothing."

"Yeah, lucky," Eddie muttered.

"Winks is right, Eddie," Cassie said, finding herself becoming a little impatient with him. "There were no witnesses. That was really lucky."

Winks pulled the Chevy to the curb in front of Eddie's house.

There, hunkered on the front stoop, illuminated by the light from inside the open front door, stood two blue-uniformed policemen.

7

"Keep driving! Keep driving!" Eddie cried, leaning forward, grabbing the back of Winks's seat and shaking it with both hands.

"I can't!" Winks told him. "They've already seen us. Look!"

All four teenagers looked at the house. The two policemen, one tall and rangy, the other squat and overweight, had turned away from the front door and were staring expectantly across the yard at them, hands on hips.

"They're going for their guns!" Eddie cried, his face pressed against the car window.

"No, they're not," Cassie assured him. "They're waiting for us to get out."

"Come on. Let's go," Scott said, reaching for his door handle.

"How did they find out?" Eddie wailed, not moving. "How did they get here so quickly?"

"Just act natural," Winks advised, cutting the headlights, then turning back to Eddie as he opened the car door. "Act natural. You can do it, man."

Eddie didn't reply.

"Take a deep breath and count to ten," Cassie instructed him. "Then come out."

She waited for him to follow her advice. Then she followed him out of the car.

The two policemen had walked halfway down the small, treeless yard to greet them. "Hey, how's it going?" the short one called amiably.

The four teenagers stood in a row at the curb, trying to look calm, trying to look normal.

"Any of you live here?" the squat policeman asked. The tall one took off his blue cap, then rearranged it on his blond hair.

"I do," Eddie muttered.

Cassie could feel him trembling beside her.

The two policemen ambled together the rest of the way down the sloping front yard until they were standing about two feet in front of the four friends.

"How long you been away?" the tall one asked Eddie, glancing at the car behind them.

"Not long," Eddie said, shifting his weight awkwardly. "A few minutes."

"Is there a problem?" Winks asked, nervously pushing up his glasses.

"Huh-uh," the tall policeman said, turning his gaze on Winks. "Just that we saw the front door wide open, and no car around, so we thought we'd check."

Scott giggled, relieved. The others remained silent.

"I must've forgot to shut it," Eddie said, glancing at Cassie. "We just went to McDonald's."

"You must've been hungry," the short policeman said, snickering.

His partner remained somber-faced. "You should always lock the door. Especially on Saturday night. It's a bad night for break-ins."

"Thanks," Eddie said, forcing a smile. "That was really nice of you to stop."

The police radio blared suddenly in the patrol car, which was parked across the street. The tall policeman touched the brim of his cap. "Have a nice night," his partner said. The two of them hurried to their car and sped away.

Cassie, Scott, and Winks went inside with Eddie. They spent nearly an hour reassuring him, calming him down, getting him to promise he wouldn't tell anyone about the accident. Then they wearily walked to their homes.

Cassie was pleased to see that her parents had already gone to bed. She really didn't feel like making small talk with them, having to lie about how she spent the evening.

"Oh, we took Eddie's parents' car out for a ride

and ran over a man. Yes, he died. But don't worry, Mom and Dad, no one saw us."

Oh, that would go over real big, wouldn't it? Cassie thought ruefully.

Real big.

It took her a long time to fall asleep and when she finally drifted off, she dreamed she was driving.

Driving and driving and driving down an endless dark road.

She didn't know where she was headed.

She wanted to stop, but she couldn't.

She was lost, she knew. Terribly lost. Surrounded by swirling blackness.

She couldn't stop driving. She had to follow the road wherever it went.

And the road was so bumpy.

So many bumps. Big bumps.

The car was bumping up and down, each bump bouncing her head against the roof with a hard jolt.

Bump bump bump.

So many bumps in the road.

Were the bumps all bodies? she wondered as she drove.

Could she really be driving over so many bodies?

If only she could stop. . . .

But there was no way.

She woke up bathed in sweat, and squinted at the alarm clock beside her on the bed table. Five-twelve.

So early.

But she knew she couldn't get back to sleep.

She didn't feel at all rested. The dream was still vivid in her mind. The endless, black road. The bumps in the road.

"Ohhh," she moaned aloud, and wondered if her three friends were awake, too.

Poor Eddie.

Eddie Katz. Scaredy Katz.

Well, he had reason to be scared now, didn't he? Didn't they all?

No, she decided.

It'll take a while to forget. But it's over.

Over.

The dead man's face loomed up in her mind, but she quickly forced it away.

The Cubs cap. The blue-and-red Cubs cap lingered in her thoughts. And then she saw the gray, staring eyes again.

Accusing her. Accusing them all.

Well, she decided, it's going to be harder than I thought to force the hideous pictures out of my mind. It'll take time. Maybe a lot of time.

But I'm going to do it.

It's over. Over.

Just a nightmare. Like my bumpy-road nightmare.

But now it's over.

She stayed in bed, wide awake, until she heard

her parents rustling about downstairs. Then she got dressed quickly, pulling on a pair of gray sweatpants and matching sweatshirt. She checked herself out in the mirror and was surprised to see that she looked exactly the same.

Her green eyes stared back at her inquisitively. I feel so different, she realized. I feel like an entirely different person. How weird that I should still look like the old me.

She pushed at her blonde, crimped hair until it looked a little less disheveled, then headed down to breakfast.

"What did you do last night?" her mother greeted her from the breakfast table, a steaming cup of coffee in her hand.

"Not much," Cassie said.

The Sunday paper had nothing in it about a hit-and-run killing on Route 12. Cassie listened to the radio that afternoon and watched a local TV newscast at six. Still no report.

Is it possible that the man's body hasn't been found? she wondered.

There wasn't a whole lot of traffic on Route 12. But, surely anyone passing the Hanson Underpass would see a man's body lying on the side of the road.

Puzzled, she called Scott, but he couldn't talk. His parents were standing right there.

Monday morning, Cassie hurried to the front

porch in her nightshirt, and unrolled the newspaper, certain that the story would be in it by now.

Shivering in the morning cold, she quickly scanned the headlines. There were reports of three different traffic accidents in Avondale, and two others just north of the city. But no story about a body being found; no story about a hit-and-run murder.

Murder.

Shivering from more than the cold, she hurried inside and slammed the door.

That night after dinner, Cassie told her parents she was going over to Scott's to study. But as she walked to Scott's house, she knew there was no way they could concentrate on their homework.

"What is going on?" she asked in a low whisper when she and Scott had finally managed to be alone in the den. "It's like the body *vanished* or something." She tucked her legs under her on the red leather couch.

"Maybe no one found it," Scott suggested, pacing back and forth in front of her. "Maybe it's still lying there."

"For two days? In broad daylight?" Cassie asked, forgetting herself and raising her voice.

Scott put a finger to his lips and glanced toward the den door.

"Don't worry. Your parents just think we're making out," Cassie said. "They won't come in."

Scott giggled mirthlessly. "You're right. They

would never suspect we're talking about a murder."

"An accident," she corrected him. "Don't start talking like Eddie."

"How's Eddie doing?" Scott asked.

Cassie shrugged. "I haven't seen him."

"Do you want to try and study?" he asked, leaning heavily against an oak bookshelf.

Cassie shook her head. "I want to drive out to that spot on Route 12 and see if he's still lying there."

"No way," Scott said, making a face.

"Why not?" she demanded.

"In whose car? My parents are home, remember? We can't say 'Give us the car keys. We're going for a ride. See you later.'"

"We could sneak out," Cassie suggested.

"Don't be lame," Scott said sharply. "We couldn't back one of the cars down the driveway without them hearing it." He sighed and pushed himself away from the bookcase. "Listen, Cassie, it's a good thing there've been no news stories."

She stared up at him. "Why do you say that?"

"It means no one is looking for us. We're not in any trouble." He stretched his arms, arching his back, reaching up toward the low, paneled ceiling, his sweatshirt riding up on his stomach.

"How can you be sure?" Cassie asked.

A knock on the door interrupted the conversation.

"What is it, Mom? We're studying," Scott said irritably.

But the door opened, and Eddie walked in. "Hope I'm not interrupting anything." His face turned beet red.

"We're just talking," Cassie said. She motioned for him to close the den door. Across the hall in the living room, Scott's parents were watching some sitcom on TV.

"What's happening?" Eddie asked, glancing at Scott, then Cassie, as he walked toward the couch.

Cassie scooted over to make room for him. The color was fading from his face, but his cheeks were still pink.

"Cassie's all pushed out of shape because our . . . accident hasn't been on TV or anything," Scott said quietly.

"Me, too," Eddie confessed. "It's so weird, isn't it?"

"I want to drive out and see if the body is still there," Cassie said.

Eddie's breath seemed to catch in his throat. He coughed. "Not me," he said finally. "I'm not going back there."

"But aren't you curious?" she demanded. "Don't you want to know if the body was found?"

"No," Eddie said. "I've been forcing the whole thing out of my mind. At least, I've been trying to. I don't want to go back there. I really don't, Cassie.

It'll make me see it all over again. It'll make it fresh again. I won't go. I won't."

"Whoa. Hold on," Scott said sympathetically. "Cool your jets, man. We're not going back there. None of us."

Cassie's face filled with disappointment. "What *are* we going to do? Nothing?"

"Yeah," Scott said. "Nothing." He stopped short. Then stared at Eddie. "I just got an idea," he said. "Eddie, what about your cousin?"

Eddie looked up from the couch, confused. "Jerry?"

"Yeah. Your cousin Jerry. The one who works at the morgue."

"What about Jerry?" Eddie asked. "He wouldn't know why a story didn't get in the newspaper."

"No. But he'd know if the body was found — wouldn't he?" Scott asked excitedly.

"Right!" Cassie cried, jumping up from the couch. She walked over to the desk and picked up the phone. "Here, Eddie — call him."

"But — wait — " Eddie protested.

"Just ask him if someone named Brandt Tinkers was brought in," Cassie said, shoving the phone receiver into his hand.

"And what do I say if Jerry asks me why I want to know?" Eddie demanded, staring unhappily at the phone.

"You'll think of something," Cassie said, "Quick — dial."

"Wait," Scott said, moving in front of Cassie and pushing a button on the phone. "Let's put it on the speaker phone so we can all hear."

"I don't have the number," Eddie whined, reluctantly taking the phone from Cassie. "And I don't know if Jerry works Monday nights."

"It's worth a try," Scott said, leaning over the desk, hovering beside Eddie.

"Oh . . . all right," Eddie said grudgingly. He called Information and got the number for the city morgue. Then he punched in the number.

Leaning in close, all three of them listened to the ring on the speaker phone. They listened to the hoarse voice of the receptionist. Then a few seconds later, Eddie's cousin Jerry came on the line.

They "How's-it-goinged?" each other for a minute or so. Then Eddie got to the point and asked Jerry if a dead man named Brandt Tinkers had been delivered to the morgue.

"Yeah," Jerry replied, his voice rising with surprise.

Cassie gasped.

The three of them glanced at each other, then stared straight ahead at the speaker phone.

"Yeah," Jerry repeated. "The cops brought him in late Saturday night. Still warm. A hit-and-run. He was crushed up really bad. They found him out on some highway. You know the guy, Eddie?"

"No. No, Jerry," Eddie uttered weakly.

"He's a businessman. Some kind of banker or

something," Jerry continued. "The family is keeping the whole thing quiet. To help the cops. I guess the cops are working real hard to find out who ran over the guy." Jerry paused.

The silence seemed heavy.

"That's all I know, Eddie," he continued finally. "How'd you hear about this guy? It hasn't been in the paper or anything."

"Oh . . . I know a kid who knows the guy's kid," Eddie lied, staring at Cassie as he said it.

When he got off the phone, Eddie's face was filled with fear. "Did you hear what Jerry said?" he asked. "He said the police are after us. We're going to be caught. I just know it!"

And at that moment, they heard a hard pounding on the front door.

8

Scott tore open the den door and raced through the front hallway to the door. Cassie and Eddie followed reluctantly behind.

"Don't run!" Scott's dad called, appearing from the living room. "What's your hurry, guys? It sounded like a cattle stampede."

It's the police, thought Cassie.

How did they find us so quickly? And how did they find us here at Scott's house?

Scott pulled open the door. "Oh. Hi, Mr. Olson." Scott sounded almost disappointed. It was his next-door neighbor, a bald, friendly-looking man with crinkly blue eyes. He was holding a red metal tool-box by the handle.

Scott pushed open the storm door.

Mr. Olson stepped into the entryway, stamping his feet on the doormat. "Just wanted to return this," he said, talking to Mr. Baldwin over Scott's shoulder.

"Thanks. Come in, Ed," Scott's dad said, squeezing past the three teenagers to take the box from his neighbor.

Cassie, Eddie, and Scott made their way back to the den.

"That was crazy," Scott said, carefully closing the door.

"I really thought it was the police," Cassie said, slumping back onto the leather couch.

"We've got to calm down. We've *got* to," Scott said heatedly.

"But how *can* we?" Eddie cried, his cheeks bright scarlet. "I *killed* a man!"

"There was no reason to think that was the police," Scott said, keeping his voice low. "The police aren't going to find us. They haven't got a clue. So we've got to stop driving ourselves crazy."

"Scott's right," Cassie said quickly.

Eddie was standing by the window, staring out at the house next door. It was obvious to Scott and Cassie that he hadn't heard a word they'd said. He was off somewhere in his own world, a frightened, confused world.

"I know what I'm going to do," Eddie said suddenly, very softly, not turning around.

"What?" Cassie asked.

"I'm going to turn myself in."

"No, you *can't*!" Cassie insisted, jumping up from

the couch and joining Eddie by the window.

He didn't look at her. Instead, he pressed his forehead against the cool glass. His entire face, she saw, was flaming red.

"You can't," Scott echoed. "We're all in this together, Eddie."

"I was driving," Eddie said, pressing his face against the glass.

"But we were all there," Cassie told him. "We all decided to leave rather than stay and face the consequences. We all were there without a license. All of us."

"If you turn yourself in, you're turning *us* in, too," Scott said.

"No," Eddie insisted, spinning around to face Scott. "I'll tell them I was alone. I'll tell them I took the car myself. There was no one with me. They'll believe that. No reason not to."

"Don't," Cassie pleaded, putting a hand on Eddie's slender shoulder. "Don't mess up your life. Wait a few days, Eddie."

"Cassie's right," Scott said. "Wait a few days. It'll all blow over. You'll feel better. We all will. I know it."

They led Eddie to the couch and sat him down between them. They talked to him for more than half an hour, calming him, reassuring him, pleading with him not to go to the police.

"We just have to wait this out," Cassie said sympathetically. "Sure, it's rough, Eddie. It's roughest for you since you were driving. But you've got to keep remembering that we're all in it together, and we're all with you."

"I keep thinking this is just one of Winks's horrible practical jokes," Eddie said sadly, his hands clasped together tightly in his lap. "I keep thinking that any minute, Winks is going to laugh and yell, 'Gotcha!'" He closed his eyes. "But it isn't a joke," he said softly. "It isn't a joke."

Scott went to the kitchen and returned a few minutes later with three Cokes and a bowl of potato chips. Setting the tray down on the big oak desk, he glanced at Cassie, who returned his glance with a faint smile.

At least we've talked Eddie out of going to the police, her expression told Scott.

The phone rang. Scott picked it up.

The speaker phone was still on. All three of them heard Jerry's voice. "Is Eddie there? His parents said he was with you."

"Yeah, I'm here, Jerry," Eddie called. "What's wrong?"

"Well, you won't believe this, Eddie," Jerry said. "I just had to call you back."

"What's going on?" Eddie asked, his expression tight with worry. Scott and Cassie froze, listening intently to the voice coming through the small speaker.

"You know that corpse you called me about? That Tinkers corpse."

"Yeah, Jerry. Yeah?" Eddie couldn't hide his impatience.

"Well, the corpse was here when I talked to you," Jerry continued, sounding baffled. "But it isn't here now."

"Huh?" Scott cried, leaning over the phone.

"It disappeared, man," Jerry said. "Gone. I mean, like it got up and walked out."

9

Tuesday morning, Cassie found it impossible to concentrate in class. Mr. Miller called her name three times before she realized he was talking to her. Everyone laughed.

She felt as if she were surrounded by fog. Her friends and classmates appeared to be drifting, their smiling faces far away in the mist, their voices distant and muffled.

She had lunch in the cafeteria, finding a spot at a corner table with Scott and Eddie.

"What *is* that on your plate?" Scott asked, pointing with his fork at the yellow-and-white substance.

"Macaroni and cheese, I think," Cassie said, making a face. "I should've just taken an apple or something."

"What happened in Miller's class this morning?" Eddie asked. "He practically stood on his head to get your attention."

Cassie shrugged. "Just thinking about things," she said, mushing her fork around in the macaroni but not lifting any to her mouth. "I didn't hear him call me."

"Didn't sleep last night?" Scott asked. "You should've called me. I was up, too."

"I guess none of us are sleeping too well," Eddie said, gazing at the ham sandwich his mother had packed for him. He raised his eyes to Cassie. "I keep thinking about that corpse disappearing."

"Don't think about it," Scott said curtly. He took a big bite of his turkey sandwich. Mayonnaise ran down his chin.

"Jerry was really freaked out about it," Eddie said.

Cassie gingerly tasted the macaroni. It wasn't bad. She took another forkful.

"Know what I keep thinking?" Eddie asked, his cheeks reddening.

"Can we change the subject?" Scott demanded, glaring at Eddie impatiently. "It's enough already. We're okay, Eddie. There's no problem. It's time to stop talking about it."

"Give him a break, Scott," Cassie said quietly. "Why are you so pushed out of shape this afternoon? Let Eddie talk."

Scott scowled at her and rolled his eyes.

"Know what I think?" Eddie repeated, ignoring Scott's impatience. "I think this sounds like something Winks would do."

"Huh?" Scott's mouth dropped open, revealing a white gob of chewed-up turkey.

"You mean steal the corpse?" Cassie asked, not understanding.

"Yeah." Eddie nodded. "Don't you think?"

Cassie and Scott didn't reply immediately.

"I mean, he's always playing really mean jokes on me," Eddie said, nervously folding and unfolding his lunch bag. "He just thinks it's a riot to embarrass me, or make me squirm and feel like a total fool."

"Whoa," Scott said, holding up a big hand as if to hold Eddie back. "Winks just likes practical jokes, that's all. He does it to everyone."

"That's not true," Eddie replied sharply. "I'm his number-one victim, and you know it."

"I don't think Winks would go this far," Cassie interrupted softly, hoping to stop their argument before it got out of control.

"Hey, Katz! Scaredy Katz!" a boy named Gary Franz called from a table across the room. A milk carton came flying onto their table, landing in Cassie's macaroni.

Cassie grabbed it, jumped to her feet, and angrily prepared to heave it back. But Miss Meltzer, the lunchroom monitor, was staring at her from the center of the room.

Cassie sat back down. She heard raucous laughter from Gary Franz's table. "He's a creep," she muttered, tossing the milk carton aside.

"Everyone gives me a hard time," Eddie said,

almost mournfully. "But Winks started it. He was the first one to call me Scaredy Katz. And he's the only one who — "

"Winks might take an eyeball," Cassie interrupted, gesturing for Eddie to calm down, "but I don't think he'd take an entire *corpse*."

"No way," Scott said, shaking his head. "Why would he do it?"

"Just to scare me," Eddie replied. "He would. I know he would."

"Well," Scott said thoughtfully, "there's only one way to find out."

Cassie and Eddie stared back at him.

"Ask him," Scott said. "We'll go ask him."

They didn't see Winks all afternoon. After school, Cassie and Eddie hung around doing homework in the library while Scott had wrestling team practice in the gym.

Scott emerged a little before five, red-faced and weary, his blond hair wet and matted down on his head. He tossed his backpack over the shoulders of his bulky blue-and-gold letter jacket and led the way out the front door of the school.

"Coach gave us a real workout," he explained. "Had us doing laps all afternoon. Good conditioning, I guess. But I didn't sign on for track — I signed on for wrestling."

"Poor boy," Cassie said in a tiny voice, patting him on the back with mock sympathy.

Eddie scurried to keep up with them, walking in thoughtful silence.

It was a damp, gray day. The whole world seemed to be laid out in shades of gray. No color anywhere to be seen.

They walked to Winks's house, not saying much.

Winks pulled open the front door, a startled expression on his face. "A surprise?" he exclaimed. "Is it my birthday already?"

No one laughed.

"What's wrong?" Winks asked, turning serious.

"Can you come out for a while?" Cassie asked, seeing Winks's mom hovering behind him in the hallway. "Hi, Mrs. Winkleman," she called, waving to her.

Winks's mom waved back and called out a greeting.

"I can't," Winks said softly. "I'm — I'm kind of grounded. In fact, you guys have to go."

"Grounded?" Eddie asked suspiciously. "How come?"

Winks turned to check behind him. His mother had disappeared into the kitchen. "The eyeball," he said, making a sour face. "I took it home. My mom was cleaning my room and — "

Scott giggled. "She found it?"

Winks nodded.

Everyone laughed.

"It's not funny," Winks said. "She nearly lost her

lunch. I meant to get rid of the thing. It didn't keep too well. You could practically die from the smell alone. Anyway, when I got home, she shoved the box into my hands. And asked me to explain what it was doing in my room."

"What did you tell her?" Cassie asked.

"I said it was for a science experiment," Winks replied. "For extra credit. But she didn't buy it. She grounded me." Hearing footsteps, he looked behind him. "You guys have got to go."

He started to close the storm door, but Eddie pulled it back open. "Winks — did you take the corpse from the morgue?" he asked.

"Ssshhh!" Winks raised a finger to his lips and checked behind him once more. "Why don't you let the whole neighborhood hear, Katz?"

"Did you?" Eddie repeated, a little softer. "Did you take the body?"

"Yeah. I've got him up in my room," Winks replied.

"Huh?" Scott cried.

Cassie and Eddie stared at Winks in surprise.

"That's a joke, guys. An eyeball is enough. You know?" Winks shook his head. "It got me in enough trouble."

"You didn't take it?" Eddie repeated, unable to hide the suspicion from his voice.

"No way," Winks said heatedly. "I'm not a *ghoul*, Katz."

"Who's not a ghoul?" Mrs. Winkleman asked, appearing behind Winks in the doorway.

"I'm not," Winks said, flashing her a phony grin.

"Yes, you are," his mother said. "If you go by what you keep in your room. You're *definitely* a ghoul."

"Very funny, Mom," Winks said, sighing.

"We're all very funny in this family," she said, frowning at Winks. "You kids have to go, I'm afraid. Sorry to be rude. But the uncool ghoul here is grounded. That means no visitors."

"We were just going," Cassie told her.

"See you guys," Winks said.

"No, he won't," Mrs. Winkleman said, pulling the storm door shut.

"He doesn't have the corpse," Scott said to Eddie as they walked down the driveway. "You need a better theory."

"No, he doesn't," Cassie said. "No more theories, Eddie. No more ideas. No more thoughts about the missing corpse. Just force yourself to think about other things."

"Cassie's right," Scott said, putting his arm heavily around her slender shoulders as they crunched over the gravel. "It's all over. Done with."

"A done deal," Eddie said. "A done deal." But his expression remained thoughtful, his eyes on the gray distance.

That night, just after eleven, Cassie was struggling through her chapter in the government textbook, trying to get her eyes to focus on the blur of type, when the phone rang. She picked it up after the first ring. "Hello?"

"Is this Cassie Martin?" a woman's voice asked.

"Yes."

"This is the operator. I have a collect call for you from Brandt Tinkers. Will you accept the charges?"

Cassie nearly swallowed her bubble gum. Her mouth dropped open, but no sound came out.

"Will you accept the charges?" the operator repeated impatiently.

Brandt Tinkers?

What's going on here? Cassie wondered.

Her heart began to thud against her chest. Her hands went ice cold.

"Uh . . . yes. Okay," she managed to reply in a shaky voice.

"Go ahead, please," the operator said, and then clicked off.

Cassie heard crackling on the line.

"Hello?"

More crackling. And then a sound like a gasp, a dry gust of wind.

"You can't run away."

The voice wasn't a whisper. It was a breeze. A burst of air.

A burst of foul air.

"You can't run away."

And then the line went dead, leaving Cassie trembling and cold.

10

"Cassie!"

Cassie slammed her locker on her finger. "Ow! Eddie, you scared me!"

"Sorry." His face turned crimson.

Cassie shook her hand hard, then sucked on the throbbing finger.

It was a little after eight-thirty on Wednesday morning. The bell for homeroom would ring in less than five minutes.

Eddie was wearing navy-blue corduroy slacks and a faded Bart Simpson T-shirt. He gazed at her with concern. "Is your finger okay?"

"Yeah, I always slam it in my locker to wake myself up," Cassie said sarcastically. Seeing the hurt look on his face, she softened her tone. "It's not broken."

"I got a phone call last night," Eddie said, leaning close and whispering confidentially.

"Hey, Katz — why don't you kiss her?" someone yelled, then laughed and disappeared around the corner.

"So did I," Cassie said, blowing on the still-painful finger. She was wearing an emerald-green sweater that matched her eyes and made her blonde hair seem to glow. Using her good hand, she straightened the hem of the sweater, pulling it down over the faded denim miniskirt she wore over heavy black tights.

"What — do you think?" Eddie stammered, staring hard into her eyes, as if trying to read her thoughts.

"I think it was some stupid practical joker," Cassie said angrily.

Eddie's face fell in disappointment.

Cassie snickered. "Come on, Eddie, you didn't really think it was a dead man calling, did you?"

He avoided her stare.

"You really are gullible," Cassie muttered, then immediately regretted it when she saw his features tighten and his face redden. "It had to be a joke, Eddie," she said, putting a hand on his shoulder.

"But who?" he asked, in almost a plea.

She shrugged. "It sure as heck wasn't Brandt Tinkers."

The bell rang. Cassie lifted her backpack to her shoulder.

Eddie didn't move. "The voice on the phone said, 'You can't run away.' "

"Same as my call," Cassie said, turning her eyes down the rapidly emptying hall.

"And then he said, 'I know you were driving,' " Eddie told her.

Her mouth formed a small O of surprise. Then she shook her head as if shaking it all out of her mind. "Just a stupid joke. Someone being dumb."

"But the four of us — we're the only ones who know," Eddie said.

"We're going to be late," Cassie said, staring down the empty corridor. Classroom doors were closing all down the hall.

"I don't care!" He grabbed her shoulder. "I — I can't think about class. This is just too weird, Cassie, too creepy."

"What are you going to do?" Cassie asked. His hand was cold through her sweater. She could see that he was trembling.

He really is a scaredy-cat, she thought, and then silently scolded herself for being so cruel.

"I'm going to cut this morning," Eddie said. "Come with me?"

"No," Cassie replied, pulling away from his grip. "I can't. I mean, I don't want to. We have to go on with our lives, Eddie. As if nothing happened. We have to."

"Please?" he asked, pleading with her with his solemn dark eyes.

"No. And you shouldn't cut, either. Come on. Come to homeroom. Please."

The second and final bell rang. Cassie saw the door to her homeroom close. She shifted her backpack and began jogging toward it, her sneakers thudding loudly on the hard floor.

"Eddie, come on!" she called, her voice echoing in the empty corridor.

But he shook his head. Then he turned and disappeared around the corner.

What's he going to do outside by himself? Cassie wondered. Is he just going to wander around all day, having morbid thoughts, scaring himself even more?

As she opened the door and hurried to her seat, she felt guilty for a moment. I should have gone with Eddie, she thought. He asked for my help, and I refused.

She settled into her seat, let the backpack drop to her feet, and glanced up to the front row where Scott sat. He grinned back at her. He was wearing a hideously bright, fire-engine-red sweater. Cassie hoped he hadn't picked it out himself.

After attendance had been taken and a few announcements had been made, the bell rang for first period. Cassie picked up her heavy backpack and waited for Scott at the door as everyone piled out of the room.

"Hey, how's it going?" he asked cheerfully, deliberately bumping into her.

She caught herself against the wall. "Did you get a phone call last night?"

He shook his head. "From you? No, you didn't call me. Where were you?"

"No, not from me," she said, giving him a playful shove out the door. "A . . . scary phone call."

He shook his head again, his blond hair still wet from his morning shower.

"Eddie and I got weird phone calls," Cassie told him as they headed up the stairs to their first-period class.

"Me, too!" Winks cried, and grabbed each of them by a shoulder.

Cassie cried out in surprise. Scott, also startled, swung his body around, nearly toppling Winks down the stairs.

"You're dead meat, Winks," Scott said, making a fist. "Don't sneak up on me again!"

Winks ignored him. "I got a call, too, Cassie," he said, his face turning serious. "From the dead guy."

"What?" Scott uttered his high-pitched giggle.

"It isn't funny," Cassie snapped at Scott.

"Are you guys freaking out?" Scott asked.

They stopped at the top of the stairs. "What did he say to you?" Cassie asked Winks.

"He said, 'You can't run away.' "

"To me, too," Cassie told him. "He called Eddie, too."

"Weird you didn't get a call," Winks said to Scott. "You're the only one."

"Hey, you're blocking traffic!" someone yelled, bumping into Cassie.

The bell rang.

"Later," Scott said, starting to jog.

"Someone's trying to scare us," Winks said, following Cassie.

"They did a pretty good job scaring Eddie," she confided.

"So what else is new?" Winks exclaimed and, tossing his shaggy, brown hair, disappeared into the classroom.

Cassie had just finished helping her father with the dinner dishes when the phone rang. It rang once, then stopped. Her mother, she realized, must have picked it up in the other room.

"Cassie, it's for you!" Mrs. Martin called. "Don't talk too long. You said you've got a ton of homework tonight."

"I know, I know," Cassie muttered. She picked up the phone — and felt a heavy stab of dread in her chest.

Is it the dead man?

"Hello?"

"Hi, Cassie, it's me. Are you still eating dinner?" It was Eddie, sounding frightened, as usual.

"No. Just finished. I've got so much homework, I — "

"Cassie, come over. You've *got* to."

"Eddie, I can't," she insisted. "I just told you — "

"No. Please. Come over right now," Eddie said. Something in his voice told her she had no choice.

"Hi, Cassie. How've you been?"

"Hi, Mrs. Katz. I'm fine."

Eddie's mother was short and more than a little plump. She looked like a very round version of her son. She had the same blushing cheeks as Eddie, and the same black, curly hair, which she wore cut boyishly short. Even though it was only seven-thirty, she was already in a flannel nightgown and bathrobe.

"Aren't you feeling well?" Cassie asked, then felt foolish.

"Pardon this old bathrobe. I get so tired after work, I like to get comfortable," Mrs. Katz said, her cheeks reddening.

"Hi, how's it going?" Eddie asked, entering the tiny, hot living room.

"Okay," Cassie replied uncomfortably.

"Eddie said you two were going to study together," Mrs. Katz said, ushering Cassie over to the dinner table, which, since there was no dining room, occupied one corner of the living room.

"Oh, yeah. Right," Cassie lied, glancing at Eddie, as if to say, what's going on here?

"Well, come have some dessert before you start," Mrs. Katz said, pulling Cassie by the arm. "I made a cake. It's from a mix, but it's very moist. You like yellow cake?"

"Yes. Fine. I mean, thank you," Cassie stammered.

The three of them sat down and had slices of cake and cups of tea. Eddie kept staring meaningfully at Cassie. It was obvious that he was dying to tell her something.

But Mrs. Katz kept up a stream of conversation, and wouldn't take no for an answer after offering seconds on the cake.

"Mom, we've really got to start studying," Eddie said, his cheeks aflame, his second slice of cake only half-eaten.

"So who's stopping you?" she replied. She grinned at Cassie. "You liked the cake?"

"It was very good," Cassie said. "Very moist." She patted her stomach.

Mrs. Katz grinned. "So what are you two studying?"

"Math," Eddie said.

"Government," Cassie said at the same time.

"Oh, right. Government. Mom, we really don't have time to discuss it," Eddie said impatiently.

Mrs. Katz jumped to her feet, an offended look on her face. "Excuse me for living," she said sarcastically. "I was just trying to show an interest."

She gathered up the three plates and carried them into the tiny kitchen.

"Come upstairs," Eddie whispered.

Cassie followed him up the narrow, uncarpeted stairway, the stairs creaking under their feet. Eddie's room was the entire upstairs. It had been a storage space, but Eddie's dad had finished it off to provide Eddie his own room. Cassie had to duck her head. The ceiling was low and followed the sloping eaves.

"After dinner, I was carrying the garbage down to the street," Eddie said excitedly. "And look what I found hooked on the handle of the front door."

He pulled something out from under his bedspread and held it up for Cassie to see.

It was a red-and-blue Cubs cap.

Cassie gasped.

"There was a note tucked inside," Eddie said. He pulled it out of the cap and read it to her.

"My hat is off to the driver who killed me."

11

Saturday morning as Cassie was finishing her French toast, the phone rang. "Who would call this early?" Mrs. Martin, still in her nightgown and flannel bathrobe, asked.

"Only one way to find out," Cassie said. She lifted the receiver off the kitchen wall phone. "Hello?"

"I'm having a bad morning."

"Scott? What's your problem?" Cassie asked. She turned to her mother. "It's Scott."

"I dropped my toothbrush in the toilet," he said. Cassie laughed.

"Not so loud!" her mother pleaded, covering her ears. Mrs. Martin couldn't stand loud noises in the morning.

"You *what?*" Cassie exclaimed.

"You heard me," Scott replied grumpily. "I dropped my toothbrush in the toilet."

"How?"

"It wasn't easy," he muttered.

Cassie laughed again. "Did you really call this early just to tell me what an incredible klutz you are?"

"I'm sick, too, I think," Scott said, his voice hoarse and scratchy.

"You're definitely a sicko," Cassie joked.

"No. Really. I think I have the flu or something," he insisted. "I may not be able to meet you guys tonight."

"Boo-hoo." Cassie pretended to sob.

"You could at least be sympathetic," he snapped. "I mean, I'm sick, and I dropped my toothbrush in the toilet."

"Did you fish it out?" she asked.

"Not yet."

"Cassie, your French toast is going to be ice cold," her mother called from the table.

"I've got to go," Cassie said, turning her back on her mother. "I'm sorry about your toothbrush."

"What are you doing today?" he asked.

"Helping my dad. We're scraping the paint off the porch. So he can paint it."

"Thrills," Scott said.

"I promised him weeks ago," Cassie said.

"Cassie, your breakfast," her mother called.

"Call me later," Cassie said quickly. "Feel better."

She hung up and returned to the table. She

stabbed her fork into a square of French toast, dipped it in syrup, and raised it to her mouth. "Mom," she complained, "this French toast is ice cold!"

"Very funny," her mother said, rolling her eyes. "What did Scott want?"

"Nothing. He wanted to tell me he dropped his toothbrush in the toilet." Cassie wiped syrup off her chin with a paper napkin.

"You and those three guys certainly are close," Mrs. Martin said, staring at Cassie as if examining her.

"What's that supposed to mean?" Cassie asked edgily.

"Nothing. Not a thing," her mother replied quickly, raising both hands as if to hold Cassie back. "I just mean it's unusual for a girl your age to be so close with three boys."

"I don't think it's so *unusual*," Cassie said, pronouncing each syllable of unusual as if it were a foreign word. "They're nice guys."

"I didn't say they weren't," Mrs. Martin said defensively. "Let's just drop the subject, okay? I wasn't trying to get you upset."

"I'm not upset," Cassie told her. She shoved the plate away. She couldn't eat another bite. French toast for breakfast made her feel as if she weighed a thousand pounds.

The kitchen door opened, and her father came in, his face red from the cold, carrying two large brown shopping bags from Charlton's, a nearby lumber store. "I'm back," he declared.

"We can see that," Mrs. Martin said sharply. "Close the door. You're letting in the cold."

"I rented an electric sander, and I got a ton of sandpaper and a new plane," he announced.

"Does this mean you're serious about working on the porch?" Cassie asked, grinning. She knew it was a foolish question.

She and her father worked all morning and most of the afternoon. "I'll never get the paint dust out of my hair," Cassie complained, just after lunch.

"It looks good," her father joked, wiping the perspiration off his forehead with the sleeve of his sweatshirt. "Gives you some sparkle."

"I hate sparkle," Cassie replied.

As she worked, sanding the corners the electric sander couldn't reach, she thought about Eddie. The poor guy was just about having a nervous breakdown.

It had taken all of her convincing skills to keep him from calling the Avondale police and telling them about the accident. Scott and Winks had worked on him, too, reassuring him, explaining to him what a mistake it would be, and then, finally, pleading with him not to do anything, to wait it out.

On Thursday night, Eddie and Winks had received another phone call, supposedly from the corpse. This call was the same as the first — the dry, airy whisper of a voice over the crackling phone line. The same words — *you can't run away*.

So far, Scott was the only one who hadn't received a call.

Or a visit.

The red-and-blue Cubs cap flashed into Cassie's mind. It was so creepy holding it in her hand, running her fingers over the brim, stretching the elastic, knowing that it had been worn by a dead man.

A man they had killed.

Who left the cap on Eddie's door?

Who was making the calls?

Her suspicions had immediately fallen on Winks. But this was too ghastly, too cruel and sick, even for him. And, she saw Winks was just as frightened as the rest of them, even though he kept insisting that the accident was old news and that he didn't care about some joker making stupid prank phone calls.

Some joker.

Which joker?

Was someone on the Hanson Underpass that night? Had someone been standing on the old bridge when they hit Brandt Tinkers? Had someone witnessed the whole thing?

If so, it would have to have been someone who knew them, Cassie realized. Someone who recognized them, who knew where they lived, where to phone them.

And that was impossible.

The Hanson Underpass was miles out of town. There would be no reason for anyone they knew to be on that bridge that night.

What a mystery.

What a frightening, puzzling mystery.

"What are you thinking about?" Her father's voice interrupted her thoughts.

"Huh?"

"You looked a million miles away." He smiled at her, but his expression was apprehensive.

It had taken Cassie a while to come out of her thoughts, to realize that the whir of the electric sander had stopped, to see that her father was staring at her expectantly.

"Oh. Nothing," she replied. "Just thinking about school, I guess."

"When's your spring break?" he asked, turning his eyes to a spot on the ceiling he had missed.

"April," she told him. "First week in April."

"I'd like to plan a vacation," he said, moving the aluminum ladder. "For all three of us. Where'd you like to go?"

"Someplace far, far away," Cassie replied, without thinking.

She phoned Scott after dinner. He had the flu. He couldn't go out.

Cassie replaced the receiver, feeling disappointed. She knew she felt something more than friendship for Scott. She could tell he felt the same way.

In some strange way, the horrible accident and all that had followed had brought them even closer together, Cassie thought.

Wishful thinking?

She was pondering this when the phone rang in her hand, startling her.

The heavy feeling of dread weighed in again.

She felt it now every time the phone rang. It could be the dry, dead voice on the other end.

"Hello?"

"Hi, Cassie. It's me. Eddie."

"Are we meeting at the tenplex?" Cassie asked. "Did you check to see what's playing?"

"I — I'm not coming," Eddie said hesitantly.

"Huh?"

"I feel kind of bummed out," he said. "I'm just going to stay home and veg out. Watch the tube."

"Okay, Eddie." Cassie couldn't conceal her disappointment. After working all day, she really felt like going out. "You know, Scott's sick. Flu."

"My mom's got it, too," Eddie said. "Maybe that's why I feel so bummed out. Maybe I'm coming down with it, too."

"Hope not," Cassie said. "Talk to you tomorrow."

She hung up and groaned loudly. First Scott, then Eddie. I don't want to go out just with Winks, she thought. She liked Winks. But she mainly liked him when the others were around.

She decided to call him and tell him that no one felt like getting together, that she was going to stay home with her parents.

When she called, Mrs. Winkleman answered the phone. "Is that you, Cassie?" she asked. "Winks just left. I thought I heard him say he was heading over to your house."

"Oh. I see. I thought I'd catch him," Cassie replied. She thanked Mrs. Winkleman and hung up, trying to decide what to do.

What the heck, she thought. I'll go to the tenplex with Winks. I've got to get out of the house.

Winks lived five blocks away. She decided to start walking and meet him halfway. Pulling her down jacket out of the front closet, she yelled, "I'm going out! See you later!" to her parents and headed out the door.

It was a clear, cold night. Cassie glanced up at the full, white moon, zipping her jacket as she jogged down the drive.

She turned left, cutting across the Culbertsons' front yard, heading toward Winks's house, her sneakers thudding softly over the frozen ground.

Somewhere down the block, a little boy was calling to his mother.

He's out awfully late, Cassie thought. She glanced at her watch. It was only seven-thirty.

It's as dark as midnight, she thought, wishing winter was over.

A dog barked. A door slammed.

When she turned the corner onto Mulberry, she expected to see Winks.

The bright lights made her stop in surprise. She raised a hand to shield her eyes from the sudden glare.

What was going on?

The owners of the corner house, the Roths, had all of their front-yard floodlights on. The entire corner was bathed in harsh yellow light, brighter than daylight.

It took a while for Cassie's eyes to adjust to the brightness. When they did, she saw Mr. and Mrs. Roth and three of their children, huddled in the street.

None of them were wearing coats.

Cassie moved forward and saw something in the street.

A pile of clothing?

No. Someone was lying on the pavement.

And Mr. Roth was leaning over the person.

"Hey!" Cassie called.

She started to run.

The porch lights went on in the house across the street. A man came running down the driveway.

"Is he going to be okay?" Cassie heard one of the Roth kids ask. The little kid was crying. His mother picked him up.

"What happened?" Cassie asked, stepping up beside them. She looked down and gasped. "Winks!"

He was on his back, his head tilted at a strange

angle. His eyes were closed. There was blood on the front of his blue denim jacket.

"We called the ambulance," Mr. Roth told her. As he said this, they could hear sirens approaching from the distance.

"But what *happened*?" Cassie screamed, staring down at her unconscious friend.

"I was at the window," Mrs. Roth said. "He was walking at the curb. A car hit him. And then sped off."

"A hit-and-run," her husband said quietly.

12

The hospital walls were pea-soup green. The fluorescent lights on the low ceiling made everything — and everyone — look even greener.

What is that odor? Cassie wondered, stepping off the elevator and searching for the Intensive Care Unit. It smelled like medicine, like alcohol or ether or formaldehyde mixed with detergent, an odor found only in hospitals.

White-uniformed nurses passed by without looking at her. Two doctors in green lab coats were talking softly against a wall. The corridor was narrow, almost tunnellike. Cassie had to squeeze past them.

Down the corridor, past a deserted nurses' station, she saw Mrs. Winkleman, in a tan cloth coat, a big, black box of a pocketbook in her lap, sitting on a folding chair, her chubby hands clasping the handle of the bag tightly.

She didn't look up until Cassie was standing right in front of her. "Oh. Hi," she said. Her eyes were red. Her round cheeks revealed tear tracks running down both sides.

"What did the doctors say?" Cassie asked, standing awkwardly in front of Mrs. Winkleman's chair, trying to decide what to do with her hands. "Is Winks — ?"

"Still unconscious," Mrs. Winkleman said, avoiding Cassie's stare. Fresh tears formed in her eyes.

"But the doctors — ?" Cassie wasn't sure what to ask.

"I'm all alone," Mrs. Winkleman said, her voice in a whisper. "Dan is in Detroit. On business. I tried to call him, but he wasn't at his hotel."

"Would you like me to call him for you?" Cassie asked, eager to help in some way, any way.

Mrs. Winkleman shook her head. She wiped a tear from one eye with a finger.

"I'm sure Winks will be okay," Cassie said, realizing it sounded phony.

"He has some broken ribs. A broken arm. Some internal injuries," Mrs. Winkleman said. Her hands were pale white against the black pocketbook.

A cart went by, filled with small brown bottles, pushed by a white-smocked man with a grizzly white beard. He dipped his head in a nod as he passed by.

"Mrs. Roth saw the car. The car that hit him," Winks's mother said, her voice trembling. She sighed and wiped away another tear. "But she didn't know what kind of car it was."

"Did she — ?"

"She said it hit him and just kept going," Mrs. Winkleman said, shaking her head.

"How awful," Cassie muttered, crossing her arms protectively over her chest. It seemed about a hundred degrees in the hallway, but she still felt chilled.

"I can't believe it. I just can't believe it," Mrs. Winkleman said, sobbing.

"Where is Winks?" Cassie asked.

Mrs. Winkleman pointed to the door. And as she pointed, it swung open and a serious-faced young doctor with slicked-back brown hair, wearing a green surgical gown, stepped out.

"Mrs. Winkleman?" He spoke in a soft but deep voice.

Mrs. Winkleman jumped to her feet. "Is Bruce — ?"

"The internal injuries don't look serious," the doctor said, glancing at Cassie as he spoke. "We're encouraged. We're not certain we've stopped all the bleeding, though."

Mrs. Winkleman gasped.

"But we're keeping a close eye on him. We'll be monitoring him for the next couple of days."

"Is he awake? Can I see him?" his mother asked eagerly.

"Not yet," the doctor said somberly. "He hasn't

regained consciousness yet. It has us a little concerned. We did a brain scan. No sign of any problem there. It'll just take a little time. We're watching him. All of his vital signs are good."

Cassie stared at the doctor, trying to determine if he was telling the whole truth or if he was making Winks's condition sound better than it was. She decided the doctor had no reason not to be honest with Winks's mom.

"There's a waiting room just around that corner," the doctor told them, pointing. "You might be more comfortable there."

"No. I'll stay here," Mrs. Winkleman insisted. "If it's okay."

"Yes, it's okay," the doctor said, nodding to another green-gowned doctor who hurried past. "We'll let you know if there's any change in Bruce's condition."

He disappeared through the door to the Intensive Care Unit.

Mrs. Winkleman dropped back into the folding chair with a loud groan. "I can't believe it. I just can't believe it," she said, more to herself than to Cassie. "Saturday night, and look where I am."

"He sounded pretty encouraging," Cassie said. "He said — " She stopped, recognizing the two figures hurrying through the narrow, green corridor toward them.

"Eddie! Scott!"

The two boys, Eddie in his blue down vest, Scott

in a heavy wool parka, came up to her, their expressions set, squinting in the harsh, green light.

"How is he?" Scott asked eagerly.

"We don't know yet," Cassie told them.

"I just can't believe it," Mrs. Winkleman muttered, gripping and releasing the handle of her bag.

Scott turned away from them and sneezed violently. "Sorry," he said, searching his jeans pockets and pulling out a wad of tissues. "I'm really sick."

"You shouldn't have come," Cassie told him. "They don't want sick people in a hospital." What a bad time to make a joke like that, Cassie thought. What's *wrong* with me, anyway?

She was glad Scott had come, she realized. She was glad both boys had come. It helped her feel a little less alone, a little more like things were normal.

Normal?

She wondered what that word meant. She wondered if she would ever feel normal again.

"Where did it happen?" Eddie asked, unzipping his vest and leaning back against the wall.

"Just a few blocks from my house," Cassie said.

"He was walking to Cassie's," Mrs. Winkleman said quietly, glancing at Eddie. "One minute he was walking. The next minute . . ."

Cassie put a hand on her shoulder.

"Did the doctors say he'd be okay?" Scott asked.

"They don't know. He's still unconscious," Cassie said.

Eddie let out a gasp. "He isn't awake?"

Mrs. Winkleman shook her head. "The doctor said his brain is normal, thank God."

Normal, Cassie thought. There's that word again.

The door to the Intensive Care Unit opened, and two doctors walked out. "Any news about my son?" Mrs. Winkleman called as they passed by.

"No change," one of the doctors said brusquely, and the two of them continued down the hall.

Cassie and the two boys stayed with Mrs. Winkleman outside the Intensive Care Unit for another couple of hours. But when the doctor came out to report that Winks was stable but still not conscious, they decided they had to leave for home.

Scott was coughing and wheezing. Cassie felt his perspiring forehead. He definitely had a fever.

Eddie had pulled into himself like a frightened turtle. He had been silent the whole time, staring down at the floor. He seemed very relieved to be leaving, and practically ran to the phone booth to call his dad to come pick them up.

"Shall I drop you guys at your houses?" Mr. Katz asked as they piled into the old Chevy. He had to repeat the question. Being in the car again, the car that had hit and killed someone, gave both Cassie and Scott the creeps.

"Well, guys?" Mr. Katz repeated, a striped wool

ski cap covering his slender, bald head.

"Uh . . . bring them to our house, Dad," Eddie said. "That okay with you guys? We can talk a little."

Cassie really wanted to go home, but she recognized the panicky expression on Eddie's face. Realizing he needed their help, she reluctantly agreed. "Just for a few minutes," she told Eddie. "Scott has to go home and get back into bed."

Scott sneezed as if to demonstrate the truth of her words.

Mr. Katz asked about Winks, shaking his head, repeating again and again that he didn't think such a thing was possible in a quiet, peaceful community like North Avondale.

"Imagine. A hit-and-run," he said, pulling the car to the curb in front of their tiny house. "What kind of a person would do such a thing? Don't they have any kind of conscience at all?"

The three teenagers didn't reply. They glanced at each other, sharing the same thoughts, sharing the same memories, the same horrifying pictures flashing through their minds.

Eddie's shoulders shook. He looked about ready to confess to his dad that he was a hit-and-run driver, too.

We're *all* hit-and-run drivers, Cassie thought. We're all killers.

Eddie's father slammed the car door and went

running over the small square of a front yard and disappeared around the back. The three teenagers lingered at the curb.

"Poor Winks," Scott said, his voice a deep croak. He started to cough.

"A hit-and-run," Eddie said. "It couldn't be an accident."

Cassie's mouth dropped open. This was stretching things a bit far, even for Eddie. "Don't try to make this into more than it is," she warned Eddie. "It was an accident."

"No way," Eddie said, kicking at a clod of dirt with the toe of his sneaker.

"What are you saying, man?" Scott asked, wiping his nose with a tissue. "You think it *wasn't* an accident?"

Eddie didn't reply for a long while. "You tell me," he said finally in a low whisper. "You tell me. You think it's just a coincidence that we kill someone in a hit-and-run, and the next week Winks gets hit?"

"Yes, I think it's a coincidence," Cassie said heatedly. "Of *course* it's a coincidence. Don't be dumb, Eddie. It's one thing to be frightened. But don't get totally *dumb*."

He recoiled as if her words had stung him.

"I've got to get home. I feel like I'm dying," Scott moaned.

"A few more minutes," Eddie insisted. "Come inside. It's cold out here. I'll make you some tea. Come on. Please," he pleaded.

Scott glanced at Cassie. Cassie looked back at Eddie. "Hot tea would feel really good right now. I'm frozen." She pulled Scott by the arm. "Come on, sicko. Tea is what the doctor ordered."

They headed up to the house. And stopped on the front stoop under the bright porch light when they saw the large envelope tucked in the storm door.

"Oh, no," Eddie said quietly.

Cassie pulled the envelope out from the door. It was blank on both sides. No name or address. "What makes you think this is something terrible?" she asked Eddie.

"This is where I found the Cubs cap," he said, swallowing hard.

"That doesn't mean anything."

"Just open it up, will you?" Scott cried impatiently. "I really have to get inside. I'm shaking all over."

The envelope was sealed tightly. Cassie had trouble pulling it open. Finally, she ripped it, tearing along the top. Then she reached her hand in and pulled out a sheet of white, lined notebook paper.

"What is it? What's it say?" Eddie asked eagerly, his voice revealing his fear, leaning close over Cassie's shoulder.

She held the note up to the porch light. Scrawled in purple crayon were the words:

ONE DOWN, THREE TO GO.

"Oh, man," Scott said, shivering inside his big parka.

"I knew it," Eddie cried. "I knew what happened to Winks wasn't an accident."

Cassie stared at the words, reading them again and again until they blurred together, until they made no sense at all.

She grasped the envelope tightly. "There's something else inside it," she said.

Her heart thudding in her chest, she reached inside and pulled out a glossy, cardboard square.

A Polaroid photograph.

Cassie held it under the porch light. All three teenagers squeezed close together to stare at it.

"Hey, what's going on?" cried Scott, gaping at the Polaroid shot. "It — it *can't* be!!"

13

The photograph slipped from Cassie's hand and fluttered off the stoop. Scott and Eddie both grabbed for it. Then Eddie dived off the stoop and scooped it up from the grass.

Even though it was no longer in her hand, Cassie still saw the horrifying image. It was an image she knew she would never be able to forget.

The Polaroid showed Scott's parents' car, the silver Volvo. The photo had been snapped to show the driver's side of the car. She knew it was Scott's silver Volvo because of the dark scratch on the driver's door.

Sitting behind the wheel, his head turned to face the camera, was Brandt Tinkers.

The corpse.

Smiling at the camera.

Sitting behind the wheel of Scott's parents' car.

So clear. The picture was so clear.

You could see that the corpse's eyes were sunk back in its head. You could see the purple tinge of its skin. The dark, unnaturally dark, lips.

The blank, unseeing stare as it faced the camera.

Sitting behind the wheel.

Of Scott's car.

Scott.

Cassie stared at Scott, who was trembling under the big parka, beads of perspiration on his forehead, his features drawn back in disbelief, in utter bewilderment as he stared at the photo, holding it close to his face with a trembling hand.

"I don't get it," Scott said, his voice hoarse. "I don't get it." He raised his eyes to Cassie. "This is impossible," he told her.

Cassie thought of Scott's new Polaroid camera, the one they had teased him about.

"I — I don't know how this happened," Scott said, suddenly realizing that both of his companions were staring at him. "Really. I have no idea."

Cassie believed him. She threw her arms around him, holding tightly to the parka, to show him that she did. "We have to get you home," she said softly. "Your face is so flushed. You're burning up."

"He's going to kill us all," Eddie muttered, still staring at the Polaroid, holding it close to his face under the porch light. "The corpse. He's going to kill us!"

"Eddie, stop!" Cassie cried.

"Well, who took this picture?" Eddie demanded,

staring at Scott. "How did the corpse get in Scott's car?"

"I don't know," Scott said weakly. "I'm telling you, Eddie — I don't know."

Suddenly the front door opened, startling all three of them. Eddie gasped and shoved the Polaroid into his vest pocket.

Mr. Katz pushed open the storm door. "What are you doing out there? You'll freeze your buns off. Are you coming in or not?"

"Uh . . . no thanks," Cassie said quickly. She took Scott's arm and tugged. "Come on. Got to get you home."

Eddie cast her a pleading stare, as if begging her not to leave. But enough was enough, Cassie decided. She wanted to get poor, sick Scott home. He seemed nearly dazed as she led him to the curb.

And she wanted to get home where she could think about everything quietly by herself.

Half an hour later, after depositing Scott like a heavy bag of laundry at his doorstep, and saying good-night to her parents, who were dozing off in the den with *Saturday Night Live* blaring on the TV, Cassie tucked herself into bed, turned off the bedtable lamp, and settled down on her pillow to think.

Staring up at the shifting shadows on the ceiling, like dark, playful ghosts over her head, she tried to put things in order, tried to step back and see things clearly.

But as much as she tried, her thoughts swirled about, much like the shadows she was staring at, one picture blurred into another, none of them as clear as the horrifying Polaroid of the corpse in the car.

Scott's car.

Scott's Polaroid?

No.

There were too many ugly pictures. Too many ugly questions.

Who had mowed Winks down? Who was trying to terrify them?

It couldn't be Scott. He was a big, lovable teddy bear. He wouldn't hurt a fly.

It couldn't be Eddie. He was too frightened, too scared of his own shadow, to pull anything this horrible.

And of course it couldn't be Winks.

So it had to be someone else. Someone who knew them. Someone they knew.

Someone who knew what had happened.

The corpse?

Cassie swallowed hard.

The corpse was the only other person who knew what had happened.

The dead man, Brandt Tinkers. There he was, crossing the highway when they hit him. There he was. Again, she saw his staring face caught in the headlights of the silver Volvo.

The corpse . . .

The only one who knows . . .

Before she realized it, Cassie had drifted off into a restless sleep.

A while later, she awoke suddenly, bathed in perspiration, the bedclothes twisted around her waist. Glancing at the bedtable clock, she saw that it was a little past three-thirty in the morning.

The ghostly shadows still swirled above her head.

Pale moonlight filtered in through the curtains on her window.

Only half-awake, Cassie sat up and took a deep breath.

And realized that she had figured it out.

She knew who was doing this to them.

14

Before breakfast Sunday morning, Cassie called the hospital. After being transferred to three different nursing stations, she was told that Winks was still in stable condition, but that he hadn't regained consciousness.

No change from the night before.

Was that good news or bad news?

Cassie wished there were a doctor in her family, someone she could talk to about Winks, someone who could reassure her that he was going to be okay.

Still in her nightgown and robe, she punched Scott's number. His mother answered and said that Scott was too sick to talk. His temperature was 102 degrees, and he had terrible laryngitis, so he could barely make a sound. He had gone back to sleep, his mother said. She added that she'd probably keep him out of school the next day.

Cassie got dressed, pulling on a long-sleeved

green top over a pair of gray sweatpants. She pulled back the curtains and peered out of the window. The sky was a solid blue. The sun was shining. Across the street, the two Finnegan kids were chasing their big Irish setter across their yard.

A cheerful day, almost springlike. She pulled open the window, wishing she felt more cheerful.

She picked up the phone receiver and punched Eddie's number. A busy signal. She sat on her bed, staring at the billowing, white curtains, then tried again.

This time, Eddie picked up after the first ring. He had been trying to call the hospital, he told her, but hadn't been able to find out anything about Winks.

Cassie told him what she had learned from the nurse.

"I guess no change is good news," Eddie said.

"I guess," Cassie replied. "Listen, Eddie, does your cousin work on Sundays?"

The question seemed to catch him by surprise. "You mean Jerry?"

"Yeah. Jerry. The one who works at the morgue."

"I think so," Eddie said. "I could call him and find out. Why do you want to know?"

"I have a theory," Cassie said casually.

"You don't think Jerry has anything to do with what's going on, do you?" Eddie asked.

"Maybe," Cassie replied. "He's the only other

person who knows anything about the corpse. And he knows that you were interested in the corpse."

"But Jerry is a good guy!" Eddie exclaimed heatedly. "He wouldn't do anything like that. He wouldn't run down Winks. Jerry likes Winks!"

"Eddie — "

"Sure, Jerry likes to joke around sometimes. But you'd joke around, too, if you worked where he does." Eddie sounded very upset.

"Eddie, stop!" Cassie cried. "I'm not accusing your cousin of anything. He was the last person to see the corpse — right?"

"Right," Eddie reluctantly agreed.

"So I just thought maybe we could go talk to him."

"You mean go to the *morgue*?" Eddie cried, his voice rising several octaves.

"You don't have to come if you don't want to," Cassie said.

She didn't like the idea of going to the morgue, either. But she had an idea that Jerry might know what was going on, or be able to help them in some way.

"Uh . . . I'll call Jerry," Eddie said and hung up quickly.

Cassie pulled on her white Nikes and tied them tightly, then paced back and forth across her room, waiting for Eddie to call back.

I'm right about Jerry, she thought, pausing to peer out the window. The two Finnegan kids were wrestling in a mud puddle near the curb. The Irish setter was sitting on its haunches watching the bout.

Jerry knows something. Jerry has something to do with this.

Jerry is a bigger joker than Winks.

The phone rang. She dived to the bed and picked it up before the first ring had ended. "Hello?"

"Hi, it's me."

"Is Jerry at work?"

"Yeah," Eddie replied. "Jerry said that dead people don't take Sunday off."

"What a riot," Cassie said sarcastically. "Are you coming with me or not?"

"You mean you're just going over there? Right now?"

"Yeah. I'm taking the bus," she told him. "You coming?"

"I've got a lot of homework," he said.

"It won't take long," Cassie assured him.

"It's very cold in there," Eddie said, "and there are dead bodies all over the place."

"Big surprise! It *is* a morgue!" Cassie exclaimed, and laughed. She knew she shouldn't laugh at him, but he sounded like such a total coward.

He was silent for a long time.

"Eddie, are you still there?"

"I'll come with you," he said. "Meet you at the bus stop."

Cassie hung up and hurried down the stairs. Her

mom stopped her as she was heading out the front door. "Hold on — where are you going?" she asked, pulling Cassie back by tugging on her long, red wool scarf.

"Uh . . . just going to see Eddie," Cassie replied.

"Are you going to the hospital?" Mrs. Martin asked, brushing Cassie's hair back off her forehead.

"Maybe later," Cassie replied.

She had a sudden impulse to tell her mother she was going to the morgue.

She had a sudden impulse to tell her mother everything, to ask for help, to allow her mother to wrap her up in a protective hug and hide her.

"Your dad thought you might like to practice your driving today," Mrs. Martin said, rearranging the scarf around Cassie's neck.

"My driving?"

"Well, you *are* taking your driver's exam after school tomorrow," Mrs. Martin exclaimed. "Don't tell me you forgot. I thought you said it was the most important day in your life." Still holding on to the scarf, she stared suspiciously at Cassie.

How could I have forgotten about my driver's test? Cassie thought.

I've been so obsessed with Winks and the corpse and the horrid phone calls, I completely forgot!

"Of course I didn't forget," Cassie lied. "Tell Daddy I'll be home in a few hours. We can go driving then." She kissed her mom on the cheek and hurried out the door.

* * *

"Nice day," Eddie said, his hands shoved into his jeans pockets, his black hair still wet from the shower.

Cassie found him waiting for her on the corner, leaning against the blue-and-white bus pole.

"Nice day to visit the morgue," Cassie said dryly, watching an enormous crow hop along the sidewalk and onto the grass. "What's that — a buzzard?"

Eddie didn't laugh.

"Just trying to keep it light," she said.

"You want to go see Winks after the morgue?" he asked, his eyes on the crow. Another crow, identical in size, glided down beside the first one.

"I don't know," she told him, looking up to see the dark blue bus approaching. "My dad might take me driving. My test is tomorrow after school. I forgot all about it. Do you believe it?"

"My test is Friday," Eddie said, his cheeks reddening. He bent down, picked up a flat gray stone from the curb, took aim, and tossed it at one of the crows.

The stone hit the ground hard a few feet from the birds. They both squawked angrily and flapped up into the nearest tree.

The bus squealed to a halt. Cassie followed Eddie through the door. "Try to squeeze in," the bus driver joked. The bus was completely empty.

Cassie and Eddie walked all the way to the back. "Friendly, huh?" the driver called, watching them in the big rearview mirror. He pulled the bus away from the curb and headed toward the civic center.

"Have you ever been to the morgue before?" Cassie asked, watching the houses and yards roll past the window.

"Yeah. Once," Eddie said, resting his knees on the back of the seat in front of him. "Jerry showed me around. I had bad dreams for a month."

"Oh, great," Cassie said, rolling her eyes.

"This is a stupid idea," Eddie said. "Jerry isn't the one who ran down Winks. Jerry's just a goof. He isn't a killer."

The bus turned onto Civic Drive, its tires squealing. Up ahead through the windshield, some of the tall, new civic buildings, including the new state office tower, came into view.

"I just have this feeling we should talk to Jerry," Cassie said impatiently. "I told you, I don't think he's a killer."

"Well, don't tell him too much," Eddie said, his expression serious, staring hard into her eyes.

"Huh? Why not?" Cassie stared back at him.

"You know Jerry," Eddie replied quietly. "He makes a joke out of everything."

"Well, he won't joke about this," Cassie said. "I mean, Winks is in the hospital, and the rest of us have been threatened, and — "

"Just don't tell him too much," Eddie repeated.

They reached their stop. Eddie pulled the cord.

The bus pulled to the curb. "Y'all come back now, ya hear?" the bus driver called.

Cassie laughed as she stepped down to the curb. "Guess he's pretty lonely," she said.

Eddie's expression remained serious. "I wish we weren't doing this," he said, staring up at the gray office buildings.

Cassie ignored him and started walking. "Is that it, over there?" she asked, pointing to a low brick building, the only old building among all the new skyscrapers.

"Yeah," Eddie said, hurrying to keep up.

The new state office tower was made of enormous glass panels, and the glass reflected the sun back down to the street. Cassie shielded her eyes with one hand to shut out the bright glare as she crossed the street.

"It's deserted here," Eddie said, turning to look in all directions.

"No one works here on Sunday," Cassie said.

"Except Jerry," Eddie added.

Etched in a granite block beside the broad wooden entrance were the words: CITY MORGUE. 1952. Cassie tried the door, expecting it to be locked, but it pulled open easily.

They stepped into a wide, circular reception area, lit by one overhead light near the far wall. The reception desk, cluttered with papers and magazines, was unattended.

"I guess we can walk right back," Eddie said, whispering for some reason. "Jerry's area is way in back. With the stiffs."

He held back, allowing Cassie to lead the way. They walked through the empty reception area and into a long, narrow corridor with closed doors on both sides.

"Look out," Cassie warned, stepping carefully through the dark, narrow hall. "Hey — what's that?"

It was a stack of body bags, made of heavy, black plastic, piled in front of a closed office door. "They're empty," Eddie said, sounding very relieved.

Cassie shuddered. "They look like garbage bags, only they zip up."

The corridor led into a large, open room the size of a small gymnasium. There were metal examining tables in the center of the room, and what appeared to be wide, gray metal lockers built into all four walls.

"Hey, Jerry?" Eddie called. His voice echoed against the walls.

"At least there are no bodies just lying around," Cassie said, now whispering, too. "What is that sour smell?" She held her nose.

Eddie looked green. "Chemicals they use. Decaying bodies. It's all so disgusting."

Light poured in from narrow windows up near the high ceiling. They stepped into the center of the

room, their sneakers thudding loudly on the concrete floor.

"Hey, Jerry! Where are you?" Eddie called.

Cassie stopped and uttered a shriek when she
saw Jerry. She grabbed Eddie's hand and stepped
back.

Eddie saw him, too.

Jerry was lying on his back on one of the low
examining tables. His arms were crossed on his
chest. His eyes were wide open, unblinking, staring
lifelessly up at the ceiling. His head was surrounded
by a wide pool of dark red blood.

15

"Jerry!" Eddie cried, and turned to Cassie, his face gripped with horror.

"This can't be happening!" Cassie exclaimed, holding on to Eddie's arm, squeezing it hard without realizing it.

"What can't be happening?" Jerry asked. He sat up, a wide grin crossing his face.

Cassie gasped.

"Gotcha," Jerry said and started to laugh.

Cassie and Eddie didn't join in. "Jerry, that wasn't funny," Eddie said, his voice just above a whisper. He sat down on the floor, his cheeks flushed. He looked about to faint.

"You really scared us," Cassie said angrily.

"Yeah," Jerry said, his grin growing even wider. He slid off the table and stood up. He held up the sheet of dark red cellophane that he had used for blood.

Jerry was tall and broad-shouldered, built like a fullback. He had long, frizzy blond hair that fell unbrushed around his round, usually grinning face. It was a mischievous face, Cassie thought. Jerry never looked serious. He had a diamond stud in one ear. He was wearing a faded blue work shirt, and gray denim, straight-legged jeans over black cowboy-style boots.

"I really thought — " Eddie started, but his voice caught in his throat, and he couldn't finish his sentence. He swallowed hard a couple of times, glaring angrily at Jerry.

"That was really unfair," Cassie said sharply. "You knew we'd be scared coming here and everything."

"Yeah," Jerry repeated, still grinning, enjoying his triumph. "Got to keep a sense of humor around here, you know. Otherwise, things get pretty dead." He snickered at his own bad joke.

Eddie, still sitting on the concrete floor, shook his head.

"So you guys want to see a corpse, huh?" Jerry asked. Without warning, he reached over to one of the wall lockers and pulled the handle.

"Jerry, stop!" Cassie pleaded.

But she was too late. A wide drawer slid out. On it, only partially covered by a white sheet, was the nude body of an old man.

"Come on, man, put it away!" Eddie screamed.

Jerry giggled.

"Yuck." Cassie felt sick. The smell was overpowering.

Jerry reached down to the dead man's feet. "Tickle, tickle." He tickled the sole of one foot. "Hey — not ticklish!" he cried, turning to Cassie and Eddie. "Here, want to try?"

"Jerry, *please!*" Cassie begged.

"Okay, okay," Jerry said grudgingly. He shoved the drawer. It clanged shut, the sound echoing off the high ceilings.

"It smells so gross," Eddie said, slowly climbing to his feet.

"You get used to it," Jerry replied. "It's not so bad after a while." He turned his attention to Eddie. "You okay?"

Eddie still looked shaky.

"Eddie doesn't like my jokes," Jerry told Cassie.

"Gee, what a surprise," Cassie replied sarcastically.

Jerry led them over to the desk in the corner. There were three wooden chairs lined up against the wall of lockers. They sat down.

"I heard about Winks," Jerry said, rubbing the back of his neck. "How's he doing? Have you heard?"

"He's still unconscious," Eddie said.

"I'm going over to the hospital later," Cassie added. "The doctor says he's stable, whatever that means."

Jerry *tsk-tsked* and shook his head. "Did they get the guy who hit him?"

"No," Cassie told him. "But something very strange — "

"We want to ask you something," Eddie interrupted, casting an uncomfortable glance at Cassie. "About the corpse."

"The one that's missing," Cassie said.

"Yeah. Wasn't that weird?" Jerry shook his head again. He pushed his frizzy blond hair back off his face.

"Do you know anything about the corpse?" Cassie asked.

"Huh-uh," Jerry said quickly, glancing at Eddie. "You sure you're okay? Can I get you a glass of water? Or maybe some formaldehyde?" He laughed, slapping the knees of his jeans.

"I'm okay," Eddie said quietly.

"His name was Brandt Tinkers, right?" Cassie was determined to pursue this. She was sure Jerry knew something that could help them.

"Yeah. And he was a businessman. That's all I know," Jerry said. "I wasn't here when they brought him in. I don't know where he came from. He was in an accident or something. That's all I know."

We *know* he was in an accident, Cassie thought. *We* killed him.

Again, the scene on Route 12 played through her

mind. The bump. The horrifying bump. The wide-eyed stare of surprise on Tinkers's face. The corpse by the side of the road.

"Really. That's all I know," Jerry repeated. "And, then, the stiff just disappeared. He was here when you called me, Eddie. Here one minute. Then gone the next."

"Like he walked away," Eddie muttered. "That's what you said, Jerry. You said it was like he walked away."

"Well, maybe I said that," Jerry replied, brushing back his hair again, "but I saw the condition he was in. Believe me, Eddie, he was not ticklish. Not ticklish. There was no way that stiff could get up and walk out of here. Unless — "

"Unless what?" Cassie asked eagerly.

"Unless he's a zombie!" Jerry cried. "The Living Dead!" He whooped with laughter.

"That's not funny," Cassie said quietly.

"Let's go," Eddie urged her. "Let's get out of here."

"You didn't see anyone come in here?" Cassie demanded, ignoring Eddie. "What about Tinkers's family? Don't they want to know what happened to his body? What about the police?"

Jerry shrugged. He burped loudly. "Sorry. Talking about stiffs always makes me hungry."

Neither Cassie nor Eddie smiled.

"You guys sure are serious today. Guess you're upset about Winks, huh?"

"Yeah, we're upset," Cassie said.

"Me, too," Jerry said. "But I don't see what it has to do with the missing stiff."

"I'll show you," Cassie said. She reached into her bag and pulled out the Polaroid snapshot.

"Hey!" Eddie cried in surprise. "You brought that?"

Cassie handed it to Jerry.

Jerry squinted at it, studying it. "That's the stiff!" he cried. "Where'd you get this?"

"It was left for us," Cassie told him. "Someone wants us to think that Tinkers was driving the car that hit Winks."

"We've got to go," Eddie said, jumping to his feet. "I feel really sick."

"I don't get it," Jerry said, staring hard at the snapshot.

"There was a note," Cassie told him. "It said, 'One down, three to go.' "

"Whoa," Jerry said, his face filled with confusion.

Eddie grabbed the photo from him. "Come on, Cassie." He started toward the door.

Cassie saw that Jerry had a very upset look on his face. "Eddie — " he called.

Eddie, halfway across the large room, turned.

"Eddie, I'll call you later," Jerry said. He nodded to Cassie. "See you. Tell Winks I'm pulling for him."

Cassie followed Eddie out of the room and through the long, narrow corridor to the building exit. The sour smell, the smell of death, followed them out into the street.

They didn't say anything to each other until they had walked a couple of blocks and the smell had begun to evaporate. "Jerry sure looked upset," Cassie said thoughtfully.

"I think it's because he saw I was feeling really sick," Eddie said.

"No, I think it was more than that," Cassie replied.

The sun was high in a cloudless sky. The air was crisp and cold. Cassie took a deep breath, then another.

"Sorry I had to get out of there so fast. I just couldn't stay another second," Eddie said as they crossed the street to the bus stop. "I thought I was going to puke my guts out."

"That's okay," Cassie replied. She wasn't thinking about Eddie. She was thinking about Jerry. "I think Jerry got upset when he saw the snapshot because he knows something he's not telling us," she said.

Eddie shrugged. "He said he didn't know anything at all. I really don't think he does."

"When he calls you later, see what you can find out," Cassie instructed.

"Okay," Eddie said. His cheeks were red as usual. But he looked as if he were starting to revive.

* * *

After lunch, Cassie practiced driving with her father. He seemed really nervous, even though she drove slowly and carefully. Sitting beside her in the front passenger seat, he kept slamming his foot down, as if he were applying the brake.

"I think you're going to pass easily tomorrow," he said after she had successfully parallel-parked twice without any trouble.

"You're just desperate to go home," she teased.

He admitted that practicing with her made him a little nervous. Obligingly, she turned the wheel over to him. He dropped her off at the hospital.

The news there was good. Mrs. Winkleman greeted Cassie with happy tears in her eyes. Winks was awake. He was still somewhat groggy. But he was awake. He had several broken ribs, a broken arm, and a sprained knee. Aside from that, he seemed to be fine. He was going to be okay.

"That's wonderful!" Cassie exclaimed, hugging Winks's mother joyfully.

Winks wasn't allowed any visitors yet, so Cassie called her dad to come pick her up. He let her drive home. Cassie couldn't wait to call Scott and Eddie and tell them the good news about their friend.

That night, she tried to push away thoughts of the driver's test so that she could concentrate on her government textbook. It was a little after eleven. Her parents had gone to bed early. She was the only one still up.

She had changed into her warmest, most comfortable nightgown and had just started reading the opening paragraph on the separation of powers when she heard the sound from outside.

A scrabbling sound.

A scraping.

The squeak of a door.

It sounded like the front porch door. She had noticed that squeak the day before when she and her dad spent the day out there sanding.

Curious, Cassie ran to her bedroom window, pushed aside the curtains, and looked down.

"Oh!"

Someone in a dark coat was running across the front yard.

She could only see his back as he disappeared into the shadows of the tall hedges.

Gripped with fear, she stood staring down at the front yard for several seconds after the dark figure had disappeared. Then she reluctantly made her way down the stairs, walking silently so as not to wake her parents.

She hesitated at the front door.

And listened.

She heard a scraping sound. Repeat itself. Again. Again.

Was he out there?

Had he come back?

No. She had seen him run away.

He had definitely been on the porch.

Most likely, he had left something there.

Something frightening? Another ugly photograph? Another threatening note?

She raised her hand to the doorknob. She unlocked the door.

She started to turn the knob — but then stopped.

Should she open the door?

16

Cassie clicked on the porch light. Then, holding her breath, she pulled open the heavy wooden front door.

And stared out through the glass of the storm door.

No one there. The porch was empty.

But the scraping sound continued.

Beyond the porch, trees bowed and trembled in a strong, gusting wind. Dead leaves rustled across the yard.

Hesitantly, she pushed open the storm door.

Her legs were shaking, she realized. She still hadn't dared to breathe.

She leaned forward into the rectangle of yellow light.

The scraping sound — she could see now what was causing it.

A large, brown oak leaf was caught in the porch

screen. The wind kept scraping it against the screen.

Cassie finally breathed, exhaling noisily.

A sigh of relief. But the relief lasted only until she saw a large, brown envelope tucked into the porch door.

She had been right.

Whoever had been darting away into the shadows had left an envelope.

Cassie peered out into the darkness, trying to make sure that he hadn't come back, that he wasn't lurking there by the side of the porch, waiting to grab her when she came out for the envelope.

She didn't see anyone.

The leaf scraped against the screen. The wind swirled.

Letting go of the storm door handle, she dashed onto the porch, the cold floor against her bare feet sending a chill up her entire body.

She grabbed the envelope, tugged it out from the porch door, and leapt back into the safety of the house.

Holding the envelope under her arm, she silently closed the front door and carefully locked it. Then she tiptoed up the stairs to her room, shivering, the sound of the rushing wind, the scraping leaf, following her up the stairs.

Shaking from the cold, and from her fright, she climbed into bed, hoping to get warm there, holding the envelope in one hand, tugging the covers up with the other. Then, with a trembling hand, she tore open the envelope.

As she had imagined, it contained another Polaroid photo and another note.

She gasped as she held the snapshot under her bedtable lamp.

There he was again. The corpse. The wide-eyed corpse, posing for the camera.

He was standing on Cassie's front porch. One hand was on the doorknob of the front door.

He was here, Cassie realized.

At my house. Standing on my porch. Standing at the door.

"And then I saw him run away," she said aloud.

So he isn't dead, she realized.

Brandt Tinkers isn't dead. He's alive. And he's trying to terrify us.

No.

He *is* dead.

We saw him. We saw his sunken eyes.

I could smell that he was dead, she told herself.

He was at the morgue. Dead. Dead. Dead.

But then he left the morgue. . . .

This wild, unconnected thinking was leading nowhere. She closed her eyes, counted to ten.

The note. She had forgotten to read the note.

It was on a folded-up sheet of lined notebook paper.

It didn't take long to read. It contained only two words, scrawled in crayoned block letters:

YOU'RE NEXT.

She knew she wasn't thinking clearly. But she had to talk to someone. She was too scared to go to sleep, too scared to sit there shivering under the covers, seeing the corpse standing on her porch, seeing the two scrawled words, seeing the threat again and again.

She couldn't tell her parents.

Then they would have to be told everything, about how Cassie and her friends had taken Eddie's car and gone out driving without any licenses. How they had hit and killed Brandt Tinkers and left him beside the road, desperate not to get into trouble.

Trouble.

Trouble seemed like such a weak word for what was going on.

No, she couldn't tell her parents, even though she really wanted to. It wouldn't be fair to the others.

So whom could she call? Eddie? No. She didn't want to frighten him more. He was already to the breaking point.

Winks? No. Of course not.

She had to call Scott.

She didn't care what time it was. She just had to talk to him.

Scott would calm her down. Scott would understand. Maybe she and Scott could come up with a plan. Maybe they could figure out what was going on.

Her hand was shaking so violently, it took three tries to punch in Scott's number. Sitting up in bed, she listened to the phone ring, gripping the top of the blanket tightly with her free hand.

It rang four times before someone at Scott's house picked it up. Then it took a long while before the voice finally said, "Hello?" in a sleep-fogged voice.

It was Scott's mother.

"I'm sorry to call so late, Mrs. Baldwin," Cassie said in a shrill voice she didn't recognize. "But can I talk to Scott? It's pretty important."

"Who is this? Cassie?" Scott's mother wasn't entirely awake.

"Yes. Could I please talk to him? I'm really sorry."

"But, Cassie, he's asleep. His fever hasn't broken."

"Yes. Please. Please wake him up. I just need to talk to him about . . . something. Please," Cassie begged.

The line was silent for a long time.

All Cassie could hear was her own rapid breathing.

"Well, I'll see if I can wake him," Mrs. Baldwin said finally.

"Oh, thank you."

Cassie heard the phone clank, as if hitting the

floor. Through the phone she heard footsteps, the groan of floorboards, the sound of Mrs. Baldwin going down the hall to wake Scott.

It seemed to take forever.

Cassie sat rigidly in her bed, her back against the hard headboard, her hand still gripping the top of the blanket, the phone receiver pressed tightly to her ear.

Finally, she heard footsteps approaching the phone, then the sound of someone fumbling for the receiver on the other end.

"Cassie — " It was Mrs. Baldwin, sounding wide awake now, and very frightened.

"Cassie, Scott isn't there! He's gone!"

17

Cassie stepped out under a dark, threatening sky.

She shifted her heavy backpack on her shoulders and, bowing her head against the wind, trudged down the driveway and headed toward school.

It had rained during the night. The ground was soft and puddled.

"I should've worn boots," she said aloud, glancing down at her sneakers.

She hopped over a large gray puddle and stepped into the street. A stream of water rolled down the curbside, flowing like a small river into the drain.

It must've rained really hard, she realized. Funny. I didn't hear it.

She always liked to lie in bed and listen to the soft whisper of rain on the roof. It made her feel so warm and protected.

Shifting the backpack again, stepping around a

deep, muddy puddle in the street, she felt unsettled now.

So many troubling thoughts.

So many fears pulling her one way, then another.

She realized she felt weary, even though she had just woken up.

A horn honked behind her.

Cassie let out a startled yelp and leapt to the curb as the North Avondale bus rumbled by. She recognized several kids on the bus. She waved, but they stared back at her, faces distorted in the window glass, and didn't wave back.

It's so cold and windy, she thought, rewrapping the red wool scarf around her neck. I should've taken the bus.

Only two more blocks to walk.

A dog barked from the front stoop of an old red brick house across the street.

The sky grew even darker. Two cars passed, their headlights cutting through the morning darkness.

What day is this? Cassie asked herself. Is it Monday?

Why couldn't she remember?

Such a simple thing. Why couldn't she remember what day it was?

She was still trying to remember when she realized the car was following her.

She turned her head, the backpack straps straining against her chest.

It was a black car. A big black car with heavy chrome all over the front. Its headlights were dark. The windshield was dark. She couldn't see the driver.

It pulled up behind her, then slowed.

Cassie moved to the curb.

The car didn't speed up. Didn't pass her.

Who is it? she wondered, staring hard into the darkened windshield. What do they want?

She started to walk faster.

The car picked up speed.

She started to run.

The car picked up more speed.

Gripped with fear, Cassie tried to utter a cry for help. But no sound came out.

She tried again to scream.

Silence.

She leapt over the curb, her sneakers splashing through tall grass, and onto the sidewalk.

To her horror, the car roared off the road, bumped over the curb, and came after her over the sidewalk.

Help!

She tried again to cry out.

Again, no sound came out of her mouth.

It was closing in on her, going to run her down.

She was going to be mowed down, struck — just like Winks.

YOU'RE NEXT.

The words of the note came back to her.

YOU'RE NEXT.

Help me! Won't somebody help me!

The car was inches behind her. The engine roar seemed to surround her, swallow her up.

Help me!

She tossed off the heavy backpack and kept running.

The car rolled over it, making a loud crunching sound as it closed in on her.

Where is everybody? Won't somebody help me? Cassie wondered.

And then, without thinking about it, she spun around.

And peered through the windshield only a few feet from her face.

And saw the corpse behind the wheel.

"Cassie!" he called, his dark eyes aglow, his voice a dry rush of wind.

"Cassie!" he repeated. "Cassie! Cassie! Cassie!"

The throaty whisper of death.

As he moved to run her over, the dead man repeated her name again and again.

"Cassie! Cassie! Cassie!"

18

"Cassie! Cassie! Cassie!"

Cassie felt hands on her shoulders. Someone was shaking her.

"Cassie! Cassie!"

Cassie blinked, struggled to keep her eyes open.

Her mother hovered over her, gently shaking her by the shoulders. "Cassie — wake up."

"Huh?" She coughed, blinked again. Bright sunlight filtered through the curtains at the window.

"I've been trying to wake you up for hours, but you wouldn't move," her mother said, letting go of her shoulders but not backing away.

Cassie sat up and rubbed her eyes.

"You'll be late for school," her mother said, walking over to the window, pushing the curtains aside, and pulling the window open a crack. Cool air immediately rushed into the room.

"I had the *worst* dream," Cassie told her mother,

finally realizing that walking to school, being chased by the corpse in the car, was all a dream, a horrifying dream.

"I couldn't wake you. It was unbelievable," her mother said, picking up a pair of jeans from the floor, folding them, and putting them over a chairback. "Didn't you sleep well last night?"

"No, not too much," Cassie confessed, swinging her legs around and climbing out of bed. Standing up, she felt as if she weighed a thousand pounds.

She stretched.

"Well, hurry up and get dressed. I'll make you some toast you can eat on the way," Mrs. Martin said, heading to the door. "Hurry. You're really late."

Who cares? Cassie thought glumly, watching her mother leave.

She dropped back down onto the bed and buried her face in her still-warm pillow. She'd been wide awake all night, until about five o'clock when she finally succumbed to sleep.

All the while, she'd been thinking about Scott.

Puzzling about Scott.

Torturing herself about Scott.

She knew it couldn't be Scott who had run Winks down. It couldn't be Scott who was terrifying Eddie and her, threatening them, threatening to run them down, too.

It couldn't be Scott. No way.

But all the evidence pointed to Scott.

Where was he last night when Cassie had called?

He was supposedly sick in bed with a very high fever. But when his mother went to wake him up, he was gone.

Where?

Cassie knew where. He was out putting a frightening photo and note on her porch.

Where did he get the corpse? Why was he using the corpse to scare them? Why had he tried to kill his good friend Winks?

Why did he want to kill her next?

Those questions Cassie couldn't answer.

But she knew why he wasn't in his bed last night.

She had seen him scampering into the hedges after leaving the brown envelope for her.

There were other signs that also pointed to Scott.

The Polaroid pictures. The three of them had teased him about his new Polaroid camera.

And in the first photo, the corpse had been sitting in Scott's car.

And Scott was the only one who hadn't received any frightening phone calls or notes.

It all added up to Scott.

But why?

It made no sense. It couldn't be Scott, she told herself.

Couldn't. Couldn't. Couldn't.

Still not fully awake, still feeling unsettled, flashes of her terrifying dream lingering in her mind, Cassie sat up and reached for the phone.

She hesitated for a second, then took a deep breath and punched in Scott's number.

She had to ask him why he wasn't home in bed in the middle of the night. She had to ask him where he was. She had to know.

She let the phone ring twelve times.

No one answered.

"Cassie, where are you?" her mother called from downstairs.

She replaced the receiver and forced herself to stand up. "I just want to stay in bed," she said to herself in the mirror over the dresser.

But she couldn't. For one thing, she had her driver's test that afternoon.

This was supposed to be an exciting day, she thought miserably, pulling on some clothes without even noticing what she had selected.

A few minutes later, she was half-walking, half-jogging to school, chewing on the slice of buttered toast her mother had handed her as she hurried out the door.

At least I'm not being pursued by a corpse in a big black car, she told herself, looking behind her just to make sure.

She arrived at her locker just as the second homeroom bell rang, and spotted Eddie at his locker across the hall. "Hey, Eddie — wait — " she called.

"We're late," Eddie called to her, slamming his locker, turning the combination on his lock. "See you later!"

"No, wait!" she cried and hurried over to him. "I know who it is, Eddie!"

"Huh?" His cheeks turned bright pink as his mouth dropped in surprise.

"I know!" Cassie declared.

"Eddie, are you coming in? I'm closing the door now." Mr. Murphy, Eddie's homeroom teacher, peered out from the doorway.

Eddie gave Cassie a helpless shrug. "Gotta run. Later — okay?" He started toward his room. "What are you doing after school?"

"Taking my driver's test," Cassie called, disappointed that she didn't get to confide in Eddie, didn't get to tell him about last night.

The door closed behind him.

She stood in the middle of the hall for a while, uncertain of what to do.

It was going to be a long day.

Cassie's driver's test seemed to be over almost before it had begun.

To her surprise, the test was given by a young woman. She made Cassie feel comfortable right away. Cassie drove a few blocks, made a few right and left turns, made a successful U-turn, and parallel-parked between two poles.

"That was easy, wasn't it?" the young examiner said, unbuckling her seat belt and climbing out of the car. "Go see the man in window eleven for your temporary license. Your real license will be mailed in six weeks."

"You mean I *passed*?" Cassie asked, stunned, still sitting behind the wheel.

The examiner laughed. "That's all there is to it. Drive carefully." She hurried to meet her next test-taker.

"Drive carefully," Cassie repeated to herself. What a joke!

For a few minutes, while taking the test, she had managed to shut out all the frightening events of the past few weeks. But now those two words — "Drive Carefully" — had brought it all rushing back to her.

This is a big day in my life, she told herself. I should go out and celebrate tonight.

But she certainly didn't feel like celebrating.

Her parents noticed her lack of enthusiasm at dinner. "Aren't you thrilled about passing your test the first time?" her mother asked.

"Guess we'll never see you anymore," her dad said, only half-joking. And then he added, "I thought you'd be more excited."

Cassie struggled to swallow a piece of chicken. "I — I guess I don't really believe it yet," she replied. It was a lame excuse, she realized, but her parents seemed to buy it.

She hurried up to her room after dinner, intent on calling Scott.

But the moment she started to lift the receiver, the phone rang. "Oh!" she cried, startled, and picked it up, somehow expecting it to be Scott on the other end.

"Hi, Cassie." It was Eddie.

"You scared me," she said. "I was just going to call Scott and — "

"Did you pass it?" he asked eagerly.

"Yes. It was easy," she told him. "I couldn't believe how easy it was."

"You got it? You got your license?"

"Yeah. They give you a temporary card right away," she replied.

"Well, can you take me driving tonight?" he asked.

"Huh? Tonight? Eddie — "

"My mom said if you passed your test, she'd let me borrow the car tonight if you wanted to take me to practice. My test is Friday, see."

"Well, I don't know. . . ." Cassie said reluctantly.

"Please," he begged. "It's my only night to practice before my test."

"I'm really tired," Cassie said truthfully. She'd barely been able to keep her eyes open during dinner.

"Pretty please," Eddie pleaded. "You said you wanted to talk to me, remember? This morning when we were late?"

"Yeah, I guess," Cassie said. She did want to tell Eddie about Scott, and about the photo and note she'd received. "Okay. I'll be right over," she said wearily. "But we'll just drive for a short while, okay?"

"Great! Thanks!" Eddie replied gratefully. "Hurry!" He hung up.

She put down the receiver, then picked it up and punched in Scott's number.

A busy signal.

Well, at least someone was home.

She'd try him again later, she decided, after she discussed everything with Eddie.

It was a clear, cold evening, an orange moon still rising in the navy blue sky. Cassie walked to Eddie's. He lived too nearby to drive there. His parents weren't home. They climbed into the old Chevy, Eddie behind the wheel, and took off.

Eddie seemed more excited than usual, his cheeks blushing, his wiry body tense, hyper. As they drove through town, Cassie described the driver's test to him, step by step.

He agreed that it sounded like a breeze.

He pulled too quickly through a four-way stop. Cassie told him to be more careful.

Before she realized it, they were past town and heading along Route 12, nearly deserted as always.

"Let's not go too far, okay, Eddie? I really am tired tonight. Didn't sleep," Cassie said, glancing at the dashboard clock.

"I talked to Winks," Eddie said. "He called me. Isn't that great?"

"How did he sound?" Cassie asked, very pleased.

"Like Winks," Eddie replied. "He sounded the

same. He's going to be okay. He said he might even get sprung from the hospital next week."

"Oh, that's great news!" Cassie exclaimed. "A little more to the right, Eddie. You're going over the center line."

"Oh. Sorry. I wasn't paying attention," he apologized, turning the wheel. "Tell me what you were going to tell me this morning. You said you know who's scaring us."

"Yeah. I mean, I think I know," Cassie said. "The only problem is, I don't know *why* he's doing it. It doesn't really make any sense."

"Well, why don't you keep a person in suspense?" Eddie said sarcastically, slowing down as an oncoming oil truck roared past.

Cassie took a deep breath and then told Eddie about the night before, about the note and the snapshot, seeing the figure run across her yard, trying to phone Scott, Scott being missing in the middle of the night.

Eddie's face froze in surprise. He kept shaking his head as he drove. "I don't believe it," he muttered. "How could Scott do that to Winks? I mean — "

He started to say something else. But a sudden explosion — like a burst of gunfire — rocked the car.

Cassie screamed.

Eddie hit the brakes as the car careened out of control.

19

The car squealed to a stop on the soft dirt shoulder of the highway and bounced a few times.

Eddie, both hands gripping the wheel, his eyes wide with shock, stared straight ahead through the windshield.

Cassie waited for her heart to stop pounding, then turned to Eddie. "We're okay."

"Yeah," he said, swallowing hard.

"I think you've had a blowout."

He looked very bewildered. "You mean — a tire?"

"Yeah. A flat tire," Cassie said. She pushed open her door. "Let's take a look."

She stepped out into the darkness. She could see immediately that the right rear tire had gone flat.

"Hey, aren't you coming out?" she called. Eddie hadn't moved from behind the wheel. In the dim light from the car ceiling, she could see him staring straight ahead, as if thinking hard, concentrating on something.

"Eddie?"

He spun around, finally hearing her. "Oh. Sorry."

Shaking his head, he climbed out of the car and came around to her side. "Oh, no," he groaned.

"It's just a flat," Cassie said, surprised by how upset he was. "We can fix it real fast. All those tire-changing practices in driver's ed will actually come in handy."

"No," Eddie said softly.

"Huh?" Cassie started around to the driver's side.

Eddie said something from behind the car, but she didn't hear him. She reached under the steering wheel, turned off the ignition, and pulled the key out.

"No," Eddie said, holding his hand up to stop her as she came back around to the trunk.

"Really, Eddie," she said impatiently. "It's just a flat tire. It's not the end of the world."

"We can't fix it," Eddie insisted, his eyes wild.

He's still frightened from the blowout, Cassie thought. It *was* pretty frightening. The first thing I thought was that someone was shooting at us. How awful! Poor Eddie must've been really scared, too.

"Tell you what," she offered. "Help me haul out the spare, and I'll change the tire. Do you have a flashlight in the trunk? You can hold the light on it. It's so dark out here."

"No," Eddie repeated.

"No, what?" Cassie asked, bewildered.

"I don't have a spare," he said.

"You don't?" she cried, surprised. "You must have one. Come on. Let's check."

She put the key in the trunk lock.

"No!" Eddie cried, and lunged toward her. "I don't have a spare, Cassie. Don't open the trunk."

"Eddie — "

"Don't open the trunk!"

He made a desperate grab for the key, but he was too late.

Cassie turned the key in the lock, and the trunk lid popped open.

She peered inside.

Then she raised both hands to her face and started to scream.

20

Folded neatly in the trunk, its arms and legs tucked in like a laundered shirt, the corpse stared up at Cassie with its dull, lifeless eyes.

Its gray face held a distorted smile. Some stitching on the lips had popped open. A piece of skin on the forehead had peeled back, revealing dark bone.

"No!" She screamed and took a step back.

"I warned you," Eddie said softly.

"Eddie — " She couldn't take her eyes off the corpse, folded so neatly, so carefully in the center of the trunk. "Eddie — it's been *you* all along!"

Eddie had moved behind her and blocked her path. "I'm real sorry," he said, his voice barely a whisper. "I'm real sorry, Cassie."

She whirled around to face him, but the staring dead eyes of the corpse stayed in her mind. "Eddie — I don't understand."

"I'm real sorry," he repeated, his dark eyes staring hard into hers. "I wasn't ready for you. This wasn't supposed to happen yet."

He took a step toward her, his eyes unblinking, as unblinking as the dead man's, his expression tense, studying her face.

"But, why?" Cassie managed to ask. "Why have you been doing this to us?"

A small pickup truck roared by without slowing. There was no other traffic in sight.

A cold wind swirled about them, bending the tall grass in the fields on both sides of the narrow highway.

Cassie was too frightened, too confused, to notice the wind.

"Why, Eddie? What are you doing with this — this corpse?" she asked, not recognizing her shrill, frightened voice.

"It was just a joke," he said softly, his hands stiffly at his sides. "Just a joke. At least it started out that way."

"A joke?" Cassie glanced into the open trunk, then quickly away.

The corpse stared out at her. The dim trunk light made its skin a hideous green.

She felt sick. Her legs were shaking. Her whole body trembled.

"Everyone hates me," Eddie said, without any emotion at all, his eyes staring straight ahead at her, his face a blank. "Everyone hates me. No one cares. No one."

"That's not true — " she interrupted.

But he raised a hand to silence her.

"It *is* true," he insisted, raising his voice to a shout. "Why else would they play all the jokes on me? Winks and everyone else. Always trying to make me look like a fool, always trying to scare me to death."

"But, Eddie — "

"I *know* they all call me Scaredy Katz," he continued heatedly, balling and unballing his fists. "I know they all laugh at me, think I'm a chicken. Winks and Scott — and you, too, Cassie."

"Eddie, people only play jokes on people they *like*," Cassie said. She knew it was lame, but the hatred on Eddie's face, the uncontrolled anger, was really terrifying her.

"That's a stupid lie!" Eddie screamed. "Everyone makes fun of me. Everyone makes fun of Scaredy Katz. Everyone tries to frighten me, tries to make me feel like I'm some kind of poor, timid freak."

"Eddie — "

Cassie didn't know what to say.

In a way, Eddie was right. They had all been cruel to him. But no one realized how deeply he had felt the pain from their jokes.

They were just jokes, after all.

"So I decided to show *you* what it's like to be scared. Really scared," Eddie said, his face filled with menace now as he took a step toward Cassie. "I worked it all out myself. My own little practical joke. First, I borrowed the corpse from Jerry. Then — "

Cassie gasped. "Wait a minute, Eddie," she cried, raising both hands to her face. "Wait a minute. Do you mean that we didn't kill this guy? We didn't hit him that night in your car?"

A pleased grin spread slowly across Eddie's face.

"You were all so stupid," he said scornfully. "We didn't kill him. He'd been dead for days. He was so stiff, he stood up by himself."

21

Eddie shook his head, grinning at her.

Cassie suddenly felt weak.

All that guilt, she thought. All those nightmares.

We all felt so terrible. Like criminals.

And Tinkers had already been dead.

He'd been dead for days.

"Jerry helped you do this?" Cassie cried, her voice revealing her fear, her confusion.

"He was up on the underpass," Eddie said, still grinning, a grin of triumph. "Jerry stood the corpse in the road when he saw my car coming."

"But — but who *is* he?" she demanded, glancing to the open car trunk.

"Some homeless guy," Eddie replied, shrugging his narrow shoulders. "No one claimed him. So Jerry let me borrow him."

"So that you could terrify us? So that you could

mow Winks down? So that you could *kill* us?"

The grin faded from Eddie's face. "I wanted you to know what it's like to be afraid, really afraid."

"But, Eddie — "

"I wanted you to think that the corpse was coming after you, that it had come back to life, that it wanted to take its revenge. But you were too smart for that. You didn't believe it was the corpse."

He closed his eyes. He let out a long cry, a cry of anger mixed with sadness. "So I decided to do more than frighten you. I decided to pay you back. For all the jokes. For all the laughter. For all the times you frightened me and made me feel like a cowardly baby!"

He was shouting now, his dark eyes blazing, his face quivering, out of control as his fury escaped.

"I got Winks. Scaredy Katz got Winks. I showed him. Now, it's your turn, Cassie!"

"No!" she cried, her mind spinning desperately, trying to think of something to say to him, something to calm him.

But it was too late.

He had reached into the trunk and pulled out a tire iron. "Your turn, Cassie," he said, raising it menacingly over his head, moving toward her quickly. "Your turn!"

"Eddie — no!" she screamed, raising her hands in front of her as if they could protect her. "No!"

He stopped, holding the tire iron high. "Don't

worry. I'm going to give you a chance." He gestured with the tire iron, swinging it wildly. "Go on. Get going. Run!"

"Oh!" Cassie spun around, trying to focus her eyes on the dark countryside. There was nowhere to run. Nowhere to hide. Stretching on both sides of the deserted highway was nothing but flat, open grassland.

"Run!" Eddie screamed, his voice raw and threatening behind her. "Run!"

Cassie started to run down the highway, bending low into the swirling wind.

"Run! Run!"

She could still hear Eddie screaming.

And then the screaming stopped. And the only sound was the rapid *thud* of her sneakers against the pavement.

She heard the roar of the car engine.

Spinning around, the white light of the headlights caught her, trapped her, blinded her for a moment. She stood paralyzed, like a frightened rabbit.

The lights grew brighter.

The car roared forward.

He's going to run me down, she realized.

22

The lights grew brighter, blindingly bright.

Cassie tried to run, but it was too late.

Even with its flat tire, the car was coming too fast. The roar of its engine drowned out the *flap flap flap* of the empty rear tire, drowned out all of Cassie's thoughts, seemed to encircle her, pull her in.

She cried out as she heard the crash.

I'm dead, she thought.

I'm hit.

He's killed me.

She waited for the pain, the overwhelming pain, waited for the darkness to fall over her.

But the crash continued behind her.

The crush of metal against metal.

The crunch and tinkle of shattering glass.

The squeal of tires as they skidded over the pavement.

I'm not hit, she realized.

I'm okay!

She turned to see that another car had barreled into the side of Eddie's Chevy. Another car had collided with the old Chevy, pushed it off the road onto the soft shoulder.

A silver Volvo.

Scott's car.

The driver's door opened, and Scott climbed out. "Cassie?"

She ran to him. "Scott! Scott! I'm here!" She threw herself into Scott's arms, pressing her face against his down coat. "It was Eddie," she cried. "Eddie. He wanted to kill us."

"I know," Scott said softly.

It took Cassie a while to realize that someone else had climbed out of Scott's car. It was Jerry. He ran to the Chevy and dragged Eddie out of the car.

"Jerry — what are *you* doing here?" Eddie cried, his face filled with confusion. "Why'd you wreck my car?"

Jerry pulled Eddie roughly over to Cassie and Scott. The four of them stood spotlighted in the Volvo's headlights. Jerry held Eddie tightly by the shoulders.

"It was supposed to be a joke, Eddie," Jerry cried angrily. "You said it was going to be a joke. You never said anything about running people down, hurting people."

"It *was* a joke," Eddie said, his dark eyes wild, darting from one of them to the other. "It was a big joke."

"People got hurt, Eddie," Jerry said, holding on to his cousin tightly. "Winks is your friend. You nearly killed him."

"No one is my friend," Eddie said bitterly.

"How did you find us?" Cassie asked Scott, still leaning against him, still feeling as if she needed his protection. "How did you know where we were?"

"I took a guess," Scott replied. "Jerry called me. He said he was real worried about Eddie."

"Yeah," Jerry interrupted, looking at Eddie. "When I saw those Polaroids yesterday when you came to the morgue, I knew something was wrong. I knew Eddie was up to something bad. I've been trying to reach him ever since."

"Eddie's mom told us you took him driving," Scott said, his arm around her, warming her, calming her. "So I just figured we'd find you here on Route 12."

"I'm so glad," Cassie said, sighing.

But then she suddenly remembered something. She pulled away from Scott and eyed him coldly. "Scott, I have to ask you something."

"Huh?"

"Where were you last night? In the middle of the night? I called you. Your mom went to look for you, and you were gone. I was so frightened, I started to think — "

Scott put a warm hand over her mouth to cut her off. "I was sleepwalking," he told her. "Sometimes I do that when I have a high fever. It's really kind of scary. Mom found me walking behind the garage. She led me back to my room."

"Sleepwalking?" Cassie cried.

"I don't remember it at all," Scott said.

"I tried to call you this morning — " Cassie started.

"Mom took me to the doctor first thing," Scott told her. "But he doesn't have a cure for sleepwalking. It's happened to me a few times before. It's so scary. Luckily, my fever is down."

"You're weird," Jerry told Scott.

"Let me go," Eddie insisted, struggling to break away from his cousin.

"Take it easy," Jerry insisted. "We're going to get you the help you need, Eddie."

"Help? I don't need help!" Eddie cried.

"We'll have to take my car," Scott said, walking toward the two cars. "Eddie's car is pretty banged up."

"And it has a flat tire," Cassie told them. "That's how I discovered the corpse. I opened the trunk and — "

"The corpse? It's here?" Jerry asked, surprised.

"In Eddie's trunk," Cassie said, picturing the torn forehead, the dull, sunken eyes.

"Well, let's get it out so I can return it," Jerry said, still holding on to Eddie, but moving quickly toward Eddie's car. "Okay if we put it in your trunk, Scott?"

"I guess," Scott said reluctantly, a sick look on his face.

Jerry pulled open the Chevy's trunk, and they all peered inside.

The corpse was gone.

23

Two weeks later, Cassie, Scott, and Jerry were gathered at Winks's house. Winks was still confined to the house. They were doing their best to entertain him and keep him from going stir-crazy.

"And no one ever found the corpse?" Winks asked, raising the cast on his arm so that he could scratch his side with his good hand.

"No." Cassie shook her head.

"Eddie kept insisting it was alive, really alive," Scott said. And then he added, "Poor guy."

"He's getting treatment from good doctors," Jerry said, slouching down on the leather armchair.

"Well, a corpse can't just get up and walk away, can it?" Winks asked, puzzling over this story.

"This one did," Jerry said, shaking his head. "I've handled a lot of corpses. I've had some snorers and some groaners, but this is the first walker."

"Yuck," Cassie said, making a face. "Can't we talk about something else?"

"Hey, Jerry," Winks said, pushing himself up with the cast on his arm, "will you lend me another eyeball when I go back to school?"

"No way, man," Jerry said, holding up his hands. "No more jokes for me. I've learned my lesson. No more jokes" — and then he added slyly — "if I can help it."

Everyone laughed.

"Hey, I've got to get some sleep," Scott said, glancing at his watch. "I've got my driver's test tomorrow." He stood up. "When's your test, Winks?"

"Forget it," Winks said glumly. "From now on, I'm taking the bus."

They all headed to the front door, Winks walking slowly but deliberately, limping only slightly. He pulled open the door for them.

And then they all screamed in horror.

The corpse was standing in the doorway, his face pressed against the storm door. His sunken eyes stared blindly into the house. The skin flap on his forehead had pulled further open, revealing more skull.

"No!" Cassie cried. "This is impossible!"

"How did he find us?" Winks cried.

Jerry's face filled with amusement. "One last joke, guys!" he exclaimed. "Sorry." He couldn't contain his laughter, which burst out as he surveyed their reactions.

"I found it on the side of the road that night," he explained. "In the tall grass. Eddie must have tossed it out of the trunk before he came after you, Cassie."

"So you went back and got it?" Cassie demanded.

Jerry nodded. "I've been saving it for just the right moment," he declared.

"Well, this wasn't it!" Cassie said.

"Let's get him!" Scott cried.

Jerry pushed open the storm door, toppling the well-traveled corpse, and started to run full speed down the drive, with Cassie and Scott in close pursuit.

Winks watched them chase Jerry down the block.

Then he stepped out onto the stoop and propped the corpse back up in front of the door.

"Hey, Mom! Dad!" he called, stepping back into the house. "There's someone at the door who wants to see you!"

Point Horror Fans Beware!

*Available now from Point Horror are tales
for the midnight hour . . .*

THE *Point Horror* TAPES

Two Point Horror stories are terrifyingly
brought to life in a chilling dramatisation
featuring actors from The Story Circle and
with spine tingling sound effects.

Point Horror as you've never heard
it before . . .

**HALLOWEEN NIGHT
TRICK OR TREAT
THE CEMETERY
DREAM DATE**

available now on audiotape at your
nearest bookshop.

Listen if you dare . . .

Point Horror

Are you hooked on horror? Are you thrilled by fear? Then these are the books for you. A powerful series of horror fiction designed to keep you quaking in your shoes.

Titles available now:

The Cemetery
D.E. Athkins

The Dead Game
Mother's Helper
A. Bates

The Cheerleader
The Return of the Vampire
The Vampire's Promise
Freeze Tag
The Perfume
The Stranger
Twins
Caroline B. Cooney

April Fools
The Lifeguard
The Mall
Teacher's Pet
Trick or Treat
Richie Tankersley Cusick

Camp Fear
My Secret Admirer
Silent Witness
The Window
Carol Ellis

The Accident
The Invitation
The Fever
Funhouse
The Train
Nightmare Hall:
The Silent Scream
Deadly Attraction
The Roommate
The Wish
Guilty
Diane Hoh

The Yearbook
Peter Lerangis

The Watcher
Lael Littke

The Forbidden Game:
The Hunter
The Chase
L.J. Smith

Dream Date
The Diary
The Waitress
Sinclair Smith

The Phantom
Barbara Steiner

The Baby-sitter
The Baby-sitter II
The Baby-sitter III
Beach House
Beach Party
The Boyfriend
Call Waiting
The Dead Girlfriend
The Girlfriend
Halloween Night
The Hitchhiker
Hit and Run
The Snowman
The Witness
R.L. Stine

Thirteen Tales of Horror
Various
Thirteen More Tales of Horror
Various
Thirteen Again
Various

Look out for:

Nightmare Hall:
The Scream Team
Diane Hoh

The Forbidden Game III:
The Kill
L.J. Smith

Fatal Secrets
Richie Tankersley Cusick